Keri Arthur recently won the *Romantic Times* Career Achievement Award for Urban Fantasy and has been nominated in the Best Contemporary Paranormal category of the *Romantic Times* Reviewers' Choice Awards. She's a dessert and function cook by trade, and lives with her daughter in Melbourne, Australia.

Visit her website at www.keriarthur.com

D1471495

520 966 61 5

Dangerous Games

KERI ARTHUR

piatkus

PIATKUS

First published in the US in 2007 by Bantam Dell
A Division of Random House Inc., New York
First published in Great Britain in 2007 by Piatkus Books
This paperback edition published in 2011 by Piatkus
Reprinted 2012

Copyright © 2007 by Keri Arthur

The moral right of the author has been asserted.

*All characters and events in this publication, other than those
clearly in the public domain, are fictitious and any resemblance
to real persons, living or dead, is purely coincidental.*

All rights reserved.
No part of this publication may be reproduced, stored in a
retrieval system, or transmitted, in any form or by any means, without
the prior permission in writing of the publisher, nor be otherwise circulated
in any form of binding or cover other than that in which it is published
and without a similar condition including this condition being
imposed on the subsequent purchaser.

A CIP catalogue record for this book
is available from the British Library.

ISBN 978-0-7499-5503-8

Printed and bound in Great Britain by
Clays Ltd, St Ives plc

Papers used by Piatkus are from well-managed forests
and other responsible sources.

MIX
Paper from
responsible sources
FSC® C104740

Piatkus
An imprint of
Little, Brown Book Group
100 Victoria Embankment
London EC4Y 0DY

An Hachette UK Company
www.hachette.co.uk

www.piatkus.co.uk

I'd like to thank

everyone at Bantam who made this book possible—
especially my editor, Anne, assistant editor Joshua,
and copy editor Madeline.

I'd also like to thank the lady who made
all this possible—my agent, Miriam.

This book is dedicated to my family.

Dangerous Games

Chapter 1

I stood in the shadows and watched the dead man.

The night was bitterly cold, and rain fell in a heavy, constant stream. Water sluiced down the vampire's long causeway of a nose, leaping to the square thrust of his jaw before joining the mad rush down the front of his yellow raincoat. The puddle around his bare feet had reached his ankles and was slowly beginning to creep up his hairy legs.

Like most of the newly risen, he was little more than flesh stretched tautly over bone. But his skin possessed a rosy glow that suggested he'd eaten well and often. Even if his pale eyes were sunken. Haunted.

Which in itself wasn't really surprising. Thanks to the willingness of both Hollywood and literature to romanticize vampirism, far too many humans seemed to think that by becoming a vampire they'd instantly gain all the power, sex, and wealth they could ever want. It wasn't until after the change that they began to realize that being undead wasn't the fun time often depicted; that wealth, sex, and popularity *might* come, but only if they survived the horrendous first few years when a vampire was all instinct and blood need. And of course, if they *did* survive, they then learned that endless loneliness—never feeling the full warmth of the sun again, never being able to savor the taste of food, and being feared or ostracized by a good percentage of the population—was also part of the equation.

Yeah, there were laws in place to stop discrimination against vampires and other nonhumans, but the laws were only a recent development. And while there might now be vampire groupies, they were also a recent phenomenon and only a small portion of the population. Hatred and fear of vamps had been around for centuries, and I had no doubt it would take centuries for it to abate. If it ever did.

And the bloody rampages of vamps like the one ahead weren't helping any.

A total of twelve people had disappeared over the last month, and we were pretty sure this vamp was responsible for nine of them. But there were enough differences in method of killing between this vamp's nine and the remaining three to suggest we had a second psycho on the loose. For a start, nine had met their deaths as a result of a vamp feeding frenzy. The other three had been meticulously sliced open neck to knee with a knife and their innards carefully removed—not something the newly turned were generally capable of. When presented with the opportunity for a feed, they fed. There was nothing neat or meticulous about it.

Then there were the multiple, barely healed scars marring the backs of the three anomalous women, the missing pinky on their left hands, and the odd, almost satisfied smiles that seemed frozen on their dead lips. Women who were the victims of a vamp's frenzy didn't die with *that* sort of smile, as the souls of the dead nine could probably attest if they were still hanging about.

And I seriously hoped that they *weren't*. I'd seen more than enough souls rising in recent times—I certainly didn't want to make a habit of it.

But dealing with two psychos on top of coping with the usual guardian patrols had the Directorate stretched to the limit, and that meant everyone had been pulling extra shifts. Which explained why Rhoan and I were out hunting rogue suckers on this bitch of a night after working all day trying to find some leads on what Jack—our boss, and the vamp who ran the whole guardian division at the Directorate of Other Races—charmingly called The Cleaver.

I yawned and leaned a shoulder against the concrete wall lining one side of the small alleyway I was hiding in. The wall, which was part of the massive factory complex that dominated a good part of the old West Footscray area, protected me from the worst of the wind, but it didn't do a whole lot against the goddamn rain.

If the vamp felt any discomfort about standing in a pothole in the middle of a storm-drenched night, he certainly wasn't showing it. But then, the dead rarely cared about such things.

I might have vampire blood running through my veins, but I *wasn't* dead and I hated it.

Winter in Melbourne was never a joy, but this year we'd had so much rain I was beginning to forget what sunshine looked like. Most wolves were immune to the cold, but I was a half-breed and obviously lacked *that* particular gene. My feet were icy and I was beginning to lose feeling in several toes. And this *despite* the fact I was wearing two pairs of thick woolen socks underneath my rubber-heeled shoes. Which were *not* waterproof, no matter what the makers claimed.

I should have worn stilettos. My feet would have been no worse off, and I would have felt more at home. And hey, if he happened to spot me, I could have pretended to be nothing more than a bedraggled, desperate hooker. But Jack kept insisting that high heels and my job just didn't go together.

Personally, I think he was a little afraid of my shoes. Not so much because of the color—which, admittedly, was often outrageous—but because of the nifty wooden heels. Wood and vamps were never an easy mix.

I flicked up the collar of my leather jacket and tried to ignore the fat drops of water dribbling down my spine. What I really needed—more than decent-looking shoes—was a hot bath, a seriously large cup of coffee, and a thick steak sandwich. Preferably with onions and ketchup. God, my mouth was salivating just thinking about it. Of course, given we were in the middle of this ghost town of factories, none of those things were likely to appear in my immediate future.

I thrust wet hair out of my eyes, and wished, for the

umpteenth time, that he would just get *on* with it. Whatever *it* was.

Following him might be part of my job as a guardian, but that didn't mean I had to be happy about it. I'd never had much choice about joining the guardian ranks, thanks to the experimental drugs several lunatics had forced into my system, and the psychic talents that were developing as a result. It was either stay with the Directorate as a guardian, so my growing abilities could be monitored and harnessed, or be shipped off to the military with the other unfortunates who had received similar doses of ARC1-23. I might not have wanted to be a guardian, but I sure as hell didn't want to be sent to the military. Give me the devil I know any day.

I shifted weight from one foot to the other again. What was this piece of dead meat waiting for? He couldn't have sensed me—I was far enough away that he wouldn't hear the beat of my heart or the rush of blood through my veins. He hadn't looked over his shoulder, so he couldn't have spotted me with the infrared of his vampire vision, and bloodsuckers generally didn't have a very keen olfactory sense.

So why stand in a puddle in the middle of this abandoned factory complex looking like a little lost soul?

Part of me itched to shoot the bastard and just get the whole ordeal over with. But we needed to follow this baby vamp home to discover if he had any nasty surprises hidden in his nest. Like other victims, or perhaps even his maker.

Because it was unusual for one of the newly turned to survive nine rogue kills without getting himself caught or killed. Not without help, anyway.

The vampire suddenly stepped out of the puddle and began walking down the slight incline, his bare feet slapping noisily against the broken road. The shadows and the night hovered all around him, but he didn't bother cloaking his form. Given the whiteness of his hairy legs and the brightness of his yellow raincoat, that was strange. Though we *were* in the middle of nowhere. Maybe he figured he was safe.

I stepped out of the alleyway. The wind hit full force, pushing me sideways for several steps before I regained my balance. I padded across the road and stopped in the shadows again. The rain beat a tattoo against my back and the water seeping through my coat became a river, making me feel colder than I'd ever dreamed possible. Forget the coffee and the sandwich. What I wanted more than anything right now was to get *warm*.

I pressed the small com-link button that had been inserted into my earlobe just over four months ago. It doubled as a two-way communicator and a tracker, and Jack had not only insisted that I keep it, but that all guardians were to have them from now on. He wanted to be able to find his people at all times, even when not on duty.

Which smacked of "big brother" syndrome to me, even if I could understand his reasoning. Guardians didn't grow on trees. Finding vamps with just the right mix of killing instinct and moral sensibilities was difficult, which was why guardian numbers at the Directorate still hadn't fully recovered from the eleven we'd lost ten months ago.

One of those eleven had been a friend of mine, and on my worst nights, I still dreamed of her death—even though the only thing I'd ever witnessed was the bloody patch of sand that had contained her DNA. Like most of the other guardians who had gone missing, her remains had never been found.

Of course, the tracking measures had not only come too late for those eleven, but for one other—Gautier. Not that he was dead, however much I might wish otherwise. Four months ago he'd been the Directorate's top guardian. Now he was rogue and on top of the Directorate's hit list. So far he'd escaped every search, every trap. Meaning he was still out there, waiting and watching and plotting his revenge.

On me.

Goose bumps traveled down my spine and, just for a second, I'd swear his dead scent teased my nostrils. Whether it was real or just imagination I couldn't say, because the gusting wind snatched it away.

Even it wasn't real, it was a reminder that I had to be extra careful. Gautier had never really functioned on the same sane field as the rest of us. Worse still, he liked playing with his prey. Liked watching the pain and fear grow before he killed.

He might now consider me his mouse but he'd yet to try any of his games on me. But something told me that all that would change tonight.

I grimaced and did my best to ignore the insight. Clairvoyance might have been okay if it had come in a truly usable form—like clear glimpses of future scenes and happenings—but no, that was apparently asking too much of fate. Instead, I just got these weird feelings of upcoming doom that were frustratingly vague on any sort of concrete detail. And training something like that was nigh on impossible—not that *that* stopped Jack from getting his people to at least try.

Whether the elusiveness would change as the talent became more settled was anyone's guess. Personally, I just wished it would go back to being latent. I knew Gautier was out there, somewhere. Knew he was coming after me. I didn't need some half-assed talent sending me spooky little half-warnings every other day.

Still, even though I knew Gautier probably *wasn't* out here tonight, I couldn't help looking around and checking all the shadows as I said, "Brother dearest, I hate this fucking job."

Rhoan's soft laughter ran into my ear. Just hearing it made me feel better. Safer. "Nights like this are a bitch, aren't they?"

"Understatement of the year." I quickly peeked around the corner and saw the vampire turning left. I padded after him, keeping to the wall and well away from the puddles. Though, given the state of my feet, it really wouldn't have mattered. "And I feel obligated to point out that I didn't sign up for night work."

Rhoan chuckled softly. "And I feel obliged to point out that you weren't actually signed up, but forcibly drafted. Therefore, you can bitch all you want but it isn't going to make a damned bit of difference."

Wasn't that the truth. "Where are you?"

"West side, near the old biscuit factory."

Which was practically opposite my position. Between the two of us, we had him penned. Hopefully that meant we wouldn't lose him.

I stopped as I neared the corner and carefully peered around. The wind slapped against my face, and the rain on my skin seemed to turn to ice. The vamp had stopped near the far end of the building and was looking around. I ducked back as he looked my way, barely daring to breathe even though common sense suggested there was no way he could have seen me. Not only did I have vampire genes, but I had many of their skills, as well. Like the ability to cloak under the shadow of night, the infrared vision, and their faster-than-a-blink speed.

The creak of a door sounded. I risked another look. A metal door stood ajar and the vamp was nowhere in sight.

An invitation or a trap?

I didn't know, but I sure as hell wasn't going to take a chance. Not alone, anyway.

"Rhoan, he's gone inside building number four. Rear entrance, right-hand side."

"Wait for me to get there before you go in."

"I'm foolhardy, but I'm *not* stupid."

He chuckled again. I slipped around the corner and crept toward the door. The wind caught the edge of it and flung it back against the brick wall, the crash echoing across the night. It was an oddly lonely sound.

I froze and concentrated, using the keenness of my wolf hearing to sort through the noises running with the wind. But the howl of it was just too strong, overriding everything else.

Nor could I smell anything more than ice, age, and abandonment. If there *were* such smells and it wasn't just my overactive imagination.

Yet a feeling of wrongness was growing deep inside. I rubbed my leather-covered arms and hoped like hell my brother got here fast.

"Okay," Rhoan said eventually, the suddenness of his soft voice running through my ear making me jump. "I'm around at the front. The main door is locked, but there's several broken windows. I'm going in."

"Can you smell anyone other than our vampire?"

"No." He paused. "Can you?"

"No. But there's something—or someone—else here that feels evil."

He didn't question my certainty. Over the years, my instincts for trouble had saved us from as many situations as they had gotten us into. The only difference now was the fact that my developing clairvoyance gave us some warning of the type of trouble we were heading into rather than us discovering it the hard way.

Which I guess made it of some use, no matter how frustrating it was otherwise.

"Use the laser, then," he said. "Better safe than sorry."

I reached into my coat pocket and slipped the weapon into my hand. It was the latest in laser technology—a palm-sized weapon that packed enough power to blow the shit out of the thickest brick wall. Needless to say, it had a pretty nasty effect on humans and nonhumans alike.

"Jack will have our skins if we laser that vamp before he questions him about his maker." Because the maker had the responsibility of care, and by letting his baby go rogue, he'd basically signed his own death warrant.

"I'd rather face his wrath than have a dead sister."

I grinned. "You just don't want to face doing the laundry by yourself."

"I can sweet-talk Liander into doing my laundry. It's your charming early-morning cheeriness I'd miss."

"I'm fine as long as you feed me coffee first thing," I replied mildly. "And I wouldn't be placing bets on Liander doing your clothes. He sounded pretty pissed off with you last time I talked to him."

"Yeah, well, he shouldn't try placing unreasonable restraints on me."

"Didn't we have this very same discussion four months ago?" I did a quick peek around the doorway. Nothing but darkness. I blinked, flicking to the infrared of my vampire vision. Still nothing but rubbish-strewn emptiness. "I'm ready to head in."

"Me, too." He paused. "And yeah, we did have this same discussion."

"So, did you talk to him like I told you to?"

"Sort of."

Meaning he'd gone for the ignore-everything-and-give-good-sex option. No wonder Liander had a smile a mile wide the next morning.

And no wonder he was back to being an unhappy camper now.

"Can I remind you that a good man is hard to find?"

"Can I remind you you're here to capture a vampire, not to lecture your older, more experienced, brother?"

I grinned. He'd beaten me into this world by a whole five minutes. "Heading in now."

"Me, too."

I snuck around the corner, keeping low and close to the wall as I scanned the immediate surroundings. The room was large, and had a wide platform running around the edges. It looked like a loading bay, one where the trucks just reversed to the ramp and the goods were wheeled directly out. Two double-swing doors were visible, one directly ahead and one to my left. The left one swung slightly—an obvious indication that someone had gone through it recently.

So why did the scent trail lead straight ahead?

I wasn't sure, but I wasn't trusting visual evidence, not in a place that smelled so much like a trap. I padded right, keeping to the walls, following the muted odor of death up the ramp and through the door.

A long hallway dotted with doorways greeted me. The air here was close, and had a stale, almost rotten smell. Like something had been decaying here for a very long time.

I wrinkled my nose and hoped like hell it was just putrid rubbish of the non-flesh kind, even as my wolf senses told me that at least *some* of the smells weren't.

Obviously, there'd been more victims snatched by the baby vamp and perhaps his maker than had been reported.

I continued on, opening each door and trying to ignore the more tangible signs of decay and death in each room as I went. The baby vamp couldn't be working alone, that much was obvious. There were at least ten whole bodies, as well as an assortment of various body parts—limbs, heads, and organs—scattered throughout the rooms. Even a newly turned vamp at the height of his feeding frenzy couldn't consume *that* much blood.

I eventually reached another swinging door. The scent of death was stronger here, meaning the baby vampire was closer. Much closer. Like just beyond the door. Trying for an ambush, perhaps? If so, he might have considered a shower first. His natural odor was a dead giveaway to anyone with a decent honker.

I stepped back a little and kicked the doors open. As they crashed back, I dove through, rolling onto my feet and sighting the laser's target on the vamp in one smooth movement.

He was younger than I'd presumed—a teenager rather than someone in his late twenties. This close, the veins under his pale skin were very visible, and were the healthy blue of a well-fed bloodsucker.

His sudden laugh had goose bumps fleeing across my skin. Not because of the low, chilling sound, but because his laugh reminded me of another's.

Gautier.

Did that mean our rogue guardian was the kid's maker? It would certainly explain how he'd escaped the Directorate for nine kills.

The thought had barely crossed my mind when awareness surged, prickling like fire across my skin.

He was here. Gautier was here.

Fuck.

Panic surged, but I thrust it down ruthlessly. To give in to panic would be playing into Gautier's hand. He loved fear. Fed on it.

But I couldn't deal with Gautier and keep an eye on the baby vamp. I'd fought and beaten more than one vampire at a time in the past, but Gautier was the most successful killing machine the Directorate had ever trained. The one time we'd fought, he'd beaten the crap out of me.

I wasn't even sure that Rhoan and I, as a team, could defeat him.

"Rhoan, we have a problem."

"Don't tell me we've lost him. I do not want to spend another night in weather like this."

"I have the vamp. The problem is bigger than that." Bigger and closer. A chill ran over me, but I resisted the urge to look over my shoulder. But my senses told me the darkness that was Gautier was moving forward from the far side of the room.

"Bigger in what way?"

I gave in to temptation and looked over my shoulder. "I know you're out there, Gautier."

The words were barely out of my mouth when the baby vamp attacked. He was on me like a rash—a spindly whirlwind of arms, legs, and desperation. I staggered back under the force of his attack, somehow managing to get my arm between us. His teeth slashed my palm rather than my neck, and sliced deep. Pain roiled white hot through my body. I hissed, but it was his greedy sucking that got to me more than the pain. I wasn't about to be *any* vampire's last meal. I swung my fist, hitting him over the head with the body of the laser as hard as I could. The force of the blow tore him from my flesh, and with a grunt of effort, I thrust him away from me. He landed on his back and slid along several more feet, until he was close to the still-shadowed Gautier.

"Kill him," Rhoan said. "Gautier's probably his maker, and if he's not, we'll worry about it later."

I blew out a breath and hoped like hell he was right— otherwise, Jack was going to be extremely pissed. I raised the laser and fired the weapon, sweeping the bright beam from left to right across the vampire's bony neck. Skin and bone sliced as easy as paper, and the smell of burnt flesh stung the air.

My stomach flip-flopped, but I ignored it, concentrating on Gautier's unseen presence. A presence that seemed even darker and more menacing than usual—and that was something I'd never thought possible until now. "You really can stop hiding, Gautier. I know you're here. Your rotten stench always gives your presence away."

His chuckle ran across the night, a low sound that set my teeth on edge. He walked free of the shadows hiding his form, and strolled toward me. Gautier was an even longer, meaner stick of vampire than the vamp who lay on the ground, and his flesh was just as pale. But like the baby vamp, there was nothing translucent about Gautier's skin—he too had the wholeness of a vampire who ate often and well.

I remembered the stink in the hall, the decaying bodies and many body parts in the various rooms. A chill ran through me. Apparently, Gautier was off the Directorate leash in more ways than one.

"I'm on the landing above and to your left," Rhoan said. "The minute he comes into range, we both fire."

Sounded like a perfectly acceptable option to me. Jack might want to interrogate this sick bastard and uncover what other macabre games he'd been playing since leaving the Directorate, but I was perfectly happy to disobey orders when it came to Gautier.

Though I very much doubted he'd fall into our hands so easily.

As if to give emphasis to this thought, he stopped just near the body of the baby vamp—tantalizingly close to the required laser range—and gave another low chuckle. The sound crawled over my skin and made me shiver. Gautier in a happy mood boded no one any good.

"Shame on you for killing my little friend," he said, tone oily and amused. "Don't you know the Directorate likes to question baby vamps and get the name of their maker first?"

"We both know who the maker is, Gautier," I replied, itching to pull the laser's trigger even though I knew it would be useless. "Though I am at a loss to know why you'd bother with such a poor specimen."

"Good help is *so* hard to find these days."

Especially when the employer was a bloodthirsty psycho. "So, does your appearance here tonight mean you've finally come to your senses and decided to give yourself up?"

He raised an eyebrow, expression mocking. "Do you really think I would make it so easy for you?"

Well, no. But it never hurts to be hopeful. One of these days fate might actually throw me a gift rather than a spanner. "Then what game are you playing, Gautier?"

"A dangerous one. For you, and for the inventive fellow who has been torturing the others."

Something akin to fear prickled across my skin. How did Gautier know about the other killings? Was he involved? It wouldn't be surprising if he was—after all, like tended to attract like, so it made sense that Gautier would gravitate toward other evil little psychopaths. He wasn't the world's greatest thinker, even if he was a killer born and bred. "So you know the person behind it?"

"Of course. And I have a lot of admiration for his methods."

I just bet he did.

"I'm going to flank him," Rhoan said. "Keep him talking."

"Have you forgotten, Gautier, that the Directorate specializes in capture of nonhuman criminals? That we guardians are judge, jury, and executioner? We will find the man behind these killings, and we will take him out." I gave him a nasty smile that was more than a little bluff. Gautier scared the crap out of me, and I didn't mind admitting it to myself. But I'd never, ever admit it to him. "And guess what, stinko? You've already been judged, and have been found extremely wanting. Whether you're involved or not, you're a dead man."

His smile faded a little, and the sensation of danger swirled around me. "It's nice to know recent events haven't knocked the bravado out of you. It is something I have always wished to do myself."

"Yeah, yeah, you're the big bad vampire we all have to fear. I've heard the song before. Just get on with whatever shit you're here to deliver."

"Impatient to play the game. That's nice." He paused, and his gaze went to the floor above. In that moment, I knew *he* knew Rhoan was up there, and something inside me froze.

Everything was about to go to hell in a big, bad way.

"But first," he continued, voice all oily smoothness, "tell your roommate that if he takes one more step, the child dies."

Oh God, oh God . . . child? What the hell was Gautier talking about? I licked my lips, and tried to control the fear churning my gut. That was what this sick bastard wanted—fear—and I'd be damned if I'd give him it so easily.

"What shit are you talking now, Gautier?" Rhoan said, voice harsh as he stepped out of the shadows and came closer to the railing. I was glad to note he kept near one of the support beams. It'd give him cover if Gautier suddenly whipped out a weapon.

After all, his hands *were* behind his back for a reason, and Gautier didn't do *anything* without a reason.

"I talk of the child who hangs above us."

"That has to be the oldest trick in the book, Gautier." And one I'd used myself—successfully—on my brother. "I'm surprised you'd sink to something less than . . . creative?"

He gave me another of his flat smiles. "Oh, I am not above using old tricks. However, I do like putting new spins on them. Take the old money-or-the-box question, for example."

What the hell? "Has being off the leash totally fried your brain cells? Because you're not making the tiniest bit of sense at the moment."

"It's simple, really. It's all about options. What do you want more: to capture me, or to save the life of the child above us?"

"What child?" I asked again.

I tensed as one hand came out from behind his back, but all he did was casually lean sideways and press a switch. Lights flickered, throwing uneven spats of brightness across the shadow-filled room. Not that any of us actually needed lights. It was just done for effect.

"Fuck," Rhoan said softly.

I didn't look up, as much as I wanted to. I was closer

to Gautier. I was the one who had the chance of hitting him if he moved.

"Tell me," I said flatly.

"There's a little girl above us with a rope around her neck. She's standing on her toes on a thin board."

"Dead or alive?" If she was dead, I was going to charge Gautier and kill him, no matter what he had hidden behind his back.

"Alive." Rhoan paused. "Blood still flows, and I can hear a heartbeat. Just."

He was more vampire than me. He had to drink blood during the rise of the full moon, and was therefore more attuned to the thud of life. Still, the news that she was alive didn't do anything to ease the tension riding my limbs. Quite the opposite, actually.

Just because she was alive now didn't mean that Gautier intended to keep her that way. Or that he'd allow us to help her.

"How long her heart continues to beat is up to you." Gautier moved his other hand and finally revealed what he'd been hiding. The biggest fucking laser rifle I'd ever seen. "One move, Riley, and your pack-mate dies. This rifle has a wide-fire beam that will treat flesh much the same as it treats concrete. With complete disdain."

"Gautier, if you've got a damn point, please come to it," Rhoan snapped.

Gautier's smile was lazy. Obviously, he had this all planned out to the nth degree, and he wasn't about to hurry.

"Do you know anything about hanging?"

"No. But if you'd like to volunteer, I'd gladly experiment on you."

I might as well have not spoken. The great Gautier was on a roll, and there was no stopping him. And as much as I wanted to help the little kid, I believed what he said about that laser.

For good or for bad, I wasn't about to risk my brother's life on the off chance of stopping Gautier.

"Hanging with little or no drop, which is the case with the kiddy above us, usually results in death by strangulation. Asphyxia, to use the correct terminology. The kiddy struggled the usual one to three minutes after suspension, then became as you see her now. However, there have been recorded cases of people being successfully revived even after thirty minutes." He paused and glanced at the watch on his free hand. "Which gives you precisely nineteen minutes."

"You're a bastard, Gautier."

I said it with venom, and he laughed. "Well, I would have thought that was a given."

"And the point of this whole charade?" Rhoan said, voice flat—a sure sign his control was close to the edge.

"As I said, it's all about options." He paused, smiling like a cat who knew the mouse was his. "Option one. Play my game and save the child. Option two, come after me now and let the child die."

"You forgot option three—kill you and save the child."

"There is no option three. You move, Rhoan dies. Rhoan moves, he dies. Either way, I win."

Because he knew we were pack-mates. He might think that Rhoan was a wolf who'd become a vampire, but that didn't matter. He knew that for wolves, the *true* death of a close pack-mate could incapacitate for weeks, if not months. Particularly with us, because Rhoan wasn't only my pack-mate, he was my twin. We were two halves of a whole—and, truth was, I really didn't know if either of us would *want* to live without the other. We were too much a part of each other's lives.

I crossed my arms. Which meant the laser was no longer aimed at the monster in front of me and left me somewhat vulnerable, but I wasn't worried about him shooting me. Far from it. He'd drawn us here for a reason, and it wasn't so he could kill us. "What game is it you wish to play, Gautier?"

"I was hoping you'd choose that one. As much as I like listening to life slowly slipping away, the game has the potential to offer us both so much more."

"For God's sake, just get on with it," Rhoan said.

Gautier's smile faded. The sensation of danger that had been swirling around me sharpened abruptly, and sweat broke out across my skin.

"Jack often commented in the past on how good Rhoan was, and how good he expected you to be, Riley, when you finally gave in and joined the ranks. So I think it only fair that we have a little test to see who truly is the best guardian. And the test is, of course, stopping the madman behind the recent killings."

"I feel inclined to point out that, a, you're no longer a guardian, and, b, you said earlier you know the man behind the killings. That gives a rather good head start, doesn't it?"

He gave me a grin that was all teeth. "I never said the game would be easy for *you*."

And he had every intention of making it even harder, if the gleam in his eye was anything to go by. Not that

that was so surprising. "So, we play this little game of yours and both hunt The Cleaver. What does the winner get—besides the termination of said killer?"

"Well, you both get the satisfaction of knowing you beat me."

"Lucky us."

He nodded. "And, of course, I would leave the state."

And I'd grow wings and fly. "And if you win?"

"Then we begin another game. Me hunting you and all you hold dear, while you try to survive."

Which is precisely what he'd promised to do four months ago. "I can't speak for Rhoan, but if you leave right now, I accept the challenge."

It was worth it, just for the chance to save the kid.

"Leave now, and I agree," Rhoan said, voice little more than a venomous hiss of air.

Gautier smiled. "I thought you'd see it my way. I'll see you on the battlefield." He gave us a salute with the laser.

Then he shot the board out from under the kid.

Chapter 2

No!" The denial was wrenched from me as I sidestepped the falling halves of the plank.

Gautier's laugh echoed even as the shadows swept him from sight.

I looked up for the first time, saw the tiny body dangling almost directly above me. Saw her bare and filthy feet, toes that were so tiny, so fragile. Not a teenager as I'd for some reason presumed, but barely older than a tot.

Bastard. Fucking evil bastard . . .

"Rhoan—can you shoot the ropes from where you are?"

"Yes. Get ready to catch."

I shoved the laser into my pocket and positioned myself under the little girl. "Ready."

A bluish beam bit through the half-darkness, cutting through the rope and blowing out the window above and behind me. Glass exploded, raining down in deadly shards. I caught the girl with a grunt, her limp little arm whacking me in the nose as I hunched over her and tried to protect her from the rain of glass.

Razor-sharp shards thudded into my back, but the leather coat protected me from the worst of it. I waited until the last of the glass had fallen, then carefully placed the little girl on the ground.

She was still alive—her pulse fluttered underneath my fingertips. But God, she was so little, so fragile . . . so cold.

There was a soft thump, then footsteps. I looked up, but could barely see Rhoan striding toward me through my tears.

"I'll take care of her," I said. "You go after Gautier."

"Keep aware." Rhoan's voice held all the fury I was desperately trying to contain. "He might have made other vamps. They might be hidden around somewhere."

If they were, I couldn't sense them. But I nodded, and as Rhoan ran off, I looked down at the little girl again and noted the bluish tint to her lips. The cause could have been asphyxia, or it could have been blood loss, but in all likelihood, it was a combination of both. Especially given the fang marks on her neck. If she was to have any hope of survival, I had to get help here fast. I stripped off my coat and sweater and wrapped them around the little girl's body and legs. It wasn't much, but at least they were warmer than the thin nightie she had on. Then I got out my cell phone and called in a mica-unit. The micas were ambulances designed to cater to medical emergencies on a street level. It was the little girl's biggest chance. Maybe her only chance.

Five minutes, they said.

I hoped the little girl *had* five minutes.

I gently brushed tangled tendrils of brown hair from her face, the chill in her cheeks so very evident against my warmer fingertips. Christ, why hadn't the Directorate received any reports about a missing kid? It was routine for the cops to pass on reports of kidnappings and disappearances, as rogue vamps often found easy victims in the young and the frail. A good majority of the reports *weren't* vamp related, of course, but the Directorate always had them double-checked, just for the one or two percent that *were*.

But maybe this snatch had been very recent. Maybe her poor parents weren't even aware that their little girl was missing.

God, what a hell of a way to greet the morning—an officer on your doorstep telling you your baby had been kidnapped and murdered.

I bit my lip again, fighting the fresh spurts of anger and tears. And I knew, deep down, that they stemmed not only from the horror of the situation, but from the fact that *I* couldn't have children. Would never feel life grow within my belly. My vampire genes had overrun my wolf ones in that area and left me a mule—not just barren but with a womb that would not support a life. Of course, there was still hope of motherhood via a surrogate, as some of the eggs I'd had frozen *had* been tested and were apparently still viable. But that choice was one I'd hoped to avoid.

Of course, the rest of my body was still a battleground,

and no one could tell me how my vampire genes might yet affect my future. I might become more vampire, like Rhoan, or I might not. And then there was an added element of uncertainty—the cell-changing ARC1-23 drug now running through my bloodstream.

"Gautier's long gone." Rhoan's voice rose out of the darkness, the suddenness of it making me jump. I'd been too busy trying to help the little girl, and that was a mistake that could have gotten us both killed if Gautier had doubled back.

Rhoan stopped close by, then stripped off his jacket and handed it to me. I wrapped it around the girl's body. Her skin felt no warmer, even with the coats and sweater I'd already wrapped around her. Maybe she'd lost too much blood.

"Why would he do this?" Rhoan asked softly. "It makes no sense."

I swiped at a tear trickling down my cheek and looked up at him. "Gautier's a psycho, and psychos don't need a good reason to do things."

"Gautier's not your average psycho, and he doesn't do *anything* without a good reason."

"Enjoyment of the kill is the only reason he's *ever* needed."

"And yet he didn't kill this little girl. She wasn't his escape route—Gautier's confident enough in his own abilities to believe he could escape us without problems." He nodded down at the girl. "He let us save her when it is more in his nature to offer us hope then snatch it away. Something else is going on here."

I frowned. "It's also in his nature to want to prove

himself better than everyone else. Why can't it be that? Why does it have to be anything more?"

"Because Gautier *is* a killer. It makes no sense for him to draw us here, offer us this 'game,' then let us save the little girl."

Who we hadn't actually saved yet. I shifted a little and glanced at my watch. Two more minutes before the mica-unit got here. God, I hoped they would hurry. The air was getting colder and death seemed to be stirring out there in the darkness. Death that was real and forever, not death that walked in vampire form.

"Then what do you think he's up to, if you don't believe his game is real?"

"Oh, I think the game is real, as far as it goes. But I also think it's a diversion."

"He said he knows the real killer."

"Which might, or might not, be a lie."

"It didn't sound like a lie."

"Maybe. But can you really imagine Gautier allowing some other psycho free space to do as he pleased in what he considers *his* playground?"

"Well, no. He's not exactly the caring and sharing type."

"Precisely. So what the hell is he really up to?"

"Until we catch the bastard, that's really an unanswerable question." And a worrying one.

Rhoan shifted, his gaze going to the door I'd entered through. Undoubtedly he smelled the aroma of garbage and death, though it was nowhere near as strong here as it had been in the hall. "Jack's here."

And he wasn't alone, thankfully. I stepped aside as the emergency team from the mica-unit tended the little girl, watching for a couple of seconds to reassure myself she was still alive, then turned and walked down to the steps. Jack had squatted next to the young vampire I'd killed.

I stopped beside him and tried to ignore the smell of death. I felt no remorse over killing the baby vamp—not after spending so long tracking him down. Not after having to deal with the aftermath of both his and his master's feeding frenzies.

Jack looked up. "Did you read his mind before you killed him?"

I shook my head. "Didn't need to. Gautier is his maker."

"If you didn't read his mind, how do you know that?"

"Because Gautier himself confirmed it."

"He was here? And you let him go?"

Jack's voice held an edge of anger, and I held up a hand. "We didn't 'let' him do anything. We had the option of taking a life or saving one. We chose the latter."

"Which was the wrong choice." His gaze slid past me. "Your softer side is going to get you killed one day, Riley."

"Saving a child is never the wrong choice, Jack." And I couldn't have lived with myself if I'd done anything else.

"And yet, because you saved the child, many others may die."

He was obviously trying to make me feel guilty and, in some ways, succeeding. Truth was, it was very possible that others *would* die because of the choice we'd made here tonight. And yet, what other decision could I have made? None—not if I wanted to retain my sanity, my soul. Surely it could never truly be wrong to try and save such a young life, no matter what the price might ultimately be.

Though I had *no* doubt that Jack would disagree with such sentiments. Regardless of the fact he was a basically decent guy, he was still a vamp, and they all tended to have strange ideas when it came to the value of life.

"We did manage to have a nice little chat with the creep." I rubbed my arms as I spoke. It was becoming so damn cold in the warehouse that I might as well have been standing there naked. "He said he knows The Cleaver."

Jack raised an eyebrow. "And he offered you the information?"

"No," Rhoan said, as he walked up and stopped beside me. "He offered us a contest."

"What sort of contest?"

"We play a game—the first one to track down and kill the serial killer wins."

Jack raised an eyebrow. "Gautier does realize he's no longer a guardian, doesn't he?"

"Oh yeah," I muttered dryly. "And I think you'll discover he's relishing the fact if you take a little look in those back rooms."

"Then why would he make a deal like this? Especially when it benefits the Directorate rather than himself?"

"Maybe all he wants is the satisfaction of knowing he is better than us." I shrugged. "He said you used to rave about how good Rhoan is, and how good I could be. He wants to prove to himself and to us that this is not true."

"Yeah, right." Jack snorted softly and glanced at Rhoan. "Are you buying that?"

"Not in the least. He may well know the identity of our killer, but I fear there's a darker reason behind the offering of this contest. Gautier's a killer, and he's long believed in his own superiority. He doesn't need a contest to prove it. He never has."

"Exactly. Which means we need to kill him before whatever plan he has comes to fruition."

Like we hadn't been trying to do that for the last few months? Gautier was the best guardian the Directorate had ever produced—expecting second-raters and the barely trained to hunt him down and kill him swiftly was nothing short of irrational.

"Gautier's not a fool," I commented. "He knows there's an execution order out on him. He's not going to provide us with an easy target."

"No. But if either of you do get the chance, I want you to take it." He looked at both of us, green eyes bleak. "Regardless of who or what gets in the way."

Rhoan nodded. I didn't react. On a scale of things I could handle in my life as a guardian, killing an out-of-control baby vamp was stomach-turning but survivable. Ending the life of someone who got between me and Gautier was a *totally* different thing. I'd killed, there was no denying that, but each time it was in either self-defense or defense of my pack—which, in my case, was Rhoan.

I guess some would argue that blowing Davern's brains out was a cold-blooded action, but then, he'd not only tortured my brother, he was the brains and the brawn behind the whole cloning and crossbreeding venture that had been responsible for so many deaths. Not to mention the reason behind the ARC1-23 drug being injected into my system.

Play with fire and you'll end up getting burned, my mom used to say. Well, Davern had played with me and Rhoan just a little too often, and he'd finally gotten his comeuppance.

"Riley? Did you hear me?"

I looked at him. "I heard."

"And?"

"I won't kill in cold blood for you, Jack."

"Even if it's Gautier?"

"Gautier I'll kill the minute I get the chance. But I won't jeopardize the lives of others to get him."

"Still fighting the inevitable to the very end?"

"And I'm so glad it's still amusing you."

He chuckled softly. "Why don't you two go home and warm up? Report in at nine, and we'll see where we go from here."

Rhoan spun and headed toward the door, but I walked over to check the little girl first. There was still very little color in her cheeks and a lot of frantic activity on the part of the medics. Chill fingers of dread ran down my spine. Death seemed to hover far too close, and deep inside I knew that if I reached out psychically, I would feel her fate. Feel the death that was waiting out there in the shadows.

I shivered and turned away. There was hope yet. I had to believe that, if nothing else.

One of the medics looked up as I moved, and tossed me the coats and sweater. "Get the bastard who did this."

"I will." I walked away. There was nothing else I

could do or say. Except hunt Gautier down and blow his rotten brains out.

I caught up with Rhoan, tossing him his jacket and donning my own. The second we stepped out of the warehouse, the weather hit, the wind so cold, so forceful, that it snatched my breath away. Rhoan wrapped an arm around my shoulder, holding me close, sharing his body heat as we made our way through the rain-soaked night.

Unfortunately, neither of us had a car to walk toward, because baby vamps usually didn't use them. I have no idea why, but suspected it might have something to do with the flood of new sensations that enveloped the newly turned. It had to be hard to concentrate on mundane things like driving when the whole world had become a playground filled with blood hunger, lust, and easy targets.

Which meant, of course, that if the vamps walked, we did too. Not that I had a car to drive—I still hadn't replaced the one I'd apparently driven into a tree four months ago—but Rhoan did, and it would have been nice just to climb inside his old Ford and drive home to warmth and safety.

Thankfully for my chilled body, we did eventually find a cab.

"You go," Rhoan said, as the cab drew to a halt outside our apartment building. "I feel like relaxing at the Blue Moon for a few hours."

The Blue Moon was one of the five werewolf clubs in Melbourne, and the one favored by us both. I studied him for a moment, then said, "You should ring Liander."

"Dammit, Riley, don't give me a lecture. Not now. I

just feel like blowing some steam and that's exactly what I intend to do."

Liander would be more than willing to accommodate any steam-blowing my brother required, and we both knew it. I wondered why he was so resistant to making any sort of real commitment to Liander—but the edge of anger so evident in his gray eyes suggested now was not the time for this topic.

But he had to be aware that he was running the risk of losing the man who was probably his soul mate. He had to be—no one else but a soul mate would put up with the sort of shit Rhoan had been pulling of late.

"Be careful" was all I said. I leaned forward and gave him a kiss, then climbed out of the cab.

He waved as the cab zoomed off. I smiled and walked up the steps to our building.

Jack wasn't happy that we were still living here. After Gautier's initial threat, he'd insisted we shift into a more secure building. Only it hadn't stopped Gautier. I don't know how he'd gotten into the apartment given the fact that vampires couldn't cross thresholds uninvited, but he'd left us a bloody rose and a simple message:

The best kill is one that is fully appreciated beforehand. The hunt has not yet begun.

After that, we'd come back home. Which didn't mean we relaxed our guard any, but Gautier had proven his point. He could get us anywhere, anytime, so there was no purpose in hiding.

I thrust open the old glass and wood front doors and began to climb the stairs. This old brick building had originally been a warehouse, but for the last fifty years, at least, it had functioned as an apartment building. And though both the building and the apartments had become as run-down as the entire Sunshine area, it was close to the city and transport, and the apartments were bigger than anything they built nowadays. Not to mention the fact that it was cheap.

Of course, the old biddy who owned the building hated nonhumans of *any* kind, but it was against the law to discriminate. Which didn't actually mean she had to accept us as tenants—humans could always find ways to circumnavigate laws if they wanted to—but having werewolves in the building also meant there was never a problem with rats. And in a rat-infested area, this was a good thing.

Though why those beady-eyed little bastards hated us so much was anyone's guess. It certainly wasn't because we had a habit of eating them. They tasted as ghastly as they looked.

Rhoan and I lived on the sixth—and top—floor, and there was no elevator, only these stairs. I ran up them— the one regular form of exercising I did outside the training they forced on us at the Directorate—then pushed open the stairwell door and strode down the hall toward our apartment. I have to admit, my thoughts were not on safety at that point. I just wanted to get inside, have a hot shower followed by several gallons of hazelnut coffee. Which I'd neatly top off with a block of my favorite chocolate—black forest.

One of the many good things about being a werewolf was the fact that our metabolic rate was so efficient, we could basically eat what we wanted and not put on weight.

I opened the door, threw off my coat, chucked my keys on the phone table, and began stripping off as I headed for the bathroom.

A soft chuckle ran across the silence.

My heart froze and, for one horrible second, I thought I'd made the mistake that would end my life. Then the voice registered and my heart did a strange little leap. I couldn't help the smile that touched my lips as I turned around.

Quinn O'Conor, ancient vampire, billionaire businessman, and one of my two permanent lovers, stood near the window, his arms crossed as he leaned casually against one pane of the glass that lined the entire outside wall of our living room.

As window dressings went, he was mighty damn fine.

Tonight he wore a navy shirt that emphasized the width of his shoulders and dark jeans that drew the eye down the lean, athletic length of his legs. His hair—once shoulder length but now cut shorter—was night dark, and so thick, so lush, that my fingertips itched with the need to run through it. Unlike most vampires, he could stand a lot of sunshine, so he was as far from white as a vampire could actually get, his skin possessing a warm, almost golden glow. And to say he was handsome would be the understatement of the year. I swear even angels would be envious of his looks, and yet he was in no way effeminate.

But it was his obsidian eyes that always caught me, and right now they were filled with a heat that instantly began to warm the chill from my skin. And, as ever, as our gazes met, something passed between us, an awareness that made my heart stutter and caused goose bumps to prickle across my skin. It was an awareness that had been present from the very first time we'd met, and it seemed to be getting stronger with every passing month.

The last time I'd seen him was two weeks ago—when he'd left me high but far from dry after a delicious dinner date. Why he'd refused all my efforts to get him into bed—or anywhere else, for that matter—I have no idea. But I very much suspected it was all part of a larger plan.

All I had to do now was uncover what that plan was. Not an easy thing when he'd had over twelve hundred years of practice at keeping secrets.

"Well, this is a pleasant surprise," I said, continuing to strip off wet clothes and drop them on the floor as I walked toward him.

His eyes gleamed with heat, and desire swirled around me—a teasing, lusty aroma that had my blood racing even harder through my veins. If it was anything to go by, he would not be playing hard to get tonight.

"I heard you liked surprises," he said, a smile teasing his lush lips as he lightly touched my shoulders and leaned forward to kiss my forehead.

Not exactly the type of kiss I was hoping for.

I pulled away from his light touch, undid my bra, and tossed it toward my discarded shirt. As tosses went, it was pretty lame, but at that point, I wasn't really caring.

"So is the surprise you appearing uninvited in my apartment, or have you something more interesting in mind?"

He smiled, his finger warm against my skin as he skimmed my cheek and lightly outlined my lips. I opened my mouth slightly, drawing in his fingertip, sucking on it briefly. Heat flared brighter in his dark eyes, and the sweet aroma of lust sharpened, until it felt like I was being crushed under the weight of it. But oh, what a way to go.

"I thought you might like to go out for dinner," he said, the Irish lilt in his rich voice suddenly more pronounced.

"Me eating food and you eating me?" I raised an eyebrow, a smile teasing my lips. "We could do that now, if you'd like."

Even as I said it, I skimmed my hands down the muscled planes of his chest and stomach, wishing he was naked so I could actually feel skin. When I reached the button of his jeans, I played with it lightly, one finger skimming underneath, brushing the top of the erection straining against the denim. All it would take was one quick tug of the zipper, and he would be free and mine.

But before I could put thought into action, he caught my hands and brought them back up to his lips. The kiss he dropped on the top of my fingers was light, almost impersonal, and yet there was nothing impersonal about the way his gaze met mine. This vampire wanted me as much as I wanted him, and I'd be damned if I knew why he was resisting. It wasn't like either of us were new to the game of lovemaking.

And it certainly wasn't as if we were new to each other. We'd been making like rabbits for months. Well, at least up until the last few weeks, when this whole "let's frustrate Riley" mode of operation had come in.

"You're wet and cold," he said, matter-of-factly.

"My skin may be cold and I may be wet, but trust me,

I'm warm where it counts." I closed the gap between us and pressed my breasts lightly against him. The silk felt so good against my nipples that I rubbed them back and forth across his shirt, enjoying the smooth coolness of the material. "Would you like to feel just how warm and wet?"

"What I would like," he said, and leaned forward to drop a quick kiss on my lips, "is for you to have a shower and get dressed so we can make our dinner reservation."

"Meaning no fun beforehand?"

"No."

"Damn."

He smiled, and my heart did another weird twist in my chest. I'd known lots of good-looking men over the years, and many of them had great smiles, but Quinn's was in a league of its own.

"What if I promise it will be worth it?" he said.

"Dinner will only be worth it if you come as dessert."

"Maybe I will. Maybe I'm not taking you to dinner at all, but somewhere where there is no chance of interruption so I can ravish you senseless. But if you do not get ready, you will never know."

I admitted momentary defeat and stepped back. "Then I'm guessing you don't want to share the shower with me?"

"I'd love to share a shower, but I suspect it would end up being an extremely *long* shower."

"And there's something wrong with that?"

"Absolutely nothing." He gave me another killer smile. "Go get ready, woman."

I went. And while I usually lingered in the shower, enjoying the sting of the water jets against my skin, there was nothing leisurely about *this* shower. I was out and dried in record time. I waltzed naked from the bathroom and headed for the bedroom. Quinn had his back to me, staring out over the myriad of city lights so visible from our windows. But, like moths drawn to a flickering flame, our gazes met in the glass.

I stopped, and for several seconds did nothing more than stare at him. It was rare for me, that. Werewolves seldom held still for any amount of time—the energy of the beast, barely contained, was Rhoan's theory. But in this instance the urge to move had fled, consumed by the force of the vampire in front of me, lost in the emotive swirl of want and desire and something else—something that ventured close to determination and yet was a whole lot more powerful.

Then his gaze left mine and slid down my body, becoming a sensual and yet excruciatingly slow exploration that had pinpricks of sweat breaking out across my skin. And suddenly it was all I could do not to run across the room and jump into his arms. Take or be taken.

He smiled at that moment, and I knew he'd read the emotion behind the thought, if not the thought itself. Quinn was both a strong empath and telepath, and while I had mind-shields strong enough to keep most vampires out, there was something about *this* vampire that left my senses reeling and my defenses down.

And it wasn't just the link we'd formed to allow communication between us in psi-shielded areas. It was more—had always been more, even before we'd shared blood.

But he was a vampire, not a wolf, and no matter how much my own body might betray my white-picket-fence-

and-kids ideal, no matter how deep the connection between us became, there was no escaping the fact that we came from two very different worlds. I could never be only with him like he wanted, and he could never provide what I wanted. I might not be able to carry children but, at this point, my eggs were still fertile. But Quinn could never give me those children. He was the undead.

Nor would he stand for someone else giving me what he could not provide. God, he hated the fact that I had other lovers, that I still went to the clubs and danced with whom I wanted, even though he knew that was part of a werewolf's nature—and something we would not give up for anyone less than a soul mate.

And while I might feel a deep connection with Quinn, he wasn't a wolf and he could never be my soul mate.

No matter how much he might think otherwise.

His gaze went back to the lights, freeing me from stillness but leaving me hot and achy and more than a little frustrated. I mightn't have any idea about the game he was playing, but I'd be damned if I'd put up with it for much longer. He might have centuries of secrets behind him, but I was a werewolf and sensuality was an inherent part of who we were. Sex was as important to us as blood was to a vampire, and if Quinn expected me to simply play along with whatever he had planned, then he was in for a rude awakening.

I continued into the bedroom and headed for the wardrobe, which wasn't as sparse as it had been a few months ago. Rhoan had gone on another of his spending sprees, and as usual, he'd bought clothes for me. I think he figured I wouldn't tell him off as much if he shared the loot. And I have to admit, his taste was far better than mine, even if his love of bright colors sometimes had me wincing.

"Do I need to dress casual, elegant, or upmarket?" I yelled out as I studied options.

"Comfortable," he answered, amusement evident in his deep tones.

Damn. It was hard to do seductive in comfortable clothes. After several minutes of indecision, I simply grabbed a pair of jeans and a thick woolen sweater. If I couldn't do sexy, I might as well be warm. I grabbed socks and undies, but didn't bother with a bra. The moon was blooming, and the moon heat—which was what we wolves called the seven-day period before the full moon—was only days away. This was the time when the power of the moon surged through our veins with ever-increasing strength, and our hunger for sex became a call we could not—dared not—ignore. The heat didn't usually hit me as hard as it did full-blooded wolves, but every couple of months I suffered all the outward symptoms. Like my breasts feeling fuller, and becoming overly sensitive. And me feeling hornier than a bitch in heat.

Which I guess was what I was.

I dressed, dragged a pair of shoes from the grip of the dust bunnies under my bed, then walked back into the living room. He looked me up and down, then said, "Perfect."

"I know." I resisted the urge to do a sexy pose—a hard thing to pull off in jeans and a floppy woolen sweater anyway—and grabbed my apartment keys and wallet, shoving them both in my pocket. "So, give. Where are we going?"

"It's a surprise." He herded me out the door and down the stairs. Outside, the wind was strong, ripping the door from my grip and slamming it back against the outside wall.

The night was still freezing cold, but at least the rain had stopped. A white limo waited at the curb. The driver stood near the rear door, and opened it as we approached. Once we were seated, the driver climbed back in, started the car, and zoomed off. Obviously, he was in on the plan, whatever the plan was.

I ignored the seat belt and slid across the soft leather seat until I was practically sitting on Quinn's lap. "I've never made love in a limousine," I said softly, sliding my hand provocatively up his leg.

"Then perhaps that can be another outing," he commented, stopping my hand before it got to the interesting bits.

"You know, if you're planning to frustrate me, you're succeeding."

Amusement glittered in his obsidian eyes. "Good."

"No, it's not. I'm a wolf, remember, and the full moon is rising."

"I haven't forgotten."

"But the million-dollar question is, do you plan to do something about it?"

Just for a moment, the heat and the need I could smell haunted the dark shadows of his eyes. My hormones did excited cartwheels, though in all honesty, I have no idea why, because all he said was "Be patient."

"Patience was never one of my virtues."

He chuckled softly, then wrapped his arm around my shoulder and pulled me close. Such intimacy *without* sex wasn't something I was really accustomed to, and it felt both strange and good at the same time. I leaned into him, my head resting against his shoulder, enjoying the closeness even while wishing it was a whole lot more.

We'd been driving for a good ten minutes before I realized we were headed for Essendon airport. Excitement stirred. I didn't get out of Melbourne too often these days, and while our casual dress suggested our destination wasn't somewhere too exotic, the airport meant it was at least going to be somewhere different.

It was a few minutes after that that the driver lowered the glass between us and him, and said, "Sir, I believe we are being followed."

"Same car as before?"

"Yes. A white Saab, with two occupants."

"Pull off at Airport West and see if we can lose him in the side streets there."

I pulled away from his arm and sat up. "How long has someone been following you?"

"We picked up the tail when I arrived at the airport earlier this evening. I thought we'd managed to lose them."

"Perhaps they've bugged the car." Fear ran through me even as I said it. One person who might want to do such a thing was Gautier. I had no doubt it was part of his plans to kill all I held dear before he killed me. If he *did* know about Quinn and *was* behind us being followed now, it meant that Rhoan had been right and Gautier was playing a game far deeper than what he was admitting. "Was it dark when you flew in?"

Quinn frowned. "Twilight. Why?"

I told him about the events of the night and Gautier's proposition.

"And you believed him?" he said, voice holding a hint of incredulousness.

"I really don't know what to think."

"So why ask the question about time?" He grabbed my arm, holding me steady and stopping me from sliding across the seat as the driver took a sharp left then accelerated.

"Because if you flew in at twilight, it confirms the fact it couldn't have been Gautier."

Because he might be the best guardian ever seen, but he was still a vampire and therefore couldn't escape the standard restrictions facing all vampires. And because he was a clone, he was too young in vampire years to be able to face *any* sunlight.

"He mightn't be able to risk fading light, but he's more than capable of employing people who can."

"Trust me, Gautier doesn't work with other people."

"All vampires work with others when the need arises. Even the Lone Ranger had help."

Amusement bubbled through me. "The Lone Ranger? That's a character from a cruddy old TV series, not real life."

"I'm rather a fan of that series," he said stiffly, but humor sparked his dark eyes.

"I *know*." After all, we'd spent boring nights watching the damn show. Well, until I managed to distract him, that was.

"You, young pup, will get a cuff over the ear if you do not show more respect for the old classics."

"That a promise?"

He shook his head, as if in disgust, but the effect was somewhat spoiled by the amusement playing across his lips. "Maybe. But first we need to find out who our followers are, and who hired them."

"When you promised an exciting time, I wasn't expecting *this* sort of excitement."

My voice was dry and, with a smile, he leaned forward and kissed me. I'm sure he meant it to be short and sweet, like all the other kisses we'd shared tonight, but my hormones had had more than enough of *that*. As his lips met mine, I ran a hand through the silk of his hair and lightly clenched a handful at the back of his head to stop him from pulling away. Then I deepened the kiss, taking my time, exploring and tasting and teasing. By the time I released him, we were both breathing heavily.

"The wolf gets her revenge," he said softly, his breath hot against my lips.

"Only partial revenge. I'll take the rest of it when we uncover who's tracking us."

"I think my plans for the evening are about to go ass up."

"Totally." I kissed him again, this time lightly. "Let's do it."

"Harry, next side street, stop long enough to let us out. Then continue into the next street and block the road."

The driver nodded, obviously unfazed.

Tension curled through my limbs as the car began to speed up. Those following us *had* to know they'd been spotted. The mere fact we'd entered an industrial estate would surely have given the game away, let alone this sudden burst of speed.

The driver wrenched the car left into another street then stopped. We scrambled out, barely getting the doors closed again before he was off. Lights pierced the night, lighting up the main road, drawing close fast. I wrapped the shadows around myself and ran for the semi-enclosed doorway of the nearby warehouse. Quinn joined me, squeezing into my shadow-filled corner, his body pressed close and hard against mine. My heart skipped, then began to race. Danger was a very powerful aphrodisiac to a wolf, and the wild part of my soul rose with a vengeance. Desire rushed through me, fueled by his nearness, by the hardness of his erection pressed so invitingly against my groin. And, most of all, by the danger of what we were about to do.

I closed my eyes, trying to ignore the needs of my body, trying to concentrate on the approaching car. The rumble of the engine was close, so close.

But Quinn was closer still.

I lifted my face and his mouth was there, crushing mine, the kiss deep and hungry and powerful. Everything our kiss in the car had been and more. And oh, so glorious.

The tires squealed as the second car came around the corner, then the engine gunned and the car sped off.

Quinn pushed back immediately. "Let's go."

His voice was curt, and I wondered if the source was the tension of the hunt, or anger that he'd responded so strongly to my closeness. He wasn't a man who liked to lose control. Not in *any* situation.

He was off in an instant, running with the speed of

the wind after the car. I followed, staying to the left of the road, barely keeping up with him despite the fact that I had a vampire's speed.

The car sped around the next corner with us close on its tail. Up ahead, the limo had stopped sideways across the road, as instructed.

The Saab slowed to halt. I stopped, and saw Quinn do the same. There was no movement from inside the car. Indeed, I couldn't even see the shadowy outline of the driver or the passenger through the darkened windows. The car just sat there, idling quietly.

I glanced across at Quinn, felt the caress of pressure against my psychic shields. I opened the door we'd created between our minds and said, *I'm not getting any feedback from my senses.*

Nor I with infrared.

I switched briefly to infrared. He was right. There wasn't even the faintest hint of blood heat in the confines of the car. *Could they be shielded against it?*

Maybe, though I've never heard of such a thing. Let's approach cautiously.

I blew out a breath, then nodded. The closer I got to the car, the more tension curled through my limbs. Still no movement from inside, and definitely no sign or scent of life.

They *had* to be there, somewhere. Had to be hiding. Two people couldn't just up and disappear without even opening doors.

I edged along the side of the car and wished I'd brought my laser with me. The whole situation would have felt a lot more manageable with a weapon in my hand.

Which just went to show how far along the road I was to full acceptance of becoming a guardian. Once upon a time, not so long ago, I'd sworn that I would never pick up a weapon for the Directorate, let alone use one.

How long would it be before I actually caved in and killed for something other than self-defense or defense of pack?

A shiver ran across my skin. I ignored it and reached for the front door handle. The window was open slightly, allowing a tight-angled but clear view of the inside of the car. Even this close, there didn't appear to be anyone there. After a quick look at Quinn over the top of the car, I wrenched open the door and stepped back, out of the immediate path of a firing weapon.

I shouldn't have bothered.

The car was as empty as it had appeared.

Chapter 3

That's impossible." I stepped closer and waved a hand through the space of the passenger seat. It met with no resistance. No invisible beings sitting there, then.

"Apparently not, because the car is empty." He opened the back door and felt inside. His hand, like mine, found no resistance.

He slammed the door shut and the sound echoed across the windswept night. He didn't say anything, just stood there, his hands on his hips as he studied the nearby buildings and shadows. After a moment, he walked over to the limo.

While he talked to the driver, I grabbed my vidphone and dialed the Directorate. Jack would undoubtedly still be at the warehouse, but Salliane, the vamp who'd taken my place as a guardian liaison and Jack's main assistant, was on duty.

"Sal, it's Riley Jenson," I said, when her dusky features came online. "I need you to do me a favor."

"That depends." Her husky voice was reserved, as it usually was whenever she was talking to me. "On whether you can be bothered using my real name or not."

I rolled my eyes. Vampires—even the ones that washed—could be fucking annoying at times. But as far as battles of wills went, this was one I was willing to cede. Though what her damn problem with me was I had no idea. And Jack was no help—he kept insisting I was imagining things.

Which was just more evidence to support my theory that he was in lust with his caramel-haired liaison.

"Salliane, I need you to do me a favor."

"What?"

The glint in her brown eyes was evident, even down the phone line. She liked the fact I'd backed away. Enjoy the moment, cow, because it sure as hell won't be happening again.

"I need a plate traced." I gave her the details.

"This guardian business?"

"Yes."

"I'll check with Jack."

Not just a cow, but a bitch as well. "Fine. Just trace the plate."

"Hang on."

I did, my gaze moving to Quinn, watching as he turned to study a small alley to the right of the limo.

Sal came back online. "It's registered to a Karen Herbert."

"You want to do a background check on her for me?"

"You sure this is Directorate business?"

"Yes," I said, even as I was thinking, Just do it, bitch. But I wisely held my tongue.

"I'll see what I can find and give you a call back."

"Thanks."

I hung up and called Jack immediately, but got switched to voice mail. Maybe the cow had him on speed dial. I left a message telling him why I'd asked for the trace and the background check, then hung up and walked across to Quinn. "The car belongs to a Karen Herbert. She's not a disgruntled ex-girlfriend, is she?"

"Never heard of her."

Didn't think the answer was going to be *that* easy. I glanced at the alley he was continuing to study. Something scratched at my senses—a presence that was there, and yet not. Which didn't exactly make sense. I frowned and looked at Quinn again. "So who wants to kill you now?"

He smiled at that. "I'm a very successful, often ruthless businessman, and a vampire besides. Those two alone give me more enemies than most."

"It would be helpful if you could narrow the field a little."

He glanced at me, eyes again obsidian stone, in which there was no life, no warmth. He suspected someone, that much was obvious. But he wasn't about to tell me, and I had to wonder why. He might have a trunk-load of secrets that he chose to keep, but this *shouldn't* have been one of them. I had the right to know, simply because I was now involved.

But all he said was "Something hides in that alley."

It drew my attention away from him again, as he'd

undoubtedly intended. My senses crawled outward, and the sensation of being watched by something indefinable increased, until my stomach flip-flopped in reaction. "What is it?"

My voice was a whisper, and he answered in kind. "A presence I haven't felt in centuries."

I raised an eyebrow. "What sort of presence?"

He shook his head. "Wait here."

I caught his arm, halting him as he stepped away. "You can't go in there alone."

"I must. He will not speak if you are with me."

"Why not?"

He touched my face briefly, his fingers so warm against my suddenly chilled skin. "Just trust me, and stay here."

I did trust him. I was just afraid for him, and besides, two was always better than one when in a fight—a fact I knew too well after a childhood of misadventures.

I crossed my arms and watched as he walked into the alleyway. The shadows wrapped around him as gently as a lover, whisking him from sight. He wasn't even visible through infrared. And it took every ounce of will I had to remain near the car, to wait as he'd asked. To trust that he knew what he was doing.

Which he did, of course. You didn't get to be over twelve hundred years old without gaining more than a little common sense. Not to mention some usable fighting skills.

After a while, the wind died down again and the night grew colder. Within minutes of that, it began to rain—not as hard as before, but rain was rain.

I shivered and rubbed my arms, torn between the

need to charge into the alley and see what was taking so long and the desire to get into the limo and out of the weather. I'd just about decided on the former, when Quinn walked out of the alley.

He was whole and unhurt, and relief swept through me. But it only lasted a second, because his anger hit me, the force of it a tidal wave that crashed over my defenses and left me struggling for air.

"Quinn," I somehow managed to gasp.

The wave of emotion stopped immediately. "Sorry."

I took a deep breath, blew it out slowly. My limbs were shaking and weak, as if I'd been winded by several hard blows. In many respects, that's exactly what had happened—only the blows were empathic rather than physical.

Odd that it only ever seemed to happen with *this* vampire.

"What happened?"

"Nothing much."

His voice was distant, his gaze, though it was on me, vacant—as if he wasn't actually seeing me or our surroundings, but something else altogether. Something internal.

"What do you mean, nothing much? Who was in the alley? What did he want?"

"Nothing that concerns you."

I crossed my arms and glared at him. "So we're back to that old bullshit, are we?"

He blinked at that, and life came back into his dark gaze. "This is a different type of bullshit, believe me."

"I'd love to, Quinn, but it seems that any time I ask a hard question—like, where were you born or what the hell was in that alley—you revert to the same old song. Well, it's not good enough. Not if you want to be something more than just another fuck."

His gaze hardened. "There are some things I cannot explain. And there are promises made long ago that bind me—much as I might not want them to."

"Meaning?"

"I am forbidden to speak to you about who was in that alley, and what I now must do."

"Why? I thought the only people who could order you to do anything were vamps older than you. And whatever it was in that alley, it wasn't a vampire." Or anything else that I recognized.

"No." He hesitated, stepping forward and reaching for me with one hand.

I jerked away from his touch and stepped back. "I've only ever asked one thing of you—the truth. And it seems to me you are as unwilling as ever to give me that."

"This is *not* my story to tell." His soft voice was as angry as I'd ever heard it. "Nor have I the time to stand here and argue. I must go."

"Then let's go."

"Not you. Me. You can take the other car—"

"Like hell I will!"

He sighed. "Riley, please. I don't want to force you to do what is sensible."

"What is sensible is for you to explain what the hell is going on!"

He hesitated, then said, "Those things in the car were not human."

"Well, I gathered that. Humans don't up and disappear into thin air."

"They weren't nonhuman, either."

"Then what the hell were they?" I mean, what else was there when it came to humanoid entities?

"Demon."

I blinked, not sure I heard him right. "What?"

"Demons. Creatures from the vaults of hell itself." He paused. "These particular demons were low-class demons—good for following and harassing, but not much good for killing anything more than humans. I'm actually surprised they were sent after me at all."

I stared at him, wondering if whoever it was in the alley had hit him over the head and loosened a brain cell or two. "Demons don't exist."

"As angels don't exist?" He snorted softly. "You have lived a sheltered life, indeed."

I stepped forward and touched his arm. "I think you'd better sit—"

He shook my touch off irritably. "I'm not crazy. Demons are creatures of mist and malevolence, and if two are loose in this city, we need to know who summoned them, and why."

"So let's get our asses into the car and start investigating."

"I will. You will be going home."

"I believe we have been through this already. The answer is still no."

He stared at me for several seconds, and a chill ran over my skin. There was suddenly something very old, very deadly, and decidedly *unhuman*—in a way that went far beyond being a vampire—in his eyes. Something I'd never seen before.

"Don't make me force you, Riley."

I opened my mouth to refute the statement then closed it again. What was the use of saying no way, when it was more than probable he *could* force me? We'd shared blood once, and if there was one thing I was certain about, it was the fact that it would have had more consequences than he'd actually mentioned. And I really didn't want to know if it was possible for him to make me obey him completely or not.

Because once I knew for sure, that would be the end of us. I couldn't be with a man who could—would—use psychic force against me in a relationship.

"Fine." I waved a hand irritably at the car. "Piss off and don't bother coming back for a while."

"Riley, please, just trust me that I have no choice in this." He reached for me again, and again I stepped away.

"Don't," I said. "Because right now, I'm angry with you and I may say something we'd both regret. Just go."

He did.

Without a backward glance.

I, however, swore like an old sea dog as I watched the limousine's taillights disappear into the night. Part of me hadn't actually believed he'd go.

One of these days, that stupid, romantic part of me was going to learn *not* to get her hopes up. Either that, or I was going to have to stop saying things if I didn't actually mean them.

I stomped a foot, then spun around and glared at the alley. I still couldn't see or feel anything in that shadowed, misty darkness—and yet, something was there. Something that teased the outer reaches of my senses, like an itch I couldn't quite scratch. I needed to investigate. Whatever it was Quinn had seen and spoken to was still in there. And while he might have believed whatever it was wouldn't speak to me, could I actually trust he'd been truthful in that?

What if it was just another ploy to keep me in the dark?

What if it was a ploy to keep me safe?

I shivered and rubbed my arms again. I was getting soaked by the softly falling rain, but at least my sweater was wool. The majority of me was warm, even if wet.

But it wasn't the rain or the wetness that caused the shiver. It was the thought of facing whatever was in that alley.

Because it was definitely waiting for something or someone.

And considering I was the only something or someone in the near vicinity, that meant, by default, it was probably waiting for me.

I lightly chewed on my bottom lip, contemplating my options, then forced my feet forward. Fortune favored the brave—and the very foolish. The latter classification had fit me often enough in the past and probably would here, as well. But it didn't matter, because I just had to find out what—or who—Quinn had been talking to.

The closer I got to that alley, the colder I became. It wasn't the night, nor was it the fact that I was soaked. This particular coldness came from deep inside, from the place where the very essence of my wolf soul rested, and it flooded outward, making my steps more and more reluctant.

Whatever hid in the darkness, the wolf feared it. And if that instinctive part of me did, then I certainly should.

As I neared the alley's entrance, mist began to gather in the darkness, stretching ethereal fingers in my direction. Without thought, I stepped back. Quickly, and in fear—though of what, I have no idea.

The mist hesitated, then began to recoil.

I drew in a deep breath and blew it out slowly. This was no way to get answers. I had to meet the mist, had to go on.

Had to.

I licked my lips, wondering why the hell I was so afraid of something as harmless as *mist,* and stepped forward. Again the ethereal fingers formed and reached for me. This time, I ignored them and kept on moving. Their touch was almost exploratory and yet, at the same time, pressing, as if they intended to halt me gently. I'd expected the mist to be cold and clammy and, in some ways, it was. Yet it burned against my skin, like the sting of lemon juice against a cut. And the farther I tried to go into the alley, the fiercer that sting got.

It was that, more than fear, that stopped me.

And still my senses could feel nothing, see nothing. There was just that itch, telling me it was there, that it was watching.

"What are you?"

My voice came out croaky, and the mist in front of me stirred gently.

No answer came from the darkness of the alleyway beyond the mist. I tried again. "I know you're there. I can feel your presence."

The little wolf has courage.

The voice was male, and came from everywhere and yet nowhere. It hung on the misty air and yet reverberated through my mind. Was gentle, and yet, at the same time, harsh.

Weird, to say the least.

"The little wolf is scared shitless, but she also wants answers." I could see no harm in admitting the truth in this instance. Besides, something told me anything else could be dangerous.

Amusement rolled across the night, in much the same manner as the words had.

I can see why he likes you.

"Quinn? Oh yeah, he just loves ordering me around, and trying to make me do things I don't want to do."

We were protectors born, little wolf, and that instinct is hard to shake.

I raised an eyebrow. "Meaning Quinn is somehow connected to you? In more than an employer-employee mode, that is?"

That is a question I am not free to answer.

"Why not?"

Because you do not ask the right person.

"Well, it's next to useless to ask Quinn. He never tells me anything."

Vampires live a long time, and there is fun to be had in taking time to unravel the mystery.

"Sorry, but patience has never been a virtue of mine."

Again the amusement swam around me, but this time it was accompanied by an odd sense of approval. Why was anyone's guess.

"Okay, so if my first question was the wrong one, will you then tell me who you are?" What, who, where—the basic questions of interrogation, as defined by the Directorate. Of course, they rarely asked so politely.

The presence seemed to consider my question for an extremely long time. Or maybe wariness and fear just made it seem that way.

I am a high priest of the Aedh.

"I've never heard of them."

I am not surprised. Few of this time would know us.

This time? As in, this century? Or longer? Something in the way he said it suggested the latter rather than the former. "And you came here to talk to Quinn?"

Talk? No.

"Then what?"

That is for him to explain if he wishes.

"He says he was ordered not to explain."

Given the Aedh died long ago, that rule no longer binds. Unless he wishes it.

Why I was surprised by that I had no idea. After all, Quinn had a long habit of keeping his secrets—and using fair means or foul to avoid answering questions about his past. "How could this Aedh of yours have died out if you're a high priest of it?"

Again the amusement swirled, this time tinged with sadness. *I am all that is left.*

"Then what is Quinn's connection to you and the Aedh?"

He once trained to be one of us.

Quinn had once trained to be a priest? The mere thought made me smile—and yet, it certainly explained his somewhat old-fashioned views when it came to sex. "And you were his priest teacher?"

No, I was not.

"Then what's your connection to him?"

Once again, that is for him to explain. The presence paused. *Do not get too curious in this matter, little wolf. You may find you do not like the answers.*

Not liking answers hadn't ever stopped me from asking the questions. And I had an odd feeling that he knew that—and that he was deliberately trying to provoke me into action I might later regret. "Did you tell him about the things in the car? Order him to hunt down the person who summoned them?"

I inform. I can no longer order.

So why was Quinn so angry? Why did he seem to think he'd been ordered? "And were the things in the car really demons, as he said?"

I take it from your tone you do not believe in demons?

"Frankly, no."

He laughed, and it was suddenly such a creepy sound I backed up a step before I realized what I was doing and stopped. Up until that moment, I'd felt no real malevolence from whatever it was hiding in the mist, but right then it seemed like I was teetering on the precipice of an endless pit. And that he was behind me, ready to push.

You will believe in demons by the end of all this, little wolf. And you will learn that not all demons are creatures of myth or magic, but rather of flesh and blood.

And with that, he and the mist were gone.

As quickly and as suddenly as the things in the car.

With the mist and the presence gone, awareness of the night and the weather returned full force. The rain was falling harder, meaning I was soaked to the skin and shivering like a newborn pup. Though I wasn't entirely sure the shivering was a result of the cold.

I scrubbed a hand across my face to wipe the rain

away—uselessly, as it turned out—then turned around and splashed my way back to Karen Herbert's car.

Thankfully, the keys were still in it. Maybe demons couldn't carry them in wraith form—who knew? Certainly not me. Hell, I still wasn't sure what to think when it came to *that* revelation.

I climbed in, started the car up, and turned the heater on full blast. But I didn't go anywhere because I wasn't entirely sure where to go. Part of me wanted to go home, get warm, and consume the coffee and chocolate I'd been anticipating earlier.

But the other half of my soul hungered for pleasures far more carnal. The full moon was near and the moon heat was rising. Quinn might be happy playing his games, but I wasn't about to sit around waiting to discover the point of it all. I had base needs, just like he did.

So why was I not roaring off to one of the werewolf clubs right now?

Damned if I knew—except for the fact that I wanted *him* tonight, not some random encounter with a stranger.

Which was probably the whole point of his "let's frustrate Riley" mode of operation. He wanted me to want him, and only him.

Which meant he was aiming for exclusive, even though he knew well enough that exclusive wasn't something I wanted with a vampire. Particularly seeing he could never fulfill the one desire that had been mine for as long as I could remember.

Kids. A family of my own.

I thumped the wheel in frustration, torn between wanting him and *not* wanting to want him. Between needing to ease the ache and wanting to undertake the journey with him even if the destination wasn't where I wanted to go.

In the end, the ornery part of me won out. Whatever I might or might not desire, there was one thing I could never change. I was a werewolf and sex was part of our nature, part of my soul. Whatever else happened in my life, that was the one thing I could never change.

The one thing I didn't *want* to change.

But even so, I didn't immediately head to the clubs. Quinn might be the one I wanted right now, but he wasn't the only man in my life. And if I didn't want to play with strangers—which I didn't—then I had only one other option.

So I picked up the phone and rang Kellen.

"Sinclair speaking." His voice was gruff, and edged with a tiredness that had my eyebrows raising. I knew he'd been working hard of late, trying to get his freight business fully moved down to Melbourne so he and I could spend more time together, but right now, he sounded like he hadn't slept in days.

"Kellen? It's me."

"Riley?" he said, and the tiredness in his voice was suddenly overrun by a warmth that had my heart doing odd little flip-flops. I might want Quinn more than could ever be good for me, but there was no denying my growing connection with this wolf. It might not have the same strength as the connection that Quinn and I shared, but we'd also had a whole lot less time together.

Something, I thought in sudden annoyance, Quinn had been doing his best to ensure. Something I'd done very little to fight, despite earlier intentions to see them both equally.

Which was odd, really.

"I didn't expect to hear from you for a few more days," he continued softly. "Thought you'd be out with O'Conor."

The way he said Quinn's name spoke volumes, but then, they'd been less than chummy long before I'd come on the scene.

"He's got business to attend to. I thought I'd give you a call instead." Which sounded like he was second choice, and I guess in some ways, that was nothing but the truth. Even if Kellen was more of a possibility when it came to fulfilling my dreams than Quinn could ever be.

He didn't say anything for a moment, but I could almost taste the annoyance he was undoubtedly trying to control. Kellen liked being second about as much as Quinn did.

"I'm not up to going to the clubs tonight," he said. "I've been working for the last forty-eight hours, and the movers have only just left. The place is a mess and I need to get my office in working order for tomorrow."

He'd bought an old five-story hotel on Spencer Street—just several doors down from the Southern Cross railway station—a few months ago, and had been busy renovating ever since. The last time I'd been there—which was only two weeks ago—the four office floors had been completed, but the fifth-floor living quarters were nothing short of a mess. But if he was finally moving in, then he must have finished them.

"I wasn't suggesting a club. I thought I might buy some wine and pay you a visit."

Again he paused. "Will you stay the night?"

"That depends."

"On what?"

"On whether you intend to worship my body as it deserves to be worshipped."

He laughed, a low, throaty sound that had my blood racing. "I did promise that last time, didn't I?"

"Right before you fell asleep."

"Riley, we had ten hours together."

"And you couldn't manage eleven?" I teased lightly. "Your stamina is sorely lacking, wolf."

"Well, I doubt I could even manage ten hours in my current state, but I do promise suitable body worship and good sex. Will that do?"

"Nicely." I glanced at my watch. "I'll be there in twenty minutes."

"Hurry."

I did. I pulled up in front of the grimy bluestone building in precisely seventeen minutes, and stopped my borrowed car right behind his gleaming new Mercedes. It was a four-door rather than a two-door—he apparently preferred the room in the back. It was room we'd put to good use on several mind-blowing occasions.

Anticipation shimmered across my skin as I climbed out of the car, a heat not even the chilly night air could temper. I walked up the steps, pressed the buzzer, then glanced at the security camera.

"Come straight up," he said, as the front door buzzed open.

I walked through and headed for the waiting elevator, then went up. When the elevator stopped and the doors swished open, I walked across the secure area, but before I could press the buzzer, the metal security door opened and Kellen stood there.

He was a lean and muscular brown wolf, though he was more chocolate in coloring than the muddy tones so often seen in the brown packs. His face was sharpish but handsome, his eyes the most delicious shade of gold-flecked green. Right now, those eyes were filled with a hunger that ripped across my senses and made my blood boil.

I stopped and raised a hand to his whisker-covered face, even though all I wanted to do was inhale the thick spicy scent of him, let it fill my lungs and soul as he wrapped his arms around my body and claimed me thoroughly.

"You look a mess," I said softly.

"That's because I am a mess." He caught my hand and drew it down to his lips, kissing it lightly. "You think you can deal with that?"

"Messy is a very sexy look for you."

"I'm glad you think that," he said, stepping backward and drawing me through the door. He slammed it shut, then drew me into his arms. His body was warm and hard against mine, his gaze fierce.

"I have so needed to do this," he added, then his mouth was on mine, plundering, our tongues tangling, tasting, urgent and hungry.

It was a kiss that had my heart racing and body aching. A kiss that made my soul shiver and stir. A kiss that had the urgency rising, until I couldn't think, couldn't breathe. Could only want.

And I did want.

Badly.

He pushed me backward until I hit the wall, then his hands were on me, his fingers scorching my flesh as he stripped off my clothes. I tore off his shirt, unbuttoned his pants. We touched, caressed, and teased each other, until the already raging desire reached boiling point. And then he was lifting me, filling me, liquefying me, and his thick groan of pleasure was a sound I echoed. He began to move, and there was nothing gentle about it. His body plundered as his lips had plundered, and the rich ache grew, becoming a kaleidoscope of sensations that washed through every corner of my mind. Then the shuddering took hold and I gasped, grabbing his shoulders, wrapping my legs around his waist and pushing him deeper still. Pleasure grew again as he thrust and thrust and thrust, until a rapturous, mind-blowing orgasm hit us both and sent us sliding into blissful satisfaction.

When the tremors finally eased, he laughed softly and rested his forehead against mine. "So much for taking time to worship your body and seduce you senseless."

I laughed, resettled myself on the floor, then ran a hand down his hot, scratchy cheek. "We have the rest of the night—are you trying to tell me you can't manage a bit of worship and senseless seduction in all that time?"

His grin was all cheeky, dangerous charm. The sort of charm that could melt a girl's heart and have her panties off in a second. Not that I had panties to worry about right now.

"It's a tough task," he said softly. "But I think I'm up for it."

I skimmed my gaze down his body then gave him a saucy smile. "I do believe you are."

"Then let's not waste a moment." He grabbed my hand and tugged me across the box-filled living room and toward his bedroom.

He certainly didn't waste another moment.

And boy, did he worship.

A shrill ringing dragged me from the depths of sleep. I flopped an arm out from under the covers and groped blindly for my cell phone. I found it on the fifth attempt and dragged it back under the covers. Kellen slid his arm around my waist, pulling me closer to the warmth of his body.

I snuggled back against him, flicked the receiver on the cell, and said, "Uh?"

"Gee, I absolutely love the level of conversation I get from you when you've just woken."

And I absolutely hated the fact Rhoan could be so damn cheerful when *he'd* just woken. It wasn't decent—not before several cups of coffee, anyway.

"If you rang me to say that, I'm going to tell Liander what you did last night then step back and watch the fireworks."

"You are such a bitch."

"I'm a wolf and I'm female. Being a bitch comes with the territory. What's your excuse?"

"Living with a bitch."

I snorted softly. "What do you want, wiseass?"

"What time are you supposed to report to work?"

"Oh, crap." I was obviously late, otherwise Rhoan wouldn't be asking the question. I flicked the covers off my head and cast a bleary eye the clock's way. Nine-fourteen.

Yep, I was late.

"Jack wants to know how soon we can expect your presence."

"I'm at Kellen's." Which wasn't that far away from the Directorate, so at least I didn't have to battle too much traffic. "But I have to shower and dress, so give me half an hour."

"Don't be any later. He's in a mood."

Oh great. That meant something hadn't gone well and it didn't matter if that something was in his private life—though I actually wasn't sure if he *had* a private life—or his work life. We'd be made to pay. "I'll be there."

I hung up.

"Work?" Kellen asked.

"Yeah. They want me in ASAP."

"You want the usual coffee before you go?"

I twisted around and kissed him. "That would be fantastic."

His green eyes sparkled in the early morning light, doing all sorts of things to my hormones.

"Fantastic would be you staying in bed with me," he said.

"I can't."

"I know." He slapped my rear lightly. "Go have your shower. I'll handle breakfast."

I went. After showering and dressing in record time—which made twice in twenty-four hours I'd achieved this miracle—I had a quick cup of coffee and some toast, shared a more leisurely kiss good-bye with Kellen, then headed down to my borrowed car.

I got there only a few minutes over my half-hour deadline. But by the time I parked, went through all the scans and security checks and then headed down to sublevel three and the old conference room that had become the daytime division's temporary headquarters, another ten minutes had slipped by. Jack swung around as I entered, green eyes as stormy as I'd ever seen them. Yep, the shit had hit the fan somewhere along the line last night. Hell, being late was pretty much a common occurrence where I was concerned. It had never bothered him before and I doubt it was the cause of his anger now.

Even so, I opened my mouth to apologize, but didn't even get a chance to say the words before he was in my face and roaring.

"What the hell were you doing last night?"

"Having some of the best sex of my life." I paused a beat, then added dryly, "You obviously *weren't*."

There was a muffled snort from behind us. Rhoan. I didn't react, just met Jack's bloodshot, green-eyed stare with a calm I certainly wasn't feeling. I hadn't seen him in full rant mode often, but I *had* seen him. And if there was one thing I'd learned after nearly eight years of being a liaison and his personal assistant, it was that it was better to use humor to diffuse the situation than to fire back. Which is what my instincts were clamoring to do.

"No, I wasn't," he said. "I was being harassed by my PA because someone was using Directorate resources without permission."

Ah, so I'd been right. The caramel cow *had* been in his ear. "Boss, if you'd just fuck the woman and get it over with, I'm sure all our lives would be a whole lot easier."

He blinked, and as quickly as that, the anger rolled away. He laughed, a short, sharp sound that only hinted at the tension I could still feel in him. "You might be right there."

"When it comes to sex advice, always listen to a werewolf. We don't have many hang-ups to cloud our judgment."

"Maybe."

He studied me a moment longer, then stepped away. I beat a hasty retreat across the almost empty room. Rhoan and I were still the only official members of the daytime guardian squad. Kade was supposed to have been transferred from the military by now, but the endless rounds of paperwork were currently holding things up. Iktar, the featureless spirit lizard who'd played a part in bringing down Davern's cloning and crossbreeding empire, was currently undergoing training and wouldn't officially become a guardian for another ten months. Berna had refused Jack's "offer" and gone home. And then there were Dia and Liander, who were on the books as "consultants" rather than guardians.

I perched on the edge of my brother's desk and asked, "How's the little girl?"

"Died last night in intensive. They haven't found her parents, yet, either."

Anger swirled through me, along with a sense of guilt. We'd tried our hardest to save her, but it had all been for naught. And Gautier was still out there, ready and willing to take more innocent lives. I rubbed a hand across gritty-feeling eyes, and asked, "Has the missing person's register been consulted?"

"Yep," Rhoan said. "No dice there."

"The cops are well able to handle that situation," Jack interrupted, voice holding an impatient edge. "What about we concentrate on our own work for a change?"

I looked at him. "So, what were you saying about resources being used without permission?"

Play innocent until all facts were on the table was my motto. Hell, I had no idea *what* he'd been told. Knowing Sal, it wouldn't have been just the truth, but rather an embellishment that would make her look good and me bad. Why she felt this necessary I have no idea—it wasn't like I was a threat to her ambitions of bedding Jack. I liked him as a person and a boss, but as a sexual partner? Never.

He poured himself a coffee from the dispensing machine and downed it in one gulp. If he'd been doing that for the last few hours, it could go a long way to explain his wired state.

"Why were you using Directorate sources to trace a car?" he asked.

"Because the car was tailing Quinn and myself. It's downstairs, in the parking lot, by the way. And I did leave a message about it on your phone."

"Ah," Rhoan said, "so that explains the satisfied smile on your face as you waltzed in a minute ago."

I glanced at him. "No, it doesn't."

"Why not, when you were with him?"

"Because I wasn't with him for very long."

"Then who were you with?"

"I told you this morning—Kellen. He decided a good

body worshipping was in order last night, and I ended up staying at his place—a fact you would have known if you'd actually been home yourself."

"Bitch."

I wasn't entirely sure whether that comment was aimed at my worshipping comment or the barb, but I decided to go with the former. "Hey, you've got a man more than willing to worship your bod. You're just too chicken to go see him."

"Children, please try and concentrate on the matter at hand rather than your conquests of the night before."

I tried to restrain my grin and look dutifully interested in the topic at hand. Judging by the look Jack threw my way, I wasn't very successful.

"Quinn has more than enough resources of his own to trace cars," Jack continued. "Hell, he could probably get the information quicker than we could. You can't just use the Directorate as your own personal information center."

"Why not? I've been doing it for seven years as your PA." I paused, then added, probably unwisely, "Did Sal do the background check on the owner?"

"Yeah, but there's nothing out of the ordinary."

"Has the owner been contacted about the car? Reported it stolen?"

"No. And she's not answering the phone. We'll follow it up this morning." He ran a hand across his bald head. "So tell me, what the hell were you up to last night?"

"We were being followed, as I said. We arranged a little trap in a side street to smoke them out, but when we got to the car, there was no one inside it."

"So they escaped before you got there?"

"No one escaped from the car. No door was opened. They just vanished."

He frowned. "That's not possible."

"Well, maybe it is for a human or nonhuman, but these things were apparently low-rank demons."

"Demons?" Jack raised his eyebrows. "And just what led you to this conclusion?"

"Quinn told me."

"Quinn told you they were *demons*?" Rhoan's voice was edged with disbelief. "Why on earth would he do that?"

"Because he believed it to be true." I looked back to Jack. "What do you know of a mob called the Aedh?"

He frowned. "The name rings a bell, but that's about it. Why?"

"Because Quinn met with someone who claimed to be a high priest of Aedh. He sent Quinn off to uncover who was raising the demons."

Jack's frown deepened. "Quinn's not the type to be ordered around."

"Tell me about it." Hell, I'd tried ordering him about numerous times, and the damned man just wouldn't do as asked. Mind you, *not* doing what I asked had often led to great amounts of pleasure, so I was hardly in a position to bitch. "So, I guess my next question is, are demons *really* real?"

"And if they *are,* why are they loose in Melbourne and following Quinn?" Rhoan added.

Jack blew out a breath and began to pace the length of the room. Which wasn't a whole lot of steps, as the room was one of the Directorate's smaller conference rooms and had been designed to hold a maximum of twelve around a table. When Kade and Iktar and their desks were installed, it was going to be cozy. Not that I minded getting cozy with Kade. But Iktar—I repressed a shudder.

"Demons do exist," Jack said, "but it usually takes a mage extremely strong in the art of blood magic to conjure one. I've never heard of any mage being able to conjure two or more."

"Blood magic?" I raised an eyebrow. "You mean it's not something they made up in fiction?"

"No. Blood magic is an extremely old form of magic that uses the blood of the conjurer to boost the power of the spell. But I haven't heard of anyone doing it for years." He swung around, his craggy face deep in thought. "You know, if we do have a mage loose in the city, we need to find out why."

"Particularly with Quinn involved—"

"Quinn is more than able to take care of himself," Jack cut in. "And whether or not there *is* a mage loose, it is not your problem. You two need to concentrate on catching the person behind the ritual murders."

Being the multitalented person that I was, I pretty much figured I could do both. And I would, if only because I'd be damned if I'd let Quinn escape without explaining why he was obligated to go after the person raising the so-called demons. But I wisely kept quiet about my intentions—having Jack explode again wasn't something I was planning to see anytime soon.

"Why can't the two be connected? I mean, if a mage needs blood to raise these beasties, then wouldn't it make more sense to use sacrifices rather than their own blood?"

"It is more powerful for a mage to use his own blood rather than a sacrifice. It's a matter of risk ratio, from what I understand."

"The more blood used, the greater the risk, and the greater the power gifted," Rhoan commented. "Makes sense."

"It may make sense but that still doesn't mean the people being sliced open aren't some part of the mage's effort to raise demons."

"No, it doesn't, but I doubt it," Jack replied. "I've seen ritual blood magic, and these murders just don't have the same feel."

Meaning we had *three* kooks running loose in the city? Great. Just what Rhoan and I needed with the moon heat rising. Not that we were the Directorate's only guardians, but we *were* the only ones currently capable of moving around in daylight.

"Okay, so they're not connected. But are we any closer to the source behind the murders?"

Jack grimaced. "Not really."

I raised my eyebrows and said, teasingly, "So sexual frustration isn't the only reason for the temper overload earlier?"

He had the grace to look uncomfortable. Which was why I liked him—he acted more like regular folk than a vampire. Mostly, anyway. "Well, I'm sure it had a bit to do with it. And being nagged by my PA is never pleasant."

"And now you appreciate my do-the-work-fast-gotta-get-out-of-here attitude, don't you?"

"Yeah. Though I have to say her scenery is better."

I grinned. "She's hot for you, boss. I have no idea why you're holding back if you're so attracted."

"Mixing work with pleasure is never a good idea."

"Then she's going to keep doing what she must to keep her voice and her body in your mind."

"Meaning the tops will get more revealing?" Rhoan piped up. "Cool."

I picked up a pen and flicked it at him. "You bat for the other side, remember?"

"Never stopped me from admiring a well-stacked frame."

I looked back at Jack. "So, besides Sal breaking your balls over me putting in an unapproved search request, what else went wrong?"

"Everything." He blew out a breath and grabbed another coffee from the dispenser. "We've had a report of another body. Rhoan, I want you to check it out."

Jack grabbed two files from the top of the coffee dispenser and tossed one of them to Rhoan. "This one has been found up near the Ford factory in Campbellfield."

Rhoan frowned. "Near? The rest of the bodies have been found in abandoned factories, not near fully functioning ones."

"I know, but we have to check it out."

"What about sending cops in?"

"If this is one of ours, I don't want them fouling the area. Peri Knowles will be waiting upstairs and will accompany you. Because this death is apparently very fresh, she might be able to sense some residual magic and give us more of a clue as to the people behind these murders."

Peri? I glanced at my brother and he shrugged. Obviously, it was a new name to him, too. Rhoan slapped the folder against his thigh as he rose. "I'll report in as soon as I get there."

He walked out. Jack handed me the second file.

"I want you to go chat with this man."

The man's name was Bob Dunleavy, and a quick flick through the file's paperwork and photos revealed a petty criminal who'd scored numerous jail terms that had never curbed his thieving ways. "He doesn't seem the sharpest knife in the drawer," I commented. "So why am I going to talk to him?"

"Because Dunleavy has, over the years, provided some good information in exchange for lighter sentences. He rang yesterday evening to say he desperately needed some help and that he'd trade some information he'd picked up from his girlfriend. Information about our current case."

"So if he called yesterday, why are you only acting on it now?"

"Because I didn't have any free staff until now. And if that free staff doesn't get her butt off the desk and get it moving, I'll give it a good kick-start."

"You're such a charmer when you're sexually frustrated," I said dryly, then waved the folder in the air. "To go chat to Dunleavy, I need a car."

"You dented the last one."

"Not my fault."

"The owner of the other car is disagreeing with that assessment."

Well, he would. The idiot didn't have insurance, so he'd have to pay for the mess his car was in himself if he couldn't shift the blame to me. "It'll take me at least an hour on public transport to get to Springvale."

"I know, which is why I've asked Salliane to allocate you another car. Just try not to dent it. Or write it off."

I refrained from pointing out that I didn't actually write off the last one, and jumped off the desk. "I'll report back in once I talk to Dunleavy."

"Do that. Alex is working on the young vamp, so we might yet find out what Gautier is really up to."

I frowned. "The baby vamp is dead. How the hell can she work on someone who is dead?"

"He's a vampire. Unless you fry us with sunlight, basic brain functions—including the ability to regenerate—can survive for many hours. Some of the older, stronger ones can even survive having their neck broken. Which means there may be enough consciousness left to read."

A thought that was entirely *too* creepy. But I didn't exactly break the young vamp's neck, I severed it. I would have thought that to be an entirely different prospect. "I thought breaking a vamp's neck was the second surest way to kill them?"

"It is, except for the very old. If the old ones are in a safe enough position, they will eventually regenerate. The young and very young simply take longer to truly die."

"So someone as old as Quinn could regenerate?"

"No. Director Hunter could. Quinn would probably be on the cusp of the required age, so surviving would be a fifty-fifty proposition."

The longer I worked with vampires, the more I learned about them. And the more secretive the bastards seemed. "So what other juicy little tidbits are you vamps hiding from the rest of us?"

"Not a whole lot, I assure you."

"Yeah, believing the sincerity behind that statement."

Jack glanced at his watch rather than replying. I took the hint and quickly headed out to collect the car keys from the caramel cow.

*B*ob Dunleavy lived in a small house—or town house, as the estate agents liked to call them—a couple of house blocks down from the Springvale police station. Maybe the boys in blue wanted to keep an eye on him. Or maybe Dunleavy figured that he'd fly under their radar by living so close. Though if his record was anything to go by, it hadn't worked so far.

Smiling slightly, I rested my arms on the steering wheel and studied the town houses opposite, not only checking for indications that Dunleavy was home but also looking for hints about the man himself.

If his house was anything to go by, Dunleavy was a slob. Which pretty much explained his lengthy record— a neat thief was often harder to catch than a messy one.

This section of Springvale was an old, established area and the house blocks around here were large enough to have three smaller houses built on them. Most of the old houses in this street had already been torn down to make way for their smaller cousins, and the "for sale" signs dominating the front yards of the remaining two suggested it wouldn't be long before the whole street was shared residential.

Dunleavy's town house was the rear one—the one

closest to the back fence and the railway lines behind it. It was clearly visible from the road thanks to the fact it sat front-on to the driveway rather than side-on, like the other two. Dunleavy's neighbors had to hate that fact. While their little places were neat and tidy, his was anything but. Talk about bringing the tone of the neighborhood down.

Two of his front windows had been smashed, the holes covered by soggy-looking cardboard that was held in place by long strips of black tape. Scraggy-looking curtains hung sadly from either side of these windows, and were yellowed with age and slashed in places. The other windows were covered by taped-up newspaper. The front door was a mess of peeling paintwork and holes, and even the brickwork looked worse for wear— almost as if it had the dust of eons coating its surface.

I couldn't see anyone moving around inside, even though there'd been bursts of movement evident in the other two town houses. But that didn't mean anything. Dunleavy did most of his work at night, so he was probably asleep right now.

I grabbed my coat and climbed out of the car. The wind hit, pulling at my hair and slapping my skin with its iciness. I shivered my way into the coat and heartily cursed the winter weather. Though at least it wasn't raining yet.

After locking the car, I shoved my hands into my pockets and made my way across the road. A curtain covering a window in the first town house moved, and a face briefly peered through the glass. An older woman, her features pinched and harsh-looking. I gave her a smile of acknowledgment and she quickly dropped the curtain back in place.

Maybe the reason Dunleavy had been caught so often wasn't so much a product of his carelessness, but rather his nosy neighbor.

I continued on past the second town house. The eleven o'clock news was blasting out from either a radio or TV inside, and the smell of burnt toast hit the air. I drew it in, savoring the sharp aroma even as my stomach rumbled a reminder it had only had toast for breakfast, and made a mental note to grab a burger on my way back to the Directorate.

There was a small van parked out the front of Dunleavy's garage. A quick look through the windows revealed piles of newspapers, discarded take-out containers and, stacked neatly in a plastic box attached to the van's side, several duffel bags. Dunleavy's tools of trade, no doubt. I climbed the crumbling concrete steps and raised a hand to knock on the door. Only to freeze as a familiar smell spun around me.

Blood. Thick, ripe, and very, very fresh.

And with it came the scent of death and excrement—smells I knew entirely *too* well.

Dunleavy—or someone else—was dead inside the house.

And Gautier had been here.

Chapter 4

For several heartbeats, I didn't move. Scarcely even dared to breathe as I listened to the wind, sorting through the scents that ran with it, noting the sounds that ran underneath it. There was no hint of life—or even *un*life—coming from this apartment. Only from those behind me.

Gautier might have been here, but he wasn't now. I'd feel him—or any other vampire, for that matter.

And while part of the excrement scent was definitely his, there was more to the smell than simply his presence. It had a very human aroma to it—and the one thing Gautier had never been was human.

Meaning someone had probably shit themselves inside the town house. Of course, anyone who had *any* brains would be scared shitless by Gautier. He was one nasty mother.

I stepped back from the door. The lock was in place, and there was nothing to indicate it had been forced in any way. If Gautier *had* been here, he hadn't come through the front door to get at Dunleavy. Though the only way he could have forced his way through the door in the first place was if Dunleavy had previously invited him in. If there was one rule about vampires that was true, it was the fact that they couldn't cross thresholds uninvited.

"I called the cops, you know."

I wasn't sure what leapt higher—my feet or my heart—and even as I spun around, I was reaching for the weapon I didn't have. Mainly because I'd taken it off near the coat stand at home last night, and hadn't gone back to pick it up in my rush to get out of Kellen's door this morning. Jack would have my hide if he found out.

Thankfully, I didn't need it. The voice belonged to the sharp-faced old woman from the first apartment. I took a deep breath, trying to calm my racing pulse and ignore the fact that it could have been *anyone* who'd crept up on me. God, I was still so green at this, I was a danger to myself.

"What?" I said, perhaps more brusquely than I should have.

"I called the cops."

Great. Just what I needed to deal with on top of a possible murder. "And you'd be Mrs. . . . ?"

"*Ms.* Radcliffe." She drew the knitted shawl draped over her frail shoulders closer to her body as the wind gusted again.

"Ms. Radcliffe, I'm a guardian." When her expression showed little comprehension, I added, "With the

Directorate of Other Races." I grabbed my badge—which I always carried—and showed it to her. "I'm here to talk to Mr. Dunleavy, so there was no need to report—"

"Not now," she interrupted, expression suddenly cross. "Before. When all that racket was happening."

"Before when? And what sort of racket are we talking about?"

"Must have been seven-thirty, eight o'clock, something like that. And the noise—" She sniffed. "Sounded like they were throwing things about and smashing up the place."

"No screaming? No arguing? Nothing like that?"

"No. They were quiet this time—except for smashing things up, that is."

"They who?"

"Him and his dirty little piece."

I raised my eyebrows and somehow resisted the urge to grin at the bristling disapproval in the old girl's voice. "His girlfriend?"

She sniffed again, and somehow managed to make the sound disparaging. "If that's what you want to call her."

"What does she look like?" Not that I actually wanted to know, but I had no idea how good the old girl's sight was. Maybe she'd seen Gautier and didn't realize it.

"Thin, with big tits. Dark hair, dark skin."

Not Gautier, then. The wind swirled around us again. His scent was fading fast. If I wanted to uncover what, exactly, he'd been up to, I had to get inside. Which meant getting rid of the old biddy—and that *obviously* wasn't going to be easy.

"Ms. Radcliffe, I really need to talk to Mr. Dunleavy—"

"It ain't much use, you know," she cut in. "The noise stopped hours ago. It's been dead quiet since then."

Dead being the operative term. "Ms. Radcliffe, please go inside, out of the cold. I'll come and talk to you later, after I finish here."

"Yeah, been told that before," she muttered, but turned and went back to her town house. Though I had no doubt she'd be peering through the curtains once inside and watching my every move.

I turned back to Dunleavy's and scanned the windows. No sign of any window being forced—though really, there was no need to when all anyone had to do was push back the cardboard that took the place of two panes. But no one had—maybe because of old eagle eyes in the first town house.

The garage showed no sign of forced entry, either. Whoever had killed Dunleavy—or whoever else was dead inside—must have gone through either the side windows or back door. I walked to the end of the porch and peered around the corner. No windows in sight, broken or otherwise. Just a view of uncut lawn and a fence line that seemed far too close to the end of the building. I stepped from the porch and walked along the wall. The ground under my feet seemed to vibrate, and the wind began to rush around me. I stopped, wondering what the hell was going on, my heart going a mile a minute—then snorted at my own stupidity as the reason came into sight. A goddamn train.

Why was I so jumpy? I might be green when it came to being a guardian, but I'd always been a jump-first, look-later type. And yet here I was, letting an old woman and a train spook me.

Why?

The blood.

The answer came almost as soon as I asked the question. I might be a wolf, I might love to hunt, and I had *certainly* killed in order to protect pack and self, but I'd never loved the taste of fresh blood. It was the one thing Rhoan and I didn't share. He not only loved the hunt, he loved to rent and tear and kill. I never had, even if I *had* occasionally participated in it.

And eating and loving a rare steak was *not* the same as sinking your teeth into flesh, let me tell you. Even *if* that flesh was only rabbit flesh—which was the only thing we wolves were legally allowed to hunt these days. Steak came in plastic containers and just had to be unpacked and cooked. Steak didn't continue to struggle for life after your teeth had found its flesh.

And yet, deep down, there was this fear that one day I *would* come to love it. That one day, my vampire genes would assert themselves fully and I, too, would come to enjoy the warm rush of life that flooded the mouth when teeth sunk into fresh flesh.

The shudder that shook my body was soul deep. But in reality, there was no choice for me. My destiny was gathering speed and no one really knew just what the future held. I was a dhampire, and what I would become was already patterned in my DNA. I might currently be more wolf than vampire, but who knew what the future would bring? Especially with the drugs that had been injected into my system by the psychos who'd been hiding under the guise of lovers over the last year or so.

And becoming a guardian, being around death and destruction and blood on a regular basis, might very well be the first footsteps down the path of acceptance. It was a known fact that the more death became a part of your everyday life, the easier it was to accept. I might fight it, but for how long?

Would there come a time when I loved the hunt *and* its aftermath as much as my brother did? As much as Gautier?

God, I hoped not. Surely fate had shoveled enough shit on my plate without adding *that* as well.

I shuddered and rubbed my arms as the last of the train cars rumbled past, then walked on. Blood or no blood, I had to see what had happened in that house.

I stopped near the end of the town house and took a quick peek around. No one in sight. I ducked around, keeping low as I ran past the intact windows. There was an odd, darkened patch of soot-like substance on the concrete near the back steps. Dunleavy had obviously been burning something recently, though why he'd do it so close to his house was anyone's guess.

The back door was wide open, and the scent of blood was stronger than before. I ignored the wild part of me, the part that relished the smell if not the taste, and cautiously walked up the steps.

The small laundry beyond the doorway was shadowed and quiet. The washing machine lid was open, the tub half-filled with clothes. I glanced at them, noting the dark overalls, the faint smell of oil and petrol. Work clothes. Or, more accurately, thieving clothes. I walked through the laundry and stopped at the next doorway, tasting the air and listening. The blood scent was coming from the right—from what looked to be a bedroom—the shit smell from the left. Given I could see an up-turned TV and lounge chair, it was obvious that some sort of confrontation had happened in the living room.

So why did Gautier's scent seem to be coming primarily from the bedroom? As far as I knew, Gautier wasn't homosexual. In fact, he'd always seemed asexual to me. I got no vibes when it came to sex and Gautier. I had never seen him with a woman, never heard him speaking of women—or men, for that matter—in a sexual way. And yet vampires were inherently sexual beings. Orgasms were their gift for blood taking, and having experienced them thanks to Quinn, it had to be said that they were certainly worth losing a bit of the red stuff over.

Not that I was going to let any other vampire near my neck. Christ, a lot of them had a tendency *not* to wash, and scent alone stopped me from getting close to most.

But Gautier was a vampire created in a lab rather than via a blood ceremony. Perhaps in the process of his creation his sexual urges had been lost. Or maybe they'd been transferred to his lust for blood. There wasn't a doubt in *anyone's* mind that he got off on killing.

A soft moan ran across the silence, a sound so full of pain that the hairs on the back of my neck stood on end. I edged out into the hall. The moans were coming from the bedroom, and yet I could sense no life in that room. Though if Dunleavy was human, that was no surprise. Humans didn't show up on my sensory radar like non-humans did, though I could read and adjust their thoughts if I was close enough. I glanced over my shoulder at the living room then, as another moan emanated from the bedroom, crept toward the latter, my senses on high alert for any sign or sound of movement.

But the only sounds to be heard were my light breathing and the occasional squeak of a floorboard under my feet.

In the bedroom, I found Dunleavy.

He was lying, spread-eagle and cheek down, on the bed, but I had no doubt it was him. The height, hair color, and profile were a match for the photos I'd seen in the file.

He wasn't moving, didn't appear to be breathing, and the white sheets on which he lay were darkened by pools of blood.

Not from a wound. Or rather, not from a normal wound, like a gunshot or stabbing.

Dunleavy had been skinned.

From the base of his neck right down to his heels. Not prettily, and not particularly neatly. In some ways, it reminded me of the sort of mess an apprentice butcher might make while practicing his cuts of meats.

My stomach rose and I closed my eyes, taking quick shallow breaths through my mouth rather than my nose. It didn't help much. The stench of blood and death was so thick I could practically taste it, and the image of the bloody mass of muscle and meat seemed burned onto my retinas.

I'd seen a lot of gruesome things over the last few months, including the death of the innocent girl yesterday. I'd welcomed some of those deaths, had mourned or cried for others. But skinning a human like he was just another animal seemed oddly worse than anything else.

And the fact that the killer had draped his somewhat shredded skin neatly over the bed end, as if it were a gossamer-fine but bloody blanket ready for reuse, only made it seem worse.

I dug the vid-phone out of my pocket and called in both a medical team and a Directorate forensic team. Then I set the vid-phone on record and send, sat it on top of a nearby drawer and, ignoring my still squirmy stomach, stepped into the room.

"Mr. Dunleavy?" I pulled on a glove and pressed my fingers against his neck. No pulse. I picked up his wrist and tried again. Again, nothing. It made me wonder if I'd really heard the moans or something else. Something that stepped into the realms of the spiritual.

Goose bumps ran across my skin. I tried to ignore the odd premonition that more was to come, and reported Dunleavy's death, as well as the time, for the benefit of the taping vid-phone. As I dropped his hand back to the bed, a wisp that seemed little more than steam began to rise from his body. A chill raced across my skin, and it suddenly seemed a whole lot colder in the room, as if the emergence of the mist had sucked the warmth out of the air.

Only it wasn't just mist, I realized. It was Dunleavy's soul.

This wasn't the first time I'd seen a soul rise, though I'd certainly been hoping that the first time *had* been the last time. That it had been an aberration rather than a strange development in a recently awakened talent. I didn't *want* to see ghosts or souls or anything else along those lines. What the hell use was the ability to see dead people? Especially when it was *dead* dead rather than vampire dead? How could the dead be of any earthly help when they were no longer a part of the physical world?

As the last wisp of mist emerged from Dunleavy's bloodied body and converged with the rest, his body seemed to collapse in on itself a little and another moan escaped—this one so soft I could barely even hear it.

And it sounded like a word. *Dahaki.*

I blinked, wondering if I was hearing things. Wondering who or what the hell Dahaki was.

I glanced at the vid-phone, hoping it had been close enough to record the soft sound, then steeled myself mentally and looked at the mess that was his back.

In some areas, the layers of skin had been stripped as one, leaving muscles and meat totally untouched. In others, skin and muscles were a raw and ugly mess. There was blood, and lots of it, because the skin is the body's cover—it seals and protects, and blood runs rich under its surface. Which was why simple wounds often bled the worst. But to achieve something like this took skill, practice, and a razor-sharp knife. Why would Gautier bother, when he was one of the most efficient killing machines the Directorate had ever produced?

And yet, besides Dunleavy, there were only two other scents in the room. One was Gautier's. The other was more flowery and feminine, so it undoubtedly belonged to the girlfriend the old girl had mentioned.

So, if this *was* Gautier's handiwork, where the hell had he learned to skin a body this skillfully? Dunleavy's back might be a mess in places, but the knife work was still way above that of an amateur. Which Gautier surely would have been. He might have been off the Directorate leash for months, but was that enough time to learn the ins and outs of skinning without the benefits of a teacher?

And if he *had* been practicing, where were the bodies?

Then I remembered all the body parts I'd found in the factory. Maybe, if I'd taken the time to sort through the bits and pieces, I would have found skins, whole and not.

Maybe the bits and pieces weren't the result of a baby vamp's feeding frenzy, but rather, Gautier's efforts to learn new and terrifying skills.

I shivered and rubbed my arms. Perhaps the more worrying thought was the fact that Gautier had obviously left the town house after dawn had risen. The old girl had said the noise all stopped hours ago, which still placed the fall of silence well after dawn. And the stickiness of the blood on the sheets and on Dunleavy's body would probably match that estimate.

Gautier was a young vamp. He shouldn't have been able to go anywhere once the sun was up, and yet it looked like he had. I had a bad feeling we'd better find out how *real* fast, or the shit could really hit the fan.

I took a breath and released it slowly, and let my gaze travel across Dunleavy's body. There was no obvious sign of a struggle—neither his hands nor his feet were tied, and nothing in the room was upturned or knocked over.

Which meant Gautier had used mind control to bring Dunleavy in here, and he'd obviously used it to control the girlfriend, because the old girl in the first town house had heard no shouting. So who'd been destroying the place? And why not stop that as well? Gautier was certainly powerful enough to fully control the actions of two humans. Unless, of course, he didn't *want* to.

It was a thought that had chills skating across my skin. Gautier didn't do anything without a reason—how often had I thought that in the past?

Frowning, I lifted my gaze from Dunleavy's body and looked around. The walk-in closet was filled with a mix of women's and men's clothing, meaning Dunleavy's girlfriend either lived here, or spent a hell of a lot of time here. But there was little else in the room. Dunleavy was a man who didn't spend a lot on furnishings, because everything in this room was bargain-basement–type furniture. Either he wasn't a very successful thief, or he spent his takings on other things. Maybe the living room might hold that particular answer.

As I turned to leave the room, a tingle of awareness ran across my neck, even as the scent of musk reached my nostrils.

"Riley Jenson?" an unknown voice said. "Cole Reece, Directorate cleanup team."

I smiled at the caution in his voice. Obviously, Cole was a man who'd worked around a few too many quick-tempered—or perhaps that should be quick-reacting—guardians. "In here."

Footsteps echoed down the hall—three sets, all men. The heavy weight of their steps was as much of a give-away as their thick scent. A tall, craggy-faced man of indeterminate age appeared, his gray hair glinting silver in the harsh light streaming in through the window. His musky, spicy scent swam around me, as refreshing as an evening sea breeze in the less than aromatic atmosphere of the apartment. My hormones did an excited little shuffle—not that *that* took a lot of doing when the moon heat was rising.

His scent also told me he was a wolf, though not a were. Every species had its own particular scent—a base, if you like, that personal odors were built upon. Male werewolves tended to have sharper basic aroma than males of other species. Or maybe it just seemed that way to us females because we were more attuned to them. Werewolves might spend a lot of time enjoying sex, but there was a serious purpose to all the fun—no matter what other races might think. The desire to find our soul mate was patterned into our DNA, and few wolves settled down until this aim was accomplished. And playing around with other species certainly wasn't going to accomplish anything—except, perhaps, fun. But no wolf could survive on fun forever.

No matter what my brother thought.

The shifter's gaze swept the room, pausing briefly on Dunleavy before coming to rest on mine. Surprise briefly overran the caution in his pale blue eyes. "Agent Jenson?"

I nodded. "Not what you expected, huh?"

His sudden grin crinkled the corners of his eyes, making his timeworn face a lot more attractive than I'd initially figured. "Not in the least. Never knew we'd gained a werewolf guardian."

Two other men crowded into the doorway behind him. One of them swore lightly as his gaze fell on Dunleavy. The other didn't react at all. Both of them, like Cole, were shifters. One had a cat scent, the other was a bird of some kind. Neither tickled my hormones in the least. Which was a good thing—there was nothing worse than a moon heat that lusted after everything with a dick. Especially when there was work to be done.

Cole motioned with his chin to the body. "What happened?"

"He was skinned."

Cole studied me for a moment, the brief spark of amusement gone. "By you?"

"Hell, yeah. And after that, we danced a tango down the hall."

He raised an eyebrow, like he wasn't entirely believing. But then, if he'd worked with guardians for any length of time, he'd know full well what they were capable of.

And given I'd identified myself as one of their number, I guess he had a right to be wary.

"Some guardians do like their torture."

"I'm a werewolf," I said dryly. "I think I could come up with a better means of getting information from a suspect than using torture."

He looked me up and down, but in a purely nonsexual way. Much to my hormones' disappointment. "I bet you could."

If four seemingly innocent words could state an opinion, then *his* certainly had. He might not have called me whore straight out, but his tone had certainly implied it. If I'd been in wolf form, the hackles around my neck would be bristling right about now.

I clamped down on the rising tide of my temper, and said, as mildly as I could, "You know, werewolves get enough attitude from humans. We certainly don't need it from our own kind as well."

He stepped forward to allow the two other men entry

into the room, then said, "I am not your kind. I'm a shifter."

Thank God.

The unspoken words practically hung in the air and flashed like a neon sign. I flexed my fingers. "You're wolf, so therefore kin, whether you like it or not. And shifters of all kinds have a high sex drive, so don't try and get all high and mighty with me."

I glanced at the vid-phone, suddenly remembering it was on and recording. Great. A permanent record of unprofessional touchiness. Not that *that* would surprise anyone back at the Directorate. I blew out a breath and retrieved my phone. Cole's two assistants were setting up their own recording device, so I no longer had to bother. Of course, this brought me quite a few steps closer to Cole, and his scent spun around me, warm and tantalizing.

"If you're going to investigate the remainder of the house," he said, nostrils flaring—like he was catching a scent that both attracted and repelled—"I need to set up the mobile record units."

"Then do it quickly." I pushed past him and walked down the hall. If footsteps could sound angry, mine certainly did.

Dammit, I didn't *need* an attraction to a man who hated what I was. I had enough of that with Quinn. Of course, the moon heat didn't give a damn about that sort of thing. It just saw a craggy-faced candy it wanted to taste.

Luckily for me, the moon fever had yet to fully begin.

I stopped when I reached the living room doorway and did a sweep of the room with my still-recording phone. There had definitely been a fight in this room—furniture was upturned, the TV and glass coffee table were smashed, and books and magazines scattered everywhere. So, if Dunleavy had fought for his life, why were there no marks on his body? Or could I simply not see them because he was lying on them?

Would I even see bruises on skin that had been stripped off?

The stench of shit was stronger here than anywhere else, but again, it was more human-based than the scent I associated with Gautier. Though that was here as well, just not as strong or as fresh. As I scanned the floor, looking for the source, I saw the feet.

Female feet, to be precise. Even from where I stood, I could see the pink nail polish on some of her toes. The rest of her body was covered by the upturned couch and several layers of book and magazine wreckage.

I glanced over my shoulder. Cole was kneeling beside an open bag, setting up the mobile recording device. Though why they called it mobile when it didn't actually move anywhere, just hung from a ceiling and recorded a three-sixty view of the room, was anyone's guess.

"There's a second body in the living room. Hurry up with that thing."

"Guardians are not supposed to interfere with investigations." His voice was short, impatient.

"I don't really care what guardians are and aren't supposed to do." Which was more of a truth than Cole would ever know—and a statement that would annoy the hell out of Jack when he heard it. Not that he'd be surprised by it, mind. "How about you quit worrying about what I'm supposed to be doing, and just put a little speed into what you're supposed to be doing?"

"If you'd shut the fuck up and let me concentrate, I might be able to."

I somehow managed to restrain my grin, and looked back at the wrecked living room. A glint in the left-hand corner of the room, near one of the rear windows, caught my eye. The sun had come out briefly from behind the clouds, and in the sudden beam of sunlight, something sparkled a pretty red. It didn't look like the sort of sparkle you got with glass. Even glass covered in blood.

Frowning, I carefully picked my way through the mess. A muttered curse followed my steps, meaning Cole still hadn't got the mobile unit together yet. I kept my phone on record and knelt near the shadows.

Sitting in the dust that had accumulated behind the now upturned TV was a ring. I recorded its position with the phone, then carefully picked it up. It was thick and silver and obviously worth a bit of money. Not the sort of thing a thief usually left lying about carelessly. So, where had it come from? Gautier? I'd never seen him wear rings or jewelry of any kind in the past. But then again, I'd never known he had a hankering for skinning before today, either. I suppose the ring could have belonged to Dunleavy—only this ring was designed for a man with thin fingers. Dunleavy had fat little sausages. And if he'd stolen it, he surely would have taken more care of it.

This ring *would* fit Gautier's fingers. So, was it his? And was losing it accidental or intentional? With that psycho, anything was possible.

When I brought it into the sunlight the engraving on

the heavy, flat top revealed itself. It was a dragon with three heads, its claws wicked barbed, and body snakelike. Six bloodred rubies gleamed in the dragon's eyes.

Just looking at it had chills skating across my skin and I had no idea why.

"You are not supposed to be moving evidence."

Cole's sharp voice made me jump a little. I tried to cover the movement by turning the ring over in my hand and studying the inside of it. "I recorded its position."

"That is not the point."

"No, the point is I'm stepping into your territory and you don't like it." I looked up at him then. "Get used to it, buddy, because I'm going to be messing up your life a whole lot more in months to come."

His stance stiffened a little. No male wolf likes to be challenged, especially when the challenge was as ambiguous as mine. "When the cleanup team arrives on a crime scene, they are in charge, *not* the paid killers."

His voice was filled with cold contempt, and anger swirled through me again. People who judged en masse rather than on an individual basis annoyed the crap out of me. I was sick enough of defending my heritage to all and sundry. I didn't need to start having to defend my job as well—especially when it was a job I hadn't particularly wanted in the first place. "Well, *this* paid killer has never been one to follow the rules. Just ask Jack."

"Oh, I intend to."

I shook my head in disgust and looked back down at the ring. There was something written on the inside of the band, but it wasn't in a language I recognized. Actually, it looked like nothing more than a bunch of weird little symbols.

I took a photo of it, then rose. Cole pressed the mobile unit against the roof, waited until the suction took hold, then hit the record button. The unit whirred to life, and one of the lenses behind the black glass sphere did a circuit around the room before coming back to rest on the two of us. From here on in, any movement and all conversation would be tracked.

"What?" he said, finally looking back at me.

I held out the ring. "Do you recognize the language?"

He took the ring and studied it intently. "Looks old Persian, but I can't be sure."

I raised an eyebrow. "Persia doesn't exist as such, anymore."

"No, but old Persian cuneiform inscriptions do exist, and they look like this."

"And how do you know that?"

"I study old-language forms in my free time."

He had to be kidding, right? "So those weird little pics are actually words?"

"Yes."

"Could you get a priority transcription on it, and send me the results?"

He looked at me for a moment, then moved to the door and grabbed a plastic bag from his kit. "I'll see what I can do."

I clamped down on the irritation that ran through me, and pointed toward the body. "Do you have any objections to me checking her out?"

He glanced up at the mobile unit. "Scan all elements north side of room."

"Scanning."

I looked up in surprise. "I didn't know those things talked."

He raised an eyebrow, like he was amazed a guardian was admitting not knowing something.

Bastard.

I couldn't work up anything more than annoyance, though. The momentary twinkle in his pale blue eyes was just too cute for my hormones to ignore, and when *they* were interested in someone, everything else went out the window.

"Latest technology," he said. "I hear the labs are currently working on units that are actually mobile."

"Well, I'm sure that development will just rock your little socks off."

"Just as much as killing rocks yours, I imagine."

"Which just goes to prove some clean-team members don't have very good imaginations."

The mobile unit beeped. "Area scanned."

"Then let's go take a look, kemosabe."

He looked at me like I was weird. Obviously not a big Lone Ranger fan. I resisted the temptation to smile as he walked across the room and stopped next to the sofa covering the woman. After studying the floor for several seconds, he looked over his shoulder at me. "It's safe to move. You want to grab the other end?"

"For you, anything."

He gave me the sort of look that would surely have silenced anyone with a bit of sense. Of course, I wasn't anyone. Once again restraining my smile, I walked carefully across. This close to the woman, the scent of excrement was almost overwhelming. I wrinkled my nose and wondered how the hell Cole coped with it all. He had to hit smells far worse than this in the course of his work, which had to be a nightmare when you had a nose as sensitive as a wolf's. I couldn't imagine doing it myself—not day after day, month after month.

But then, I couldn't imagine being a guardian for the rest of my life either—and right now, that was the only option I had.

After righting the sofa, the reason for the smell became obvious. The woman was naked and lay on her back, her arms pinned underneath her body and legs akimbo. The bruising on her thighs suggested rape, and the bruising on the rest of her body said she'd fought it as hard as she could.

And whoever had raped her had ripped apart her neck and sucked the life out of her. But they hadn't been satisfied with that. Oh no. Because they'd then turned around and shit on her. The evidence of it lay between her breasts, watery and reeking to hell.

"Vampire shit," Cole said. "Very few other creatures produce excrement that diluted."

I looked up to find him studying me. "What?"

He waved a hand at the brown fluid. "That is the waste product of a vampire, and probably a baby one at that. Older vamps tend to have less color and form. Baby vamps are generally still shaking off their 'humanness' and tend to produce something vaguely resembling regular waste matter."

"Seems I learn something new about vampires every damn day." Although vampires' waste products wasn't really something I'd ever wanted to think about, let alone know.

"I've never seen a guardian look as furious as you do

right now." He cocked his head a little, expression hinting at surprise and curiosity. "It's almost as if this death offends you."

"And a senseless death doesn't offend you? It doesn't offend you that some bastard shit on this woman after he'd raped and killed her?"

He shrugged. "I've seen too much for something like this to offend me."

I snorted softly. "And you think *I'm* the cold-blooded monster?"

"Cold-blooded killer," he amended softly. "There is a difference."

Not enough to matter, I'd warrant. I looked back at the woman and saw for the first time that she had dark skin and dark hair. This had to be Dunleavy's girlfriend if the old girl in the first apartment had her descriptions right.

So, if Gautier was responsible for Dunleavy's death, who had been in here, taking care of the girlfriend?

My gaze rose to the mess of her neck, and the excrement. My stomach twisted, and an odd sense of foreboding crawled up my spine. I turned around, studying the remnants of glass and furniture scattered about the room. Eventually I found what I was looking for, facedown on the brick hearth. I rose and walked over to it.

Picked up the photo frame and saw the dark-haired woman and the child within it. I closed my eyes for a second, cursing the unfairness of fate.

"Why the interest in the photo frame?" Cole asked.

"Not the frame, but the photo within it." I turned it around and showed him. "See the child in the photo? We found her last night. She died this morning."

"So whoever did this wanted the child?"

"No, I think she was just bait." I rubbed a hand across my eyes. That's why the young vamp had stood there for so long in the rain. Gautier had wanted to ensure we'd follow. He knew we'd try and save the girl. Knew we'd try and trace her parents. Which meant, maybe, he'd wanted us to find these kills. And had wanted us to find that ring.

The question was, why?

My gaze went to the woman again, and my frown deepened. "How long has she been dead?"

Cole looked down at the body. "Rigor mortis hasn't yet set in, so she's been dead less than three hours." He met my gaze again. "Why?"

"Because the timing is all off. These two are recent kills, and yet the little girl was kidnapped much earlier." And we'd killed Gautier's little protégée last night, so it couldn't have been him doing this. Though it *was* always possible that Gautier had more than one baby vamp in his nest.

But that still left the problem of how the baby vamp had gotten out of here when the sun was up. Gautier might be a young vamp, but he still would have a touch more tolerance than any youngsters he'd turned. The slightest caress of sunlight would be instant death to any one of them.

"Maybe she was kidnapped to buy their silence," Cole said.

Maybe. Dunleavy *had* rung yesterday evening, desperate for help. This was obviously why. If Jack had acted earlier, if the Directorate had more staff, then maybe the little girl would still be alive. Maybe even her mom and Dunleavy.

It made me wonder what they'd known. Obviously it was something of extreme value, because death had come hunting them pretty damn quick. But how did whatever they'd known connect with Gautier? And how did Gautier connect to The Cleaver?

Because it was beginning to look like he *was* connected, no matter what Jack said—and no matter what Gautier's so-called contest might imply.

I glanced down at the picture. It was better than looking at the real woman lying on the floor. "I think I'll go question the neighbor again. See if she saw anything earlier. But please, save your cheering until I get out the door."

"A hard task, but I think I'm man enough for it." A smile teased his lips, making his craggy face and pale eyes suddenly seem warm and inviting.

"I think you're man enough for lots of things." I suddenly remembered the mobile recording unit, and resisted the urge to add more. Like, *but are you man enough for me?* The reality was, Cole was a wolf-shifter. He'd smell my interest. If it wasn't reciprocated, then I wasn't going to push. "You got any objections to me taking this?"

"No." He hesitated. "I'll send the transcription from the ring as soon as we get it."

"And the woman's full ID, if you could."

He nodded. I turned and headed out the door. His gaze was a heated weight that centered not on my back, but on my butt. I resisted the urge to work it, and just got out of there before I got myself into trouble.

Ms. Radcliffe confirmed that the child did belong to

Dunleavy's girlfriend. "When did you last see her?" I asked, wrinkling my nose at the overwhelming odor of cooking cabbage coming from the unit's interior.

"Yesterday, when that woman was taking her to kindergarten." She sniffed. "Her dad must have picked her up after. He shares custody, and just as well, too."

"You wouldn't happen to know his name, would you?"

"Robert Worthington. Lives over in Prahan, or someplace fancy like that. The kid's name is Ellana."

"And the girlfriend's name? Don't suppose you remember that?"

She sneered. "Trudi Stone. She's a part-time waitress, and a stripper at one of them men's clubs."

"Did you see anyone else come or go from the apartment?"

"No." She sniffed. "But he was burning something behind the town house after all the racket had died down. Horrible smell, it was."

I remembered the burned patch outside the back door. The baby vamp, perhaps? Timing-wise, it'd probably fit, even if it made no logical sense. Why would Gautier not share whatever protection he had from the sun with his own creation? Or was it simply a case of the baby vamp having done what he was taken there for, and Gautier having no further use for him? Letting him fry in the sun was one sure way of getting rid of any evidence the Directorate might be able to use.

"Ms. Radcliffe, you've been extremely helpful. Thanks for your time."

"It's always my pleasure to help you officers."

I resisted the urge to smile but couldn't help feeling

sorry for the local cops. They were going to be seriously bombarded by the old girl's "helpful" reports over the next few days.

I retreated to my car, barely getting there before the skies opened up and the rain came down. As water pounded the windshield, I threw the photo on the seat then got out my phone and called the Directorate.

The caramel cow answered.

"Sal, Riley Jenson again. I need you to trace an ID for me."

"I'm not your personal servant," she replied coolly. "There are proper channels to follow."

"I don't like proper channels, and I need this information quickly."

"Such requests have to be approved—"

"I haven't got the time for this shit, Sal. Just do it without arguing or I'll start whispering nasty things in Jack's ear about his hot-to-trot personal assistant." I quickly gave her Trudi's name and Dunleavy's address. "She apparently works as a waitress and part-time stripper. I need to know where."

"You are such an ass." Despite the annoyance in her tone, the soft tap of a keyboard was evident over the phone.

"But I'm an ass Jack listens to." Sometimes. I waited a few seconds, then said, "Anything?"

"Yeah. I'm sending you her profile."

"Including a working address?"

Salliane paused. "She works as a cocktail waitress at the Cattle Club. There's no strip joint listed."

Meaning it was probably a cash-in-hand job at one of

the underground strip joints. "Where's the Cattle Club? I've never heard of it."

"So much for you being a party animal," she said, somewhat cattily. "It's the latest hot spot."

"For weres, or for vamps who have the hots for their boss?"

"Humans, asshole. Anything else?"

"Nope. Such a pleasure talking to you again, Sal."

"Bite my ass, wolf girl."

She hung up and I grinned. I was going to get into trouble if I continued riling her, I knew that, but damn, it was fun. She was wound so tight her face would surely crack if she smiled. But at least she was efficient. I'd barely hung up, when the information about Trudi Stone came through. I studied her file for several seconds, noting there was no criminal history and seemingly nothing out of the ordinary about her.

The daughter got a mention, as did the ex. I typed in a note asking that the dad be notified about the death of his little girl, then put the Cattle Club's name into the nav-computer and got the address and driving directions.

The club sat in the middle of the city's famed King Street dance club district, an area that was basically the human equivalent of werewolf clubs—but without the free sex. Though apparently it *was* available if you had ready cash and didn't mind a quickie in the alley or a nearby car. Part of me wondered if Trudi had been a part of that scene. I wouldn't entirely have been surprised if she was. In the file photo, her eyes had held that world-weary, bleak sort of look that hookers who'd been in the game for a while got.

Had the information she'd been killed for come from a client, or from somewhere else? Was the Cattle Club the connection at all, or was it the strip joint we knew nothing about?

The only way to know was to go there and snoop. While it was now early afternoon, I had no doubt the club would be open. Most of the King Street venues now had twenty-four-hour licenses, and served food, alcohol, and the promise of a good time to any who entered. It wasn't unusual to have lunchtime lines almost as long as the nighttime ones, as those on midday breaks tried to get inside for a little action. Trouble was, I wouldn't get in dressed as casually as I was, not without flashing my ID—and I had a feeling that was something I'd better avoid until I scoped out the place.

Clairvoyance, I thought, as I started up the car, truly sucked. I mean, if it was going to feed me little warnings, it could at least add *why*.

I headed home and changed into something a little more upmarket and sexy, then grabbed my thickest coat and drove on to the club.

There was a line out the front, but not a huge one. The rain was still coming down intermittently and the wind that whipped down King Street was icy, blasting away at the flyaway ends of my long woolen coat. By the time I got to the door, my bare legs had an almost blue tinge. Considering the red hair, it wasn't a good look.

"You're looking a little cold," the bright spark manning the door said as he opened it.

"You'd better have coffee inside, or things could get ugly," I said, through chattering teeth. God, the things I did for my job.

The bouncer chuckled, white teeth positively glowing compared to his dark skin. "Fresh made on the hour and thick enough to stand a spoon in."

"And that's a good thing?"

"It'll warm the cockles of your heart right quick."

"Well, my cockles definitely need warming."

He looked me up and down, his gaze lingering just a little on the plunging neckline of my dark green cashmere sweater. "Hard for me to judge *that* with the coat you've got on." He grinned, brown eyes twinkling. "There's a cloakroom inside, if you want to ditch it."

"I do. Thanks."

He nodded and closed the door behind me. I stopped, waiting until my eyes adjusted to the sudden darkness before checking my coat and heading down the steps into the club proper.

The main room had a retro feel and was bigger than I'd expected. A primary-colored, well-lit bar curved around a good part of the room and was lined with old-fashioned silver stools. Funky disco balls sprayed rainbow colors across the large dance floor, and in the semidarkness that lined the remaining walls were sunken couches and old-fashioned diner tables, complete with booth seating. The music itself was a loud mix of dance and techno. Not my taste, but at least ignorable. Maybe they turned down the volume during the day.

I scanned the shadows. There were lots of people inside—the line outside was testament to that—but the sheer size of the room lent a feeling of space that few clubs could boast. Me, I liked my clubs crowded. All that flesh to flesh was a pleasure my wolf soul adored.

I walked over to the bar and propped on one of the

stools. The bartender walked up from the other end, a polite smile touching his Asian features. "What can I do for you, pretty lady?"

"The man at the door promised me coffee strong enough to warm the cockles." I raised an eyebrow, a smile teasing my lips. "I'm here to see if the coffee lives up to that promise."

Amusement touched his lush lips and dark eyes, and my hormones sat up and took notice. "Cold outside, huh?"

"Goddamn freezing." I let my gaze slip down his back as he walked across to the coffee machine and grabbed a mug. Good shoulders. Nice ass. Shame this wasn't a wolf club—I caught the thought and shoved it away. I was here to work, not amuse giddy hormones.

"Milk? Sugar?"

Awareness shone in the deep brown depths of his eyes. He knew full well I'd been checking him out and wasn't in the least bit fazed. Maybe even appreciated it. "White and one, thanks."

He nodded, filled the cup, then walked back. I have to say, the packaging looked just as good from the front, too. He slid the coffee across the red-lit countertop, but waved away my money. "If you're going to be here a few hours, we'll run a tab and you can pay when you leave."

"Thanks." I lifted the mug, wrapping my hands around it to warm them up. One sip proved the security guy hadn't been kidding. The coffee was like sludge—thick and strong but surprisingly tasty.

"So, it lives up to its rep?" the bartender asked, watching my expression with increasing amusement.

"I think it's safe to say I've never tasted anything like

it. But it certainly warms the cockles." I grinned and held out a hand. "I'm Riley."

"Jin."

His fingers were warm against mine, his palms calloused and grip strong. Not the hands of someone who did bartending for a living. "You tend bar here often?"

He shrugged as he grabbed a tea towel and began polishing glasses. "Couple of times a week. It's good money for casuals."

"Ah." I took a sip of the coffee. "That's probably why I haven't seen you before."

"You come here often, then?"

Something flashed on his left hand as he picked up another glass. A ring of some kind. Luckily, it was on his index finger rather than his ring finger. I hated flirting with someone who was married. Just a waste of everyone's time.

"Sometimes." I grinned. "I got personal attention from a yummy bartender then, too."

"We're the friendly type here." He studied me for a moment, interest still very evident. "That why you're here today?"

"Actually, no. I'm here to catch up with an old friend who works here part-time."

"What's his name?"

"*Her* name. Trudi Stone." I studied him but caught no reaction to her name. Though why I was expecting one, I couldn't say.

"Hang on a sec, and I'll go check when she's next on." He walked down to the middle of the bar, served a man who was giving me a more than casual look-over, then disappeared inside a small office. He came back out a few seconds later. "According to the roster, she isn't back on until tomorrow night."

"Damn, I swear she said she was on today." I put the coffee down and crossed my arms on the counter, leaning forward a little to give him a better view of my breasts. Hey, he was sexy, and I might as well enjoy myself while scavenging around for information. I certainly couldn't risk trying to read his mind here—not when there were security cameras everywhere. My telepathy might be strong, but anyone could be watching, and it would only take one person to notice the momentary stillness of the bartender as I searched his mind for things to go ass up. Better to do that sort of thing when I had him alone. "So, when are you back on?"

His gaze went from my face to my boobs and back again. Amusement curved his very kissable lips. "When do you want me on?"

"How about tonight?"

"It'd be my pleasure."

I raised an eyebrow. "It had better be mine, too."

He chuckled softly. "Oh, I guarantee it. But I do need a contact number."

"If you've got the pen, I've got the number."

He produced a pen and a bit of paper from under the desk and slid both across the counter with his left hand. For the first time, the ring on his finger was fully visible.

On the flat silver surface was a three-headed dragon with wicked claws and bloodred eyes.

Just like the ring I'd found in the dust at Dunleavy's place.

Chapter 5

*N*ice ring," I murmured after a momentary pause, then casually picked up the pen and wrote down my cell phone number.

"This old thing?" He wriggled his fingers under the lights, so that the fiery eyes of the dragon heads glittered and burned. "It's just a club ring. Not worth much, but it catches the attention of pretty girls."

If he was lying, I couldn't sense it. Not that *that* meant anything. He was human, after all. "So it's a conversation opener?"

"It always helps to have one." He picked up the paper and tucked it neatly into his shirt pocket. "What time would you like to meet?"

I picked up my coffee and sipped it again. "What time do you finish here?"

"Seven."

"Then would nine suit?"

"Perfectly. Shall we meet somewhere for coffee or just go out for dinner?"

"Dinner." I paused. "There's an Italian place over on Rathdown Street. Small and intimate. Goes by the name of Riceni's."

He nodded. "Good choice."

"I always make good choices." My voice was a low purr, and heat rose in his eyes. I gave him a slow smile. "In the meantime, would you know if the restaurant upstairs is still open?"

"It never closes. If you head up the stairs now, I'll ring the chef and tell him to look after you."

"Thanks." I slid off the stool, picked up my coffee, and headed up the stairs—fully aware of Jin's hungry gaze following me and enjoying every minute of it.

The chef did indeed look after me, giving me a steak that sliced like butter and lashings of chips and vegetables. It was one full but happy wolf who headed out onto the street an hour later.

Once in the car, I retrieved my phone, pressed the vid-enable button, then dialed the Directorate. Jack, not the caramel cow.

"Hey, boss man, it's Riley."

"Good grief, she's reporting in. Miracles do happen."

I grinned. "I can be a good little wolf when I want to be."

"Which isn't often. What happened at Dunleavy's?"

I gave him a quick roundup of events, including my thoughts on Gautier, the details about the ring, and who the little girl's mom was.

"The thing I don't get is how Gautier is getting around after sunrise."

"I don't know. He shouldn't be able to."

"Well, he is, so we'd better find out real quick just how."

He grunted. "It's a shame both victims were dead when you got there. You could have read their minds to see what information they had to pass on."

Which was my cue to tell him about what I'd seen—and heard—in the bedroom. "Well, Dunleavy was sort of alive when I got there."

"Define 'sort of.'"

"He was groaning when I walked in. As I got to his side, his body sort of collapsed, and I saw his soul rise." I hesitated again. "I swear it said Dahaki."

"Dahaki?"

"Yeah. And I'm not sure whether it was simply air rushing out of a dying body or whether his spirit was actually trying to communicate." Or whether I was as crazy as I sounded.

"Given the reports that suggest your clairvoyance is developing strongly in areas that are not the norm, I'd say there's a fair chance you *did* hear his spirit speak. Which is interesting, to say the least."

"It's creepy, that's what it is."

"Maybe. But the ability to question the truly dead sure as hell would give us an advantage against the freaks we hunt."

"Only if I'm there when they die, Jack."

"Or if their spirits hang around."

A chill ran across my skin. I did *not* want to think about spirits hanging around waiting for a chat.

"I've asked Cole to send me a transcription of the writing on the inside of the ring as soon as he can, but if you want to have a look at it, it'll be on the recordings I sent via my phone."

"I'll get Salliane to dig them up. I'll also order a check on the design and see what we come up with. What about Trudi Stone—any luck on your follow-up?"

So the caramel cow *had* gone tattle-telling. Again. "I went to the club where she worked and talked to an Asian fellow. He was wearing a ring with the same design as the ring I found at Dunleavy's."

"Could be a coincidence."

"Could be. I'm doubting it, though. I have a date with him tonight, and I'll do a little mind-probing then, but I was wondering if you could break into the Cattle Club's records and look at his file."

"What's his name?"

"First name is Jin. He was born here, because there's no trace of an accent."

"Human or non?"

"Human."

"Tread warily, then. Don't let him suspect you're something more than human."

"Boss, I think the only thing he cared about was me being a hot-to-trot female."

"Then keep it that way."

"I will." I paused and started the engine so I could turn up the heater. It was beginning to feel like a tomb in the car, and I wasn't sure whether it was the cold weather or trepidation. "How'd Rhoan's investigation go?"

"It's apparently a regular feeding kill. One of the night boys can follow it up."

I'm sure the night boys—many of whom were hundreds of years old—would be thrilled with that. "I'm heading home to grab a break before tonight. I'll e-mail my report from there."

"Make sure you do. And please, stop harassing my PA."

I grinned. "I needed information fast."

"I'm not saying don't ring for information. Just asking if you'd be less of a bitch when you do so."

"In case it's escaped your notice, I *am* a bitch. Born and bred. Just shag her, Jack, and get it over with."

"I don't suppose telling you to mind your own business will do any good?"

I chuckled. "Not in the least."

"Wolves," he muttered. "Make sure you report in after the date tonight."

"Will do, boss."

I hung up and headed home.

I had a towel wrapped around my body and was standing in front of the wardrobe, trying to decide what to wear, when Rhoan finally came home.

"Hey, sis," he said, plopping inelegantly down on my big old bed. "Hot date?"

"A hot date that's a possible lead." I pulled out a black dress and showed it to him. "Jack told me earlier that your investigation turned out to be a regular kill. You sure?"

"That dress is too formal. You want something that has him thinking about your bod and what he'd like to do with it rather than the questions you're asking." He pushed up from the bed and walked over to stand beside me. "And yeah, the case isn't connected to our Cleaver case. Peri actually thinks we've got a couple of baby vamps working as a team to feed."

"Like we need *that* right now," I muttered. "Why can't bloodsuckers keep their kids under control?"

"Most do. It's really only a few who run free of the leash."

"That's a few too many if you're one of the victims."

He shrugged and reached into the wardrobe, pulling out a lime-green ruched dress that had leg slits, a super-low-cut front, and open back. "Where are you going?"

"Riceni's. And I'll freeze my tits off in that." Not to mention glow neon bright under the subdued lighting.

"Not if you work this right, babe. He'll be throwing off so much heat and desire, you'll burn."

"That doesn't negate the glow factor of the dress."

"God, the older you get, the less adventurous you get."

"*That* is a good club dress, *not* a reserved Italian restaurant dress."

He put the outfit back. I crossed my arms, watching him flick through more dresses. It was annoying to note that most of the ones I'd bought were quickly glossed over. But then, my tastes did tend to be a little more conservative than my brother's.

"So, what did Jack have you doing today?" He pulled out a dark green stretch-satin dress with long sleeves and cutouts on the shoulders and sides, and held it against me. "Perfect. Sexy without being too revealing."

"Checking out a source, which turned out to be a crime scene." I took the hanger from him and walked over to the bed. "The little girl we found turned out to be the daughter of the source's girlfriend."

"Both dead?"

"Yep. And Gautier was the cause."

His gaze met mine, cold and angry. "We will get that bastard, you know."

"I know." I wriggled the bottom of the dress over my hips and smoothed down the material. Stretch satin wasn't something I would have picked myself, but I had to admit, it felt smashing against my skin.

"Very nice rear view," Rhoan commented. "I'd skip the undies and the stockings if you can stand the draft. As Liander would say, we don't want ugly panty lines marring the outfit."

I snorted softly. "Liander's not the one who has to put up with the aforementioned drafts." I slipped my heels on. "And speaking of Liander, have you seen him lately?"

"Had dinner with him." He raised an eyebrow. "And if we're going to get all nosy, how about Quinn and Kellen?"

"Quinn's still off hunting demons, and you know Kellen's the reason I was late this morning." I smiled, re-membering our early morning chat over my quick breakfast. "He wants to whisk me away somewhere se-cluded next weekend."

Rhoan grinned. "That man is determined to pry you away from your vampire, isn't he?"

Most definitely. And when the result of his determi-nation was a really good time for me, who could actually complain? "I said no to the weekend because of the case, but I said yes to a three-week holiday somewhere exotic afterward. Jack owes me time off."

"Man, that'll piss Quinn off no end." And Rhoan's grin suggested this was no bad thing. He and Quinn might be friends, but my brother was more than a little annoyed with Quinn's behavior over recent months.

Not that he particularly wanted me to be dating him in the first place.

"Quinn left me stranded in the middle of Airport West and hasn't said boo since. He can go take a long jump off a short pier for all I care right now."

Rhoan chuckled. "I love it when you two argue. It's always such fun watching the shit fly."

"Glad we're amusing you." I grabbed a dark green handbag then walked over and kissed him on the cheek. "You take care, big brother."

"You too. And don't forget the condoms if you're pretending to be human. Wolves may be resistant to sexually transmitted diseases but humans aren't, and he may think it strange if you allow sex without raincoats."

I grinned and patted the side of my handbag. "Bought them before. Ribbed, studded, and ice."

He raised his eyebrows. "Ice?"

"Blurb says they give a sensation that increases body heat and feels like ice at the same time. I'll let you know if they're worth the effort."

"Please do. I'm always looking for a new experience."

"Heard that about you."

He swatted my rear. "Be polite to your elders. And get going, before you're unfashionably late."

I went.

The rain was still pelting down and the roads were

slick. Of course, that didn't stop idiots tearing past at a hundred miles an hour. I found myself wishing time and again I had a cop light to stick on the roof, just to scare the bastards.

By the time I'd found parking and splashed my way to the restaurant, I was about fifteen minutes late. The maître d' met me at the door, helped me out of the soggy coat, then led me to a rear table where Jin waited. He stood up as I approached, revealing a dark blue suit and a pale gray shirt that looked absolutely smashing against his complexion. His gaze swept my length and came back full of heated approval.

I grinned and leaned forward to kiss his cheek. His skin was satiny smooth against my lips, his aftershave a delicious mix of exotic woods, lime, and tangerine. "Lovely to see you again."

He smiled, waiting until the maître d' had settled me before sitting down himself. "They actually asked me to work a second shift tonight. I said no way."

"I'm glad."

"So am I." He looked up as the table waiter approached. "Would you like a drink? A white wine, perhaps?"

"Perfect."

And really, the wine, the food, and the company were all that and more. We chatted about everything and anything, teasing and flirting and generally having a good time. I liked him—liked his sense of humor, the way he effortlessly moved the conversation from one topic to another. Even the brief silences were comfortable. I kept putting off questioning him until the desserts were cleared and I could delay no longer.

"So," I said, swirling the wine around gently in my glass. I'd probably had a little more than I should have—I could feel the warm buzz running through my veins. Or maybe that was just the excited hum of my hormones. "Tell me, what do you actually do for a living?"

As I asked the question, I lowered my shields and reached out with my mind, carefully feeling for his thoughts. But I hit a protective wall as strong as anything I'd come across in the past—only it didn't feel like the natural shields of a psychic.

Oddly enough, it didn't feel like a nanowire, either. The nanowires were the latest development in nanotechnology and protected the wearer against psychic intrusion. I didn't know how they actually worked, but I did know that they were somehow powered by the heat of the body and offered up an extremely faint electronic tingle when in use.

So if his shields weren't natural and weren't technological, what were they? What else was there?

I didn't know, but I sure as hell intended to find out.

In the meantime, I'd have to uncover my information the old-fashioned way—through sex and snooping—because there hadn't been anything more useful than a home address listed on his Cattle Club personnel file. Even a full search had revealed little more than the fact he had no criminal record, and had studied psychology at a local university.

Of course, it was only five months ago that I'd been so determined *not* to fuck the enemy for the Directorate. And yet here I was, ready and willing to do that very thing. Though it did help that he was cute. And that I was getting no reading on him along the psychic lines. If he'd looked good but felt bad, it would have been a different story.

Maybe.

He raised his eyebrows. "Is there something wrong with bartending for a living?"

I smiled. "No. But you just don't look like a man who'd be satisfied with a lifetime of bartending."

"Ah." He hesitated a moment, then shrugged. "I'm floating at the moment, doing a bit of this and that. I did the whole college thing, then couldn't be bothered going into the field I trained for."

"So you have other part-time jobs as well?"

"I work at the Hunter's Club." He looked at me like I was supposed to know it. "It's a health club in the city. Runs yoga, Pilates, massage, spa therapies, gym. Stuff like that."

A smile teased my lips. "Don't tell me—you double as a masseuse, just to feel up all the pretty girls?"

He reached across the table, picking up my hand and turning it over. He ran a gentle finger from my palm to my wrist and back again, sending little shivers of delight scampering up my arm. "Only the very special ladies get my attention. I normally work in the gym area, as one of the fitness trainers. Did a course in one of my floating years."

"So the ring is a Hunter's Club ring?"

"Not really." His grip tightened on my hand, crushing my fingers a little. It was an odd combination—the heated caress of his finger and the wispy ache of pain—and it had a slight tremble running through my limbs. As if I was on the verge of discovering something new. Which was weird, because there wasn't much that was new to me when it came to the realms of basic sex. "Would you like to order coffee here, or would you prefer somewhere more intimate?"

He met my eyes as he said it, and in those warm brown depths I saw desire, barely controlled. And yet I couldn't help noticing the change of subject. He didn't want to talk about the ring—not in detail, anyway. Which was interesting considering he used it as an ice-breaker. I raised a teasing eyebrow. "And just where is this 'somewhere more intimate'?"

His smile was slow and sexy, and my ever-ready hormones did their usual little shuffle. "My place. It's actually only a block away."

"Ah, well." I paused, pretending to consider it. "I have no idea whether this 'coffee' will be worth the race through the rain."

"Then perhaps you would like a teaser taste?" He pulled back on my hand as he said it, gently forcing me to lean across the table.

"Love to," I murmured, a heartbeat before his lips met mine. Our kiss was slow and tender, an explorative type of kiss shared by strangers who intended to soon be a whole lot more. Neither of us were breathing very steadily by the time we'd finished.

"So," he said, his breath warm against my lips, "do I pass the test?"

I licked my lips, drawing his taste, his breath, into my mouth. "I think you could."

"Then we'll leave immediately." He released me and motioned to the waiter for the bill. Once we'd paid, he helped me into my coat then guided me out, his hand resting in the middle of my back. Warmth pooled where his fingers rested, even through the thickness of the coat.

It was still raining outside, but the pelting force of earlier had at least eased to a fine drizzle. The night was still bitter, but between the amount of alcohol I'd consumed and Jin's heated presence, I certainly wasn't feeling it.

But we'd barely walked half a block when a familiar chill made me realize we were not alone.

Vampires stalked us.

Great. Just great. How was I supposed to deal with them without giving the game away to Jin?

I stopped and took off a shoe, shaking it lightly as I tried to pinpoint the location of the vamps. They were across the street, keeping the shadows wrapped around them as they hurried to get ahead of us. Their hunger mingled with their scent, stealing like a thief across the night, filling my nostrils and sending chills scampering across my skin. Their smell was of the freshly dead. Baby vamps, not mature ones.

So, were they the same ones who'd left the mauled body Rhoan had been sent to investigate, or two completely different ones? And who was making all these vamps and then setting them free?

For no real reason, Gautier's image flashed through my thoughts. It actually made a sick sort of sense for him to be doing this. He knew the Directorate was short staffed. He knew it'd stretch us to the limit and therefore cut down our ability to hunt *him*.

Jin swung around, his gaze searching the night before coming back to mine. "What's wrong?"

"Stone in my—"

I didn't get the chance to finish, because the two vampires shook off the shadows and attacked. Jin made a sound low in his throat, then pushed me out of the way. I staggered backward for several steps, then caught my balance and ducked under the fist of one of the vamps. He chuckled softly, an amused sound that grated against my nerves. As the vamp came at me a second time, I kicked off my other shoe, caught it midair, then whirled around and smacked the wooden heel of the stiletto across his chin. Flames trailed where the wood touched flesh, and the smell of burned skin caressed the air. He frowned and glanced down at the shoes I held in surprise.

Obviously, he didn't realize the heels were wood, and I didn't give him the time to work it out. I kicked him, with all the force I could muster, in the goolies. Air left his lungs in a whoosh of sound that was all agony, and as he hunched forward, I swung a fist, hitting his chin hard and knocking him out cold.

I whirled around to help Jin, only to stop in shock. The other baby vamp lay at his feet, moaning in agony, his legs and arms bent at odd angles. Jin was barely even breathing fast, but as I watched he closed his eyes and inhaled deeply, as if the scent of the baby vamp's pain was somehow fueling his body.

Which was a very weird thing to think. But chills scampered across my body anyway—if only because no lone human should have been able to defeat a vampire. Not even a baby one.

So, did that mean Jin was something other than human? And if so, why were my senses still reading him as human? Or was it merely a case of him having psychic talents at his disposal? I glanced down at the vamp, at the pain and fear etched on his face. Psychic talents that broke limbs? I'd never heard of something like that before, but I was by no means an expert. I couldn't even define my own talents, for Christ's sake.

I grabbed my cell and made a quick call to the Directorate to order in a cleanup team—though I made out for Jin's sake that I was just reporting the attack. I'm sure the caramel cow thought I was crazy. But then, she undoubtedly thought that *long* before this phone call.

Jin blew out a soft breath as I hung up, then opened his eyes and turned around to fully face me. There was a spark in his dark eyes that spoke of something almost alien. Otherworldly. Another chill ran across my skin and yet, perversely, the wolf in me reacted with fierce desire. The strongest alpha in the pack was always the most desirable, and this man, alien eyes or not, had me wanting him so badly it was painful.

As his gaze met mine, he smiled. It was a ferocious thing to witness. The thought of retreat flashed through my mind, but before I could decide, he took five quick steps, wrapped a hand around the back of my neck, and kissed me. Hard. His other hand slid around my waist, pulling me against him, so that the thickness of his erection pressed against my groin. It felt so very, very good.

"I want you." His voice was a harsh growl filled with a passion every bit as fierce as mine. The hand at my back slid down my spine, past my butt, onto thigh. Goose bumps flitted across my skin and I wasn't entirely sure whether its cause was desire or the unnatural warmth of his caress. "Here, now."

"Not here." His fingers had slipped under the stretch

satin, and it was all I could do not to move, to guide those fingers to where it ached so badly. "Your place. It's warmer."

He made a low sound of frustration then grabbed my hand and pulled me forward, forcing me into a run. Water splashed across my bare legs, but if they were chilled I couldn't feel it. Jin's heat and desire and something else—an energy I could sense but not name—pulsed over me in waves, causing perspiration to dot my skin and my blood to boil through my veins.

If he had been were, I would have thought he was using his aura to make me compliant and ready. And, God help me, I *was* ready, for whatever he wanted to dish up.

We turned left into a side street. Three houses down, he pushed open a gate and raced me up the front steps. I had a brief glimpse of a white painted, classic double-story Victorian town house, then the paneled door was opened and I was all but pushed through.

"First right," he said, as he slammed the door shut.

I walked into the lounge room, stripped off my coat, and tossed it onto the nearest chair. My shoes were flung in the same direction, but I kept my purse long enough to grab some condoms.

Though I heard no footsteps—despite the wooden floors—he was suddenly behind me, his hot hands briefly brushing my thighs as he grabbed my dress and pulled it roughly over my head.

He made a low noise of appreciation, then pushed a hand against my spine and propelled me across the room toward the back of the big old leather sofa.

"Grasp it," he ordered.

I did. He grabbed the condoms from me, kept one,

then tossed the rest onto the sofa. After kicking my legs farther apart, he began to explore, his touch so fierce it was almost bruising as he pinched and caressed and teased, until the need to have him inside was so intense I thought I'd surely explode.

And then he bit me, hard, on the shoulder. Somewhere in the last few minutes pain and pleasure must have become one, because I gasped aloud at the exquisiteness of it.

"You like it rough," he commented, breath harsh and fast against my shoulder.

"No," I somehow managed to say. "But that felt good."

Why was the question. I'd never been into the whole pain-for-pleasure routine, though I had played around the edges of it a few times.

This was already further than I'd ever stepped before. Further than I'd ever *wanted* to step. And yet I couldn't stop it, didn't want to stop it, and some deep down part of me worried about that. Worried if it was willingness and pleasure or something else that was allowing previously set boundaries to slide.

But that tiny spark of worry had no hope of stopping events. Not when the tide of pleasure was rising.

His teeth scraped my skin, nipping and teasing as he moved down, then he bit again, this time on my rump. I shuddered, unable to hold back a thick groan that was part pleasure, part pain.

He drew a deep breath, as if sucking in the sound. His fingers trembled against my skin, evidence of the control barely maintained. "Perhaps a little bit rougher?"

Part of me shuddered at the thought but I didn't say anything, too caught up in the moment to protest now.

He slapped my rear. Like the bite, it was hard, and sent little jolts of stinging electricity skating across my skin. I groaned, seesawing between desire and pain, part of me wanting to push it further, part of me resisting and wanting to hit back.

"How good does that feel?"

He gave me no chance to answer, but slapped again, harder still, leaving my butt stinging and my body quivering.

"Very good," I gasped. So why was I suddenly so willing to push the limits here with Jin? I had no idea, and that in itself was scary.

Then I remembered the odd energy I'd sensed earlier. Was Jin using an aura the same way a wolf might? But how was that possible if he was human?

"And this?" His sudden bite was brutal, but the swell of pain was met with a kiss, his heated lips somehow easing away the ache. My knees just about buckled under the flood of sensation.

"Good, good," I somehow said.

He slapped again, this time my thigh, and sharp enough to have tears stinging my eyes. And then he was in me, driving deep, the icy feel of the condom an almost painful contrast to the warmth of my body. Yet it felt so good I moaned.

His grip bruised my hips as he held me still and thrust and thrust, until it felt as if the cool, latex-covered heat of him was trying to claim every single inch of me.

My breathing was fast, urgent, the air thick with need and desire that was both mine and his. The low down pressure built under the sweet assault of his body, and all too quickly reached boiling point.

We came as one, his roar mingling with my cry, his body slamming into mine so hard the whole sofa seemed to shake.

Then it was over and I was trembling, sweating, my limbs so weak they seemed barely able to support my weight. I took a deep, shuddery breath, and released it slowly. "As coffee went, that was damn fine."

He chuckled and kissed my shoulder. "Perhaps we should make our way down to the kitchen and get the real thing."

"We should." Though I doubted it would calm my pulse rate or ease the odd quivering still running through my limbs.

He took my hand and guided me down the dark hall to the kitchen. He tossed the condom in the trash, then put on the kettle and pulled a rich-looking chocolate cake out of the fridge. Surprisingly, despite the fact that I hadn't long finished a three course meal, I was famished.

We drank and ate and chatted. After nearly an hour, he pulled me to my feet and led me back down the hall to his bedroom. We had sex, harder and rougher than before, leaving me drained and yet satisfied.

It set the pattern for the rest of the night.

When I finally woke, it was to the unfamiliar sensation of an aching body. It felt like I'd run a marathon, and I suppose in some respects I had, yet I was a were-wolf, well used to all night sex-a-thons. Sex with a human shouldn't have left me *this* weary. But it wasn't only aching muscles that plagued me. Hot spots dotted my body, little pinpoints of agony where Jin had bitten or slapped too hard or too often.

And yet there were several times during the night when I'd felt his need to go further, harder.

I was damn glad he hadn't.

I groaned softly and opened bleary eyes. Light flooded the room, an indication that dawn had well and truly come and gone. I shifted, briefly enjoying the caress of silk as the sheets slithered over my naked body, and glanced at the clock. Nine A.M. Guess I was going to be late for work again.

I rolled onto my back. There was very little in the way of sound in the house. No movement, no whistling kettle, nothing to indicate there was anyone here. I frowned, listening more intently, and caught a noise that had me puzzled for several seconds. Then I realized what it was—someone snoring.

So, I wasn't alone in the house. But Jin's scent was a distant thing rather than active—an indication that he wasn't actually in the house.

Frown increasing, I tossed off the blankets and got out of bed. The aches intensified briefly, and I winced. Damn, if sex with Jin was an everyday affair, I'd be black and blue before a week was out. Not that I *had* the stamina for a week of him—which was a *very* odd thing for a werewolf to admit.

The bedroom door squeaked as I opened it. I winced and waited tensely for some reaction. Nothing happened. Other than the soft snoring coming from behind the door opposite, the only other sound to be heard was the soft hiss of warm air coming from the vents in the ceiling.

I grabbed a robe from the back of the door, putting it

on and lashing it around my waist as I padded softly down the hall.

Jin wasn't in the kitchen, either, but he'd left a note propped up against the salt shaker in the middle of the table.

Sorry to run out on you, Riley, but work called and needed my help urgently. Grab something to eat, or a shower, or whatever you want before you go. I'll ring you tonight.

If not for his snoring mate, the perfect opportunity to snoop through Jin's things and find out a little more about him had just presented itself.

I bit my bottom lip for a moment, contemplating the kettle and whether my desire for an early morning coffee was bad enough to risk waking the housemate.

The answer was a definite no. I spun around and padded lightly back to the living room, collecting my things and taking a quick look around. There didn't seem to be anything odd or strange in the room, and nothing that snagged the interest of my instincts.

I blew out a breath and headed back to the bedroom. I needed a shower, but given the running water might wake the snorer, it was probably better to do a bedroom search beforehand.

I carefully closed the door, then tossed my things on the bed and began to quietly—and carefully—go through his drawers. One fact I discovered straight-away—Jin was a man who liked fine things. His boxer shorts were silk, for heaven's sake.

The only thing I found that snagged my interest was

a stack of business cards in his neatly sorted sock drawer. They were black, with the name Hellion Club printed in red, and Jin's name underneath. I took one of the cards, then gathered my clothes and headed for the shower.

Thankfully, it didn't wake the snorer. I just wasn't up to dealing with a stranger right now. I needed to get home, send Jack my report, then grab some rest, because I was feeling shakier than a newborn pup.

The rain had cleared away during the night, and the morning was one of those crisp, sunshine-filled ones that Melbourne often got in winter. It was still cold enough to freeze the balls off a dog, but at least the sun was out.

I gently closed the door, then did up my coat as I padded barefoot down the steps. At the gate, I stopped long enough to put on my shoes, then headed for my car.

I'd barely gone two house blocks when a hand wrapped itself around my arm. I reacted instinctively, kicking backward at the heated presence I could feel behind me.

Then realized who that presence was.

Quinn.

Chapter 6

He released my arm and jumped out of the way of my kick. I turned around. He was dressed in black from head to foot, a shadow that looked out of place in the brightness of the morning. Just seeing him again had my hormones stirring—though with a whole lot *less* vigor than normal. Weird. "What the hell are you doing here?"

"I was about to ask you the same thing." His warm voice was edged with displeasure.

I snorted softly. "I'm dressed in last night's party clothes, and I'm coming out of a house not my own. You do the math."

"Oh, I get the equation, I'm just wondering whether it's for your own pleasure or for the Directorate."

"If you're not going to answer my questions, why the hell should I answer yours?" Especially when my answer would only result in having grief flung my way. Quinn might have decided he had to be in the race to win the race, but that didn't mean he was at *all* happy about me taking other partners. Especially when those other partners were complete strangers.

I spun on my heel and walked away before he could answer. I didn't need this crap now. I just wanted to get home.

"Riley, wait." He touched my arm again, but his grip was gentler this time, less demanding.

I paused and looked at him. "What?"

He tugged me around to face him, then looked intently into my eyes. "Are you all right?"

I tried to shake free of his grip but it tightened imperceptibly. "Of course I'm all right. Let me go."

He didn't. "You look drained."

Something resembling fear slithered through me. "What?"

"I said you looked—"

"I know what you said, but what the hell did you mean?"

"It means someone has been feeding off you."

That feeling of fear intensified. "As in vampire type feeding?"

He nodded, and with his free hand, touched my chin and gently guided my head from one side to the other. "No bite marks evident there. What about elsewhere?"

Everywhere, babe. I pulled free from his grip and stepped back. "The man I was with was not a vampire."

He frowned. "You sure of that?"

"He *was* human."

The expression on his face suggested he wasn't believing. "You remember the time in the plane, when you all but forced yourself onto me?"

I crossed my arms. "You didn't put up much of a fight, believe me."

"No. But I took too much blood, remember?"

Like I could forget? "So?"

"So, do you remember the resulting feeling afterward?"

"Washed out, shaky." I paused, finally catching his drift. "He didn't take any blood from me, Quinn. Trust me on that."

"Blood vampires are not the only type of vampire out there."

I blinked. "They're not?"

"No." He lightly touched my cheek, his fingers warm against my cooler skin. "You need to eat then rest. Immediately."

"Well, I was planning to do both before some rude person stopped me in the street."

His sudden smile didn't erase the concern in his eyes, and part of the anger I'd been feeling over his desertion in the middle of a dark night and hot date evaporated. But only part.

"What if I offer to buy you breakfast then drive you home?"

I eyed him for a moment, the desire to be with him warring with the need to get back at him for dumping me so abruptly the other night. "So what about the person you followed here?"

He smiled. "Should have known you'd guess."

"Not hard to. I mean, unless you're out whoring

around as well, the only other logical reason for being here is the fact that you were following someone."

"I do not whore around—"

"Ah, yeah," I interrupted. "You're a billionaire who doesn't have to pay for it. Which makes it okay for you to fuck all comers and not me."

His sigh was a sound of pure frustration. "Can we not do this here? You really do need to replenish your strength."

I stubbornly remained where I was. "And what about the man or woman you were following?"

"I think my target will sleep most of the day. She prefers night, anyway."

And how would he know that? Doing a little non-whoring of his own, perhaps? "And your target is currently in the house I came out of?" Meaning the snorer was a woman?

"Yes." He paused. "I take it your date was the man who left at dawn?"

"Yes."

"There was something odd about that one."

"Tell me about it," I muttered, then turned on my heel and began walking toward my car. Quinn kept close, as if he were afraid I would topple over at any minute. I was shaky, but not *that* shaky.

"He did read as a human, but there was also an other-worldliness that suggested something more." He cast me a sideways glance. "What was the sex like?"

I raised an eyebrow. "What was the sex like for you?"

"I haven't had sex for several days." A smile touched his lips. "Now, last week I was with this stunning red-head—"

"Who is still extremely upset about being dumped the other night, and who does not want to be fucked around anymore."

He met my gaze for several seconds, then looked away. His smile faded, and his vampire face came online. "Riley, I do what I think best to protect you."

"And yet the shit headed my way always seems deeper when you do. You have to learn to trust me, Quinn."

Surprise flitted briefly across his impassive face. "I do—"

"No, you don't. Not out of the sack, anyway."

"Riley, you should not take the risks that you do."

"And you should not keep secrets from me if you want to be a serious part of my life." I fished my keys out of my purse. "So, answer the question. Did you have sex with the woman you were following tonight?"

His smile held an edge of bitterness I didn't understand. "No, I did not."

"Why not?"

"Because that would be *extremely* wrong, and because her brand of sex is not something I have ever desired."

"Why would it be wrong? And have you had sex with her in the past? Or at least watched her have sex?"

"No, and no." He plucked the keys from my hand and guided me around to the passenger side of the car. "And it would be wrong because she is something I abhor."

"Then how do you know about her brand of sex?"

"I have a good imagination." He slammed the door shut, walked around to the driver's side, and climbed in.

Once he'd started the car, he added, "She owns a sex club."

"As in, werewolf type club?"

"No. A punishment center."

That raised my eyebrows. "Meaning she charges people for the privilege of being spanked?"

"It's not spanking. That's far too vanilla for this club. It's all about torment, humiliation, and suffering. About the despair of knowing there is nowhere to go and nothing you can do."

"And people get off on feeling something like that?"

"Some do."

"I guess it takes all kinds." And while it might not be my kind of fun, I wasn't about to look down on those who liked the darker stuff. Hell, I *knew* what that felt like. I crossed my arms and studied the road ahead. "So why were you following the whip wielder?"

He glanced at me. "Why were you fucking the human?"

"Quinn, just give with the information for a change."

A smile twitched his lips again. "I'm looking for the person who raised and controls the demons. Given such types are usually drawn to the darker emotions, my best bet is to follow the woman who runs one of three clubs catering to dark needs in Melbourne and see who she interacts with."

He was lying. Or rather, not telling the entire truth. I'm not sure why I was so positive—not sure if it was intuition or merely past experience—but whatever the reason, I was sure there was more behind his reasons for following this woman than what he was admitting.

"Might not your demon master be drawn to one of the other two, though?"

"Perhaps. But my target's club is the biggest, and therefore would have the stronger pull to those who relish such things."

I remembered the card I found in Jin's drawer. "Don't suppose this club is called the Hellion Club?"

"Yes." He glanced at me again, expression concerned. "How do you know of it?"

"Found a business card in Jin's drawers."

"If you were going through his drawers, then he is a target rather than just a good time."

"Well, he was originally a good time, until I saw he was wearing a ring similar to one found at a crime scene." I paused. "Have you been able to access the personnel files of the Hellion Club?"

"I have people working on it. Again, why?"

"Because the business card I found had Jin's name on it."

He looked at me briefly, expression unreadable. "Then this Jin likes his sex rough?"

"A little. Not to the extent that the club apparently caters to, though."

"Even so, I was under the impression you didn't like it rough."

"I don't. Jin controlled himself." I looked at him sideways. "And it's not as if anyone else is bothering to cater to my needs in *any* way at the moment."

"Sex isn't everything, Riley."

"It is to a werewolf when the moon is rising." I shook my head. "You're never going to get it, are you?"

"From your expression, I'm guessing probably not."

He had *that* right. I glanced around as he turned left into an unfamiliar street, and realized we were heading away from my apartment rather than toward it. "Where the hell is this restaurant you're taking me to? I need to eat, and I need to sleep." Not to mention report to Jack.

"You wanted breakfast. I thought I'd cook it for you."

"You cook?"

"Twelve hundred years does tend to give one a lot of time to practice the skill."

"So where is this palace of yours located?" In all the time we'd been going out, he'd never taken me to his Melbourne home. We'd either gone back to my place, or his plane, or whatever plush hotel room he'd rented for the night. But never anywhere that was personal to him. "And why take this step now?"

He shrugged. "Because I owe it to you. Because you're right in saying that I need to share more of myself if we are to become anything more than fuck-buddies."

"Wow. This has to be a first—the vampire actually admitting I was right about something."

"I can still go somewhere else, you know."

I did the wise thing and shut up.

We ended up in Warrandyte, a small but extremely trendy "arty" community situated on the outskirts of the city, right next to the Yarra River and a state park. It had the reputation of being conservation-minded and neighborly, and was not the sort of place I figured a security-conscious, privacy-seeking billionaire would want to live.

His house was another surprise. A white picket fence lined the front yard, and the small, weatherboard home looked in serious need of not only a good lick of paint, but the services of a gardener. To say the plants had over-run the garden was the understatement of the year.

"Where's the mansion?" I said, as he helped me out of the car. The luscious scent of lavender and eucalyptus spun on the air and I breathed deep. Some of the tired-ness clawing at my body eased under the freshness of the air.

"The mansion is in Brighton. That's my house. This is my home." He wove his fingers through mine and led me down the steep steps. The deck's wooden flooring creaked as we walked across it and I warily looked down as he stopped to open the door. "Is this thing going to support the weight of two people?"

"It's old, not rotten." He pushed open the door. "Welcome to my world."

His world was warm and comfortable, and totally the opposite of anything I'd ever imagined him living in. The house itself was tiny, consisting of little more than two bedrooms, a kitchen, bathroom, and living room. And yet there was nothing claustrophobic about the place. Between the Baltic pine floorboards, stonework, and rich paintwork, the whole house exuded a warm airiness and peace that just felt . . . right. And this feeling was aided and abetted by furniture that was well-worn and yet comfortable.

"Lovely," I said, wandering over to the back win-dows. His yard sloped down to the banks of the Yarra it-self, and the view beyond was incredible. If not for the occasional glimpse of a roofline, it would have been easy to believe we were alone in the wilds.

"What would you like for breakfast?" he said from the kitchen. "Pancakes? Bacon and eggs?"

I looked over at him and smiled. "Would both be greedy?"

"Both it is." He grabbed a frying pan from under the bench and started messing about. I watched for the sheer pleasure of watching a gorgeous man cooking, then shook myself into action and said, "I've got to ring Jack. What's the phone reception like out here?"

"There's no phone in the house. If you're using your cell, you'd better go outside."

He threw me a key. I dumped my handbag onto the nearby chair, grabbed my phone, then unlocked the door. Outside, the sunlight dappled through the trees and the air was quite cool. Somehow, the tranquility of the setting more than made up for any chill.

I walked down to the far end of the balcony, then leaned on the banister and called Jack.

"Well, good to see you're back to bad habits," he said, by way of greeting.

"Boss, don't expect miracles. Especially when I've been working my ass off on behalf of the Directorate." Which was no less than the truth. My ass *still* smarted. I gave him a brief rundown of events, then asked, "You found out anything more about Karen Herbert yet?"

"There's been no sign of her, and she's been missing from work for several days. But given our workload, she's currently listed as low priority."

Meaning he'll only start to worry if she turns up dead somewhere. Bastard. "What about Gautier?"

"What about him?"

"Do you think he's behind the sudden rise in baby vamps, and would he be doing it just to piss us off?"

"Probably."

"So have you figured out how he managed to walk out of that apartment when it was past sunrise?"

"All he needed to move around in was a van with blacked-out windows."

"If there was a van around, the old biddy next door would have seen and reported it. She didn't, so there wasn't." I paused. "Dunleavy and his girlfriend must have known something pretty vital to be killed the way they were. Did a full background check reveal any clues?"

"No. But the security tapes from the Cattle Club show Trudi and Jin working together on several occasions. Maybe she overheard something she wasn't supposed to."

Maybe. But that was something we'd never know now. I scratched at an itch on my leg irritably. "Here's another odd one for you, boss. How can Jin, who's listed as human and feels human, defeat a vampire?"

"I don't know." He paused, and I could almost hear his brain ticking over. It wasn't hard to guess in what direction. Eventually, he said, "But I think you need to hang around him and find out."

"Like that's a surprise."

He snorted softly. "Hey, you admitted you enjoyed yourself."

"That's beside the point. There's something more going on with his brand of sex, Jack. There's an odd energy in the air—something I've never felt before."

"Does it feel dangerous?"

"No. But—" I hesitated, not sure I could fully explain the odd mix of unease and desire Jin's energy inflicted. "I'm a werewolf, Jack. There is no known way sex with a human should leave me as shaky as I was feeling this morning."

"Unless he's some kind of emotive vampire."

"Meaning he feeds off emotion?" Which is what Quinn was probably getting at when he said blood vamps weren't the only kind out there.

"Yes. Some feed off pleasure, some feed off pain. Some like a mix. Jin sounds like the latter type."

"So why does he read as human?"

"I don't know. He shouldn't."

"If he *was* an emotive vamp, could he beat a regular blood vamp? One who wasn't a baby?"

"As a general rule, no. Emotive vamps are more energy beings than physical beings."

Well, Jin was *definitely* physical. "So how can I protect myself against his feeding?"

"You can't. You just have to ensure you take a break between sessions and get some food into you. The richer the better, because it refuels your energy faster."

Which was why Jin had been feeding me gooey chocolate cake last night, obviously. "So, even though he's sucking down emotions, I have to eat to keep my physical energy up, same as with regular vamps?"

"Afraid so. Though emotive vamps do tend to leave you a little more strung out emotionally for a few hours afterward."

I must have slept through that period of recovery, because I was feeling okay by the time I'd left Jin's. "And if I don't eat and refuel? Can it become dangerous?"

"Well, he could drain you to the point that you're physically unable to defend yourself, but he can't kill you with his feeding as a blood vamp can." He paused. "See if you can grab some hair samples. We'll run some tests and see exactly what we're dealing with."

"He said he'd ring tonight, so I'll see what happens." I paused. "Have you decoded whatever was written on the inside of the ring?"

"Not yet. It appears to be some form of glyphs. We're trying to find a match."

"Anything else of interest in Cole's report, then?"

"Yeah, you were being a pain in the ass at the scene. Not that *that's* a surprise."

"Hey, I was just asking questions. He needs an attitude adjustment." And a good dose of werewolf sex. "How did Dunleavy actually die?"

"Heart attack."

I raised my eyebrows. "Really?"

"The initial attack happened during the skinning, the fatal one after eleven."

Which was about when I'd been entering his apartment. The poor man probably thought I was Gautier coming back to finish him off. "What about the time of death of the woman?"

"About eight. Which means Gautier had to have some means of getting out of there without facing sunlight, even if the old girl next door didn't see it."

"Logically speaking, I'd agree. But I've just got a feeling something more is going on."

"You tried to clarify that feeling?"

"I can't clarify something that's as tenuous as a feeling."

"Yes, you can. You just need more training."

"What I need is more sleep. Especially if you want me out with Jin tonight."

"Take the day off, but keep your phone on in case I need to contact you."

"Done deal."

I hung up and headed back inside. The smell of hazelnut coffee swam through the air and I just about drooled. "You've been preparing for my visit."

He nodded as he dished up several pancakes. "It's the only reason I have food in the house. Normally, I don't."

I propped on a stool and leaned my arms against the bench. "So it's been a while since you invited another woman here?"

He added bacon and eggs to the plate, slid the lot across the bench, then looked me in the eye. "I've never invited a woman here before."

I raised my eyebrows, even as a warmth I couldn't even begin to explain spread throughout my body. "Never, ever?"

"Never, ever."

"Wow." I picked up my knife and fork. "Thank you for the honor."

His sudden smile was filled with warm amusement, and once again my hormones stirred to sluggish life. Jin had better be a short-term job, because I sure as hell *wasn't* liking the impact he was having on my sex life. I mean, normally I'd be jumping over the bench after a smile like that.

"At least you can no longer say I don't share anything of myself."

I wanted to point out that this was just a house, even if it *was* his sanctuary, and that what I'd been talking about was *him*. His past, his hopes, his dreams—everything that had made him the vampire he was today. But I didn't. It was a step forward, and for now, that was enough.

"So, are you just planning to tease me with that delicious coffee smell?"

His smile stretched, then he turned to grab a cup and pour the coffee. I admired the view, wished I had more energy, and began consuming the meal he gave me.

After breakfast, coffee, and gentle small talk, he took my hand and led me down the small hall to his bedroom. "You need to sleep." He pulled down the handmade patchwork quilt that covered the big old wooden bed, then gave me a stern look. "Alone."

"Well, that's never any fun."

He touched a hand to my cheek, his fingers warm and tender against my skin. "Perhaps not. But you need to rest."

Despite myself, despite stirring desire, I yawned. Hugely. He chuckled, and leaned forward to drop a sweet kiss on my lips. "If you feel like fun, I'm sure we'll have time later."

"I'll hold you to that." I stripped off my dress and climbed into his bed. The cotton sheets were cool and soft against my skin, the pillow cradling my head as gently as a lover. I was asleep before I could even say good night.

When next I woke, it was once again to the sound of silence. I yawned and stretched out the kinks, noting with relief there was little in the way of remaining twinges, then opened my eyes and looked about. Quinn wasn't in the room, but his warm, sexy scent still teased the air. Weak sunlight peeked around the corners of the thick curtains covering the windows to my right,

suggesting the better part of the day had slipped by. I
shifted to get a better view of the clock on the bedside
table, and saw it was just after four.

"Quinn?"

My voice seemed to echo through the small house. I
frowned, flipped off the covers, and got up. Quinn wasn't
in the living room, nor the kitchen, nor the bathroom. In
fact, he wasn't in the house at all.

An odd mix of worry and anger ran through me. I
spun on a heel and walked back into the bedroom. My
clothes weren't on the floor where I'd left them. Anger
began to overrun the worry as I walked back to the living
room. My purse, shoes, and phone were also absent.

The *bastard*.

He hadn't brought me here to give me a glimpse of
his life. He'd brought me here to keep me away from a
case *he* considered too dangerous.

I should have known.

Should have guessed it was too good to trust.

I picked up the small nude figurine sitting on the
kitchen table and threw it against the far wall with all the
force I could muster. It shattered against the stone, sending shards of fine white porcelain spearing through the
room. I hoped it was expensive. *Fucking* expensive.

I took a deep breath in an effort to control the rage.
Running around breaking things might make me feel
better, but in the long run, it wasn't going to help me
much. First things first—check whether I still had a car,
look for replacement clothes, then get the hell out of
here.

A peek through the front curtains provided the un-
startling information that my car had also gone. I resisted

the urge to rip the curtains from their tracks, and let them fall back into place.

Next up, clothes. As it turned out, not only had my clothes gone, but all his. Not that running around naked particularly worried me, but the night was promising to be a cold one. The chill was already in the air.

The third item in my list proved to be just as elusive—the front door had been key-locked. So were all the windows as well as the sliding door out onto the patio. The key he'd used earlier was gone. Which, while not considered a fire code violation by the law, was a very stupid thing to do.

"Bastard, bastard, bastard."

I'd have to break out. There was nothing else I could do. Without even thinking any more about it, I picked up a chair and threw it through the window. It smashed through the glass, hit the patio, then bounced up to crash through the railing and disappear over the side.

I shifted shape and leapt through the hole. Part of me was hoping like hell someone noticed the window and used it to steal all his fine—and undoubtedly expensive—bits and pieces.

He deserved that, and more.

I followed the riverbank, enjoying the feel of the damp earth under my paws, the freshness of the breeze against my coat, even if they did little to ease my foul mood.

As I got closer to central Warrandyte, I left the riverbank and moved into the streets, padding quietly along the sidewalk. Few people took notice of me. Most were in a hurry to get home, and in the dusky light, I looked like just another stray dog anyway. Under normal circumstances, the magic that helped me change would also have taken care of any clothes I might be wearing—just don't ask me how, because it was a magic I didn't question, just accepted. Of course, once we were back in human form, the clothes were usually a shredded mess, so while the magic might conceal the clothes when we were in wolf form, it certainly didn't look after them. Lucky for me, that wasn't going to be a problem on *this* occasion.

Was he ever going to get a piece of my mind when I caught up with him.

When I found a main road and was free of the trees, I shifted shape and pressed the com-link button in my ear. "Riley to base—anyone listening in?"

Silence was my only response—not that I'd really expected anything else. The trackers were long range, but the communicator part of the units were far more limited. With the hills and the trees, I pretty much figured it would be a miracle if I got through.

I tried a couple more times, just for the hell of it, but eventually conceded I'd have to contact them the old-fashioned way. I walked down the street until I found a phone booth. Thankfully there weren't that many people out, meaning I didn't have any immediate worries about someone reporting my nakedness to the police. I picked up the handset, rang the Directorate's emergency number, and got put through to Jack.

Wouldn't you know it, the caramel cow answered instead. "Guardian division. Jack Parnell's phone."

"Sal, it's Riley. Where's Jack?"

"In a meeting with the Director. What do you want?"

For you to get back into whatever annoying coffin

you crawled out of. I cleared my throat, and said, "I need a car and clothes at my current location."

"You lost your clothes?" Amusement crawled through her cool tones. "Though I suppose it wouldn't be the first time. You wolves do tend to get careless about such things."

"Maybe, but not this time. It was done to prevent me working a case."

Sal sniffed. It was a superior sound if ever I'd heard one. "I've located your call position. We have a car in the area and I've sent an order for them to pick you up. They'll take you home to retrieve some clothes."

Better than nothing. Though if the increasing edge of amusement in Sal's voice was anything to go by, she wasn't being as helpful as it seemed. "Can you transfer me to the following cell number?" I reeled off Jin's number. "I need to call my target and explain why I'm late."

"Consider it done, wolf girl. I shall tell Jack of your predicament."

And enjoy every moment, undoubtedly. "Tell him it was Quinn, and that I'll report once I make contact with my target."

She didn't answer, just transferred the call. As I waited, a teenager walked by and almost broke his neck doing a quick double take. I gave him a wave and he grinned, his feet seemingly glued to the spot as he got out his cell phone and began dialing. Given the grin, I very much suspected it wasn't the cops he was dialing, but his mates. I suppose it wasn't every day a teenage boy found a naked woman standing in a phone booth. What were the odds I'd soon have an audience?

I smiled and, as he pointed the phone at me, gave him

a thumbs-up. The answering wows and ahs were audible even from where I stood.

"Hello?"

Jin's easygoing tones came on the line, and I snapped my attention back to my job. "Jin, it's Riley."

There was a brief pause, the squeak of a chair, then footsteps and a door opening. Then he said, "Hello, dear Riley."

His voice had dropped several levels, and slid across my skin as smoothly as silk. A warmth that was part desire, part trepidation flooded my senses, as if just by speaking he could call to the wildness within me.

"When you didn't answer your phone," he continued, "I began to fear I'd scared you off."

"I'm not that fragile." Despite the fact that accurately described my state when I first woke up. "I misplaced my phone, that's all."

"Ah. I'm glad you rang, then." He paused, and I heard voices in the background. One male, one female. Accompanying them was a slapping sound that sounded an awful lot like a leather belt against skin.

And given the business cards I'd found, it probably was.

"I'm afraid when I couldn't get you earlier," Jin continued, "I agreed to work. But we could go out afterward, if you like."

"I'd like," I said absently, trying to tune in to the soft noises behind him. The slapping sound was now accompanied by soft sounds of distress rather than enjoyment, and there was something about it that just snagged at my instincts. "Where would you like to meet?"

"I'm not entirely sure what time I'll finish here, as we've a bit of work to do yet."

Yeah, and I was betting it wasn't serving customers alcohol.

"I could just wander into the club and wait for you to finish."

Though if he was at the Hellion Club, I was backing out. Slapping and biting and even being restrained I could handle, but torture and humiliation just didn't rock my sexual boat.

"I'm not at the Cattle Club."

I swore internally. What was I going to do to get out of the date tonight? There was no way on this green earth I was going to go anywhere near the Hellion Club. I wasn't *that* damn dedicated to the job.

"I'm at the Hunter's Club," he added.

Curiosity stirred. The Hunter's Club was a fitness club, so what sort of exercise had people making choking noises? "Well, I can come along and watch all the pretty men exercise while I'm waiting for you."

"Or you could come along for a massage and spa treatment. On the house."

"So you don't want me watching all the pretty men?"

He laughed. "To be perfectly honest, no. Besides, watching men sweat will probably get boring after a while."

Not for a werewolf. I grinned. "What time do you want me there?"

"If you're coming for a treatment, how about in an hour? It takes a few hours to go through both."

"Are you going to be my masseur?"

"You can bet on it, babe."

Anticipation thrummed through me, and suddenly it was all I could do to remember that this boy was bad, that he could be dangerous, and therefore had to be treated with caution. And *that* caution should be applied equally to the club, especially if those odd noises were anything to go by.

"I've gotta go home and change first, so I might be longer than an hour."

"I'll be here waiting," he said simply, and hung up.

I replaced the receiver and turned around to discover my teenage ogler had gained a couple of mates—all armed with phones. A wise werewolf would have been discreet and shifted shape but I couldn't see the harm in giving a few boys a cheap thrill.

A blue Ford pulled to a halt beside the phone booth and for a moment I thought my flashing days were about to be cut to a sudden halt by the long arms of the law. Then the passenger door was flung open and a rough voice said, "Get in."

And suddenly I understood Sal's earlier amusement. The voice belonged to Cole. Obviously, she didn't realize she was actually doing me a favor. Grin widening, I blew the boys a kiss then climbed into the car.

He took off before I was even buckled in. "Those boys are going to have wet dreams for the next fortnight."

"If it's only for a fortnight, I'll be most disappointed."

He chuckled softly, and I raised my eyebrows. "The shifter is amused, not annoyed?"

He glanced at me. Despite his amusement, wariness still held sway in his pale blue eyes. "Oh, I'm pissed off about having to rescue a damn wolf careless enough to lose her car *and* her clothes, but at least I'll get overtime."

"So I'm not going to get a lecture about wantonly flaunting myself in front of a couple of young males?"

"I was a teenage boy once myself, you know. Those kids are going to be heroes to their peers." His gaze swept down my body, lingering long enough on my breasts to send a warm flush through my system, then he looked back at the road. "There's a coat in the back if you're getting cold."

"I'm aroused, not cold."

"I know." He glanced at me. "I'm just being polite."

"Are all wolf-shifters as uptight as you?" I twisted around to grab the coat, making sure my breast brushed his arm as I did so.

His eyes narrowed slightly, but all he said was "You want to punch your address into the nav-computer?"

"Before or after I cover up?"

"Before." He looked at me, amusement twitching lips that suddenly looked lush and kissable. "I never said I *wasn't* enjoying the view."

"So there's hope for you yet?" I leaned forward and punched my address into the computer, aware all the while of his gaze lingering on my breasts. The shifter was a boob man, obviously. Just as well I wasn't built in the stick-thin mode of most weres.

"There's always hope for me. But for you? Not a chance."

I grinned and leaned back, curving my back a little to show off my assets to full advantage. "Never challenge a werewolf, Cole. You'll always lose."

"In this, I think not."

"Game on, then."

He looked at me, clearly amused. "It takes more than a good set of breasts to get into my bed."

"So the challenge is to discover what else it takes? I think I'll enjoy that."

He shook his head and didn't reply. The rest of the trip was spent in silence. I didn't bother putting on the coat, just draped it over my lap and legs to keep them warm. The atmosphere in the car was pleasant, and yet filled with an underlying tension that was all arousal and desire. The shifter might not *want* to want me, but he did. While I took great delight in knowing that, I didn't push things. Cole obviously was going to be a long-term project—but one I had no doubt I could win over.

He pulled to a halt in front of my place, leaving the car running as he glanced up at the old warehouse building. "Looks as though you have plenty of room up there."

"We do. And big windows." And a great big bed you'd look good lounging naked on.

He met my gaze, the scent of his lust spiking sharply. "In which you undoubtedly flaunt yourself."

"And why not? The neighbors don't complain."

"No surprise there." He looked away. "I'll see you at work sometime."

"You will, shifter. I'll make sure of it."

He looked at me again, but didn't reply. I climbed out of the car and walked up to the steps, aware of his gaze following my naked butt and this time working it for all I was worth.

He roared off as I opened the door. I grinned to myself, anticipating the challenge he presented, and ran up the stairs to my apartment. The door was locked, but a hard punch in just the right spot soon fixed that. Neither Rhoan nor I could see the point of good quality locks when the door itself was thinner than cardboard and the old lady who owned the building refused to ante up for better ones.

Of course, locks didn't keep out vampires, either—a point made obvious when I spotted my handbag, cell phone, keys, and clothes sitting neatly on the coffee table. I had no doubt my car would be parked up the street somewhere. How nice of Quinn to return them all.

I had a quick shower to freshen up, then pulled on my gym gear and filled a bag with a couple of dresses, some toiletries, and some makeup. I had no idea where Jin intended to go after my treatments, so it was better to cater to all eventualities.

I grabbed my purse and cell phone, then called a cab. Ten minutes, they said. Knowing from past experience that it was more likely to be twenty than ten, I headed for the kitchen to make coffee. The doorbell rang before I could take two steps. I opened the door to find Cole standing on the other side, his hands in his pockets and looking more than a little put out.

"Don't tell me," I said, raising my eyebrows, "that you've decided to taste a little werewolf action after all?"

"Hell will freeze over first," he muttered. He thrust a hand through his thick silvery hair. "Jack just called. There's been another body discovered and he wants us both there."

Chapter 7

The woman lay on her back, her arms and legs spread wide, like a starfish. She was naked, and there was an almost rapturous expression frozen onto her dead features. As if the manner of her death had aroused her to the point of fulfillment.

Just like the other women we'd found.

A shiver ran through me, but I wasn't entirely sure whether the cause was horror, or the odd chill in the air. A chill that spoke to an awareness deep within, one that suggested we were not alone in this warehouse.

That dead things abided here.

I rubbed my arms and let my gaze slide down the woman's white body. Like the other victims, she'd been opened up from neck to knee, and all her main internal organs removed. There should have been a lot of blood after a kill like this, but there wasn't—and in many ways that was far worse. Because it meant someone had drained her—drained her while they sliced her and removed her organs. Drained her while she lay there with that rapturous look on her face.

I shuddered, suddenly glad I hadn't eaten anything since breakfast. I don't think it would have stayed down at that point.

I forced my gaze from the destruction of her body and looked at her left hand. Like the other victims, she was missing half her little finger. The wound, though healed, looked extremely fresh.

And for some reason, her missing a finger made me feel colder—sicker—than anything else that had been done to her. Which was an extremely odd reaction, even for me.

I looked past her. Jack and Cole were standing in the far corner of the old factory, talking softly. If I concentrated, I could probably hear what they were saying, but it felt like too much effort when I could just ask Jack later on. I studied the immediate surroundings instead. Cole's team had been here for a good half hour by the time we'd arrived, so the few clues evident were already tagged. Like before, the sooty remains of a pentagram was visible on the concrete, and droplets of black wax littered the ends of each point. While I didn't know much about magic, I knew black candles indicated the darker paths rather than the light.

Though the mutilation of the body was enough to indicate *that*.

I looked back at the woman as something stirred. A wisp of thick air. Smoke, perhaps, curling softly in the air, barely visible against the bright lights the clean-team had set up.

Another chill ran through me.

It wasn't smoke.

It was her soul.

And as it found shape, it found voice, words. *Dahaki,* it said. *Azhi Dahaki.*

The chill got fiercer, until it felt like fingers of ice were creeping into *my* soul. As if the woman's soul brought with it the fierce cold of the underworld. *Who the hell is Azhi Dahaki?*

I wasn't entirely sure whether I said that out loud or telepathically. Wasn't sure if the woman's spirit would even answer.

It stirred softly, a body of smoke with no features that gently rotated. But with every turn, energy built in the air, until the small hairs along the nape of my neck were standing on end. Only then did the words come again. *You must stop him.*

With that statement, the energy fell away, and the soul disintegrated, fleeing to whatever region of afterlife it was bound for.

I took a deep, shuddering breath. It was bad enough that I was seeing souls—now the fucking things were beginning to *talk* to me.

"Riley?"

Jack's voice was soft, filled with caution, but I jumped all the same. I looked up, saw that he was standing only a few feet away. Cole stood beside him, a concerned look on his face. I hadn't heard either of them move.

"It talked to me, Jack." I rubbed my arms. "It actually damn well *spoke.*"

"I did warn you that might happen."

I snorted softly. "Yeah, well, I was hoping you were wrong." I looked down at the body, to where the soul no longer hovered. "I don't want to be talking to the spirits of dead people, Jack. It's just too creepy."

Cole's eyebrows rose. "You can converse with spirits? Cool."

I gave him an annoyed glance, and concentrated on Jack. "It said a name—the same one Dunleavy's soul gave me. Only this time it was *Azhi* Dahaki. A full name, perhaps?"

"It's quite possible. It's an odd name, though."

"Well, it's an odd talent." And *that's* precisely why Jack had brought me down here tonight. He'd been hoping I'd see something. "Have you got an ID on her yet?"

"Karen Herbert," Cole said, looking down at the PDA in his hand. "Twenty-two years old. Lived alone. Parents currently holidaying in Queensland."

I looked at Jack. "*The* Karen Herbert? The one I asked for a background check on?"

He had the grace to look uncomfortable. "Afraid so."

"Well, if that isn't proof positive there's a link between Quinn's case and ours, I don't know what is."

"Which is why, when you see him next, you will be questioning him."

Yeah. Like that was going to result in anything useful. I waved a hand at Karen's face. "She didn't die in terror. There were no drugs found in the systems of the other women, and I doubt there will be here. It once again suggests she came here willingly, Jack."

"Or that there was psychic influence. That can't be traced after death, remember."

"Jin's not psychic, so maybe I'm following the wrong person."

"If Jin's blocking you telepathically, he's a psychic of some sort. Plus, he shares a house with the woman Quinn is following, he works at the same place as Dunleavy's girlfriend—who was killed by Gautier because she'd seen or heard something—and he has a ring the same as one found at a murder scene. It's too much of a coincidence. Everything is connected. We're just not seeing the complete picture yet."

And we needed to, before the next woman was murdered. My gaze went back to the body. "So are these ritual killings or sacrifices?"

"My guess would be sacrifices. For what, I'm not sure."

"Blood *and* organ sacrifices," Cole corrected, then looked at me, "which is a darker and more powerful magic altogether."

"It's still ending up with dead women, buddy-boy."

Annoyance flared in his pale eyes. "The nature of the magic is often a direct indication of the nature of the magician."

"Doesn't take much of a genius to guess we're dealing with someone who's *very* black in nature."

"No, but the fact that there's blood and organ used means we are dealing with an extremely strong type of black magic. And if the mage is adding his own blood, then we are dealing with someone who's raising a power capable of doing far more than calling a couple of demons."

"Meaning, you don't think Quinn's hunt and ours are merging?"

"Meaning, they may well be merging, but our boy is doing more with his power than releasing a couple of demons to harass a vampire." Jack eyed me for a minute. "You don't seem overly perturbed about Quinn locking you up."

"You haven't seen his house." I glanced at my watch. If I didn't get going soon, Jin was going to start wondering what the hell was going on. "Look, if you don't need me, I've got a suspect to meet."

"Go. But be sure you hit the com-link if things get rough and you need out."

I raised my eyebrows. "Why tell me that when I know for a fact you don't say it to other guardians?"

"Because the other guardians are dealing with regular old psychos. I've got a feeling your particular psycho is off the scale even by our standards."

"Well, gee, that's a comforting thought." I eyed him for a minute, then added, "And besides, you don't want me dead yet because you want to see where the drugs take my talents."

"Precisely." He smiled and threw me a set of keys. "Seeing Cole drove you here, take my car. But I want it back in one piece."

"You give me your keys, you take your chances." I grinned, tossed them lightly in the air, then headed out.

Night's curtain had well and truly fallen, and though the air was cold, the night was clear. The moon hung fat and yellow in the sky, not quite full but not far off it. The heat of it sung through my veins, a surging desire that was only going to get worse over the coming nights. It was, I thought grimly, probably the *best* time to get landed with the job of fucking a bad man.

And when I finished doing him tonight, I was going to ring Kellen. I had a bad feeling I'd need some tender care and gentle loving to wipe the foulness of Jin's touch from my mind.

I found Jack's car and headed into the city. It was a Monday night, so the streets were quiet and parking easy to find. I grabbed my bag and headed back up the street toward the club, discovering the number he'd given me was actually that of a multistory building and the club was on the nineteenth floor.

Which was pushing my phobia to the limit.

I took a deep breath and forced a smile on my face as I approached the guard. "Hi," I said, acting all cheery even though my stomach was doing a rebel dance. "I'm here for the Hunter's Club."

"You got a membership pass?"

"No."

"Can't get in without a membership pass."

Obviously, this security guard wasn't paid to be helpful. Either that, or he was just bored and having himself a little fun. "My name is Riley Jenson. I'm here as a guest of Jin Lu."

He glanced down at a sheet sitting on his desk, then picked up a book and placed it on the desk. "Need you to sign in there," he said, pointing to a space. "And write your name after it."

I did. He took the book, got a pass out of his drawer, writing a number beside my name before handing it to me. "This will work the elevator and get you past the foyer doors. You'll need to return this pass and sign out when you finish."

I nodded, grabbed the pass, and headed toward the

elevator. The swift journey upward had a tremor running through my limbs, but thankfully my stomach decided to stay where it was. The entrance to the club was all gold-and-white luxury, the carpet plush enough that I had to resist the temptation to rip off my shoes and run barefoot through it. But I couldn't help a wry smile when I spotted the sign emblazoned over the front doors. Not only did it say "Hunter's Club" in great big fancy letters, but it had "humans only" underneath it.

Charming.

Humans were still trying to legislate a rule that would outlaw the "no-human" rule in the werewolf clubs, but it was just fine and dandy for them to outlaw *us* willy-nilly. The sooner we got some nonhuman representation in the government ranks, the better.

The doors swished open as I approached, and in that instant, I saw the sensors lining the doorframe. They really *were* serious about the club being humans only.

And it meant if I went through, I would be outed as something other than human.

I swore under my breath and glanced at the blonde manning the reception desk. She was one of those sexy athletic types guaranteed to set on edge the teeth of any normally built woman, but more important, she hadn't appeared to notice that I'd stopped short of the doorway and was just standing there. She wasn't wearing a nanowire—unless they were now making them in designer earrings—and there didn't look to be any other psychic deadeners in the room. Not that they could actually stop me anymore.

I blew out a breath, then opened several shields and let my mind sweep into hers, taking control in an instant.

I might not be able to "sense" humans, but I sure as hell could control them. I made her turn off the alarm, figuring the club would be safe for the few hours I was here. And just in case someone higher up noticed, I had her pull the plug out of the wall. That was the trouble with sensor units installed after the building had been completed—a careless movement could very easily break their connection. Which is why many of them were now being directly wired into power mains.

I released my hold on her, then went through the door and approached the desk. I still had a telepathic finger on the pulse, so to speak, just to hear her thoughts and ensure there were no lingering doubts about what had just happened.

She blinked, like a dreamer waking from a dream, then gave me a bright smile.

"Well, hello there," she said, her welcoming tone as fake as her tan. "New to the club, are we?"

"We are." I showed her the pass. "I'm a guest of Jin Lu's."

Something flickered in her eyes—an emotion too fast to pin down—though the smile never dimmed. But her thoughts gave away what her eyes only hinted at—that her opinion of Jin was low. Indeed, she thought he was an arrogant pig who got altogether too rough during sex. She'd even had to lie to her boyfriend because the bruises had taken *forever* to fade.

Obviously, she wasn't a big believer in monogamy while in a relationship. I restrained my smile and accepted the pen she gave me, signing in a second time.

"I'll just call him," she said, handing over a locker key. "If you'd like to wait on the sofa."

I glanced at the sofa, then at the wall of glass beyond it, noting with some pleasure it looked out over the main gym area. There were lots of men inside, working out on various machines, skin gleaming with sweat and muscles rippling. As views went, it was pretty damn fine, and I walked over to make the most of it.

Jin's name was announced over the speaker system. Five minutes later, awareness raced across my skin. Though I couldn't hear any footsteps—probably because of the thick carpet—I knew it was Jin. The heat and scent of him called to the wildness within, even from a distance.

I glanced over my shoulder. He strode toward me, wearing black gym pants and a black tank top. His skin gleamed with sweat and heat, and he looked sexier than any man had a right to. Desire surged, but my gaze caught his and it fled as quickly as it had risen. His dark eyes gleamed with a ferocity I'd never seen before—a ferocity that was both ancient and inhuman. As if, in that one brief moment, I was viewing his soul and it was nothing that belonged in this time.

Nothing that belonged on this earth.

Then he blinked and smiled, and the strangeness was gone, leaving me wondering if communicating with the dead woman had shaken me more than I'd presumed. I mean, Jin mightn't be human, per se, but he had to be at least a subspecies or some sort of nonhuman. Didn't he? What else was there?

A comment Quinn had made a few months ago floated through my thoughts. He'd said that while he was raised as a human, technically he was only partially so. That the other half of his being was something that no longer existed.

If a half-breed from a race that no longer roamed this earth could survive through the ages, then other, darker things surely could.

The chill that raced through my soul this time was one of foreboding. I didn't want to know about those other darker things. I really didn't. But I had a bad, bad feeling that not only was I fucking one of them, I was stepping deeper into their world the longer I stayed by Jin's side.

He stopped and leaned forward to kiss me, and it was all I could do not to recoil. His mouth was cool and quick against mine and, for that, I was grateful. Right then, anything more passionate would have been too much.

"Hi," he said softly. "Nice to see you again."

He smelled of musk and man and dark spices—all scents normally guaranteed to set my hormones a-dancing. And admittedly, despite the chills and foreboding, desire did stir. I was a wolf, after all, and danger was an aphrodisiac.

But running underneath his lust-worthy scent was a trace of sex and blood, mixed in with a hint of jasmine. I couldn't help wondering if his exertion had been more the rough horizontal kind—involving straps, whips, and naked, perfumed flesh—rather than mere gym work.

"Looks like I've come here at a bad time."

He shrugged. "There's a gym and spa special running at the moment, so we've a bigger crowd than normal tonight. I'm afraid I can't give you that massage I promised, but I'll get Terri to start you off with the treatments, and I'll see if I can grab a break in the next twenty minutes or so."

"Look, if you'd rather I leave and come back—"

"No."

His grip tightened on my arm and the alien light gleamed briefly, starkly, in his dark eyes.

"I have no idea how long I'll be," he continued, "but I'd rather you wait."

"Then I'll wait."

He nodded and pulled me forward, kissing me hard. It was very much a signal of intent and part of me quailed—if only because it suggested that last night was only a teaser. That tonight I'd get a more in-depth introduction to his darker needs and desires.

How far was I willing to go for the sake of the Directorate and tracking down a killer?

I didn't really know anymore, and that was perhaps the scariest thing of all. If my determination *not* to do what the Directorate and Jack wanted me to do had slipped so much in a matter of months, what would I be like a year down the track? Would I become the willing fighting and fucking machine Jack wanted me to be? Was it as inevitable as the cycle of the moon?

A tremor ran through me. Jin broke off the kiss, and smiled. "I shall try to hurry," he said, trailing one hot fingertip down my neck. His touch paused near the pulse point, and his smile widened. "I'd hate to waste such delicious excitement."

"Then don't." I stepped back. "The sooner you go, the sooner you can be back."

He laughed, then turned and walked away. I repressed another shiver and tried to ignore the humming of hormones that just *loved* the danger Jin represented. Sometimes being a werewolf was a pain in the ass.

I looked across to the receptionist. Her face was carefully neutral, but her distaste rode the air. Resisting the urge to tell her I actually sympathized, I said, "Where do I go for my treatments, then?"

"Just follow the door to your right. Terri will take care of you."

I followed the directions and pushed through a set of swinging doors. A meaty-looking black woman possessing slick, tied-back hair and hands big enough to snap a bus in two approached from the opposite end of the hall. She stopped when she saw me, well-shaped eyebrows rising almost in alarm. It wasn't hard to guess why. She knew what I was, simply because she wasn't human herself.

I stopped several feet in front of her, and looked her up and down. I'd only ever met one bear-shifter before, but this woman left Berna for dead when it came to sheer muscles and size.

"How did you get past the monitors at the door?" she asked, her voice a low growl that was more curious than antagonistic.

I met her dark gaze with a raised eyebrow of my own. "Probably the same way you do."

"You're a half-breed?"

"Yep."

She nodded. "The sensors read us half-breeds as humans. Kinda handy in a situation like this."

It would have been if I'd actually been half-human. "When we want to go where the rules say we can't go?"

She grinned. "The club rules say no nonhumans. Doesn't say anything about us half-breeds." She motioned me down the hall. "I've set you up in cubicle three. I'll give you the massage, then Raj will show you to the spa. There's a twenty-minute limit, unfortunately, because we're full tonight."

"Can I be nosy and ask why you're working here? It's a bit of a risk, isn't it?"

She shrugged. "The worst they can do is fire me. And the pay here is better than other clubs. Gotta go with the money when you've got a family to feed, you know?"

I nodded, taking in the scents and sounds as we walked down the hall. Hints of sweet oils and feminine musk rode the air, mingling with the tangy spice of male and the faint scent of chlorine. No jasmine, though. No hint of sex.

Whatever Jin was doing, he wasn't doing it in this section.

"Are you the only nonhuman working here?"

"Yep. All employees have to present a birth certificate as evidence of humanity, but mine says human, so I'm okay."

I raised my eyebrows. DNA tests at birth had been mandatory for at least thirty years, and Terri looked a lot younger than that. "And how did you manage to achieve that?"

She grinned. "My old man worked in the labs and fudged the evidence."

"Dangerous stuff." And worthy of at least ten years' jail time if it ever came to light.

She shrugged. "He's dead now, so what can they do to him?" She opened the next to last door on the left. "You want to strip down and place all your valuables in the locker? I'll wait out here."

"And am I supposed to walk around in nothing but my skin?"

She grinned. "I've heard tell you wolves make a habit of it."

"Well, yeah, but humans get quite antsy about it."

"Which is why you put on the robe hanging next to the locker you've been assigned."

"Ah. Thank you."

The changing room was on the small side, and smelled faintly of lemon and ginger. There weren't many other lockers in use, meaning there weren't a whole lot of women in tonight. After quickly stripping down and putting everything in the locker, I grabbed the robe and walked around the room, sniffing the air lightly. And found the scent of jasmine coming from a locker on the far side of the room.

I glanced at the door, wondering if I should take the chance of breaking into the locker. I needed to find out who the woman behind that scent was, if only because she might be one of Jin's regulars, and therefore might know something more about him. Like what he really was.

I checked out the ceiling, but couldn't see any cameras. Not that cameras were usually found in changing rooms but I couldn't take the risk of security seeing I was up to no good.

I slipped my locker key in between the locker door and the frame, and jimmied the door out enough to grab it with my fingers. Then I gave it a quick, hard tug. Locker doors just weren't designed to withstand the strength of a werewolf, let alone one who also had the might of a vampire behind her as well.

With the door open, the scent of jasmine was more powerful. The woman had stacked her clothes in a neat pile, and had hung her handbag over the single hook on the side. I opened it, then searched through the mess of tissues, makeup, and keys until I found the holder containing her credit cards and photo ID. Her name was Jan Tait, and she was a pretty woman with green eyes and blond-highlighted brown hair. I memorized her Carlton address, then flicked through the rest of the holder, seeing more credit cards, a gold card for the cinemas, and a picture of a black-and-white cat. Which probably meant she was single. Attached or married women usually had pics of their other half or kids.

I shoved everything back into the bag, then closed the door and gave it a light thump to force the lock back in place. After doing up the robe, I headed for the door and the waiting Terri. We only walked another four doors down before she stopped and opened another door, this time revealing a small cubicle with a lone table sitting in the middle.

"Here you go. Just strip down and lay on the table. I'll be with you in a moment."

"Thanks, Terri."

She nodded and closed the door. I took off the robe and threw it over the end of the table before lying down as directed. After about five minutes, Terri came in and got down to work. I have to say, she was damn good. By the time she'd finished, my muscles were all fluid and relaxed. Like the aftermath of fantastic sex, only without the effort and fun.

"Okay," she said, doing up the massage oil bottle lid, "I'll just buzz Raj and he can take you down to the spas."

"They're not on this floor?"

She shook her head. "Next one down, near the administrative areas."

This place had to be bigger than it appeared if they had a second floor just for the office crew and the spas. "That's inconvenient, isn't it?"

She shrugged. "It's only a set of stairs."

I guess so. I put the robe back on and lashed the front together. Raj, a pimply teenager who looked no older than seventeen or eighteen, strolled in a few seconds later and gave me an insolent wave to follow. We walked down a set of carpeted stairs and into another wide hallway that was lined with doors. From behind each came the sound of bubbling water and soft music.

"Individual spas?" I said, taking a quick glance up and down the hall. No security cameras here, either. Very convenient.

The kid nodded and threw open a door. As he did so, a pass-card swung out from under his shirt. It had a bar code across the bottom, suggesting that if I wanted to go anywhere less public, I might need a pass to get into it.

Bugger.

"Customers seem to prefer individual spas," the kid said, "and it gives management a chance to charge extra." He grinned and waved a hand toward the small cubicle dominated by a large bath. "Shower before you get into the water. The controls for the jets and music are on the left panel. Light controls on the right."

"And the toilets?" I lowered a shield and telepathically felt for his mind. His thoughts were bright and swift, reminding me of one of those com-games teenagers seemed addicted to these days.

Taking his pass and ensuring he didn't remember it was altogether *too* easy.

"Toilets are down the hall and to the left," he said, without a pause or a blink that would have given anything away to unseen watchers. Not that I thought there were any, but you never could be too careful. "You got twenty minutes, then someone will be back for you."

"Thanks."

He nodded and headed back toward the stairs. I stepped inside the room and closed the door. After stripping off the robe and dropping both it and the stolen pass on top of the small stool sitting in the corner, I had a shower to rinse off the honey-smelling oil, then quickly dried off and put the robe back on. Once the music and spa jets were on, and the lights off, I headed out the door.

The corridor was empty, save for a robed woman down the far end. She paid me no heed as I strode toward her, and soon disappeared into one of the rooms. Spa jets went on as I passed by her door, an indication that she was safely occupied for the next twenty minutes. I paused at the end of the hall, looking left and right.

The right-hand corridor led out into the building's main foyer and the elevators. Not the way I wanted to go. Besides, the exit doors were locked and alarmed.

The toilets were to the left, as the kid had said, and beyond them a double glass door that said "Staff Only"—an invitation for the curious to investigate.

I looked over my shoulder, just to ensure the kid or someone else wasn't headed my way, then walked over to the card reader. I peered in through the glass, looking for cameras, then swiped the card. The reader beeped, the light flicked to green, and the door buzzed. I opened it up and slipped inside.

The big room was empty and silent. There were four doors leading off it, one of them open, revealing what looked to be a well-appointed staff lounge. Not the type of room that would hold many secrets—not the kind I was after, anyway.

I walked across to the first closed door. Opening it cautiously revealed a small corridor and several offices that were obviously occupied, given the feminine chatter coming from them. I moved on to door number two. Nothing but a large storeroom. Door number three was keycard locked.

I swiped the kid's card through the slot, but the little light stubbornly remained red. Obviously, Raj didn't have clearance for this area.

I stepped back and studied the doorframe, looking for alarms and wondering if I should risk breaking open the door. As I did, a bell rang.

Adrenaline surged and, for half a moment, I was certain I'd been sprung. My damn heart seemed to lodge somewhere in my throat, beating a million miles an hour.

I stepped back, ready to flee to cover, then realized the ringing was actually a phone. Amusement at my own jumpiness swept through me, but it didn't last long. Because when the phone stopped ringing, footsteps became audible.

They were approaching from behind the locked door. Someone was coming out.

This time I did turn and run—but just to the nearest hidey-hole, which happened to be the storeroom. But I left the door open enough to peer through.

The locked door opened, and a big blond man dressed in black stepped out. He had a coiled black whip in one hand, and a twisted bit of material in the other. I stepped back into the shadows as he approached, but didn't close the door, figuring a moving door would catch his eye more than a partially opened one.

He didn't stop, just strolled past and into the office area. I glanced back at the door that had been locked, saw that it was still closing, and ran like hell toward it, squashing my breasts against my body with my hands so they didn't brush the door as I slipped through the vanishing gap.

The door closed with a soft click that seemed to echo ominously. A long, dark corridor lay before me. Other than the soft sound of my own breathing, nothing seemed to stir. The air was still, hinting at age and mustiness and something else, something I couldn't quite place.

Something that had chills running down my spine.

I rubbed my arms, and wished I had something warmer than a robe on. Cold had never been a friend of mine, though right now I could pretty safely say the goose bumps flitting across my flesh were due to fear more than the chill.

I wrapped the shadows around me, just in case someone came out into the corridor unexpectedly, then padded down the hallway, following the scent I couldn't name.

Other scents soon joined it. Sweat. Blood. The hint of jasmine. Unless there were two ladies wearing the exact same scent, then Jan Tait was close by.

Doors loomed in the darkness. Four in total, two on

the left, two on the right. I sniffed the air, trying to catch the direction of the jasmine scent. It seemed to be coming from the first door on the right, but it was hard to tell because that unknown scent almost overwhelmed everything else. And *that* scent was coming from the second door on the left.

It was, I thought, a little bit of desperation, a lot of death, and a mix of male and female. The death scent reminded me a little of Gautier, but even then, it wasn't quite the same.

And with the mix of scents came odd mewling sounds.

Another shiver crawled across my skin. I reached for the door handle to my right. There was no way in hell I was tempted to investigate that other room or the scent emanating from it, because it just felt *wrong*. I might be a werewolf, I might often tread where only fools usually dared, but I wasn't a complete idiot. Not when I was alone and without backup, anyway.

I carefully opened the door and peered inside. The room was in complete darkness, and the only sound to be heard was the soft panting of breath. Jan Tait—or whoever it actually was—was alone in the room.

I slipped inside and closed the door, then switched to infrared. And discovered what looked like a medieval torture room. There were racks with rough wooden wheels and thick ropes, chains attached to cuffs dangling from the ceiling, a huge wooden wheel straddling a deep water trough, and rough ropes attached to wall rings.

It was from one of these that a woman dangled. Her toes barely even touched the floor, meaning her shoulders and arms had to be taking the brunt of her weight.

The pain of it had to be killing her. But as my gaze slid down, I realized the shoulders weren't even half of it. She was naked, her light brown hair tied neatly into a ponytail and a cloth, knotted at the back of her head, covering her eyes. The loose ends of the cloth trailed down her back, touching flesh that was bloody and raw. In truth, it didn't actually resemble skin anymore, but freshly shredded meat. Her breath was shuddery gasps, and yet the cause wasn't fear or pain, despite the mess her back was in, but rather arousal. It stung the air, as thick and as heavy as the scent of her blood. This woman, whoever she was, was getting off on the mess they were making of her.

I shuddered at the thought, and walked forward. The carpet gave way to tiles that were icy against bare toes, and the sound of my steps whispered across the silence.

The woman shifted her feet, so that her weight rested more heavily on her arms. The moan that escaped was a sound filled with pleasure. "More," she whispered. "I need it . . ."

I stopped behind her and studied the cuts. The welt marks evident through the raw mess indicated the whip I'd seen the man carrying earlier was more than likely the weapon used here. Which just might mean he was due to come back.

Meaning, if I was going to question this woman—or at least read her mind and grab the answers I wanted—I'd have to hurry. I lowered my shields, and slid swiftly into the woman's thoughts.

Bad mistake.

Her mind was all pain and thick arousal, and the moon heat surged to life in response. Sweat broke out across my skin, and for several seconds, it was all I could do not to spin around, go find the nearest male, and fuck him senseless.

I wrenched free of the woman's thoughts and took a deep, shuddery breath. Okay, so I'd have to get answers the old-fashioned way.

"Jan? Why are you doing this?"

"I need. I pay."

I raised my eyebrows. So the Hunter's Club *did* provide more than just gym and massage services. Interesting. "What do you pay, Jan?"

She twisted on the ropes, her wrists so raw blood dribbled down her left arm, heading for her shoulder. "Gold pass. Top of the tree. Please. No more teasing. Finish it."

There was a desperation in her voice that had the chills galloping, rather than merely stepping, across my flesh. She wanted what they were doing to her. Wanted it, needed it. I rubbed my arms, and said, "I'm not here to finish it."

She moaned and yet, oddly enough, her desire rose, sharp and tantalizing in the still air. I wrinkled my nose against the scent, not because it was horrible or anything, but because my blood was beginning to pound through my veins again, stirred to life by the seductive smell. I might not be attracted to the same sex, but the scent of desire was enough to set hormones raging when the moon heat was closing in.

"Tell me how people find out about the gold pass."

"Hellion Club," she gasped. "They realized I needed more."

Needed to be brutalized, obviously. Needed to be cut

into pieces and left hung up to suffer. Like she was just another slab of meat fresh from the slaughterhouse.

Another shudder ran through me. I might be sexually adventurous, but even I had my limits, and this was way, *way* past anything I could ever imagine wanting. And I couldn't help feeling sorry for her—though I'm sure my sympathy would be the last thing she'd want.

She obviously enjoyed what they were doing to her, so who was I to turn up my nose at another's wants or needs? Hell, that was the very reaction I'd spent most of my life fighting.

"Who from the Hellion Club recommended you come here, Jan?"

"Maisie, the owner. She saw my need. Said she understood it."

"And why did she recommend this club? Aren't there others?"

"She said her brother specializes."

Her *brother*. Another link in the chain, or just a coincidence? As I opened my mouth to ask another question, footsteps echoed in the hall outside. I waited, barely daring to breathe, hoping those steps would keep going right on by.

They didn't.

As the door began to open, I sprinted across to the huge wheel and slid in behind the cover of the water trough.

The man who came in was the man I'd seen carrying the whip earlier. But behind him was Jin. He must have taken a shower since I'd last seen him, because he looked fresh, and no longer smelled of sweat and sex and jasmine. Or maybe it just seemed that way because the tall whip carrier's scent was all blood and sweat and musky man, and it was powerful enough to overwhelm any lesser scents.

The two of them stopped just behind the woman. Jin raised a hand and casually slapped the woman's beaten buttocks.

She moaned, as if in pain, and yet the scent of desire sharpened tenfold.

"What do you want, Jan?" Jin slapped her again, harder this time. As the woman whimpered, he breathed deep, as if sucking in the sound.

A chill went through me. He'd done the same thing when he'd broken the bones of the baby vamp who'd attacked us, too.

Maybe he *was* some sort of energy vampire, as Quinn had suggested. But if that was the case, why was I still reading him as human? He couldn't be both—it just wasn't possible. Once you'd stepped over the threshold of life to undeath, you read as a vamp, regardless of what you'd been in life.

"More," Jan said, twisting agitatedly against the ropes holding her, unable to see but obviously trying to.

"I legally cannot give you more, Jan."

"But I paid," she panted. "Please—"

"No."

"Please."

It was desperate, that sound, and it made me shiver. Because it was all too easy to imagine that sound coming out of my mouth. With the full moon rising, it was totally possible for me to get *that* desperate. I'd been there before, thanks to Talon and his insane determination to get me with child any damn way he could, and I knew from that experience I would do anything—take any amount of punishment—to get what the moon and my body demanded.

And if I kept fucking Jin, that just might be where I ended up. He liked pain—could possibly even feed on it—and a werewolf was capable of taking a whole lot more in the way of punishment than a mere human.

I bit my lip, and decided, right there and then, to get the hell out of this place as soon as possible. I might want to catch the people responsible for sacrificing the women, but there were still limits to what I would do for the Directorate's cause.

The sound of flesh slapping against flesh, and the moan that followed it, had another tremor running across my skin. Jan might want what they were doing to her, might have paid big money for it, but all I wanted to do was get up and smack them all.

Then go find Kellen, who was into common old everyday sex, and fuck his brains out.

"Are you willing to pay more for your needs, Jan?" Jin asked. "Are you willing to go all the way?"

All the way? Something about that phrase had warning lights flashing. I mean, how much more could any human—male or female—take?

Obviously, a whole lot more if the sudden surge of desire and desperation coming from Jan was any indication. "Yes, yes," she said.

Jin glanced at the big man beside him and smiled. It was a cold, pleased thing, and sent ice slithering through my soul. There was nothing remotely human in that smile. Nothing even resembling humanity.

"We have another candidate, Marcus."

"We do." The big man's voice was a rich rumble that should have been sexy, but only sent more chills skittering across my skin. "I shall inform the boss."

"Good." Jin glanced at the woman. "Finish her off, then take her to the recovery room. I better go check our other patrons."

"The women in rooms two and three bleed sweetly."

Jin snorted. "But the woman in two gives no pain. No fear, and only a little desperation."

"She is lesbian, is she not? Could we use that?"

"She's bisexual, so no. Death intends to keep trying, but I think she'll become another meal for him. I don't believe she can provide what we need." He slapped the other man on the shoulder. "Don't forget to get the papers typed up for Jan once she regains consciousness."

"Will do."

Jin left. Marcus casually unfurled his whip and snapped it across the silence. I jumped. Jan merely moaned, the sound one of anticipation.

"Tell me what you want, Jan."

"Finish it. Hard."

"Tell me," he said, voice almost lost under another snap of the whip.

"Beat me," she whimpered. "Just beat me."

"As the man said, I can't do that. Not yet."

She made a gargled sound full of despair. He breathed deep, as if sucking it in. Just like Jin had appeared to be sucking in her pain.

God, was Jan the only human in this room?

"Please," she said again.

Marcus coiled the whip back up, then ran the handle end down the torn flesh of her back. "You want it fin-

ished; I want your desperation. I want to feel your torment." He reached up with one hand to grab the rope ty-
ing her left arm to the ring. "You will give me that, Jan."

Her arm flopped free. He grabbed it before it could
fall to her side, then spun her around, shoved her back
roughly against the wall, and tied her back up.

Then he fucked her, using the thick whip handle
rather than his body. All the while, the big man breathed
deep, his body shuddering in pleasure as she twisted,
screamed, and, eventually, came. Then she collapsed
against the ropes and blacked out.

Marcus leaned forward and kissed her lips, as ten-
derly as any lover, then carefully undid her ropes and
carried her out. I stayed where I was, battling the mix of
rage, disgust, and desire sweeping through me, trying to
control the twin urges of finding someone to beat senseless and finding a man to fuck the hell out of.

Right now, neither was exactly practical.

I blew out a breath then stood, knowing I had to get
back to the spa before someone came looking for me. I
padded across the room and carefully opened the door.
The corridor still lay in shadowed darkness, but it was
far from silent. Screams and grunts were now coming
from the room that held the odd scent—which was room
two, I noted, suddenly seeing the small number on the
door.

Who was the man referred to as death in that room?
Was it Gautier, or someone else? It didn't smell like
Gautier—not exactly—and besides, Gautier didn't do
sex. And whatever else was happening in that room, sex
was definitely involved.

I shuddered and got the hell out of there.

As I opened the door at the end of the corridor, a door down near the torture rooms opened. I scooted out the door as fast as I could, but not fast enough.

"Hey—"

I didn't hang around to hear what else was shouted, just ran. I hit the buzzer to open the glass doors, waited impatiently for them to open, then pushed through and ran for the spa.

Once there, I stripped down, slid the pass out of sight behind the stool, then dove into the spa. As the warm water began to take the chill from my skin, I ducked under the bubbles, wetting my hair and feeling the heat caress my face.

In the hall outside, doors opened and closed.

Someone was checking who was and wasn't around.

I leaned back and closed my eyes. A few minutes later, my door opened and Jin's thick scent filled the room. I opened one eye and looked up at him. "Twenty minutes isn't up yet, is it?" I groped for my watch, which had slid toward the little stool. It was then I noticed a little bit of the pass-card's lanyard sticking out from behind one of the stool legs.

Shit. If he took one more step, he'd be able to see it.

I grabbed my watch, then rose. I didn't step from the spa, though, just let the droplets stream down my water-warmed body. His gaze followed them, as I thought it would. Whatever else he was, he still wore the shape of a man, and all men looked when presented with nakedness. But I pressed a wet hand against his chest, just to ensure he didn't move.

"According to my watch, I still have eleven minutes left." Which was a huge shock. I mean, with all that I'd seen and done, I would have sworn at *least* twenty minutes had slipped by. "Are you trying to cheat me?"

He grabbed my hand, squeezing it harder than necessary. I winced. He smiled. "It can hardly be cheating when you're getting it for free."

I arched an eyebrow, and kept my voice low. Sultry. "And here I was thinking I was going to be paying for it all later."

He chuckled, then pulled me forward, the unexpected force of it making me slip. He caught me, his arms sliding around my body, the strength of his grip brutal.

"What games do you play, little one?" He dragged me up, out of the water; his voice was a dark whisper against my ear.

"No games." My breath little more than a pant of air, but the cause wasn't excitement. He was holding me so damn tight it was a struggle to breathe.

"You had better not be. I do not like being made a fool of."

"I'm not trying—"

"Then why were you in a restricted area?"

Shit, shit, shit. I raised my gaze to his, saw nothing but coldness in those alien depths. Whether he'd truly seen me, or merely fished, I couldn't honestly say. I'd been moving with vampire speed—most people wouldn't have seen more than a white blur.

But Jin wasn't most people.

I tossed a mental coin to decide between a lie and the truth, then said, "I went to the toilet. I didn't know it was restrict—"

He swung me around and flung me back against the

wall. Hard. Pain flared briefly, reverberating through my body, and I had to resist the fierce desire to knock him back onto his ass.

"Hey, I don't mind rough sex, but that's enough of that or—"

"Or what?" he cut in. He wrapped a hand around my neck and pressed against my carotid artery lightly. Fear swirled through me. I saw him taste it. Saw his eyes gleam in sudden pleasure. "You'll leave?" He barked a laugh. "You need what I offer, little one."

"No—"

He shook me, making my teeth rattle and cut off the words. "Yes. Shall I prove it?"

Before I could say anything, his mouth swooped to mine. It was a harsh and unrelenting kiss, a demand that briefly walked the edge of violence, then well and truly dipped over when his teeth caught my lip and bit down hard.

It hurt badly, but desire flared all the same. I couldn't help what I was, couldn't help that danger drew me like a moth to flame, and perhaps that was just as well. Because Jin was taking the lust for danger for the lust for pain, and in this situation, that was a good mistake. One that might just keep me alive.

He chuckled softly, and stepped away. I tried to ignore the throbbing ache in my lip, as well as the one lower down, and said, "You take me for granted."

"Because you want it. Because you get off on it." He flicked a puckered nipple casually. "You will wait, for as long as I want you to wait, simply because you hunger for what only I can give."

Arrogant bastard. But I kept the thought inside and

simply looked at him as he continued, "But unfortunately, I have other duties to tend to before I get to satisfying your desires."

He turned and walked out. I listened to his footsteps, the sound of doors opening and closing, the soft questions and answers.

He wasn't so sure it was me after all.

Thank God.

And his actions here just now had given me the perfect excuse to run. I'd already accused him of taking me for granted. Given his arrogance, it would be perfectly logical for me to now walk out.

Which was more than worth the price of a bitten lip.

I had a shower to wash the scent of chlorine and Jin off me, then toweled myself dry and put the robe back on. After peering out the door and testing the air to ensure Jin's scent had well and truly faded, I headed back up the stairs to the changing room.

Once dressed, I walked around to the reception area.

"All finished?" the blonde said brightly, as I handed back the locker key.

"Yes. And when Jin comes looking for me, please tell him I do not appreciate being taken for granted." I slipped into her mind as I said it, handing in the stolen keycard and making her believe a guest had found it near the stairs.

"Of course," she said, without skipping a beat. And if the amusement in her eyes was anything to go by, she'd absolutely delight in making such comments to Jin.

I nodded my thanks, but on turning away, caught sight of her computer. Would a receptionist have membership lists on her computer? She'd have to, wouldn't she?

I slipped into her mind again, making her do a search through the database. And discovered that Jan Tait wasn't the only woman who had signed up for a gold pass.

Karen Herbert, the latest victim of the serial killer, had too.

And so had every other victim.

Chapter 8

*J*ack wasn't going to let me walk out on Jin for very long, that much was obvious. Not when the club he worked at had finally provided a link between all the murdered women. Jin was a source of information not yet fully explored.

None of which changed my determination to walk out now. I glanced around to ensure no one was paying us any particular attention, then got the woman to download onto a disk all the membership files and employee details possible. The gold-pass membership files were restricted, and I wasn't about to push my luck by getting her to try and load those. Jack could order one of his tech plebs to do that. Although I'm sure the caramel cow would just wet herself at the thought of showing off her technical skills. She certainly had them: I'd caught her hacking into my files once.

I slipped the disk into my pocket, then erased my tracks in the woman's mind and headed out the door. Once I'd returned my pass to the guard and was safely ensconced in my car, I grabbed my phone and dialed Jack.

"She reports twice in a twenty-four-hour period," he said, by way of hello. "This is indeed a time for miracles."

"You've been hanging around the cow too much. You've picked up her smart mouth."

"The only woman in my employ who has the sass to backchat her boss is the one I'm talking to. And it's not nice to call someone a cow."

"It is when they have tits the size of hers. And don't tell me you haven't noticed."

"Are you ringing for a reason? Or do you just want to piss me off?"

Both, usually, but I didn't think it would be wise to admit that. "I think I've found the link between all our victims."

"What? How?"

"All four were members of the gold-pass section of the Hunter's Club, the upmarket health and fitness club Jin part-times at. From what I've seen, the gold-pass club is a word-only membership for people with special requirements."

"What sort of special requirements?"

"They need extreme pain to get their rocks off."

"All of our victims had healed scars on their backs and arms."

"They should have massive scars if what I've just seen is any indication of what they go through." I hesitated.

"It's quite possible I've met the woman lined up to be the next victim. Her name is Jan Tait."

"You got all her details?"

"I grabbed everything off their computer that I could. The gold-pass membership files will require hacking skills to get into."

"We'll handle that end. You stay on Jin."

Yeah, right. "Um . . . there's been bit of a development in that area. I'm afraid I just walked out on him."

His sigh was a sound of frustration. "Can you do nothing the easy way?"

"Trust me, I had no option. But I'll follow him for the rest of the night, see where he goes and who he talks to."

"Good. In the meantime, I'll get Salliane to dig up the dirt on the Hunter's Club and its owner."

"Jan said that she was recommended to the Hunter's Club by the owner of the Hellion Club. Apparently the two are brother and sister. And Quinn just happens to be following the woman who owns the Hellion Club."

"Interesting."

"Why?"

"Because we've been cross-checking the Cattle Club's security tapes, and have discovered Jin talking to a man named John Kingsley on more than a few occasions."

"So?"

"So, he's a very nasty piece of work who's been suspected of several murders. There's never been enough evidence found to convict him."

"That still doesn't explain why he's raised your bad-guy antennae."

"Ah, but see, he also happens to have a half sister by

the name of Maisie Foster, who owns a punishment club by the name of—"

"The Hellion Club," I finished for him. "So Rhoan's already checking this Kingsley person out?"

"Yeah." Amusement crept into his voice as he added, "Apparently he ran into Quinn there."

My eyebrows raised. "Don't you think it's a little bit coincidental that Quinn is following the woman who owns the club that is recommending people to the special services of the Hunter's Club? He obviously knows something he's not telling us."

"Which means you need to find out what you can from him."

Yeah, like he was going to tell me anything. He'd more than likely try locking me in a closet somewhere. For my own protection, of course. "You think this woman could be the one raising the demons?"

"I have no idea. Though I doubt Quinn would simply follow her if that was the case."

"He would if he had motives other than finding the person who was raising the demons." And I very much suspected that was the case. After all, the spooky guy in the alley had basically implied there was more to this than just a couple of demons.

"As I said, question him." He paused. "I did a search for that name the souls gave you."

"And?"

"Azhi Dahaki is part of an ancient Persian legend. It's said that he's the servant of Angra Mainyu, who's supposedly the god of darkness, the eternal destroyer of good, the personification and creator of evil, and bringer of death and disease."

"A real charmer, in other words." I paused. "That ring I found had Persian hieroglyphic thingies on the back of it."

"Cuneiform inscriptions, actually."

"So you've translated them?"

"Not fully."

His voice was grim, and chills skated across my skin. "What does it say so far?"

"Something about entrusting their souls to the god of darkness."

I rubbed my arms. "But it's just a legend, isn't it? I mean, a god of darkness and lies can't really exist, can it?"

"Humans once believed werewolves and vampires didn't exist."

"That's because we were covering our asses like crazy. And it's also totally different from this sort of situation."

"No, it's not. And there is no reason to believe there aren't things in this world that have chosen to remain hidden while the bolder of our races have stepped out of the shadows."

"Jack, we're talking about an ancient god here."

"Are we? Or are we merely talking about an entity that has bided his time for the right moment to come out of hiding?"

"Is there a third option? I mean, those two really suck."

He chuckled softly. "We're still researching the legend. But it's not looking good." He hesitated. "Be wary around Jin. If he *is* part of this legend, he may have powers we can't even begin to guess at."

That was something I didn't want to think about. "Anything else I need to know about Azhi Dahaki?"

"Well, he's supposedly a three-headed dragon who represented pain, despair, and death."

"Hate to break this to you, but no one I've met is a dragon, let alone one with three heads."

"It could be a figure of speech, remember that. And you're the one who mentioned Jin seems to enjoy pain."

"He seems to feed on it," I said, as I recalled the ring I'd found at Dunleavy's and the ring Jin had been wearing. Remembered the dark room and the two men. One sucking in the sound of pain, the other despair.

Fuck.

Legends *could* come to life.

"Jin and Marcus," I added. "Pain and despair. Two of the heads."

"Who's Marcus?"

"One of the club's employees, and the man working Jan Tait over."

"So, that leaves one more—death."

I hesitated. "Gautier's working for these people. Could he be the death head?"

"It's possible, but Gautier's not sexual, and that seems to be a requirement of the dragons."

"Gautier's been off the Directorate leash for a while. It's possible he's changed or evolved."

"But he would have to change his very nature to become sexual. Activate your tracker, Riley, and keep in contact."

"Will do." I hung up, then pressed the com-link in my ear to activate the tracking. I know Jack's new rules said all guardians had to be traceable twenty-four hours a day, but I'd be damned if I'd follow that particular order unless absolutely necessary. A girl needed *some* privacy. Especially with the full moon rising.

I started the car and drove around the building until I found the parking lot exit. I parked several spaces down, then hunkered down in the seat to wait.

The phone rang after half an hour. I glanced at the number ID and smiled. Jin had obviously discovered I'd skipped.

I pressed the receive button and said, "Hello?"

"Riley? Where the hell are you?"

"I'm on my way home. Where else would I be after your charming little display of machismo?"

"You liked it. You can't deny that."

"Just because I like it rough in bed doesn't mean I like it rough out of it. If that's what you like, then go find another playmate." And with that, I hung up.

The grass was *always* greener on the other side of the fence, and I was betting on the fact that Jin would be desperate to have what was now out of his reach. I wasn't the only one who hungered this night. I'd seen Jin in action, and his needs were every bit as fierce as a wolf in moon heat.

He'd ring me, and keep on ringing me, until he got me again. Because if nothing else, I was a wolf and I gave good sex.

He did ring, several more times. I studiously ignored all calls and after an hour or so, saw him pull out of the car park in a white BMW. Not the sort of car I would have imagined him in—something black, sporty, and dangerous would have been more appropriate, surely.

Once he'd passed, I pushed upright and pulled out after him. Following him wasn't hard, despite the speed he was doing. Rush hour had well and truly passed and the streets were relatively clear of traffic. In fact, the hardest thing about the whole exercise was trying to remain far enough behind that he didn't notice me without me losing him.

I wasn't entirely surprised that we ended up in Toorak. That's where Quinn was, and he sure as hell seemed to know more about this whole situation than the rest of us. And he was going to let me in on the secret, or I was going to get *really* angry. Just how much good that would do was anyone's guess.

Though zilch was an odds-on bet.

Jin pulled into the driveway of a gated residence. I stopped well up the street, and got out once the gates had opened and he'd driven in.

The cool breeze swirled around me, carrying with it a familiar scent. But not the one I was expecting.

I shoved my hands in my pockets and scanned the night behind me. "Gautier, one of these days you'll actually bathe and I'll be in deep shit."

His soft chuckle slid across the darkness as uneasily as oil across water. Chills skittered across my skin. There'd always been something particularly nasty about Gautier's laugh, but tonight it seemed ten times worse.

"And one of these days, I'm going to enjoy smacking that smart mouth from your face." He shook free of the shadows and strolled toward me. "Interesting that we both turn up at this place."

Tension rippled through my limbs. I shifted my stance a little but still felt like a sprinter at the starting block. All edgy and ready to run. "The only thing inter-esting about it is the fact I doubt it's coincidental."

He stopped well short of laser range. Not that I actu-ally had a laser to use, but I wasn't about to let him in on that little secret.

"Coincidence doesn't play a huge role in my actions," he admitted, "but I am curious as to what you're doing here."

I raised an eyebrow. "You don't know? I thought you knew everything."

"Oh, I know more than you could ever guess."

His smile was all teeth. Too much teeth, in fact. But it was his gaze that sent another chill down my spine.

There was something not quite right about his eyes.

Something almost inhuman.

Not vampire inhuman, but something more. Some-thing alien and old.

And it reminded me of the coldness I'd seen lurking in Jin's eyes.

Gautier *was* the death head of the dragon.

Sexual or not, he was definitely one of them.

I flared my nostrils, drawing in his scents, tasting the nuances and differences. It *had* changed—the differences were slight, but nevertheless there. But I couldn't say for sure that it was scent I'd smelled emanating from room two at the health club. Maybe the night, the cold, and my fear was somehow distorting sensory information.

Or maybe something else was. *Someone* else.

I resisted the urge to retreat and shifted one pocketed hand, as if clenching a nonexistent weapon tighter. His gaze flickered down and his toothy smile grew. I had a bad feeling he wasn't fooled by the ruse.

Either that, or he wasn't worried about being shot by a laser. Which was probably more likely. He was the type to think getting shot might be a good price to pay for the fruition of his aims. And it's what those aims were when it came to the immediate future and me that had me worried.

And he knew it, damn him. The quick glimmer of amusement firing his cold eyes was easy to see, even at night.

"Riley, keep him talking," Rhoan said into my ear, through my still-open link. "I'm armed and on my way."

Good, I wanted to say. Hurry.

But Rhoan was mind-blind, and I dared not use the com-link because it would only warn Gautier. I forced a smile and said, "So if you know it all, tell me why you killed Dunleavy and his girlfriend."

He raised a mocking eyebrow. "What makes you think I did that?"

"It's that smell thing I keep warning you about. It lingers, you know?"

"They died during daylight. You know I can't move around in daylight."

"I know you never used to be able to, but you've been off the leash for a while, and who knows what nasty sort of company you've been keeping? Or what talents they have that could help a foul piece of work like yourself?"

He raised a mocking eyebrow. "Nasty doesn't even begin to cover my current company, dear Riley. And you should watch yourself. He has his eye on you."

I forced a grin. "Is that concern I hear in your voice, Gautier? I'm so touched."

"You will be, if he gets his hands on you."

"So why the warning, Gautier? If you're working for these people, why warn me?"

"Because you are mine to destroy." He took a step forward. I took one back. He grinned, and it was a cold, ferocious thing. "I intend to destroy all you hold dear, and then I intend to destroy you. Slowly, and sweetly. And no one—no matter who or what they are—will stop me. Not when I get all that I am promised."

A shiver ran through my soul. There would be nothing sweet about his sort of destruction, of that I was sure. Especially not now that he'd become the death head of an ancient legend. "And just what were you promised, Gautier? Or should I guess? Let's see, what do all good little psychos want? Power?"

"You will discover soon enough."

And with that, he attacked.

It was like fighting a cyclone—he was all power, speed, and bloody force, and stopping him was next to useless. He'd been bred for fighting and killing, and I was only a new inductee. And a reluctant one at that.

I twisted away from his blows, then backed away as fast as I could. I didn't want to fight Gautier—not now, and not in the future. And especially not when Rhoan was on his way armed with weaponry that would kill the bastard once and for all.

But Gautier didn't follow my retreat. Just stopped and shook the shadows from his form again. He gave me a grin, and sucked in a deep breath.

"Ah, fear. Such a sweet, sweet thing."

A familiar tingle ran across my skin, telling me Rhoan was near. I didn't react, not even when the red light of a laser cut across the night, arcing toward Gautier.

But he must have sensed Rhoan's presence at the last moment, because he twisted away suddenly. The laser aimed at his head cut into his shoulder instead, and the smell of burned flesh spun through the air.

Gautier laughed. *Laughed.*

The man was terminally insane, there was no doubt about it.

But while he might be insane, he wasn't stupid. He gave us a respectful bow, then faded into the night and ran away.

"Never attack Riley without looking over your shoulder for me," Rhoan shouted to his fleeing form. Then he gave me a grin and casually flung the laser rifle over his shoulder. "Want to give chase?"

"As much as I enjoy a good hunt, that bastard probably has a trap ready and waiting."

"Probably. But it's all part of the fun."

"You're as mad as he is."

"Not really." He leaned forward and gave me a kiss on the cheek. "I'm not insane enough to tackle you alone."

I grinned. "Only because I'm armed with saucy secrets your lover would just adore to hear, and you know I'm not afraid to use them. I don't have that advantage over Gautier."

"The only advantage we'll ever have over him is if we tackle him together." He slipped an arm through mine and began guiding me down the street. "Next time you scent him, don't stand there waiting. Just run."

"And give him the satisfaction of my fear? No way in hell."

He looked at me, eyebrow raised. "And you call me mad?"

"Well, it does run in the family, you know."

He chuckled softly, then said, "So, give me an update on your date."

I did, including what Jack had said about the old Persian legends and my thoughts on who the dragons might be—including the fact that Gautier was one of them. And then I told him everything Gautier had said.

"And you believe him?" Rhoan asked.

"I believe that he's playing his own game, whatever else he might be doing or might have become." I shrugged. "Gautier's a killer, but he's not exactly the world's greatest thinker. It makes sense that if there was someone who was stronger and darker in town, he'd align himself with them. Even if it is just a means to an end."

"I don't understand what Gautier would get out of such a deal, though."

"Well, being the death head for a dark god would surely come with benefits. Like the ability to face sunlight. If he did kill Dunleavy and his girlfriend—and he certainly didn't deny it—then he can now move around in the day. And that shouldn't be possible for a vamp his age."

"Is there magic that can give such protection?"

"Who knows? But if magic can raise demons and a dark god, why shouldn't it be able to protect a vampire from the sun?"

He frowned as he slid open the van's door. "So now

all we have to figure out is what Gautier and his cohorts actually are—and then a way to stop them."

"Well, Jin reads as human and Gautier still reads as a vampire, but maybe that's because their shells still are. Maybe their beings have become something else entirely."

He raised an eyebrow as he helped me into the back of the van. "Spirits of some kind?"

"If I can see souls rising from the dead, and Quinn can be hunted by demons, there's really no saying that an ancient spirit can't be recalled to claim a new body, is there?"

He slid the door shut then waved a hand at the thermos of coffee sitting on a small bench filled with weapons as he moved toward the seat in front of the bank of monitors. "You know, that's an awfully scary thought."

"Yeah, I can see you're shaking in your boots."

"On the inside, I am." His smile belied any attempt of seriousness. "The Directorate as a whole has no experience in dealing with things non-substantial. I mean, how do you kill a spirit?"

"I don't know." I poured myself a cup of coffee and briefly breathed in the smell. Bliss in a cup, even if it looked like mud and probably tasted just as bad. "But I know someone who might."

He raised an eyebrow. "Who?"

"Quinn."

He glanced at the screens. "He's parked in the right corner of the back garden if you want to talk to him."

I grinned. "That's a mite worse than having fairies in the bottom of a garden."

"Trust me, I'm the only fairy around this neighborhood at the moment."

"A good thing, with the moon on the rise." I drained the coffee in several gulps, and winced a little at its bitter taste.

"True." He pointed a finger at the screen. "Check out the security lines before you go. Don't want you tripping over any alarms and tipping them off."

"Hey, I'm not a complete novice at this."

He merely grinned and pointed at the screen. So I checked it out and memorized all the hot spots. "That's a whole lot of security happening."

"Makes you wonder what, exactly, they're protecting, doesn't it?"

I looked at the other screens. There were cameras on every angle of the house, but none on the inside. "You able to hear their conversations yet?"

"Some. They've got some sort of shielding around the place. We only pick up things when they're near the windows."

"Frustrating."

"Very. But Jack's working on subverting their internal security system and fast-tracking it into ours."

"Could be handy. We need to know what those bastards are discussing." Because it would be nasty, of that I had no doubt. Whether or not it related to our investigation was the question we had to answer.

But all the indications we'd had so far certainly suggested it would.

I pushed away from the monitors. "I'm off to find Quinn. If you hear anything odd happening, give me a call." I slid the door open, then paused and looked back at my brother. "And lock this door. Gautier may have run, but he could come back. I don't trust him one iota."

"I can take care of myself, Riley."

"But that bastard is out to hurt me, and the best way to hurt me is to hurt you."

"If he wanted to take me out, he could do so without coming anywhere near the van."

Well, yeah, but Gautier was a man who liked to taste his victory. Liked to breathe it deep, and get his jollies off it. He could hardly do that if he just blew the van to pieces.

"Is it going to hurt you to lock the door?"

He rose. "If it stops you nagging, I'll lock the door. Go find your vampire, woman, and ease some of that tension I can smell."

"I have a feeling my vampire isn't going to be too compliant in that regard."

"Well, work for it, girl. It's about time you had to."

"Bitch."

"Right back at ya, babe. And don't switch the com-link off—unless you're going to get frisky with Quinn. That I don't need to hear."

I grinned and headed out. Behind me, the van door closed and locks tumbled into place. A little bit of tension ran from my limbs. While I didn't think Gautier would attack again, you just never knew. If there was one person in this world who could be trusted to do the unexpected, it was that slimy bastard.

I shifted shape in the shadows, then leapt into the nearest yard. I had no idea what sort of security any of the neighboring houses had, but at least if I tripped an alarm, all the occupants would see was a wolfy-looking dog.

I scrambled over the gate, scraping my belly on the tops of the pickets in the process, then made my way around to the back garden. Several more fences later, I was in the yard behind Kingsley's house.

Quinn's delicious scent filled the air. I sniffed it happily, drawing it deeply into my lungs, letting the aroma fill me the way I wished his body could fill me, then trotted across to him, carefully avoiding the two spots containing infrared sensors.

"Some people need to be tied up, obviously," he said, amusement warring with frustration in his soft tones.

I shifted shape, then reached under my torn sweater and shook my bra free. Lacy items just didn't handle the change as well as stretchy ones. My sweatpants were still serviceable, and while my sweater was torn, it could be tied at the front and still worn. But the bra—useless.

"Jin did enough of that the other night," I said, tossing the bra over the neighboring fence. Let them have fun trying to figure out where it'd come from. "I've discovered it isn't on my list of favorite things."

"Ah," he said, his gaze on mine and filled with a flame that was all sexual awareness, all desire. "Is that why you're here?"

"Partly. Jin tried getting rough out of bed, and I decided he needed a lesson in manners. I left, and he lost his temper and came here."

"So the whole gang is here?"

"Including Rhoan and Gautier." I studied him as I lashed the ends of my sweater over my breasts. "Have you been back home yet?"

He raised an eyebrow. "Do I need to?"

"Well, I smashed a few things, but other than that, it's in reasonable order."

"Ah." He paused. "There were some figurines amongst the casualties, I suppose?"

"One or two."

"They were worth a fortune, you know."

"Good."

"That's not very adult behavior."

"And drugging me, taking away my clothes and car, and locking me up was?"

"I was only trying to—"

"Next time," I interrupted, "try treating me like an adult. Let me make my own decisions and mistakes."

"A mistake on this case could get you killed."

"I'm well aware of that fact. But it's my decision, and my decision alone. You have no rights, and no say, in my life, Quinn. You never will."

"We'll see."

Frustration swirled through me. I wondered—and not for the first time—if continuing a relationship with Quinn was worth all the angst. Then I remembered the sex, and thought, Hell, yeah, it most certainly *was*. Still, I couldn't help asking, "Why won't you give this fantasy up? Why not settle for what you *can* have—you and me in an ongoing but not mutually exclusive arrangement?"

He raised the eyebrow again. "Are you willing to give up your white picket fences and two-point-five kids dream?"

"No—"

"Then do not tell me to give up what I desire."

"The difference is I'm not trying to force my dreams on anyone. You are."

He didn't answer, his gaze going to the house instead. Part of me figured it was little more than a ruse to avoid answering a difficult accusation, but I lowered a shield and stretched out telepathically anyway. Not toward him, which would be a stupid thing to do considering his telepathic skills could sweep mine under the nearby daisies and stomp all over them, but toward the house. Only my telepathic "beam" somehow mingled with Quinn's, and while I couldn't actually hear his thoughts because of his shields, the resulting mix triggered some sort of weird amplification between us and those within the house.

Voices sprang into focus—not just one person, but everyone in the house—in some strange sort of "conference call." I was hearing their thoughts as conversations, in real time. Weird, totally weird.

And yet another sign the drugs I'd been injected with were continuing to affect my body and my psi-skills in unexpected ways.

"We can't afford to have this O'Conor person sniffing around much longer." Jin's mental tones were filled with simmering tension—tension that was both sexual and physical. "He's getting too close."

"We're trying our best to get rid of him," another voice said, the mental tone mild and yet filled with an underlying iciness. Only it was more an inhumanity than any mere coldness, and it had my soul shivering.

"Obviously, you're not trying hard enough." The words were practically spat. Jin was a very unhappy boy indeed. The thought cheered me no end.

"The demons are having trouble tracking his life force. It's intermittent." The voice was female, and presumably Maisie Foster. Something in the way she spoke was oddly familiar—though why I had no idea.

"He's a fucking vampire—how could his life force be intermittent?"

"Because before he was a vampire he was something else. He almost destroyed me once. I do not wish to risk it again."

The annoyance I'd felt earlier increased tenfold. Quinn had already told me that before he'd become a vampire, he'd been something more than human, so that in itself was no surprise. But he'd conveniently forgotten to add that *that* something had already met this evil.

"I have my reasons for keeping secrets," he said softly, without even looking at me.

"And I've just about had enough of your secrets and lies. You could have saved the Directorate so much time and energy if you'd just told us what you knew from the beginning."

Not to mention the fact that his admission might have prevented my needing to fuck the creep. I didn't want to sleep with bad guys just to get information—and Quinn was well aware of that fact. Hell, he *hated* the fact that I was doing it, so why not come forth with information if it could have prevented it?

"Because I did not know that your case and mine were one and the same."

Mainly because he didn't bother to check. But I resisted the urge to say the words out loud. Those inside the house were still talking, and right now, getting information that might end this case was far more important than sorting out a vampire determined to get his own way—whether it be on the case or in our relationship.

"He could destroy us again if we do not proceed cautiously," the deep voice said. "He is one of the few on this earth who even remembers us as anything more than legend."

"So, we sit around and twiddle our thumbs until his life force becomes strong enough for the demons to track?"

"No," Maisie said. "I intend to conjure a stronger class of demon, but it takes time to summon them. I've had to send the sub-demons back to hell so I have the energy reserves required."

I glanced at Quinn as Jin began questioning Maisie further. "Sounds to me like we need to contain Maisie Foster."

"If we take her out of the picture, we warn the others."

"They already know you're after them."

"But they do not know the Directorate is after them."

I snorted. "If these are the people responsible for the sacrifices, then they *know* we're after them."

"But they are not yet aware how close you are to them."

"I wouldn't bet on that—we think Gautier's one of them. The death head, in fact."

He glanced at me sharply.

"Yeah," I added. "We figured out some of the history. But it'd be nice if you took some time out of your busy schedule to fill in the blanks."

"If Gautier *is* the death head, then Jin knows you're a

guardian. That makes it even more important that you stay away from him."

"He doesn't know."

"You cannot be sure—"

"I can, because the one thing Gautier wants, besides power, is my destruction at his hands. He'll give up his soul, he'll give up control of his body, but he won't give up that."

"You'd trust your life on that fact?"

"Yes." I glanced back at the house. "If we snatch Maisie, they'll just think that you took her out."

He studied me, his features carefully neutral. It was a look I'd seen many times before—usually right before he told me some lie.

"Maisie Foster is an extremely powerful sorceress. It will not be easy to take her out."

"Even so, it'd be a hell of a lot easier to remove her from the scene than one of the dragons, wouldn't it?" It was a question aimed more at Rhoan than Quinn. I had no doubt that, between me and Quinn, we could handle Maisie, but I didn't want to do anything without official approval.

"Capture her, you mean?" Quinn asked.

I nodded. "I'm sure Jack will want to chat with her."

"She will never 'chat,' nor could Jack or the Directorate contain her."

I raised my eyebrows. "Why?"

"Because, as I said, she is an extremely powerful sorceress. Magic cannot be contained by psychic powers or technical devices."

"But it can be contained via other means?"

"Yes." He hesitated. "To be honest, I do not think the

effort worth it. She will die before she tells us anything about her master."

"John Kingsley is her half brother, not her master."

"John Kingsley no longer exists. Nor do any of the other men inside that house. They are merely living, breathing receptacles for the spirits of evil."

Jin and that blond man I'd seen in the fitness club *might* be just shells, but the creepy spirit I knew as Gautier was still well and truly present. I shivered, and tried to ignore the fact that I'd been fucking something that didn't even belong on this plane of existence.

"But how can spirits march in and take over someone's body like that?"

"Magic. Blood magic." He looked at me. "And they need regular, willing sacrifices to maintain their existence."

"Hence the bodies we're finding." And the reason they were going after those with extreme sexual tastes. "Why willing victims? A sacrifice is a sacrifice, isn't it?"

"The dragons may need the taste of pain, despair, and the fear of death to feed, but the god of darkness himself grows strong on the acquiescence to evil."

"That doesn't entirely make sense considering his dragons feed on pain, despair, and death."

"But Angra Mainyu is the god of darkness, the eternal destroyer of good. He feeds on the *enjoyment* of darkness and death."

This was all getting a little weird for me. "However much these people enjoy pain, I can't see how they'd willingly go to their deaths. Have you seen what he does to these people?"

He hesitated. "Yes. But the desire for pain is often a

growing one, and these people are carefully pushed to crave more and more, until only death will bring them the ultimate satisfaction."

Visions of Jan rose. The mess of her back, the way she needed—begged—for me to finish it. How long had Jin and his cronies been working her up to that point? How long would it be before she became the next victim found neatly sliced and diced on some warehouse floor?

"Trouble is," I said, repressing a shudder, "he doesn't just feed on the joy of killing them."

"No. The flesh of heart and liver and kidney are sweet on the tongue."

"I do not even *want* to contemplate how you know that."

The smile that touched his lips was gentle, and yet somehow sad. "I have been a vampire a very long time, Riley. And all vampires, whether they admit it or not, have their dark times."

"Doesn't mean I have to know about them."

"You should, because they are a part of what I am."

"And a werewolf is part of what I am, but that doesn't stop you from trying to circumnavigate the fact."

He didn't answer, just looked back at the house. When you didn't want to answer a question, ignore it. That was Quinn's usual mode of operation, and it was getting more and more annoying.

And yet, I had to admit it was contradictory to want to know about his past, and yet not know about his dark times. I surely couldn't have one without the other. Not if I truly wanted to understand this vampire.

"And Jan?" Jin said, as I returned my attention to the house. "When will she be recovered enough to move?"

"Perhaps tomorrow," a fresh voice said. It took me a moment to realize it was Marcus, the whip-happy blond from the club. "We applied Jin's salve, and the healing is progressing satisfactorily."

"Then tomorrow night. We shall meet and see how suitable she is." He paused. "Jin, bring an appropriate partner."

"A testing may not be a wise move with O'Conor and the Directorate on our tail," Maisie commented.

"It cannot be helped," Kingsley said, voice a lash of anger. "Unless you wish to contribute your own flesh again so soon?"

Maisie's shudder ran down the mental lines, becoming my own, even though I had no idea what Kingsley actually meant—and no desire to find out. "I'm only looking out for your safety, John."

"I know. But I need a full blooding. If you raise another demon before then and kill Quinn, it should not be a problem."

"I have only so much blood in my body, John. I cannot—"

"You can, and will. I need six more victims to sustain my existence on this earth. After that, we are less vulnerable."

I glanced at Quinn. "Did you know this?"

He nodded.

"Then why have you not gone after them?"

"Because I am a vampire above everything else, and vampires have restrictions." He motioned toward the house. "If they do not move from their lair, I cannot kill them."

"Maisie moves."

"Maisie was my one and only connection to the others. I could not kill her until I had found all the tendrils of this evil."

"Then why won't you take Maisie out of the picture now that we've found all the players?"

"Because, as I've said, it would warn the others and perhaps send them undercover again."

Inside the house, Maisie said, "We cannot risk raising too much magic at the moment."

"The house is secure enough. As is the altar."

"Yes." But there was doubt in Maisie's voice.

"Just got word from Jack," Rhoan said into my ear. "If Maisie's the one raising demons, get rid of her as soon as you can."

"He doesn't want to talk to her?" I had a job to do, I knew that, just as I knew taking Maisie out would save others from suffering. But I couldn't help the reluctance to take that final step and kill on command.

Quinn gave me an odd look, then glanced at my ear and smiled grimly. Obviously, he'd forgotten I'd been permanently bugged.

"He says it's too much of a risk if she's the blood sorceress." Rhoan paused. "We can swap if you like. I'll take her out, and you take over monitoring."

"No, it's okay." It wasn't, but I wasn't about to let Rhoan step into dangerous situations just because I had issues. Hell, it wasn't as if I *hadn't* killed before, and Maisie was every bit as bad as the men whose lives I'd taken in the past.

But it was just one more step. One more slash at my futile determination not to walk that path.

I blew out a breath and looked at Quinn. "Any idea how to take out a sorceress?"

"I do not think this a wise course just yet."

"She's already raised one lot of demons to hunt you down, and she's been ordered to raise another. There's no saying she won't also send them after me or Rhoan or Jack. And unlike you, our life forces can't just conveniently fade. Nor do any of us have a clue on how to deal with a demon."

"I'm not saying we can't kill her, just saying it would be better if we delay until we find the gate through which she is bringing the demons."

I blinked. "A gate? Demons have a gate?"

His all-too-brief smile had my hormones sitting up and taking notice. Not that they ever needed much encouragement. "Spirits and demons can't tear their way into our world willy-nilly, you know."

"Well, that's good to hear." I guess. "But what about souls, ghosts, and the like?"

"Souls are the essence of people who live and die in this world. They do not hang around, but move quickly into the next life. Ghosts are souls who are pinned to this plane of existence for some reason."

Some of that I actually knew, but it was nice to have confirmation that there wasn't some permanently opened gate into the netherworld through which these apparitions could come through and taunt me. Especially given the recent developments in my clairvoyant talents. Ghosts and souls popping in for a quick chat at all hours of the night was *not* something I particularly wanted.

"So what does a demon gate look like?"

"It's not actually a gate, as such. It'll be a specially

cleansed area that contains a magic circle and most probably a pentagram. In this case, an upside-down one."

I rubbed my head. This stuff was certainly a lust killer—as he had probably intended. After all, he might want me, but he'd never been one to give in to desire when on a hunt. "So a magic circle contains the demons?"

"No. It's a sacred and purified space where magic—in this case a summoning—can be safely performed. It serves as a boundary for the power and is the doorway from this world to the spirits."

"And the pentagram?"

"An upside-down pentagram is said to be the sign of evil."

"Said to be?"

He shrugged. "A pentagram facing north can cause great problems, as north is associated with darkness and the unknown from pagan times."

"How do you know all this crap?"

His smile was almost bitter. "I am a very old vampire, and sometimes easily bored."

"Uh-huh." I had a feeling the thing I'd met in the alleyway—the thing who'd called himself a high priest of the Aedh—might also have a whole lot to do with his knowledge.

"So where might we find this circle?"

"Somewhere she feels safe. Somewhere secure."

"Her house?"

"Possibly. But I cannot enter that place to check."

"I can." And I had a somewhat legitimate excuse for being there if caught—Jin. "We can use our telepathic link. I'll describe what I'm seeing, and you can tell me how to destroy it."

He glanced at the house, then at me. "The minute we destroy the circle, she'll feel it."

"So?"

"She might get a tad angry."

I grinned. "I handle 'tad angry' with ease, vamp boy."

He didn't say anything, just looked at me, and my grin slowly faded. "Look, let's just do this, before someone else dies."

He took a moment to nod, then glanced at the house again. "Rhoan has this house tapped?"

"Yes." I didn't mention he couldn't actually hear a whole lot. I had a feeling if I did, Quinn wouldn't be going anywhere.

"Has he infrared of the rooms?"

"Not yet," Rhoan said into my ear. "Maybe in an hour or so, once Jack's team finishes hacking their security."

I repeated his words, and Quinn nodded. "Somewhere in that house, probably at a subterranean level, there will be some sort of tunnel leading into a deep chamber. We need to find it."

"Why?"

"Because that is where his power rests. That is where he sacrifices and feeds. To destroy him, we must first destroy the altar."

"I'd imagine that would piss him off more than a little bit."

"Yes, it will." There was something in his eyes—a darkness that was part memory, part ferocity—that sent a shiver down my spine. "And that is when you will understand the true meaning of the god of darkness."

"A lesson I have no desire to undertake."

"A wise decision."

That was me—wise all the way. *Not*.

"You got a car nearby?"

"Yes."

"Then I'll follow you to Jin's, if you like."

He nodded and pressed a hand to my back, gently guiding me toward the rear of the yard. Warmth shivered across my skin, and moon-spun desires sprung to fierce life. "I don't suppose—"

"No," he said, "not here. Not now."

I scowled at him. "You're just no fun."

"If the moon heat is so bad, you should not be here."

Yeah, well, there was that. "It's just an itch that needs to be scratched. Nothing urgent." Not yet.

He didn't say anything, but then, he didn't need to. He might not be able to actually smell my desire, but he was a vampire *and* an empath. He'd feel the heat of it in my emotions. Would hear the elevated rate of my heart.

I headed back to my car then followed his—a divine black Porsche Coupe—across to Jin's. I couldn't get parking anywhere close and was forced to park in the next street then lope back. Quinn, lucky bastard that he was, somehow managed to grab a prime parking spot five doors down from Jin's.

My gaze went to his house, and a tremor ran down my spine. There was something almost watchful about its facade.

Something sinister.

I rubbed my arms and glanced at Quinn. "Doesn't look as if there's anyone inside."

His gaze was on the building. "There's nothing visible on infrared, but that doesn't mean the place is empty."

I raised an eyebrow. "It doesn't?"

"Demons don't show up on infrared."

"That's a comforting thought." I paused. "So how do I combat a demon?"

"Demons can be killed when they materialize." He walked to the trunk of his car and opened it up. "All you need to do is chop off their head."

"Which will be positively easy, no doubt."

It was dryly said, and he smiled. "About as easy as chopping off a vamp's head."

I waved a hand. "A walk in the park, then."

"Yeah." He handed me a long silver knife, waited until I'd strapped it on, then gave me two bottles of water and a box of salt.

"What am I supposed to do with these?" I asked, a little bemusedly.

"Holy water and salt are both weapons and purifiers." He slammed the trunk lid shut. "They can either keep the demon off you long enough to use the knife, or contain the circle so that it cannot be used for summoning again."

"We're not going to destroy it?"

He shook his head. "By making it unusable we force her to make a second, and therefore drain her of a little more power. We need every advantage we can get."

"Can I just point out it's two against one?"

"No, it's two against five. She will call the others if attacked and they can respond quicker than you could ever imagine."

He touched my back again, sending little shivers of

delight lapping across my skin as he guided me toward the house. "How? They're in human form, and therefore restrained by human limitations."

"They can shed their human forms if they wish. It just means they have to find new bodies to take over."

"And would that be easy?"

He glanced at me, obsidian eyes giving little away. "No human can withstand them."

"In which case, there'd be no need for a willing victim acquiescing to evil, then, would there? They could just take whatever they wanted."

"There is a difference between feeding to maintain existence and taking over the body. In the first instance, one *has* to be willing; in the second, one does not."

"Could a nonhuman resist them?"

"Not if we're talking about a usurping of body ownership."

A tremor ran through me. I hadn't really wanted an answer to *that* particular question. Not when I probably had to face the bastards sooner rather than later.

I opened the gate and ran up the steps to the front door. It was locked, naturally, and a quick hunt around the nearby potted shrubbery didn't produce any handily hidden key. "Don't suppose you were a cat burglar in one of your bad periods, were you?"

"I'm a vampire, remember?"

"Oh yeah." Thresholds and all that. "Oh well."

I hit the door hard, in the sweet spot just above the lock, and it sprung open. Quinn raised his eyebrows. "That's a neat little trick."

"Courtesy of an apartment where the locks never work and the landlord refuses to replace them. It's the same sort of lock." I opened the salt and one of the bottles and held them at the ready. And felt stupid doing it.

I mean, water and salt had never been on my must-grab list when it came to weapons. When it came to unconventional weapons, give me a wooden spiked heel any day.

I took a long look at the shadow-bound hallway, then glanced at Quinn. "What am I looking for?"

"A cellar or room below ground level."

"Why below ground level?"

"Earth acts as a barrier to those sensitive to magic."

"The same way as it acts as a barrier to infrared?"

He nodded. "The door will probably be locked. Make sure it hasn't got any symbols carved or drawn onto it before you touch it."

"Symbols are bad?"

"They could be *very* bad." He touched my cheek, his fingers so warm against my skin. "Be careful in there."

"I will." I leaned forward and kissed him—just a brush of lips, a promise of heat, but even so, it had my hormones dancing with glee. I pulled back before the temptation to taste him more fully became too much, and stepped over the threshold.

The silence of the house descended like a blanket, and there was something almost surreal about it. It wasn't just the silence of a house without people. It was too watchful, too *tense,* for that.

Goose bumps ran across my skin. I gripped the salt box a little tighter and opened the telepathic link between us.

Heat swirled through my mind, desire as thick as

anything I was feeling. *My, my, my,* I said, with a mental grin. *The vampire hungers for more than just blood, I think.*

I'm standing three feet away from a bitch in heat. His mental tones were dry. *Is it any wonder I'm feeling a little horny myself?*

Well, the bitch did offer a little relief.

Not when we're working.

I sighed dramatically. *You are such an old man.*

I prefer to call it cautious. And you and I can sometimes get loud.

Yeah, but isn't it fun?

Not when we're breaking into a suspect's house, it's not.

I smiled, and took several steps into the hall. A clock ticked silently in the room to my right, and the still air was cold. Almost abnormally so. Amusement fled, and I licked my lips. *I suppose the kitchen is the most likely place for a cellar door?*

Generally.

I hadn't noticed one when I'd been here earlier, but then, I'd been more worried about getting some sustenance into my body before I passed out with fatigue. I padded down the hallway, my footsteps echoing lightly across the silence, every sense alert for the slightest twitch or abnormality. Nothing had changed, nothing had moved, since I was last here. Dust still layered the phone table, bills still covered the corkboard near the kitchen door, and plates bearing the remains of chocolate cake still littered the sink.

The only thing that was different was the atmosphere. The odd feeling that I was not alone in the house, despite the fact I couldn't scent or see anyone.

I stopped near the kitchen table and had a look

around. There was a half-glass door to my left, through which I could see the backyard. Beyond that, the only other doorway was the pantry.

Open it.

The pantry?

Yes.

I've seen it open. It's a real pantry.

His frustration swirled through me. *Can you just do something I ask without arguing about it?*

Don't think it's possible. I grinned as I walked across the kitchen. The pantry door squeaked as I opened it, and the sound crawled across my nerves. *I see shelves covered with tins and stuff.*

All of them?

My gaze slid down. *There's three spare shelves on the right.*

Squat down.

I obeyed. *And?*

Is there a button or lever on or under any of the shelves?

I shifted slightly, moving closer to the shelves. Dust stirred, catching my nose and making me sneeze. The force of the sneeze stirred several sheets of loose paper sitting on one of the half-empty back shelves, revealing a small dark handle.

Found something.

No odd symbols on or around it?

A couple of dead bugs and some sheets of paper containing recipes is about as odd as we get.

Use the lever, then. But be careful.

Tension crawled through my limbs. I rolled my shoulders, then placed the bottles of holy water in front of me and grabbed the handle. It didn't take much strength to move the lever down, and as I did, there was a harsh grating sound. The three shelves slid aside to reveal the darkness of a tunnel.

I peered inside. The tunnel was big enough to crawl into on all fours and shored up with wood, but the smell of dirt and mustiness hung heavily in the air. It was also long, dark, and scary-looking. I switched to infrared, but it didn't help any. The tunnel curled to the left as it headed downward, and while infrared could see past walls, it couldn't pierce earth.

What do you smell?

The sudden question made me jump a little.

Dampness. I hesitated, sorting through the more tenuous scents coming up from the tunnel. *Blood. Sulfur.*

Sulfur is demon scent. How strong is it?

Not very.

If it's an old scent, it's probably from past summonings. He hesitated. *Still, proceed with caution, and keep the salt and water handy.*

Just what the hell am I supposed to do with them?

Holy water burns when it hits them. The salt can act as a barrier they can't cross if you use it to create a circle around yourself.

If I have time.

If you have the time.

I blew out a breath, grabbed the bottles of holy water, doing up the loose top so it didn't spill before climbing into the tunnel.

Though there was plenty of room, progress was slow. Between tasting the air, sliding the water ahead of me, and trying to see where the tunnel was actually going, speed wasn't going to happen.

The gentle slope curved around to the left, then right, and the smell of dampness, blood, and sulfur increased. And with it came something else. Muskiness.

Animal muskiness.

Something else was down here. I stopped, drawing in a deep breath, trying to place the aroma. It was sharp and distinct, and felt old in a way I couldn't even begin to explain. And it wasn't anything I'd ever come across.

There's something here.

What?

I don't know. It smells animal, but different, if that makes sense.

Could be any manner of demon.

Well, gee, that's comforting.

Amusement drifted down the telepathic line. *There's only one way you're going to know what it is.*

Says the man who's safe on the other side of the door.

The amusement died. *If I could swap places, I would.*

I know. I shuffled on. The slope continued its gentle downward arc, and the odd assortment of smells neither increased nor decreased. After a minute or so, the tunnel began to widen, and I was able to stand.

I dusted the dirt from my hands and knees, then looked around. The room was small and on the square side of round, and, like the tunnel, shored up by wood. There didn't appear to be anything hiding in corner shadows, despite the animallike odors haunting the air.

Talk to me, Riley.

I've reached the cellar. I took a step, and the sound echoed on the wooden floor. A chill scampered across my skin, though I wasn't entirely sure why. My gaze caught a white candle sitting in an alcove to my left, and beside it sat a box of matches. I mentioned them to Quinn, and added, *Is it safe to light?*

Riley, you're a dhampire with infrared sight. You don't need candlelight.

It's a psychological thing. I think this place would feel better with a little regular light.

Do it, then.

I placed one of the bottles near the wall, out of the way, then tucked the other under my arm and grabbed the handily placed box of matches to light the wick. Yellow light flared softly across the darkness, lending weight to the corner shadows but somehow offsetting the odd chill.

There doesn't appear to be anything here.

Check the floor.

I glanced down. Up until now, part of me had been hoping that Quinn was wrong, that magic wouldn't play a part in this whole setup. But, as usual, my hopes were dashed.

There's wax remains of five black candles standing at each of the points of a pentagram that appears drawn onto the floorboards by ash or something like that. Around this, we have fist-sized black stones forming a circle.

The black stones are warding stones. They're stronger than regular protection circles, but perform the same basic functions.

I studied the nearest stones for a minute, noting the way the black surface seemed to swallow rather than reflect the candlelight. *Will the holy water or salt have any effect on them?*

On them? No. And depending on the type of spell used,

*they may even prevent you from putrefying the pentagram
and making it unusable.*

How?

*They form a physical barrier. Place your hand near the
stones to see what I mean—but be careful.*

I stepped closer to the nearest two stones and raised a
hand. Electricity buzzed across my fingertips like little
angry flies. As I got closer, mini flickers of red lashed the
air, like lightning about to strike. I stopped my hand a
whisker away from the barrier, watching the almost angry light show, letting the energy of it flow across my
skin. It felt foul. Evil, even.

Not surprising given that the pentagram it protected
was being used to call creatures from the dimension of
hell itself.

I dropped my hand, shaking it a little to get some
warmth back into my fingers and to lose the feel of the
power. As I stepped back, something stirred in the
shadow-filled corner to my right and the odd mustiness
sharpened abruptly.

A low rumble ran across the silence, making the
small hairs on my neck stand on end. I reached for the
knife, but my fingers had barely closed around the hilt
when the shadows found shape.

And what a shape.

It was big and black, with yellow eyes that gleamed
with unnatural fire in the pale candlelight and teeth as
long as my forearm.

It wasn't a demon.

It was a hellhound.

Chapter 9

Houston, we have a problem. I was gripping the knife so hard my knuckles positively ached, but I hadn't yet drawn the blade from the sheath. I had a bad feeling that if I moved, if I so much as twitched, the thing in the corner with the fearsome-looking teeth would attack.

And those teeth looked strong enough to bite me in half.

There's a demon? Quinn's tension suddenly flooded the link between us, until I wasn't sure where his ended and mine began.

If a hellhound is classed as a demon, then, yeah, one of them.

A hellhound is a stronger class of demon, and won't be stopped by the salt. It can, however, be burned by holy water.

I awkwardly began to undo the lid of the water bottle one-handed. As shields went, it didn't inspire a whole lot of confidence. Particularly when the creature lowered its head and snarled again. The sound rolled around the room, and if I'd been in wolf form, hackles would have risen. This thing might be a demon, but it was a doggy demon, and my wolf soul just didn't take to being threatened by anything canine.

Which is why I mostly kept my wolf in check. Sometimes she had absolutely *no* sense.

Do I need to slice its head off to kill it, or will any old well-placed stab work?

Slowly, carefully, I began to draw the knife from the sheath. The rumbling growl got louder, the threat in the creature's eyes sharper.

I'm afraid you'll have to take its head off.

Crap. That meant getting closer to those needle-sharp, feet-long teeth than anyone with any sort of sense would want to.

The knife finally inched clear of the sheath. The hellhound's growl reverberated again, a low sound of warning and anger. Tension crawled through my limbs and sweat broke out across my brow. With the knife at the ready, I continued my awkward attempt to undo the water bottle.

The hellhound sprang. I threw myself sideways, hitting the wooden floor harder than necessary and driving the air from my lungs. As I gasped at the shock, the bottle slipped from my hand and rolled away, spurting droplets of water that sizzled and steamed across the floor as it did so. I cursed and lunged after it, only to hear the click of sharp nails tearing wood as the creature came at me again. I rolled away and slashed sideways with the knife. The blade scraped across the hound's hide, slicing through hair but not skin.

It snarled, revealing nasty-looking gums to accompany the nasty teeth. I jumped to my feet, waving the knife in front of me, trying to catch the creature's attention long enough to try an attack. It was smarter than that. Its gaze stayed on mine, luminous and deadly. The fear stirring my stomach got stronger. I hadn't signed on to fight creatures of myth and magic. Psychos and rogue vampires were more than enough for me.

The hellhound sprang again. I twisted out of its way, slashing at the soft flesh of his neck, hoping to at least sever something vital. But it shifted at the last moment, becoming something less than substantial, and suddenly it was behind me.

Teeth sank into my flesh, spurting warmth down the back of my leg. I bit back a scream and twisted around, driving the knife blade deep into the creature's right eye, into his skull.

Blood gushed from the creature's eye socket, spurting warmly over my fingers. The creature roared and wrenched its head backward, tearing my flesh in the process. Pain flashed white-hot through my body, and my breath hissed through clenched teeth. But I kept a grip on the knife, and forced myself to move—hobble— out of the creature's immediate reach.

My knife blow had been hard enough, and deep enough, to have struck brain matter. It should have killed it outright. It didn't, because this was no ordinary beastie. Something I'd partially forgotten in the heat of battle.

The hound shook its head, spraying droplets of blood

that hit the force-warding stones and sizzled out of existence. Then it leapt, arcing across the small space that separated us. Again I twisted out of the way, but this time it must have been expecting the move, because it shifted in midair. Its body hit mine, thrusting me forward with incredible force.

I smashed into the wall face-first, crushing my nose and splitting my lip. Blood spurted, the metallic taste filling my mouth and making my stomach stir threateningly. For a moment, everything was red, and I wasn't sure if it was blood or the angry energy of the nearby warding stones. I pushed away from the wall, felt rather than saw the impetus of the hound's approach, and dropped flat and rolled. Only to remember the stones. I thrust out a hand, stopping my momentum inches from the warding circle even as I slashed at the air with the knife. The silver blade cut through the flesh of the creature's underbelly as it sailed over my length, missing the hissing wall of energy by a whisker. Black blood spurted from the creature's wound, spraying across my face and arms and stinging like acid.

I swore and scrambled away, following the line of stones, using it to protect one side of my body, in much the same way as I might have used a wall. The electricity of it buzzed across my face, and the warning flickers of red fire cut across the shadows, giving the room a sullen angry glow.

Slicing open the hound's stomach didn't appear to be slowing it down any, though I don't know why I expected it to when stabbing a knife into its brain had zero effect. As I stood there, staring at the creature staring at me, the realization came that this was a fight I was never going to win. Not playing it this way. He was too quick, too strong. And he was a demon without living restrictions.

This thing is going to tear me to pieces before I ever get near its neck.

Then use the power of the stones against it.

Won't that warn our magician that something is going on?

Yes, but if you do not think you can sever its head, then we have little other choice.

Okay. I took a deep breath, then made a sideways leap for the barrier. The hound attacked the minute I moved, slashing out with wickedly barbed claws. I twisted and dropped at the last moment, but the creature's blow caught my left sleeve and tore into flesh. It didn't matter, because it was concentrating on me rather than where it was going, and that's exactly what I wanted. The creature hit the wall of energy and the stones reacted instantly. Red fire erupted, surrounding the hellhound in a whirling, incandescent cauldron of flame, burning it, consuming it, in little more than a blink of the eye, until there was nothing left, not even ash, to scatter lifelessly down to the floor.

I blew out a breath, thankful the wards didn't appear to discriminate between evil and good. I guess that made sense, though. It was probably easier to protect the circle from all comers rather than raise a discriminatory type of magic. If that was even possible. *One hellhound dead and gone.*

Relief spun down the telepathic line. *Are you okay?*

I pushed into a sitting position and took stock. The wound on my leg was the worst—the creature's claws had sunk deep, tearing three bloody trenches down from my thigh. And it fucking *hurt*.

The scratches on my arm were no less bloody or painful, but at least the hound's claws had only caught a fraction of skin. The top was a goner, though. My lip and nose hurt, but were really the least of my problems.

The bastard got me a couple of times.

Use the holy water to cleanse the wounds then, before shifting. Demon marks can fester and not heal otherwise.

Even for a werewolf?

Werewolves aren't immune to the forces of magic—whether they be light or dark—simply because you are creatures of magic yourselves.

I shucked off my shredded top, then leaned sideways and picked up the bottle of water I'd dropped. The creature hadn't given me time to undo the lid properly before it attacked, so only a little had managed to escape. I undid the top the rest of the way, and poured some of the water over all the wounds.

About half a minute after the water hit my flesh, it turned white and began to bubble and burn like crazy. I clenched my teeth against the scream rising up my throat, and mentally swore for all I was worth at Quinn.

His amusement drifted down the mental line. *If I'd warned you, you wouldn't have done it.*

Too right, you bastard, I said, when I could.

If you had changed before applying the water, you would have carried the infection into your body. You would have died from it, Riley, because there is no cure for the poison of demon bites once it takes hold.

Not even a magical cure?

He hesitated. *There are magical cures, but I am no*

*magician, and there are few left in this day and age who even
believe in demons, let alone know the spells to cure their bite.*

*Which is odd, isn't it, when you consider we have all
manner of nonhumans still running around?* I shifted shape
as the bubbling finally eased, staying in my wolf shape
for several seconds before shifting back. It healed the
scratches on my arm, and stopped my split lip from
bleeding, but my leg was going to take several more
shifts to fully repair. And I was still going to end up with
bruising, a puffy mouth, and a sore nose, no matter what.
Thankfully, I wasn't seeing Jin tonight, because the
mouth and the nose would be a little hard to explain
away.

But magic is a skill learned, Quinn said, *and like any
skill, it can be lost.*

Like the priests of Aedh are lost? I grabbed the water
bottle and pushed upright. Pain slithered up my leg, but
otherwise it was fine. There was no more bleeding, at
least, though I had no doubt the already pretty bruising
would get worse.

The priests are not lost. They are destroyed.

That one in the alley didn't look very destroyed to me.

You did not see him. You only heard him.

True. I considered the circle for a moment, then
tossed some water toward it. The stones didn't react, allowing the water to arc right through the middle of
them. The stream hit one edge of the pentagram, where
it began to sizzle and steam.

The holy water passed through the warding stones.

*Ah. Good. That means she's set the wards to react to flesh
and blood, not inanimate objects.*

Then why did it react to the demon? They aren't real and living in the human sense of the word.

They are when they're in flesh form. Sprinkle the salt liberally across the pentagram, then use the water to form two circles around the warding stones. Make sure there's about five feet between each one.

Why? I began to spread the salt around, making sure my hand didn't actually go anywhere near the flickers of red lightning.

Because evil might be able to step over one circle, but it can't step over two.

I couldn't see why not, but then, I didn't know a whole lot about magic, holy water, and demons. Nor did I really *want* to learn anything more.

I finished spreading the salt, covering as much of the pentagram's surface as I could, then did the two circles. The water sizzled like acid as it hit the floor, burning a light trench in the wood and filling the room with whitish steam.

With that done, I got the hell out of there. Quinn pulled off his sweater and offered it to me as I closed the front door.

I looked at the sweater, then at him. "You don't like me half naked?"

"I love you naked, but you can't drive home like that because the cops will pull you over."

He shoved the sweater my way again. I crossed my arms and pointedly ignored the offer. I had clothes in my car if I wanted them. I didn't need his, no matter how deliciously warm they might smell. "Why would I be driving home?"

"Because you need to shower and rest."

"And what will you be doing while I'm showering and resting?" I knew *exactly* what he'd be doing. I just wanted to know if he'd actually admit it. Admit that he was mollycoddling me yet again. I mean, hell, yeah, I was bloody and sore and in desperate need of a bath, but it wasn't the first time and it probably wouldn't be the last. And it certainly didn't stop me from doing my job.

It was scary to think I now actually considered being a guardian my proper job. Lord, how things had changed.

"I'm going to be taking care of our magician." He placed the sweater on my shoulder.

I shifted my shoulder and let it slip to the ground. "Not alone, you won't be."

His obsidian gaze seemed to be growing darker, deeper, until it felt like I was falling into a tunnel—a tunnel I could so easily, so willingly, get lost in. This vampire might not be my soul mate, but that didn't mean there wasn't something good between us. Something special.

An alarm went off somewhere in the back of my thoughts. I blinked, but the sensation of being caught by the darkness of his eyes didn't go away.

"You will go home, Riley," he said softly, "and you will rest."

The tunnel seemed to be getting deeper and deeper, until it was all around me, swamping me, overrunning my will and my mind. All I could see was the coal-dark depths of his eyes and all I could hear were his words. The compulsion to obey them swam through me, beating at my skin, my nerves, my brain. So much so that I actually took a step back before I realized it. It took a whole lot of determination to stop a second step and remain still.

I knew then what he was doing.

Anger hit, fast and furious, momentarily weakening the force of his command. I slammed down my shields and severed the mental connection between us, but it was too late, far too late. The compulsion had already been embedded into my consciousness, a desire that beat at my senses with every rapid heartbeat.

I clenched my fists and resisted the urge to scream and rant and rave at him. It took every ounce of control I had to simply say instead, "Don't do this."

He raised an eyebrow. "Don't do what?"

My hands were clenched so hard my fingernails were beginning to dig into my palms. The pain helped keep my anger in check, and the compulsion momentarily at bay.

"Don't play me for a fool, Quinn. I warned you once what would happen if you ever tried to use your vampire wiles on me, and I meant every word."

He looked away for a second, studying the street behind me, his expression calm, giving little away. If anything, that very lack of expression only increased the fury rising inside me. I *hated* the fact I could never read him as well as he could read me.

Hated the fact he was forcing me to a decision I never wanted to make. And an action I never wanted to take.

He looked back and said, "I'd rather have you angry and alive, than dead." His fingers touched my cheek, his skin so warm against mine. "Be sensible. Go home and be safe."

I resisted the urge to press into his caress and jerked my face away instead. "No. And all you're doing is proving you still don't trust me."

"I trust you. I just don't believe you or the Directorate can handle these people."

"You can't go after these people alone."

"I destroyed them once. I can do it again."

"Quinn—"

"No," he interrupted tersely, "I have lost too many people I care about in the past to evil such as this. I will *not* lose you as well."

His command still beat inside my brain, growing in intensity, until every muscle trembled with the need to obey. I wouldn't be able to resist it for much longer, and we both knew it. "Even at the cost of never seeing me again?"

He smiled. "You're a werewolf. You can no more deny great sex than you can the moon change."

I stared at him for several seconds, shocked that he could even *think* that. And at that moment, I not only hated what he was doing, but I hated *him*.

It wouldn't last long—couldn't last long, because it was really only anger, not hate itself. But the words hurt, regardless. Did he really think so little of my integrity that he thought a good fuck could cure me of all concerns? Did he really think I *wouldn't* go through with my threat? "You have a whole lot to learn about werewolves, matey. Or at least *this* one."

"Go *home,* Riley. Rest and recover from your wounds. I'll see you in the morning."

"No, you won't fucking see me in the morning. Or any other morning."

"Riley—"

"Fuck off."

With little other recourse left, I spun and walked

away. His gaze just about burned a hole in my back, but I didn't look around. I strode up the street, around the corner, and across the road. I didn't see the car, only heard the screech of tires as the driver swung to avoid me. A beer-fueled male hung out the passenger window and made several crude comments.

I swore at him too, then shifted to my wolf shape. I wasn't in the mood for male attention of *any* kind right now—which just went to show the depths of my fury. The moon was riding high and the fever *should* have had some influence over my reaction to the comments and the man.

I walked on, wishing I'd parked closer. My nails clicked on the concrete, a soft tattoo that echoed in time with the anger beating through my veins. Which is probably why it took me several more minutes to realize the compulsion to go home was nowhere near as strong as it had been.

I stopped.

Go home, go home, go home. The words were still a mantra in my brain, looping round and round. And yet, like the moon hunger, it was a compulsion that I suddenly seemed able to push into the background and ignore. Why?

I shifted back to human shape. The force of the compulsion jumped back into focus, as strong and as sharp as the moon fever spinning through my veins. My feet moved forward without any real command on my part, padding along the pavement at a decent clip. Shifting back into wolf form seemed to once again ease both compulsions.

Well, well, well.

No one had ever told me that being in wolf shape would ease the fever, but in some ways, it made sense. Werewolves *didn't* make love while holding wolf form—at the very least, it was considered disrespectful, often an act of degradation, and, at the very worst, an act of rape. If you respected your partner, you just *didn't* mate in animal form. It was one of those unwritten rules every wolf, young or old, knew.

Besides, what sane werewolf really wanted to ease the moon fever in any other way besides the time-honored, human-style method of mating?

But how many people knew the force of a vampire's compulsion could actually be muted by changing body form? Quinn's order to go home had been embedded deep into my human brain, but wearing my wolf skin seemed to somehow transmute that order into something that could be, if not totally squashed, then at least ignored.

Which was a very handy thing to know—not that it would matter anymore when it came to Quinn. He was out of my life, whether he believed it yet or not.

The thought made me swear internally. At him, at my job, at fate in general. Dammit, why couldn't anything go smoothly?

There were a lot of things I could put up with in a relationship—hell, I'd proven that by putting up with an arrogant, self-centered asshole like Talon for so long. Quinn could be that, and a whole lot more at times, but he could also be an amazingly caring and gentle man, and so totally fun to be with. We were good together, at least when he wasn't being an ass.

But the one thing I've *never* liked is partners who

tried to use force to make me do what *they* wanted. It was simply unacceptable.

And that's the line Quinn had crossed tonight, even if he'd used psychic strength rather than physical strength.

It's not as if he didn't know how I felt. I'd warned him more than once. Now I had to back those words up with action. *Had* to. If I didn't, he'd just ride roughshod over my entire life. Give a vamp an inch, and he'd sure as hell try to take a mile, and Quinn had proven that adage true time and again.

God, why did he have to force the issue? Why couldn't he have just let me do my job, whether or not it was safe? Life itself was unsafe—death could hit anytime, anyplace. Wrapping me in cotton wool was never going to work, no matter what he thought. I wasn't the type of girl who enjoyed being pampered and fussed over twenty-four hours a day. I could *never* be that type of girl, even if I *wasn't* now a guardian. And if that's what he wanted in a relationship, then he was chasing the wrong bit of tail.

And speaking of chasing, *this* bit of tail had a job to do.

Ignoring the pang of sadness, and the deeper, darker ache that seemed centered somewhere close to my heart, I turned around and loped back toward Jin's house.

Quinn had moved from Jin's doorway and taken up residence in the shadows of a garden several houses down. I padded along on the opposite side of the street, keeping close to the cars parked along the curb, using the metal and the shadows to help hide my form. Not that I really thought he'd see me—he was watching for evil, not for a wolf. Besides, I very much doubted the possibility that I could shake his compulsion would even cross his mind.

When I was close to Jin's house, I positioned myself between two cars, keeping low and deep in the shadows, and waited. There wasn't much traffic at this hour, but the night was far from quiet. People moved in the house behind me, flushing toilets and turning lights on and off. Laughter drifted on the night air, and somewhere in the distance music heavy in bass played, making me want to tap my paws.

Quinn didn't move. Neither did I.

Time ticked by. The moon reached its zenith and began to wane. I crossed my front legs and shifted my rear ones, trying to find a comfortable position. The cold, hard pavement wasn't helping the aches any.

It had to be nearing three when a car finally pulled to a stop in front of Jin's house. It wasn't Jin—the legs that appeared underneath the car door as it opened were decidedly feminine, as was the flowery scent that spun through the air.

The car door slammed shut, revealing a short blonde wearing four-inch heels, rolled-up jeans, and a purple crop top. She was a little on the overweight side, but absolutely stunning to look at. Her keys jangled loudly and silver flashed, drawing my gaze. Two letters hung from the ring—MF. Short for Maisie Foster? If it was, she wasn't the least what I expected a mage to look like.

She made her way through Jin's gate and up the steps. I glanced at the house where Quinn hid, and felt shock ripple through me.

He was gone.

Completely gone.

And yet I'd seen or heard no movement and his car was still parked up the road.

How could he leave without me catching some hint of it? He may have vampire speed, but even if he'd moved faster than a speeding bullet, I still should have caught some hint of it. Should have seen the disappearing flare of his life force.

Frowning, I scanned the area with infrared, looking for some sign of him. Why would he wait all this time for Maisie, then run off? It made no sense at all.

Then I caught the familiar scent of sandalwood and masculinity in the air. Quinn's scent.

He *was* still here, even if I couldn't see him.

I raised my nose, drawing in the scent, trying to find direction. It was coming from high above me. Not from the rooftops, but from the sky itself.

My gaze went to the night and the stars, but there was nothing to be seen beyond the gathering clouds and the brightly shining moon.

What the hell was going on? Vampires couldn't fly—not unless they were bird-shifters in their pre-vampire life, anyway. And whatever else he was, Quinn wasn't a shifter. Of that, I was sure.

Then something he'd said a few months ago came back to me. I'd asked him how he'd gotten into Starr's compound without Rhoan or anyone else seeing him, and he'd said, *I simply ceased to exist in any term the human mind recognizes.*

Shame he'd forgotten to mention the same damn talent allowed him to *fly.*

My gaze went back to Maisie. She'd reached the front door and was searching through her bag. Obviously, she didn't keep her door keys on the same tag as her car keys. For a powerful mage, she was kinda dumb.

Quinn's scent sharpened, and I had a sudden sense of movement through the air, though there was still nothing to be seen.

At the last possible moment, Maisie seemed to sense the same thing, because she swung around and gasped. A hand formed out of thin air, chopping down hard. Maisie dropped to the steps like a stone.

Quinn's form seemed to merge from the night as he drifted down the steps, landing neatly and lightly next to Maisie's body. He studied her for a moment, then looked around, his gaze skimming past my hidey-hole with nary a pause of concern. Then he bent, picked Maisie up, and walked down the steps toward his car. He placed her in the passenger seat, then climbed into the driver's seat, started the engine, and zoomed off. I watched the car disappear, then backed out of my hiding spot and shifted shape. The compulsion and the moon heat leapt into focus, but one was now stronger than the other.

Maybe shifting into wolf shape several times had finally muted the strength of Quinn's order. Which was good, because I needed to go to the club and do some serious ache-easing.

As my steps echoed across the still night, I pressed the com-link in my ear and said, "Hello, hello, anyone tuned in?"

"I'm always tuned-in, unlike some former liaisons who shall go unmentioned."

Oh joy. The caramel cow. "And a good evening to you, too, Sal."

"What do you want, Riley?"

Pleasantry, which I was never going to get talking to her. But I guess I wasn't overly generous with it myself, so I was hardly in a position to bitch.

Which had never stopped me before.

"Jack around anywhere?"

"One moment, please."

The sound of heels clicking came through the earpiece, meaning Jack was somewhere other than his desk. "Riley?" he said, after a moment. "Did you take care of our mage?"

"Not exactly."

"What happened?"

"Quinn happened." And just mentioning his name had the barely settled anger rising again.

Jack sighed. "What's he done this time?"

"He's just kidnapped our little mage."

"What?"

"Yeah. We *did* foul the pentagram through which she was calling the demons, which according to him was better than destroying it, because it will force her to expend more energy making a new one."

"In dark spells, it's usually the magician's blood that fuels the summoning. Fouling it won't actually stop her using it; it'll just prevent her from calling through certain types of entities."

"Meaning I should have destroyed it?" That Quinn had spun yet another lie?

"She would have sensed the destruction. It might have driven her—and the rest of them—underground." He paused, and the sound of liquid hissing into a cup came down the line. He was either in the day-shift operations room or the foyer, where the other coffee machine was situated. "What happened after that? How come Quinn kidnapped the mage and why aren't you with him?"

"Because the bastard pulled his vampire wiles on me—embedded an order to go home while our telepathic line was open."

"Game man. Has he still got his balls?"

I grinned, and very much suspected there was nothing pleasant about it. Amusement wasn't high on my list of emotions right now. "For the moment. I did make an interesting discovery in the process of going home, though—becoming a wolf actually transmutes the compulsion."

"Does it? That's interesting."

"Yeah. Once I'd discovered that, I naturally headed back to see what Quinn was up to. That's when I discovered he could not only make himself totally invisible to all senses except scent, but that he could also fly."

"*What?*"

"Well, I'm not actually sure if he was flying. I couldn't see wings or anything. He seemed to be more drifting."

"Even very old vampires *cannot* fly."

"But before he was vampire, he was half-human and half something else," I corrected. "And that other half is something that doesn't exist anymore."

"Only birds—or bird-shifters—fly."

"So do gryphons. So do a hundred other things that can't be classified as birds."

"None of which Quinn is."

I raised my eyebrows. "Then you know what he is?"

"Nope. I only know what I've been told."

By his sister, no doubt, who was the next one up the

vampire ladder from Quinn. Which, in itself, was a mystery waiting to be solved, because Jack was a whole lot younger in vampire terms than Quinn and his sister. "Quinn's driving a black Porsche." I gave him the license plate number, then added, "He's got GPS in the car—don't suppose you can plug into the satellite and backtrack to see where he is going?"

"It'll take a bit of time to find his car-code and then track him, but we can try."

"And in the meantime, what do you want me to do?"

"Any word from Jin?"

"No." Of course, it was hard to get word when I had the phone off. But I wasn't about to mention that because Jack would kill me.

"Any chance that you could get an invite to their dinner party tomorrow night?"

Who'd have guessed *that* was coming? "Can't you get the infrared working?"

"No. He's got some of the most sophisticated shielding in that house that I've ever come across. We can get their body heat and positioning, but we're still only catching snippets of actual conversation."

"I can try." Turning on my phone would probably be a good start. Given the frustration burning down the telepathic line earlier, Jin was one needy little demon. And while he could go out and get himself another girl, he'd gained a taste for werewolf flesh. And it wasn't a boast to say we did hard sex better than most humans, simply because we had the stamina.

"Then try. We need to get into that house and see what they're up to."

I blew out a breath, and hoped like hell that Jin had

learned his lesson and started fucking like a normal psycho rather than an abnormal one.

Though, was there any such thing as an abnormal psycho?

"I'm heading to the Blue Moon, boss. Give me a call on the cell if you happen to track down Quinn."

"Will do."

I touched my ear once to turn off sound but not tracking, changed my clothes, then climbed into my car, and drove on to the club. As usual, there was a queue out the front, though given the full moon was still a few days off, it wasn't all that bad. I walked past them and ignored the annoyed comments thrown my way. If they were stupid enough not to make a permanent table booking in a club as popular as this one, well, that was their problem, not mine.

Jimmy, the half-lion-shifter, half-human bouncer gave me a huge gold-toothed grin as he looked me up and down. "I like the dress, but the drying blood on your arms and legs is a bit of a worry."

"You don't think it'll catch on as a fashion statement?" I paid my entrance fees and struck a pose.

He snorted softly. "No. You been in a fight again, girl?"

"Everyone knows there's nothing like a good fight to get the hormones going." I grinned and stood on my tippy-toes to drop a quick kiss on his cheek. "Anyone I know inside?"

"Kellen came through about half an hour ago looking for you."

Ah, good. I was hoping he'd be here—it saved me the trouble of ringing him and inviting him down. Jimmy opened the door, and I scooted inside. The air was rich with the scent of lust and sex, and I breathed deep, allowing the atmosphere to soak through every pore, every muscle, every bone. The desire burning through my bloodstream leapt into renewed focus, and suddenly it was all I could do not to shuck off my dress, dump my bag, and go join the sweaty, passionate crowd pressed so close together on the dance floor.

I loved this place. Always had. But in recent months, I hadn't come here as often as normal, and standing here now, I had to wonder why. I mean, Quinn had made it patently obvious he didn't like the werewolf lifestyle, didn't like our free and easy attitude toward sex, despite the fact he was a benefactor of that attitude. And he hated me coming to the clubs when he was in town.

But it wasn't until now that I realized just *how* much I'd curbed my wilder nature for him.

At least I wouldn't have that trouble any longer. I could do who I wanted, when I wanted. I briefly raised my gaze, watching the hologram stars twinkle against the midnight-colored roof as I blinked away the sting of tears.

Damn him to hell, I thought, and headed down the steps. Closer to the dance floor, the sensual beat of the music was accompanied by grunts of pleasure and the slap of flesh against flesh. The fever in my blood rose to boiling point and my breath caught, then quickened. I wanted—needed—to get out there. To lose myself in the middle of that sweating, writhing crowd, to think about nothing more than sheer and utter pleasure.

Once again I resisted the temptation to just dump everything on a table, and walked instead into the changing rooms. After a quick shower to wash the sweat and blood from my skin, I finger-combed my damp hair, then shoved my clothes into the locker. Once I'd clipped the key onto a chain around my neck, I finally headed out.

The rich aromas of hunger and desire spun around me, a living thing that stole my breath and made the low-down ache even fiercer. Despite this, I stopped, my gaze scanning the lusty crowd. The moon fever might burn, but tonight there was only one I wanted. Someone totally opposite to Quinn in every way imaginable. Someone who was warm and caring and, most important of all, dependable.

Someone who not only wanted me every bit as badly as Quinn, but who wanted me as I was, not as I could be if only I would allow myself to be that bit more malleable.

My gaze centered on the brown wolf dancing with several females on the far edge of the dance floor and anticipation zoomed through me.

I moved into the crowd, flirting, dancing, and teasing, enjoying the press of so much flesh but never stopping, my eyes always on the main prize.

He was dancing with several different females by the time I neared him, meaning he was merely cruising, waiting rather than participating. The thought had my hormones doing a happy little jig. I dropped a kiss on his shoulder blade and drew in his scent, so spicy and rich and *male,* then slid my hands around his waist and pressed my breasts against the heated flesh of his spine. As I echoed his dance moves, I skimmed my fingers down his abs, enjoying the tremor that ran through his muscles, feeling a sudden rush of power as he pressed back against me. Encouraging, demanding. My touch slid lower, caressing hair, then flesh. His penis was thick and hard, pulsing with desire. I caressed him, teased him, sliding my hands up and down his shaft as I slid my breasts up and down his back. His hunger flicked around me, a noose of heat that captured me, drowned me, making me hunger for him, making me ready for him.

I slid my hands to his hips, gently pulling him backward, guiding him deeper into the thick press of flesh, until the smell of sex was so powerful it was almost liquid, and space was at such a premium that it felt like a hundred different people were touching, pressing, caressing.

We danced, my front to his back, a slow but carnal overture of what was to come. Sweat formed where our flesh touched, and the air was so thick with the heat of our desire I could barely even breathe. Then he turned, and smiled, before his mouth claimed mine and we were kissing like our lives depended on it.

And when it all became too much, he lifted me up and onto him. Then he was in me, stretching me, filling me, in a way so pleasurable I moaned the glory of it to the moon.

He began to move, thrust, and I moved with him, riding him hard, savoring the sensations flowing through me, until the waves of pleasure rippling my skin became a molten force that would not be denied. But as the shudders of completion ripped through us both, and the warmth of his seed flooded deep inside, a tiny part of me wished I were with another.

I closed my eyes and took a deep breath. Forget him. Just forget him.

Kellen wrapped his free hand around the back of my neck, holding me still as he claimed another kiss. It was a fierce and demanding thing, and I let his hunger claim me anew, determined to enjoy myself regardless of how sad that tiny part of me might be.

"Your nose and mouth are looking a bit bruised," he said, after a while.

"I had a bit of a run-in with the wall."

"Work or an accident?"

"Work."

"Hope you made the bastard pay."

"Oh, yeah."

He touched my lip gently, sending desire quivering through my limbs. "It looks painful. Maybe I should stop kissing you."

"Like hell." I pulled him again and kissed him hard, just to prove it didn't hurt. Even though it did, just a little.

"I reserved a privacy room for us," he said eventually.

"The one with the spa, or the one with the airbed?"

"Spa. The airbed was gone by the time I got here."

"Good." I'd had enough of things floating in the air that shouldn't for one night. I kissed him gently, then said, "I'm glad you came here tonight."

"Riley, I have no intentions of letting you be with anyone else any more than necessary." He touched my cheek this time, fingers warm against my skin as he brushed sweaty strands of hair back behind my ears. "I want you to be mine, and only mine."

"Well, tonight your wish has been granted."

"I wasn't talking about just tonight."

"I know." I smiled and touched his face, cupping his cheek and letting my thumb brush his familiar lips. "And maybe I'm ready to talk about that. But not here. Not yet."

His sudden smile was so filled with happiness and warmth that my toes curled. He scooped me up in his arms and strode purposefully toward the rear of the club and the privacy rooms.

And as I leaned my head on his shoulder and listened to the steady beat of his heart, I realized that, in many ways, I *was* ready. Quinn might have hurt me tonight with his actions, but perhaps he'd also done me a favor.

And perhaps it really *was* time to give my brown wolf a chance to prove whether or not we were meant to be.

Rhoan was up and about by the time I got home. He looked out from the kitchen as I closed the door, and held up a cup. I nodded, threw my gym bag on the sofa, and collapsed down beside it.

"You look like a wolf who's had a hard night," he said, offering me the steaming mug before he sat down on the sofa opposite. "Need I ask why?"

"Kellen reserved the spa room at the Blue Moon. We made full use of both the bed and the spa."

Rhoan raised his eyebrows. "Kellen? What happened to Quinn?"

"The bastard used mind control on me."

"Ah." Rhoan took a sip of his coffee, his expression giving little away. But he was my twin, and I knew exactly what he was thinking even if we didn't share the empathy of twins. Quinn would get an earful for his actions, and I wasn't just talking about words. Rhoan didn't mind getting in the odd smack or two to emphasize his points when it came to anyone who hurt me.

I sipped the coffee, and sighed in contentment at the nutty, hazelnut flavor. Rhoan had obviously gone shopping. "Anything of interest happen last night?"

He shrugged. "My shift ended at two, and up until then they were all a model of decency. Depressing, really."

I grinned. "I'm betting you weren't the model of decency once you got back to Liander's."

"Well, no. It's amazing the fun that can be had with a rubber monkey suit."

I didn't even want to go *there*. "So, what's next?"

He sipped his coffee and appeared to consider the question. Annoyance stirred. I knew my twin better than I knew myself, and right now, he was hedging. "Spit it out, bro."

"Well, we have planned an official little raid on a certain hotel room rented by one Quinn O'Conor."

"I want in."

"Riley—"

"That *bastard* has used and abused me for the last time. It's about time he started taking me seriously."

"Slapping him in handcuffs won't make him do that."

"Maybe not, but just think of the pleasure it'll give me to watch his expression as I do it."

He snorted softly. "You haven't even asked why we're arresting him."

"Because he's with the dark mage."

Surprise flitted across his otherwise calm expression. "You knew that?"

"Discovered it last night." I hesitated. "I also discovered that changing shape mutes a vampire's compulsion."

He nodded, as if it were something he'd long known. If that were the case, he could have told me. "So you're the reason Jack was tracking him in the first place?"

"Yep." I downed the coffee in several gulps and rose. "What time is the raid planned?"

Rhoan glanced at his watch. "Jack wants us there at ten." He looked at me and smiled. "He knew you'd want in."

"I'm getting predictable, and that's just sad." I glanced across at the clock. "I've time enough to freshen up, then."

A hot shower didn't do a whole lot to shake the tiredness, but at least I felt cleaner. I grabbed some pants and a thick sweater to combat the chill of the day, then retrieved my boots from the grip of the dust bunnies under my bed. Not only did these particular boots have a nice big heel, but the heel itself was made of wood. A handy thing if a certain vampire got antsy. Not that I'd stake him with the intent of killing him, but hurting him just a little was a tempting prospect.

Once dressed, I grabbed my ID, credit cards, and cell phone, then headed out. Rhoan tossed me my gun. "If you forget it this time, Jack will kill you."

"Only if some tattletale tells him I keep forgetting it." I reluctantly strapped it on. "I don't want to start relying on these things, bro."

"I know. But sometimes, a werewolf's teeth and a

vampire's speed just aren't enough. Trust me on this." He gave me a quick hug, then ushered me out the door. "And if you *are* going to do this job—and we both know you really have no other choice—then you have to learn to use all the tools of the trade. Whether you like them or not."

Speaking of tools . . . I pulled the phone from my pocket and turned it on. To find a dozen voice messages awaiting me, all from Jin. I listened to them as I followed Rhoan down the stairs. Each was basically the same—an apology, a demand that I ring. It wasn't until the last one that he sounded anything resembling contrite.

"That's one bad boy who has it bad for you," Rhoan commented, as he opened the passenger door of his old Ford and ushered me inside.

"He just adores the way I take a slap," I murmured, concentrating on sending Jin a semi-cold text message. I might be under orders to get into that dinner party tonight, but I didn't have to be all meek and mild about it.

"A lot of bad men seem to like that," Rhoan commented, after getting into the car and venturing into the traffic. "Must be something in their makeup. They get their rocks off on giving others pain."

I looked at him. "Is that why you enjoy the job so much?"

He shrugged. "Sometimes, different is good."

"Different from Liander, you mean?"

He gave me a keen glance. "I love Liander, don't get me wrong, but sometimes, I just need more. My work gives me that, Riley."

"He's not complaining about the men you do within

your job. He's complaining about the ones outside work."

Rhoan sniffed. "Yeah, well—"

"Don't give me that 'yeah, well' bullshit. Liander's a good man, and he doesn't deserve the crap you hand out. At the very least, you should talk to him."

"I can't."

"Why the hell not?" My phone rang. I looked down and saw it was Jin. I ignored it and looked back at my brother, waiting for a reply.

He scrubbed a hand across his jaw as he looked in the rearview mirror. "Because I don't want to lose him."

I blinked. Of all the excuses I'd been imagining, *that* certainly wasn't one of them. "What?"

"If I confront the issue, he may decide to walk away. I don't want to risk that, Riley. I really don't."

I reached across and touched his knee. "Liander loves you, and he's not going to walk away unless you push him to it. And that's precisely what's happening now— he's very frustrated by your refusal to talk about the situation."

He looked at me. "Frustrated enough to walk away?"

"Yes."

"Fuck."

"Yes."

"I can't do monogamous. I don't *want* to do monogamous."

"There's always compromises in any relationship, Rhoan. Maybe this is one you and Liander have to come to." And I honestly didn't think Liander would mind Rhoan having other partners in a work situation. As long as he was committed outside of it. "If you care for him as much as you say, bro, it might pay to give a little."

He grimaced. "I don't know—"

"Talk to him. At least do that."

"Okay."

"Promise?"

"Promise."

"I'll nag you endlessly if you don't."

He laughed. "You do anyway." The phone rang again and he glanced down. "And for God's sake, answer that, before the poor man has a coronary."

"Him having a coronary could solve some problems."

"Not if he's a demon who can just go get another body." Rhoan glanced in the rearview mirror again. "Answer the damn phone."

I pressed the receiver and said "Hello," even as I flipped down the sunshade and slid aside the cover of the vanity mirror. Rhoan kept looking at something behind us, but for the moment, I couldn't see what.

"I'm sorry," Jin said, voice warm and contrite. "I acted like an ass last night."

"Yes, you did," I said coolly. "And it wasn't appreciated."

"Can I make up for it?"

"I don't know. Can you?"

"Would an expensive lunch be a start?"

Given I had no intention of spending any more time in this man's company than necessary—and I did use the term *man* loosely—lunch was definitely out. "It would be nice, but I can't today."

"How about dinner, then? A friend is having an exclusive dinner party at his Toorak mansion, and the food and company are usually excellent."

Yeah, I just *bet* they were. "I could be tempted."

"Could be?"

"Most certainly."

"Shall I pick you up?"

"I prefer to drive. That way, I have transport in case there's a sudden ass attack."

He laughed. "Then I shall meet you at my friend's." He gave me Kingsley's address. "I promise, no sudden ass attacks tonight."

He was either very sure of the attraction between us, or he was trying to regain my trust by making out like he had nothing to hide. Why else would he give me the address? I mean, he had to be very sure I wouldn't report it to someone—like the cops. "Good. What time shall I meet you?"

"Seven."

"Until then, then."

I hung up and shoved the phone back in my pocket. "One job done."

"You be careful in there tonight."

"I'll be fine. And you'll be listening in via the van—won't you?"

"Yeah, but there're still too many variables we just don't understand at the moment, and I've just got an edgy feeling it could all go ass up."

He looked in the mirror again, and I frowned. "What the hell do you keep looking at?"

"I think we picked up a tail."

I flipped down the vanity mirror again. "Where?"

"Three cars back, white Toyota."

The car wasn't hard to spot—it wasn't like he was trying to hide or anything. "You sure?"

"Not a hundred percent. It's just a hunch."

I'd back Rhoan's hunches over most people's certainties any day. "You want me to call it in?"

"Nope. You feel up to a little interrogation session?"

I raised my eyebrows, and tried to ignore my pulse's little jump of excitement. "We got time?"

He glanced at his watch. "Five minutes to spare."

I rolled my shoulders, and gave in to that flicker of excitement. "Let's do it, then."

Rhoan grinned, then flicked another glance at the mirror and swung into a side street, pressing his foot hard on the accelerator. The tires squealed as they slipped then caught, and the car shot forward. Another look at the mirror, another left, and then he was stopping. I jumped out of the car and ran into the shadows of the nearest building, hunkering down in the doorway so I was less likely to be seen. Rhoan moved off, but slower this time.

Within a minute, the white Toyota slid around the corner and accelerated. I waited until they'd almost passed, then slipped my laser from its holster and shot out both the nearside tires. Then I was up and running.

The car skidded to an awkward stop, inches away from a blue Ford parked along the curb. Up ahead, Rhoan had stopped at an angle, letting the car block the road as he scrambled out.

Two men tumbled from the Toyota. The driver headed toward Rhoan, while the passenger came running in my direction. I stepped in his path, and a grin split his strong, hairy features. "You're not going to try and stop me, are you, little girl?"

"You're right," I said, moving in so fast he barely had time to blink before my fist was buried into his gut. "I'm not going to *try* and stop you."

The air left his lungs in a whoosh, and he collapsed to his knees with an odd sort of wheeze. I grabbed him by the scruff of the neck and dragged him back toward the car. A quick look ahead showed that Rhoan had the driver under control.

I threw hairy guy into the side of the car. He hit head-first and cursed. I ignored it, patted him down for weapons, then caught his right arm and pressed it up and back against his spine. His curse became a hiss of pain.

"Ease up, girly. I ain't done nothin' to you."

"You're following a guardian. While that may not be illegal, it's certainly considered an insane practice by most. Especially us guardians."

"You ain't no guardian."

I pushed just a little bit harder on his arm, then with my free hand, got out my badge and shoved it in his face. "Proof enough, buddy-boy?" He nodded, and I put the badge away. "Why were you following us?"

"I was paid to, wasn't I?"

"By whom?"

"I don't know. I didn't talk to the contact, did I?"

"Did your friend the driver talk to him?"

"Yes."

I reached sideways and opened the passenger door. "You will get inside the car and you will not move out of it or I will cut your flaming legs off. Understand?"

He nodded. I shoved him inside, slammed the door

shut, and walked across to Rhoan. He had the driver spread-eagled against the rear of our car, and was leaning against him, one elbow planted in his back to hold him in place as he went through the driver's wallet.

"You get the name of his employer?" I asked, stopping at an angle so I could keep an eye on hairy guy.

"Not yet. He's demanding we arrest him, and that he gets his phone call before he says anything."

I raised my eyebrows. "You did tell him we're guardians, not cops, didn't you?"

"Nope. Why bother with niceties when it comes to scum?" He closed the wallet and shoved it back into the man's pocket. "You want to do the honors?"

"Honors?" the driver squawked. "What fucking honors? What the hell are you talking about?"

We both ignored him. "You know it's a pain in the ass using telepathy on crap like this—why don't you just beat it out of him?"

"Beat? You can't beat me—it's against the fucking—"

Rhoan dug his elbow in a little harder and the rest of the driver's sentence was lost to his yelp.

"He's human."

"So fucking what? Just beat him up, get the name, and let's get on with it."

"Okay, okay, I'll talk."

Rhoan gave me a grin, then wrapped his arm around the driver's neck and drew him upright. "So talk," he said, voice soft. Deadly.

"It was a man called Gautier. Met him last night. Said he needed us to follow you and report back where you went."

Gautier. Was there no getting rid of that prick? "Was that all he asked you to do?"

"Yes," the driver wheezed.

Rhoan leaned close to the guy's greasy head, and said, "You're lying."

"Trackers. We set them on your car, in case we lost you."

Rhoan tightened his grip until the man's breathing became a desperate gasp. "That all?"

"Yes. For God's sake, yes."

"Where did you have to report back?"

"He gave us a phone number."

"Then give it to me."

The man wheezed out some numbers. Rhoan spun the man around and pushed him toward the car. "You warn your employer about this little episode and I'll make sure I pay you a little visit."

The man caught his balance, then wheezed, "I won't, I won't."

"Good," Rhoan said, voice all mild. "Don't let me see you following me again, or it won't be just your tires my partner shoots out."

The man ran for his car, threw it into reverse, and left—flat tires and all. I shook my head at my brother. "You enjoyed that, didn't you?"

"And you didn't?"

I grinned. "All I need now is another coffee, and my morning will be complete."

Some part of me was scared by that admission. Scared by the fact I *did* enjoy roughhousing that scumbag. Scared by the fact it would be *so* easy to let instinct take over completely, to become the one thing I never wanted to be—a hunter as skilled and deadly as my brother.

The possibility was there. It was definitely there.

I shivered and rubbed my arms. "You want to check your side of the car for traveling bugaboos? I'll check this side."

Rhoan nodded. Ten minutes later we had five tracking bugs sitting on the front of the car. "Gautier wasn't taking any chances," I said, picking up one and crushing it under my heel. "What I don't get is why he'd even bother to employ idiots like that. Especially if he can now move around in daylight himself."

"Maybe he still has some restrictions. Maybe whatever magic he's getting from these people is only short-term. Which means he needs outside help to track our movements." Rhoan crushed several more bugs under his heel.

"Gautier mentioned something about coming after me once he gets all that he's been promised." I dropped a bug and stood on it. "I've got a bad feeling we had better stop him before that happens."

"We will. Neither Jack nor I are about to let anything happen to you, Riley."

Yeah, but my brother was only a dhampire, and Jack was only a vampire. If Gautier's warning was anything to go by, then he was becoming something more. Something deadly and not of this world.

The thought had chills skating across my skin. I ignored them and crushed the last of the bugs, scattering the metal remnants with a toe. "You want me to report the phone number to Jack?"

"Yeah. He'll have it tapped and watched, though I

doubt Gautier will be foolish enough to go there. He'll probably have a remote dial-in arrangement."

Most likely. One thing Gautier could never be accused of was dumbness in the line of duty. We got into the car, and I phoned Jack while Rhoan drove on to the hotel.

It was one Quinn and I had been to a few times in the past. I climbed out of the car and looked at the Langham's luxurious foyer, and suddenly wondered how many other women he'd escorted through the marble and crystal opulence.

Not that I minded Quinn having other women. It was just the lies. The saying one thing and doing another. Dishonesty was something I just couldn't forgive.

"Heading in now, Jack," Rhoan said, as he walked around the car and flashed his credentials at the valet people. He glanced at me. "Jack said to stop being a pain in the ass and turn the com-link sound on again."

"Oh. Yeah." I lightly pressed the little button. "Sorry, Jack."

"One of these days you're going to be tied up and in serious trouble because you've got your com-link off and can't call it in."

"I said I was sorry."

"Forget the sorry. Just quit doing it."

"Okay, okay." We entered the lower foyer and ran up the sumptuous staircase. Rhoan headed over to reception while I continued on to check out the dining area. The rich aroma of toast and sweet pastries made my nose twitch, but I tried to ignore the luscious food on display and scanned the area. No sign of Quinn or the dark mage. My gaze drifted to the food, and my stomach rumbled.

I somehow forced my feet away, and headed back to reception. "They're in six-twelve," Rhoan said. "Apparently he had food delivered half an hour ago."

"Why? He doesn't need to eat and she was unconscious."

"Obviously, that's no longer the case."

Obviously. The question was, why did he force me away and then kidnap her? What did he need to do that he couldn't let the Directorate in on?

"Quinn won't take this lightly," Jack said. "Whatever he's up to, he doesn't want us to know about, and that means he'll probably fight capture."

My stomach did an odd flip-flop. I wasn't sure whether the cause was excitement or fear. "Even against the two of us?"

"Sentimentality doesn't play a whole lot into the thinking of an old vampire," Jack said, voice dry. "Not when he's on the hunt."

"Great." I looked at Rhoan. "Let's get this over with."

We headed up. As we approached the room, I blinked, flicking my vision to infrared. Two bodies jumped into focus, one far darker than the other. Oddly enough, Quinn was the brighter one, and closer to the wall. Maisie sat near the window. I glanced at my brother.

He pointed to me, then to the right. I nodded, and pressed a hand flat against the door as he got the keycard out of his pocket. He looked at me again, and raised an eyebrow in query. I took a deep breath, then readied the laser and nodded again. He swiped the card through the slot, and I flung the door open, waiting until he was in before following him through.

There was an exclamation, a flash of red light, a blur of movement, then Rhoan was being tossed sideways like so much rubbish and that blur of heat was coming at me. I pressed the laser, aiming low, scouring the carpet and the end of Quinn's toes, not wanting to permanently hurt him. There was a brief whiff of rich spice and seared flesh, and Quinn was on me. I ducked his blow, dropped to the ground, and swept with a leg. Incredibly, I hit him, knocking him off his feet. His butt hit the floor with a thump that would have bruised the tailbone of any other man. And though I'm sure he could have moved, he didn't. Just sat there with a somewhat surprised look on his face.

At any other time, it might have been funny.

Right now, when it was just another instance of how much he underestimated me, it wasn't.

I rose and aimed the laser at him. "Move, and next time it'll be more than your toes."

The surprise melted away, and anger sparked to life, burning in his dark eyes, heating the very air around me. "What are you doing here?"

"My job. Rhoan, you okay?"

"Yeah. Bit of a bruised jaw, but I ducked the worst of it." Footsteps whispered across the carpet. "He has the mage confined."

"Good." I looked at Quinn. "You want to get up?"

He did. And the closeness of him, the rich, glorious smell of him, had my hormones doing giddy little cart-wheels. I couldn't ever imagine a time when I *didn't* want this vampire, moon-heated lust or not. But as I kept trying to tell him, while sex might play a major part in my life, there was only so much shit I could take before the enticement of good sex began to wane and frustration and annoyance took hold.

Quinn and I had passed that point ages ago.

"How did you find me here?" His voice was low, rich with the lilt of Ireland. Which usually meant he was barely controlling some emotion or other. His accent was rarely noticeable otherwise.

"I asked Jack to track you after you knocked out the mage last night."

He raised his eyebrows, surprise evident yet again. "You countermanded my order to go home?"

"I did. Fancy that." I looked past him. "You want him cuffed?"

"There is no need—"

My finger tightened reflexively against the laser and a soft whine filled the room. "I *am* itching for an excuse to shoot, you know."

"Cuff him if you want to," Rhoan said.

"I want."

"Revenge for last night?" Quinn said, amusement playing amid the anger.

"Just doing my job," I said, and met his gaze.

I'm not entirely sure what he saw in my eyes, but the amusement and the anger fled abruptly. "Riley—"

"It's too late, Quinn," I said softly. Wearily. "I'm tired of listening to your excuses, tired of the one-way traffic. I *am* a werewolf, I *am* a guardian, and it seems you can't accept either."

"We had a deal—"

"Would that be the deal you keep breaking?" I

caught the cuffs Rhoan tossed my way. "Tell me, how long have you been using our telepathic bond to curb my visits to the clubs?"

It was a guess, but a reasonable one. I certainly hadn't been restricting my visits consciously—but my reaction in the Blue Moon last night had certainly proved that they had indeed been curbed. And the wolf within wouldn't have done it willingly—hell, *she* wanted more visits, not less.

So it had to have been an unconscious decision. A decision caressed into compliance by a link so light I wasn't even aware of it.

He didn't say anything, and that in itself was damning.

"Turn around and place your hands behind your back."

"There is no need for this," he said quietly, even as he obeyed. "And there was a good reason for sending you home last night."

"I don't care if there was or there wasn't. And there *is* every need for me to do this. There are consequences for every action, Quinn. It's about time I started making you pay for yours."

"We—"

"Are finished." I looked at Rhoan. "You ready?"

He nodded, then looked at Quinn. "Don't try anything. If she doesn't shoot you, I will."

"For interrogating a suspect?"

"No. For abusing Riley's trust yet again." He picked up Maisie, throwing her like a securely cuffed sack over his shoulder. "Let's get this show on the road."

I stepped back and waved Quinn past me. He gave

me his vampire face, but the air fairly burned with his anger. And surprise.

He hadn't expected that I'd really end it. Hadn't believed that I'd meant what I said.

Now all I had to do was find the strength to really walk away.

Chapter 10

I leaned my head against my hand and barely restrained a huge yawn. "This is going nowhere fast."

Jack handed me a coffee, his expression grim. "No one said breaking a mage's defense would be easy."

I sipped at the hot liquid in the cup. It couldn't be called coffee because it just didn't look, or taste, anything like it. Still, if it served the purpose of keeping me awake, I'd drink a gallon of the muck.

I eyed our captive through the one-way glass. Maisie was currently being interrogated by both a specialist in magic and a specialist in "interviewing" techniques. I'd seen the interviewers in action on several occasions over recent months, and knew their methods could get *extremely* gruesome. Unlike regular police, the Directorate didn't have to worry about prisoner rights. If the person being questioned posed a threat to the human population in *any* form or shape, then the Directorate could basically do what they wanted to get the required answers. Except, of course, if the person involved was human or part human. Then it got trickier.

Which was probably why the techniques being used today had been pretty mild so far. Maisie might be a mage of extreme power, but she was *also* human. By law, the Directorate had to tread cautiously.

My gaze moved to the spindly woman standing in the corner of the room. I hadn't even known we had a whole section of people specializing in magic, and I'd been working here for nearly eight years. Right now, she didn't seem to be doing a whole lot, but sweat was beginning to dot her creased forehead, and the white stones surrounding Maisie had taken on a glow that reminded me vaguely of the heat shimmer that rose off a road on a long, hot summer day. Whether it was caused by our mage, or Maisie's powers testing her defenses, I wasn't entirely sure.

"How much longer do we have before Marg starts to weaken and the stones lose their ability to contain Maisie?"

Jack shrugged. "Marg will signal when her strength is giving out. As a general rule, she can last four or five hours if she's doing nothing more than boosting the strength of the warding stones."

"Why don't we just raid her mind telepathically?"

"I tried earlier, when you were talking to Quinn."

And hadn't *that* provided a whole lot of information. Quinn had never been free and easy with information, but right now he was making like a clam and getting ir- ritatingly amused when I got angry about it. Rhoan was currently in the process of having a little chat with our silent vampire, but I very much doubted he'd have any more success than I did. "And?"

"And, her shields are unlike anything I've ever come across. I've asked Director Hunter to come down and assist me."

That raised my eyebrows. After eight years of being here, I'd actually catch a glimpse of the elusive Director Hunter? "She's not exactly hurrying."

"She decided to help Rhoan with Quinn first."

"Ah." And according to the weird hierarchy and honor system vamps had going, Quinn, being younger in vampire years than Hunter—though heaven only knew if he was younger or older in real, since-birth terms—was ethically obliged to answer any and all of her questions. "She could be hours, then."

"Could be. Quinn may be younger, but I think he's almost as powerful."

"Which means what?"

"That while he may be obliged to answer, he can't be forced. It all really depends on Quinn following the rules."

And vampires never followed the rules unless it suited them. I sipped the brown muck for several minutes, then glanced at my watch. If I didn't get some sleep soon, I was going to be a baggy-eyed wreck tonight. And that was *never* a good look.

"Why don't you and I have a crack at her?"

Jack glanced at me, and I swear there was a gleam of satisfaction in his eyes. "Are you feeling up to it?"

"No, but if it's the only way to get out of here and get to bed, then I'll give it a shot."

"Good." He rose from the chair immediately, and that gleam became more pronounced. I had a sudden, very powerful feeling of falling into a well-laid trap. And it had me wondering if he'd even asked Hunter to come down and help, or whether it was a nice little ruse to get me to volunteer. But I didn't bother asking because I just didn't have the energy to get mad right now.

I only wanted to get home, even if the cost was playing Jack's game and stepping just a little bit more into the shoes of a full-fledged guardian.

"I'll hold her mind still and open," he continued. "While you weave your way inside and see what you can find."

"Okay." I drained the remainder of the brown muck then put the empty cup down on the bench. "Let's do this."

I followed him into the interview room, and stopped slightly behind him. Maisie's gaze skimmed us both, and a slight sneer touched her pale lips. "What, two people not enough to break one little blonde? We've got to add a couple more?" Her voice was sharp and irritating, and yet, once again, the way she phrased her words had that odd sense of familiarity scratching at my senses.

"And people fear the guardians," she continued. "What a joke."

Jack glanced at the specialist interrogator, and without another word, she left the room. "Last chance, Miss Foster. Are you going to answer our questions willingly, or shall we do it the hard way?"

"If you could do anything more than contain me, I think it would have happened by now. We both know

your pet magician cannot hold the strength of the circle
for long, and then I will be gone."

Power touched the air, a tingly, spidery flare of electricity that flowed like wildfire across the room. Its center was Jack, not Maisie or the Directorate's magician,
and its touch had the tiny hairs along my arms and the
back of my neck standing upright.

"People are always underestimating the Directorate,"
he said softly, as the net of power flowed up and around
Maisie. She stiffened, her eyes going wide as her body became immobile. "It is never to their benefit to do so. Go,
Riley."

I blew out a breath, then closed my eyes and carefully
shut down my other senses, until my only awareness was
of Maisie and the net of power that blazed around her.
Slowly, carefully, I touched the net telepathically. The
thrum within it was potent, a distant thunder that
seemed at once forbidding and barely controlled. Like a
storm about to break.

It was frightening, in some ways. I'd always known
Jack was powerful, but I'd never felt just *how* powerful,
even during our training sessions. And yet, he'd admitted himself that he was far less so than Quinn. In some
ways, it proved just how much Quinn had been hiding
from me—and how much more he was capable of. God,
curtailing the urges of a werewolf had to be a walk in the
park for someone with *that* much power. No wonder I
hadn't been aware of what he was doing.

I skimmed the surface of Jack's power, riding it like a
wave, using it as a ramp to enter Maisie's mind. Her
outer defenses were already laid open and bare by Jack,

her surface thoughts an easy read. But it wasn't surface thoughts we wanted or needed.

I pushed on, moving beyond the reaches of Jack's control, into the deeper recesses of Maisie's mind. It was there I discovered what Jack had meant earlier.

Maisie's telepathic defenses weren't in the form of a wall, or mental "glue," or anything else that I'd come across before. Hers were more in the form of a spider-web—interconnected, fragile in appearance, yet sticky and extremely strong. Breaking one strand didn't mean I was through—I had to break *all* the connecting strands before I could go deep into her mind. Which was why two people were needed—one to hold her, and one to break her.

Even so, it was hard work.

The web seemed to thicken near the center of the mental shield, the threads becoming more tangible, harder to break, the closer I got to the deep recesses of thought. Sweat began to trickle down my spine, and an ache began to make itself known behind my closed eyes. A migraine in the making.

During my early months of telepathic training with Jack, I'd often been left physically and mentally exhausted, but like any sort of training, time and constant practice had provided some sort of mental fitness. *This* was making me feel like a rank beginner again. Every ounce of strength I possessed was being channeled into trying to breach Maisie's unusual defenses, and my limbs were beginning to tremble with the effort.

Then, with the suddenness of a rubber band snapping, the tenuous webs gave way, leaving me mentally shaking but floating free in the rush of Maisie's deep consciousness.

Only Maisie's spirit or soul, or whatever that part of human consciousness was called, wasn't there.

Someone, or *something,* else was.

And it was aware and waiting.

The attack came with a suddenness that was staggering. I had a brief feel of femininity, a taste of ancient power, then let out a yelp as my whole body recoiled from the sheer anger and force behind the mental punch.

Hands grabbed my arm, holding me upright, then Jack was beside me—a huge cloud of power and fury that might not be as ancient as the being inside Maisie's mind but every bit as dangerous.

The ancient spark stilled instantly.

Riley. It was an order and a question, all in one, and said in a way that suggested I'd better damn well hurry.

I licked my lips, and mentally pressed forward again. The presence in Maisie's mind might have been held defenseless, but she was still very much aware.

Who are you? My question seemed overly loud in the darkness of the mind held captive, echoing as if we were in an empty cavern rather than deep human consciousness. The thought had goose bumps chasing their way down my spine, and I had no idea why.

Then the darkness seemed to stir. *I sense something familiar in your thoughts.*

The voice was old, and again, there was something in the way she pronounced words that scratched at my instincts. Something in the soft lilt to her words that was almost recognizable.

Tell me who you are, or I will kill you.

Amusement spun through the darkness. *You cannot kill me. Even* he *cannot kill me.*

I frowned. He who? Jack? *Do not underestimate our skills.*

Do not overestimate your own skills. You have no power to kill me. No skill. Those few who possessed such skills died a long time ago.

She had to mean the priests of Aedh. Why else would the spirit of the priest even be here, if not to deal with an ancient threat? Question was, how was Quinn involved in all this? What was his obligation to the priest? What was his connection to the ancient spirit holding Maisie's body captive?

What have you done with Maisie? Even though I asked the question, I had a pretty good idea that whatever or whoever Maisie had been, she was not now in residence in this body. Which, in a sense, was a good thing. We were not now restricted by the chains of dealing with a human.

And God, the mere fact that I was even thinking that made me want to puke.

The mortal who once inhabited this flesh has long gone.

Did you kill her?

Amusement ran through the void. *You cannot kill a soul. You can only restrain or destroy.* The voice paused, as if to add significance. *This incarnation will be her last.*

Another chill ran through my body, yet I couldn't really feel sorry for Maisie. Not if she was truly responsible for bringing this evil, and the others, into being. *Tell me your name.*

My name is Caelfind O'Cuinn.

Why was that name familiar? Where had I heard it . . . then it hit me. *O'Cuinn*. Quinn's real surname.

Suddenly his secretive ways were making a *whole* lot more sense.

So, you are related in some way to Quinn?

Quinn?

I formed his picture in my mind, and the presence laughed. It was a mocking, spiteful sound. *Ah, my foolish little brother. He thinks he had my mind and body frozen last night while he attempted to break me.*

As we have broken you?

You merely hold my body and defenses captive. My deep thoughts are still my own, or I would not be answering, now would I?

Couldn't argue with that, I supposed. *Why did you raise Azhi Dahaki?*

I needed the strength of the three-headed dragon to raise the eternal destroyer.

And why would someone like Maisie want to raise someone like you?

Because in darkness there is strength. Maisie wanted power. I granted her that.

Then you killed her. Or killed her spirit.

The equivalent of a shrug ran through the darkness of Maisie's mind. *There is a price to be paid for the granting of one's desires.*

And what is the price you paid? Alienation from your family? A life spent in the netherworlds of hell?

I have gained immortality. She made a disparaging sound. *And my family has dedicated their worthless lives to ridding the world of both myself and the god of darkness. They cannot see the futility. Cannot admit that darkness exists because humanity itself exists, and that to erase one, you erase the other.*

Well, I wasn't seeing the connection myself. I mean, humans could be a pain in the ass sometimes, but I very much doubted they were the sole reason for evil's existence. *So you're saying Angra Mainyu cannot be destroyed?*

He can never be destroyed. Not for as long as there is one human living and breathing on this earth.

With her words came a sense of power, of force. As if she were trying to make me believe that, and nothing else. If that was her intent, then it backfired, because all I could think of was the fact that while this all-powerful god of darkness was still alive—if a spirit could be deemed such a thing—he'd been trapped in the nether regions of hell for hundreds, if not thousands, of generations.

And if it had been done once, it could be done again.

We need to finish this, Riley.

Jack's mental tones were cracked, evidence of the struggle he was having to contain the being inside Maisie's body and mind.

I blew out a breath. *Tell me how to rid this world of your dark master, or I will kill you.*

Try. You will not succeed. Kill this body, and my spirit will simply claim another.

Annoyance ran through me. But then, overwhelming arrogance and a supreme sense of superiority *did* tend to get on my nerves. I'd put up with far too much of that during my years with Talon.

Talon. . . .

The mere thought of him had an idea sparking deep inside. A horrible, hateful idea that part of me—the part that had seen the remains of too many women mutilated by *this* evil and her so-called associates—rejoiced in. *Jack, am I technically free to do what I wish with this woman now that we've confirmed Maisie is long gone?*

Yes.

I opened my eyes and looked at the one-way glass. "Get me a threaded sheet knife."

The sheet knives were a Directorate special. Basically, they were thin, clear sheets of plastic that were as rigid as steel and could slice through just about anything—flesh, metal, or wood—with ease. The threaded sheet knives were almost identical, only they were made of a special compound that reacted with blood and disintegrated to reveal the silver strip that ran down the heart of it. Ideal for pinning werewolves and other shapeshifters to human form—a fact I knew for a certainty, having done it to Talon.

If a threaded sheet knife could hold the soul of a werewolf to human form on the night of a full moon, it could surely hold a demonic spirit to human flesh.

It was worth a shot, anyway. Talking and threatening was getting us nowhere fast.

I glanced around as the door opened, and a security officer stepped in and handed me a knife. As he left, I held up the knife.

Amusement ran through Caelfind's thoughts. *Am I supposed to feel threatened by something so flimsy?*

I thought about the bodies again. Conjured the images of the women, their flesh sliced opened, internal organs gone—eaten—while they lay there dying. Revulsion swept through me, accompanied by anger. I grabbed them both, hanging on to the strength of those emotions, using them as shields as I pressed the point of the knife against the flesh over Maisie's left breast, right above her heart.

Tell me how to rid this world of your dark master, or I will trap you for an eternity inside dead flesh.

You cannot do that. Once this flesh is dead, my spirit is free.

Even the immortal can get it wrong occasionally.

I pressed the blade into her, watching as it sliced through cloth and muscle and bone with ridiculous ease. Her eyes went wide, and pain began to fill the void. Yet it never touched me, held at bay by either the anger in my soul or Jack's steely presence.

I drove the knife deeper, ramming it through her sternum, lodging the point deep in her heart. Blood began to seep across my fingers, blood that was warm and sweet to my nose, stirring excitement through my veins.

No, no, no, part of me wanted to scream, but I pushed it away ruthlessly, concentrating on Caelfind, watching her eyes, waiting for the moment of her body's death, and the realization that she would never be free.

The knife began to disintegrate, and smoke seeped from the wound, lodging the silver deep inside. Pinning her spirit, the way Talon's spirit had been pinned.

Only she didn't scream the way he'd screamed. She merely smiled and waited, her thoughts filled with pain and yet amused.

Until the moment her heart finally gave out, and her body slumped to the floor.

Then she screamed. Screamed like a banshee, until her fury filled my mind and made it almost impossible to think.

Tell me how to rid this world of your master.

My words were little more than a pebble standing against a cyclone, yet still she heard.

He can only be banished by a priest. A priest of Aedh.

And your brother is one?

The last one.

Well, not exactly the last. But perhaps the last still retaining flesh form. *And the dragons?*

Behead them.

Can't they take over another body, as you can?

She hesitated, twisting in fury. *No. Not without my help. Now, release me, as you promised.*

I laughed—a harsh and hateful sound—and began to pull back. *All these years of serving a dark god, and you still believe in promises?*

Her fury followed me, nipping at my mental heels like a rabid dog until the force that was Jack stepped in and stopped her cold. I fell out of her mind, feeling like I was falling from a great height, and found myself on my knees, on the floor, trembling and shaking and sweating.

And then I felt the warm stickiness of blood across my hand, smelled again its metallic sweetness, and my stomach rose.

I pushed onto all fours, scrambled over to the waste bin, and lost every scrap of food and liquid I'd eaten during the day.

When there was nothing left to lose, I collapsed back against the wall and sucked in great gulps of air. It felt like I'd gone ten rounds in the training ring with Gautier, with every inch aching and bruised, and my head pounding. The only thing that was missing was the actual bruises.

It was a good five minutes before I had the strength to even open my eyes. Jack leaned against the rear wall, his hands on his knees as he sucked in air, the skin on his arms paler than I'd ever seen them and his fingers little more than skin and bone. Which just proved how much strength it had taken to hold Caelfind.

My gaze slid on to the stone circle. Maisie's body lay slumped in the middle. Blood gleamed darkly off the front of her shirt, and the thick scent had my stomach twitching again.

Or maybe it wasn't the scent of blood. Maybe it was just the realization of how easily—how very easily—I'd spilt her blood and ended her life.

I might tell myself that I would never be the killer Jack wanted me to be, but the truth was, that skill was already within me.

I *could* kill, and kill easily, when I had to. When I wanted to. When I needed to.

Bile burned my throat. I put my hand over my mouth and swallowed heavily, then forced myself to remember the lives Maisie and her cohorts had destroyed.

Because while I might hate what I had done here today, while I would probably suffer nightmares about it for weeks or months to come, the truth was, if it saved just *one* life, then part of me could not regret it.

As for the part that *did* . . . well, at least that proved there was still hope left. Today might have proven that the killer Jack wanted me to be already resided within, but accepting that part of my soul—becoming comfortable with it—was still a ways off yet.

And I had to be thankful for that. Had to cling to it, as fiercely as I could. It was my only hope.

Jack pushed upright with a thick groan. His face was gaunt, cheekbones prominent. A man in serious need of a good feed.

And the dark hunger gleamed in his eyes.

"Control it, boss," I said softly. Warily.

"If I wasn't, you'd be lunch rather than sitting there making stupid statements."

I grinned. "Good to see your sense of humor doesn't leave when the bloodlust rises."

"It will if you keep blathering. Get your butt home, and get some rest, Riley. I'll finish off matters here."

My gaze slid to the body on the floor—to the dark pool of blood beginning to thicken near her body.

Knew it wouldn't go to waste.

I shuddered, and got the hell out of there.

Four hours' sleep was never going to be enough, so when the alarm went off at six it was damn lucky it wasn't flung across the room. But the natural irritability that came with lack of sleep increased tenfold when I realized I wasn't alone in my bedroom.

And the warm sandalwood scent told me who it was.

I rolled onto my side. Quinn sat near the window, surrounded in a halo of fading sunshine, a dark silhouette of male perfection. Mother nature at her perverse best—for while the bod may be beautiful, the nature of the man left a hell of a lot to be desired.

Though I guess he'd probably say the same about me. And would probably be right.

"What are you doing here?"

"I came to thank you," he said, voice soft and oh so sexy.

"For what?" I flung off the sheet and got out of bed. Quinn's gaze slid across my skin like liquid heat, and my hormones reacted accordingly.

"For doing what I could not. Capturing and containing Caelfind."

I picked up a T-shirt from the floor, gave it a sniff to check its freshness, then pulled it on. "We would have all saved time and effort if you'd been honest with us from the start."

"You don't understand—"

"No, I don't," I said, as I stomped out to get coffee. It wouldn't help to put out the low-burning fire caused by both Quinn's presence and my own nature, but it sure couldn't hurt my grouchy mood. "There was nothing stopping you from telling me that night the priest made his appearance. Only your own ornery need to do everything your own way."

"There's the pot calling the kettle black," he muttered.

I shot him an annoyed look. Even though he was no longer surrounded by the blinding halo of sunlight, he still looked little more than a shadow because he was dressed from head to foot in black.

Even his dark eyes were shaded. Wary.

Some perverse part deep inside was mighty pleased about that. The other part, the part heated by the growing nearness of the full moon, just wanted to grab him and shag him senseless.

Because right now, the wolf within didn't really care about hurt or anger or anything else. Not when the moon fever was surging through my bloodstream. But once the full moon had come and gone, she *would* care. She *would* hurt, and she most certainly *would* regret having given in yet again.

I couldn't do it. I had to hold firm, no matter what.

Dammit, I had a wolf who cared for me. A wolf who didn't abuse my trust or my feelings. A wolf who longed for the same sort of future as I did.

That *should* be enough.

It was perverse—insane—to want more.

And yet, deep down, part of me did.

"Look," I said, my voice holding an edge of anger that was aimed more at myself than him, "if you're here to argue, you can just march right out of my apartment. I'm not in the mood right now."

"I'm not. I'm just here to talk."

"Good." I shoved on the kettle, then reached up to grab the coffee from the shelf. Luckily for everyone, there was still some of my favorite left. "Then tell me about the priest in the lane. Who was he?"

He hesitated. "My father."

Well, that certainly explained the odd questions. The old man had been quizzing his son's prospective mate. "Then I know where you got your orneriness from. Your father was as helpful as you were."

He raised a dark eyebrow. "So you actually *did* speak to him?"

"Yep. What is he? A spirit? A ghost? What?"

"He is a spirit. Of sorts." He hesitated. "He is— was—the gate master. The priest responsible for ensuring the ways into this world from the spirit world remained locked."

"All the ways?"

"Most of them. The priests are magi-sensitive. They can feel when a new gate is being formed."

"So why didn't you feel this one, if you were a priest?"

"Because I was only an initiate, and not fully trained."

The kettle began to whistle. I flicked off the power and poured the water into the cup. "Is that why you became a vampire? Because you needed eternal life if you were to hang about and wait for your sister's reappearance?"

He smiled, a warmth I felt deep inside rather than actually saw. "Yes."

"And it was Henri who turned you." It was a guess, but one I was fairly certain was correct. After all, he'd been friends with Henri all his undead life, and he'd used and abused all the rules, regs, and me to find his killer.

"Yes. He looked after me through the bloodlust."

I nodded. So many things were beginning to make sense, now. "So what, exactly, are the priests of Aedh? What are you?"

"I am—was—human."

"Humans can't fly. Nor can vampires who aren't winged shifters of some kind. You may be part human, but you also admitted a while ago that you were something else."

Surprise flickered in his dark eyes. "You saw me fly? How?"

"I didn't see you, I sensed you. Now answer the damn question—what else are you?"

He hesitated. "The priests were not human in any true sense. They weren't even an offshoot branch of the family, as werewolves and shapeshifters are. They were more an energy force than actual flesh."

"Yet they had to be able to take on human form. I mean, you're here, so they could obviously breed, and human conception has basic needs."

He smiled, and my hormones did their usual crazy dance. "Yes."

"So what sort of form did they take?"

"They were tall, golden, and winged. They were often depicted as angels in ancient texts."

That raised my eyebrows. "So where are your wings?"

"Half-breeds never got the wings."

"Just the powers?"

"Yes."

I sipped my coffee, and considered him for a moment. "Did you banish your sister's spirit after I pinned her?"

"No. What you have done is far better. She is trapped in flesh that no longer lives. She can never escape."

"Flesh rots. When it does, won't she be free?"

He smiled again, and this time there was nothing warm about it. Goose bumps ran across my skin. I had to hope that *that* smile was never directed my way.

"The body will be mummified, then wrapped in silver, and sealed with spells only another priest can undo. She will never escape. Can never return to hurt this world."

Just live in an agony of unlife for the rest of eternity. It was a cruel ending, even for a spirit hell-bent on having her dark master dominate the world. Yet I couldn't work up any sympathy. "Which just leaves us with the dragons and their master."

"Whom I can either banish or seal in flesh, once we flush out his sacrifice site."

"Why is flushing out his sacrifice site important?"

"Because I can use its power to send him back if that's what we decide to do. Then I can cleanse the site to prevent him ever using it to reenter our world."

"I thought your sister was responsible for him being here?"

"She was. But if the gate is not closed, he can come back through."

"Not a good thing."

"No." He paused, then stepped forward, until there was only a hairsbreadth between us. The heat of him, scent of him, flowed over me, through me, filling my lungs, filling my heart, filling my soul. My breath caught, then quickened, and it took every ounce of willpower to remain as I was, to not step forward, into his embrace.

"Be careful in there tonight," he said, his dark gaze on mine and filled with concern. Filled with warmth. "The god of darkness is a very powerful soul, and long practiced in seducing the unwary."

"I could never be counted as one of the unwary." Which wasn't exactly the truth. Otherwise, why would I be standing here, drinking in the scent of sandalwood and man and desire, until all I wanted to do was wrap my arms around him and hold on tight? Why wasn't I running as far and as fast as I could from this man and all the problems he represented?

Because he was my chocolate. It might be perverse, it might be insane, but he was the one temptation I could never, ever resist.

And yet time and again he'd proven he just wasn't good for my health—my emotional health.

I might want him physically, but it just wasn't enough anymore. Even with the moon in full bloom, even with desire battering at my senses, part of me was just tired of it all.

Tired of the fighting. Tired of his constant belittling of the werewolf ways. Tired of simply trying. If he wasn't at least willing to meet me some of the way—and his actions seemed to constantly prove he wasn't—what was the point of us even being together?

I'd once said sex was a very good place to start any relationship, and I still believed that was totally true. But sex wasn't the end-all of any relationship, even for a werewolf. There had to be more.

Had to be trust.

And the truth was, I just didn't trust Quinn anymore. And that, more than anything he might have said or done over the last few months, was a relationship killer.

I stepped away from him.

He frowned. "Riley—"

"No," I said softly. "I have a job to do, and I need you to leave."

"I have no intention—"

"You have every intention," I said, and a little of the anger that was bubbling deep inside came spewing up. "Do you remember a lady called Eryn Jones?"

"She was my supposed fiancée, so yeah. But what has she got to do with us?"

"You remember what you did to her?"

"I gave her what she deserved, but I still don't see—"

"She used a drug on you," I said shortly. Angrily.

"That changed the way you thought and acted. She made you fall in love with her." I crossed my arms and glared at him. "How different is that from what you're doing to me?"

"It's different." But it was softly said. He knew the point I was making. He just didn't want to acknowledge it.

"*How* is it different?" I all but shouted. "How in the goddamn hell can you stand there and say it's different?"

"She didn't care for me, just my money."

"And you caring for me makes it all right for you to try and change my very nature through mind control?"

"I was just—"

I held up a hand. "I'm tired of your excuses, Quinn. Tired of giving, tired of forgiving. Just get out."

"There's too much between us to just walk away from it. I won't—"

"You keep saying that, and yet you keep trying to change my very nature. Enough is enough. Please, just leave, Quinn."

"No—"

"She did ask nicely," Rhoan said, his voice holding an edge as he crossed his arms and leaned against the doorframe. "Leave, or I *will* make you."

Quinn's expression darkened. "This is between me and her—"

"You take her on, you take me on," Rhoan said. "Right now, she doesn't want you in this apartment, or her life. Go, as asked, or I *will* make you."

Quinn's gaze went from Rhoan to me and back again, and the sudden sense of danger had the hairs along the back of my neck rising. Even though he hadn't moved a muscle, the man standing in front of me was suddenly every inch an old and deadly vampire. Then he shook his head, and the sensation fell away.

"I never took you for a coward, Riley. I guess I was wrong."

"I guess you were." I took a sip of coffee, then added, "But then, you're the one trying to change a werewolf's nature, not me."

He gave me a look that was an odd mix of anger, determination, and regret, then spun on his heel and left. When the front door slammed shut, I sighed in relief.

"Thanks, bro."

He nodded. "You sure you want to do what you just did?"

"He was trying to change who I am, Rhoan. I can forgive many of the things he's done, but I can't forgive that."

"For ever and ever, or just for a while?"

"I don't know. I'll tell you when I figure that out."

"Fair enough." He walked up beside me and flicked on the kettle. "I'm your backup for tonight."

"No offense, bro, but I hope you're not my only backup tonight."

"Jack will be there. And the place will be surrounded." He hesitated, and added with a wry grin, "And our enigmatic vampire will undoubtedly be there, if only so he can close the gate."

"The more the merrier." I reached up to the shelf, grabbed the regular coffee, and handed it to him. Rhoan's tastes weren't as fussy as mine when it came to coffee—even if I'd drink just about anything when push came to shove.

He accepted the jar with a nod of thanks, and tossed some granules into a mug. "You worried about tonight?"

"Yes." I rubbed an arm, and tried to ignore the goose bumps that fled up my skin at the thought of stepping into the den of a dark god and his dragons. "If they felt Caelfind's entrapment, then things could get very nasty in there tonight."

"But they have no reason to suspect your involvement with that."

"No. But Caelfind was a very old being with powers we can only guess at. It's not beyond the realm of possibility that she contacted Kingsley somehow when she was caught."

"If they knew Caelfind had been caught and restrained, then they'd be on the move. So far, Kingsley hasn't stepped from the house."

"As far as we know. He might have access to underground passages or something."

"In the middle of Toorak?" Rhoan grinned. "I doubt it."

"Toorak has sewers, just like every other suburb. There's no saying he hasn't got cellar access or something."

"No, but it's unlikely."

Maybe. But we worked in a world where the unlikely was more than possible. "I'd like to go in there with a couple of hidden weapons. Just in case."

"A set of your special shoes would be sensible." His gaze went to my hair. "And I think we can attach a couple of the threaded knives to some hair clips or something. But we'll have to go to the Directorate to get them."

We had to go back there, anyway. Jack wanted me to try and place some listening devices and micro-cameras around the place. "They'll have to be short knives if we're attaching them to hair clips, and short knives won't reach the heart."

"No, but all you really need them to do is to pin his spirit to his flesh. We can use conventional weapons after that, and let Quinn do his priest banishing or containing stuff."

I nodded and glanced at the clock. It was nearing six-thirty now, and given I was supposed to meet Jin at seven, I was going to be pushing things. Still, I liked the thought of making the bastard sweat a little.

And I certainly wasn't in a hurry to get there, anyway.

I finished my coffee, then pushed away from the bench. "I'll go for a shower, then we can head off."

"Then I'll go pick out an outfit that'll guarantee they won't notice any hidden weapons."

"Great. I'm going to end up basically naked."

He grinned. "When you've got something to hide, show as much flesh as possible. Now go grab that shower, or we're going to be horribly late."

I went.

And we were horribly late.

It was nearing seven-thirty by the time I climbed out of the cab. Jin paced the sidewalk in front of Kingsley's mansion, his expression anxious. I had to wonder why—after all, it wasn't like he *had* to bring a partner or face dire consequences.

Was it?

I remembered the tone of Kingsley's voice when he made the request, and suddenly wasn't so sure.

The traffic noise from the main road began to fade, and the click of my heels against the pavement became more noticeable, carrying sharply across the night. Jin spun, and an almost relieved smile touched his lips. But as my gaze met his dark eyes, I noted the anger there. He might be putting on a pleasant and urbane front, but the creature within was furious.

A shiver ran through my soul. I didn't want to face that anger. Didn't want to feel the consequences of it.

Knew I'd probably have to do both.

He walked toward me, his gait unhurried and yet sexy, that of a man who knew he was good-looking and who knew how to work it. I let my gaze slip downward, unable to help admiring the outer package even if the being within frightened the crap out of me.

He stopped when there were still several feet between us, his gaze traveling idly down my body, making my skin burn and my blood boil. He was close enough that the heat of him, the musky male scent of him, rolled over me, briefly erasing the other scents that filled the night. I breathed deep, letting the musk of him fill my lungs, letting it fuel the moon-spun desire to greater heights. I had a bad feeling I'd need to be at fever pitch to get through this night without giving in to the need to run for the hills.

"I was beginning to think you'd stood me up." His voice was husky, deep, and in his dark gaze, lust now competed with the anger.

A shiver that was part desire, part trepidation, raced up my spine. "Couldn't escape work early, then couldn't get a cab." I shrugged casually. "I figured you'd wait."

He raised an eyebrow. "And why would you be so certain of that?"

I closed the distance between us, until my nipples—erect and hard inside the filmy confines of my little green dress—brushed the silk of his gray shirt. "Because you want me. Badly."

He made a sound low down in his throat, then wrapped a hand around my neck and pulled me close. For the briefest of moments, the memory of who and what he was rose and something inside resisted. Ruthlessly, knowing I had no other choice—that another part of me *wanted* no other choice—I pushed thought and resistance away. As his lips met mine, I kissed him urgently, giving in to the press of his body against mine, letting sensation fuel desire to greater heights.

His free hand slipped down my back, cupping my butt, pressing me hard against him. After a few minutes, he groaned softly and broke off our kiss.

"You're not," he said, his breath short and sharp, his lips brushing mine as he spoke, "wearing any panties."

"They tend to get in the way of a good time." I ran my hands down his arms, then slid them around his waist. The only way we could get any closer would be for him to slide deep inside. And part of me—most of me—wanted that. I was a werewolf, first and foremost, and sex was high on the agenda tonight. "Are you sure you want to have dinner with your friends?"

It was a question that had to be asked—a question that any normal, fiercely aroused woman would ask. If I *didn't,* he might think it odd. I just had to pray that he wouldn't take me up on the offer. I needed to get inside that house, discover what I could, and get the hell out.

Flying solo with Jin wouldn't achieve any of those. Wouldn't achieve an end to this case, and that was the one thing I wanted above everything else.

"I have to." He briefly kissed my lips, my cheeks, my chin. "But I promise, it'll be worthwhile. John has some delicious entertainment planned."

And what sort of entertainment did a three-headed dragon and his dark lord deem delicious? Goose bumps flitted across my skin, but were quickly drowned under a new wave of need as Jin's touch slipped under the hem of my dress to caress my skin, my butt.

"More delicious than being with me?"

My voice was a husky purr, and a quiver ran through the body pressed so close to mine. "Oh, I intend to be with you. Just not here. Not yet."

"If you don't hurry, I might have to find someone else to satisfy my needs."

Humor flicked through his eyes. "That, too, might yet be accommodated." He stepped back, pulling away from my loose hug, then threaded one hand through mine. "Let's go."

He tugged me toward the house, and ushered me through an open gate. Kingsley's house was one of those modern ones, all concrete and sharp angles. My gaze ran up the monolithic front of the building, and I couldn't help thinking that with its barely-there slashes of glass, it almost looked as if the building had eyes. Dark beady eyes that were staring down at me. Judging me. Eyes that knew entirely too much.

A cold chill ran across my skin. I bit my lip, silently admonishing my imagination. It was just a building. Nothing more, nothing less.

Except that it housed a dark god, intent on wreaking havoc on the world at large.

Not only was I about to step into his den, but I was going to try and bug it.

And I had a bad feeling that if I didn't watch my step, it could be the last thing I ever did.

Chapter 11

*J*in climbed the steps and pressed the buzzer beside the huge chrome-edged doors. I stopped next to him, pressing closer than I normally would have, needing the heat of his body to chase away my chills.

I couldn't escape the feeling that I was about to do something very, very bad. Bad in a much-hurt-for-Riley sort of way. And while Jin was a psycho and God knew what else, I at least had some sense of him, of what he was capable of.

The same could not be said for the man whose footsteps echoed in the hall beyond the door.

I licked dry lips, and almost felt relieved when Jin draped an arm around my shoulder. Only it wasn't a proprietary arm, wasn't meant to be comforting. His fingers dug into my shoulder almost brutally, as if he sensed my sudden uncertainty and was determined to prevent any attempt to leave.

He wasn't to know that I couldn't. Wouldn't. No matter what happened in here.

The measured steps drew closer. My heart seemed to leap up into my throat, and breathing suddenly became that much more difficult. I shifted my weight from one foot to the other, and crossed my arms. But I resisted the temptation to rub them, and had to hope Jin would think the goose bumps traversing my arms were due to cold rather than fright.

The door finally opened. I'm not sure what exactly I expected, but the thin, spectacle-wearing, almost nerdy-looking man standing in front of me certainly wasn't it. Relief hit so hard I almost laughed.

Almost.

Because when my gaze met the blue of his, I realized just how deceiving looks could be. This man might be ordinary when it came to looks, but stare into his gaze and the real man became evident.

He was power, sheer power—a power that was at once both raw and seductive. Magnetic. Though there was a good four or five feet between us, I felt the pull of it. It washed over my skin as sharp as electricity, and seemed a whole lot more dangerous.

Because it could destroy in more ways than mere death.

"I didn't think you were coming," he said, his words aimed at Jin, though his gaze continued to hold mine. "We were just about to start."

There was a low note in his voice that was urbane, se-ductive, and it invaded my senses and heated my skin. A tremor that was all awareness, all anticipation, ran through me.

I was in trouble. Big, big trouble.

I might be a werewolf, and I might be willing to use sex to get the information I needed, but this man—this dark god—had centuries of lust and unholy desires behind him. When it came to seduction, I was standing at the feet of a master.

And the master had plans for me, just as Gautier had warned. The confirmation was evident in the dark and hungry gleam in his eyes.

"Riley got held up by work," Jin explained. "I apologize."

"As indeed you should." His gaze still held mine, judging, enjoying. When he held out his hand, I placed mine in his almost without thought. He bent and placed a kiss on my palm, his lips lingering, tasting. "Welcome to my house, Riley."

"Thank you." It came out a squeak and I cleared my throat. "It's a pleasure to meet you."

"The pleasure will be mine, I assure you." He released my hand, and yet I could still feel the lingering heat of his lips on my palm. Somehow, I resisted the temptation to wipe my hand against my dress. "Jin, escort our pretty lady inside and introduce her to our other guests."

He stepped to one side. Jin placed a hand against my spine—low down, close to my butt, so that his fingertips caressed my cheeks as I walked—and ushered me inside. Desire prickled across my skin, and the low down burning became even more furious. The moon fever was still well under control—and yet, the awareness of it was there, meaning I had to have sex sooner rather than later.

Which shouldn't be a problem, I thought, shivering.

My heels clicked on the polished marble tiles, the sound echoing through the long emptiness of the hall. Kingsley obviously wasn't big on furnishings—the hall had a coat stand near the door, and an ornate cherry-wood telephone table about halfway down, but that was about it. The pale gold walls were bare of paintings, mirrors, or any other kind of decoration. The lights were ornate, but none had bulbs, leaving the hallway a wasteland of shadows. Luckily, I didn't need light to see, but I had to wonder if all the gloom and the emptiness was a ploy to play on the nerves of their guests. After all, these were men who were aroused by the darker emotions, and fear, however subtle, had to taste mighty sweet.

As we passed the telephone table, I pressed a finger against one of the minute listening devices attached lightly to the outside of my purse, then ran my hand casually across the cherrywood, carefully but quickly placing the bug under the unit's ledge.

One down, five more to go.

A door loomed on our left. It was big and ornate and had to be as heavy as hell, given the effort Jin seemed to put into opening it.

As I stepped through I realized why.

Power slid over my skin, cold fingertips of energy that briefly resisted my efforts to walk into the semi-dark room. And I realized then that had to be why the Directorate was having so much trouble reading the inside of this house. Caelfind had obviously set up her own kind of deadeners, and I had no doubt they would be both psychic and electronic. She had seemed a thorough sort of sorceress, even if she turned out to be a little over-confident in the end.

With an odd sort of sucking sensation, the energy slid over my skin then released me. I scratched at my ear, wondering if Rhoan could still hear what was going on. Wondering if the tracker would work in this room, or whether I was, for all intents and purposes, on my own.

I didn't want to be on my own. Not with these people.

If indeed they could be classed as people.

Jin touched my spine again and lightly guided me forward. The room was long, and shadows haunted the far corners. The air was a rampant mix of sharp spices, flowery perfume, fear, and desire. While I had no desire to draw the mix deep into my lungs, Jin had no such inhibitions. He sucked in a long breath, then exhaled it slowly.

"Ah, the sweet aroma of a good red. Would you like some?"

If he could smell red wine in *this,* he had a better nose than me. "A small glass would be nice."

"I'll introduce you to the others, then get you a drink."

I nodded, my gaze already roaming across the faces of people gathered near the open fire at the far end of the room. I had no idea why they huddled there, because the room was almost unbearably hot. Maybe they just felt safer near the fire—it *was* the only source of light in the room, after all.

And then my gaze hit the face of a man I knew, and I stopped. I couldn't help it.

Gautier.

Oh *God*—what the hell was I going to do now? I *should* have known, *should* have damn well realized he'd be here. If Jin and Marcus had been ordered to attend this little shindig, it was logical that Gautier—the death head of the dragon—would also have been.

Only none of us had thought about that. It was stupid. Totally stupid.

And it might very well cost me my life.

He smiled and minutely raised his glass, as if in greeting. My stomach stirred, and bile rose. I swallowed heavily.

"Are you all right?" Jin said, a touch of concern in his voice that I didn't for a minute believe.

I somehow managed a nod. "Sorry, just letting my eyes adjust to the darkness."

He touched my elbow. "I'll guide you."

I had no choice. I had to move. Had to brazen this out and test how far Gautier was going to let this play out. And I could only hope that the cavalry who waited beyond this house would come a-running when I needed them.

With tension curling through every part of my body, I forced my feet forward. We walked past a long wooden table that was set, ready for dinner—though the candles in the ornate candleholders were as yet unlit—and moved into the warm circle of light near the fire.

Sweat began trickling down my spine as we neared the fire, but I wasn't sure whether it was the heat, or simply fear of the thin-faced man who watched me with a mocking, superior smile.

I forced my gaze from him, and studied the others.

Most of the people here I already knew. The first was Marcus, the big man I'd seen terrorizing Jan at the club. At least *she* was looking a whole lot more lively than the last time I'd seen her, though she still moved with a slowness that spoke of healing wounds.

The third person Jin introduced as Raven and she was clinging to Gautier's arm in a way that was nervous, and yet very sexual. She was a thin woman with black hair, pinched features, and darting, bloodshot gray eyes. She was also a shifter and, like Jan, had a desperate, needy sort of air about her—which made me wonder if she was another victim in the making.

Then her scent triggered the memory of the club and that odd smell coming from the second room, a smell that had been a little bit of desperation, and a lot of death.

It *had* been Gautier in that room. And this woman had been with him.

Becoming the death head hadn't only given him an immunity to sunlight, it had given him sex. Dark, deadly sex.

The thought made me want to puke.

Jin touched my back lightly, dragging me out of my thoughts and fears, then moved off to fetch our drinks, leaving me to make small talk with people I had no intention of ever getting to know better. All the while, Gautier watched me like a spider, saying nothing, merely smiling that cold, venomous smile of his. Every instinct I had was screaming to get out, while I still could.

But Gautier wouldn't let me go. I knew that. Whatever game he was playing, I was caught in the middle of it, and I had no choice but to let the night roll on and see what happened. See what he planned.

When Jin slipped the red wine into my hand, I practically gulped down the first couple of mouthfuls. It didn't do a whole lot to ease the tension slithering through my limbs, but at least it was wet and soothed the dryness in my throat.

After about five minutes of inane banter about the weather and whatnot, a small gong went off behind us. As we turned around, the candles sprung to life, flickering warm light across all the crystal and silverware, and sending shards of rainbow light spiraling across the room.

Kingsley now stood at the end of the table, a king surveying his subjects. His gaze met mine and lingered, making my heart skip, then race, even harder. Worst thing was, I wasn't entirely sure whether it was due to fear, or something else. Something that had a whole lot more to do with wanting a treat that was obviously very bad for me.

"Jin, you and the lovely Riley can sit at the head of the table with me tonight."

He said it like it was granting a great gift, and indeed, that's how Jin seemed to take it. His smile was wide as he escorted me to the chair on Kingsley's immediate right. I thanked Jin as he pulled out the chair and seated me, then placed my purse on the table, casually sticking another device to my fingertip and dropping my hands. Which were shaking. Because Gautier was still watching and still saying nothing. I placed the second device under my chair and hoped like hell it still worked with the magic barrier in place.

The camera—which looked to be nothing more than a slightly larger flat silver bead on my glittery purse—

needed to be placed higher, and that, for now, was impossible.

Kingsley picked up the nearby bottle of wine and filled my glass. Then he picked up his own and raised it.

"To new friends and good times," he said, lightly clicking his glass against mine, and then Jin's.

"And a long night of passion and desire," Jin added, his gaze holding an intensity that had little flash fires dancing up and down my spine despite the deep fear that resided within.

Yet the heat Jin raised was nothing compared to the closeness of his dark master. Sitting next to Kingsley was like sitting close to a wolf with his aura set to full intensity. It made me sweat, made me want, like never before.

Had he been another wolf, I would have simply used my own aura to mute the force of his. But how did you mute the force of a dark god? Especially when he was wearing the skin of a human? I couldn't even *use* my aura, because no one here but Gautier knew I was wolf—and I very much intended to keep it that way.

If Gautier would let me.

The meals came, brought into the room by women who moved with the silence of ghosts and who looked just as pale. Not that they *were* ghosts—with my growing affinity to the dead, I would have felt that—but all the same, there seemed to be very little life in their eyes or expressions. Perhaps Kingsley had sucked all the energy and life from them.

Everyone but Gautier ate, drank, and made more small talk as the plates of food came and went. Jin was right in one thing—the food here was amazing.

As the night wore on, my head grew sort of fuzzy, in

that warm, had-too-much-to-drink-and-now-way-too-loose sort of way. I actually stopped drinking wine after the entrée, but my head didn't get any clearer. It felt odd, like I was there but not there. A watcher standing outside my own body, aware of events but not really a part of them. Even the fear of Gautier and what he was up to seemed to slide away.

Somewhere deep inside, alarm grew, but I didn't even have the energy to wrest it to the foreground for a thorough examination. It was just too much hassle. Everything was too much hassle, except sitting here enjoying.

Dessert—a mass of fudgy chocolate cake that was almost as good as an orgasm—came and went, then coffee was served. It wasn't hazelnut, but it was top shelf and absolutely divine.

Which left us with the after-dinner entertainment. Kingsley stood once the last of the coffee cups had been collected by the pale women, and the tension I'd felt earlier leapt back into the warm room. But it was accompanied by hot spots of fear, desire, and excitement—the fear and desire Jan's, the excitement belonging to Jin, Marcus, and the thin shifter. Gautier was as inscrutable as ever, and yet there was a gleam in his eyes that had distant shivers dancing up my spine.

"Shall we move on to the main entertainment?"

"Oh, please do," Jan said, her voice breathy with excitement.

Marcus gave her a hug, and my stomach stirred. Maybe eating all that chocolate cake was a bad idea. Not if the entertainment was what I was beginning to think it was.

Kingsley walked across the room to a second set of

doors I hadn't noticed before now and pushed them open. The room beyond, like this one, was ill lit, but filled with looming shadows and the sharp smell of blood and fear and death.

Jin held out his hand as Kingsley disappeared into gloom. My hesitation was brief, but nevertheless there, and part of me was mighty glad of that. At least it meant I wasn't so far gone that I'd walk into trouble without thought, without fear. Not that either would do a whole lot at this point in time.

Two by two, we walked into the room. A light clicked on down the far end, throwing pale light across the darkly stained wooden machinery filling the room. It was another goddamn torture chamber. Like before, there were rough wooden racks, chains attached to cuffs dangling from the ceiling, a huge wooden wheel straddling a deep water trough, and rough ropes attached to wall rings. But there were other machines here, truly nasty-looking ones, like metal chambers filled with spikes and other, even more deadly-looking things.

This time, I stared at them with a more dispassionate eye. Horror was there, but it was a distant thing, held back by a wall of detachment. It was odd, this feeling of being here and yet not here, and yet part of me was glad. If not for the distance, I might have been tempted to run screaming from the room.

Or would I? Truth was, I wanted to do my job. Wanted these freaks stopped for all eternity.

It was the only clear, unfuzzed thought in the whole foggy mess that was the current state of my brain.

Kingsley appeared out of the gloom. He'd taken off his dinner jacket and loosened his tie, and the lusty tension filling the room sharpened abruptly, hitting my senses like a hammer and making my knees weak.

Jin's hands slipped around my waist, pulling me back against him. His breath was heated, rapid against my neck, his thick erection pressing hard into my butt.

Kingsley stopped in front of Jan, raising a hand and gently caressing her cheek. She shuddered under his touch, and the scent of desire and need swirled around us, sharp and tantalizing in the heavy air. My breathing quickened in response, and Jin's soft chuckle stirred my hair.

"Soon," he whispered. "Soon."

"Do you understand the reason you are here?" Kingsley trailed a hand down Jan's neck and began to undo her shirt.

She pushed into his hand, offering her small breasts to his touch and his gaze. "It's a test," she said.

"A test, not an end. Do you understand that?" He finished undoing her buttons, and pushed her shirt aside, exposing her breasts but not touching them himself.

"Yes," she all but whimpered, her desperation for his caress very evident in her voice. But she didn't move. I wondered vaguely what held her in place—fear, or something in Kingsley's eyes? Something I couldn't see from where I stood?

"Then choose your machine."

Her gaze darted around the room, and came to rest on the smallest of the wooden machines. "The barrel. I choose the barrel."

"Ah, a good choice." Kingsley's gaze shifted to Marcus. "You know what to do."

The big man nodded, and led Jan across to the barrel

that was lined with tiny wooden spikes. Gautier pulled Raven close to his body, and began playing with her breasts in a way that looked crude and painful. I gulped and forced my gaze away. I couldn't handle a sexual Gautier. It just wasn't right.

Kingsley walked across to where Jin and I stood. He stopped to our left, watching us rather than his so-called show. The thick, raw scent of him wrapped around us like a blanket, making me sweat, shake.

Want.

"Do you know what is about to happen?"

"Yes." My answer was soft, breathy. Part of me hoped it was fear, but mostly I knew it was excitement.

"And are you aroused by the thought?"

"I'm aroused by Jin. Aroused by you."

He raised an eyebrow. "I think you lie."

"No."

"Then shall we watch and see?" His words held a touch of command, and I battled them instinctively.

"No."

Amusement touched his lips. "You're right, Jin. This one *is* strong. A very good choice indeed."

"Thank you," Jin said, as he slid his hands from my waist to my breasts to my shoulders.

A quiver of anticipation ran across my skin as he began to slide the straps down my shoulders.

"Watch," Kingsley ordered, and this time I had no choice.

Jan had stripped and stretched her body across the barrel. Marcus had tied her limbs to rings set in the floor, stretching her arms and legs wide and pressing her stomach down against the tiny spikes. As yet, they hadn't broken skin, because I couldn't see or smell blood, but it obviously wouldn't take much more pressure to do so.

Marcus began to strip, and even in my detached state, I could find nothing truly beautiful about him. He was just a man, all sinew and big bones, with a regular old dick. Not that I minded regular old dicks if the packaging around them was decent enough.

The sound of a hand slapping sharply against flesh made me jump a little. I blinked, and realized that somewhere along the line, Marcus had donned a leather glove on his right hand. From each gloved fingertip extended barbed strips of leather. As he slapped Jan's back, the force of his blows pressed her stomach down against the spikes and the little strips lashed out, striking her shoulders with some force.

It wasn't very long at all before her already scarred back became a raw and bloody mess, but her breaths were short, shuddery gasps of pleasure, and the air was thick and heavy with the scent of her blood and her need.

And it wasn't only hers.

The sharp smell of Raven's arousal spun through the air, filled with desperation and need. As much as it sickened me to think she was enjoying the show *and* Gautier, the scent only served to fuel my own to greater heights.

Jin's fingertips slid down my arms, taking the dress straps with them, and the dress itself was soon a puddle of green silk at my feet. He took my purse and tossed it off to one side, then slid his fingers up my stomach and firmly grasped my engorged nipples. He pinched them, hard, and the jolt that ran through me was all pleasure. For a wolf in the midst of moon heat, any touch could be pleasurable. And right now, despite the situation, despite my odd detachment—or maybe because of it—I just wanted his caress, be it hard or soft.

"Watch," Kingsley intoned, his voice seeming to echo, as if it had come from a very great distance.

Marcus was no longer just hitting her. He was between her legs and fucking her, thrusting hard and deep as she twisted, screamed, and, eventually, came. She went limp against the barrel, but the big man didn't stop, pounding and pounding and pounding his body into hers.

And my muscles were jumping, my skin quivering, as if it was me down there, and I wanted, so wanted, the release that hovered so close and yet so far.

But then Marcus came and the quivering stopped, and it was all I could do not to scream in frustration.

Kingsley laughed softly. "I think this one is ready to do more than just watch."

Jin was still pinching, still teasing. "Yes," he said, his voice a husky drawl near my ear. "She's more than ready."

"Then prepare her." He reached out, caressing my cheek. "Gautier, you may continue your pleasures with Raven on whatever machine you choose."

The woman's thick moan of pleasure followed me out of the room. I was glad I could no longer see Gautier, but I could feel his gaze on me, long after we'd left the room.

We passed through another doorway filled with the feel of resisting power, and into a small square room. In it was a set of standard wooden medieval stocks, though this one had an odd, stomach-height wooden bar set about two feet out from the stocks themselves. There was nothing else in the room. Nothing living or inanimate, anyway.

There were wisps of smoke that stirred in dark corners, and I swear they whispered of horrors I could only hope never to experience.

Fear rose briefly, and I stumbled. Just for a moment, the fog dissipated and clarity of thought made a brief appearance. Something was wrong. Something was *very* wrong. I had to get out of here. Had to.

I wrenched my arm from Jin's grasp and spun around, one foot lashing out, kicking him hard in the gut. Dragon or not, he was still wrapped in human flesh, and the human went down with a huge gasp for air.

But he wasn't down for long enough.

As I ran for the door, he lunged forward, grabbing my heel and yanking hard. I came down face-first, and my chin split open on the cold tiles. Blood sprayed, and pain exploded. I swore and twisted, kicking him in the head, trying to get him to release me. I had the strength of a were and a vampire behind me, but it didn't seem to be making a whole lot of difference. Inch by bloody inch, I was being drawn inexorably toward him.

I swore again and pushed into a sitting position, lurching for one of his fingers and yanking it backward brutally. Bone snapped and he screamed—a sound filled with fury and pain and desire.

He hit me with his free hand, the blow landing hard and snapping my head backward. I hit the tiles a second time, and for several seconds I saw stars.

By then he was on me, his weight pinning me, his legs pushing mine apart as he grabbed my wrists and held them above my head. "I thought you didn't like it too rough," he said, his hand between us, yanking at the zip on his pants.

I struggled against him, but when he thrust deep inside, I couldn't help the tremor of pleasure. The moon was high, the fever raged, and I wanted sex. Any sex. Even his.

But I wasn't so far gone that I'd let pleasure overwhelm the need for safety.

"Rough is one thing. Force is another."

I somehow managed to buck my body, threw him off me, then scrambled to my feet and ran again for the door. Straight into the warm and naked body of John Kingsley.

It was like hitting a steel wall, and I rebounded off him with a gasp. Before I could recover my balance, he lashed out with one hand, hitting my bloody chin and throwing me across the room. I hit the wall with a grunt and slithered to the floor.

"Enough," he said. "You will fight no more."

I wanted to, desperately wanted to, but it was as if someone had pulled the plug on the sink that was my anger and desperation. It all just floated away, and the odd detachment came back full force.

"Jin, place her in the stocks."

He picked himself up off the floor, then roughly grabbed my arm and yanked me upright. Without ceremony, and with very little care, he thrust me toward the wooden stocks. The reason for the stomach-height bar soon became evident. I was made to lean over it, and then my head and arms were placed securely locked into the stocks and my spread legs chained to either leg of the stomach rest. It was a position that was uncomfortable, a position that left me open for invasion, a position that stretched every muscle to its limit, and one that would soon have me screaming in pain.

Which is what they wanted. Precisely what they wanted.

But not *all* that they wanted.

Jin stood behind me, his thick cock resting against me, teasing but not entering. Kingsley moved to the front of the stock. Though he was naked, his cock was flaccid. Some deep down part of me prayed like hell it stayed that way.

He stopped. The heat, the acrid, male scent of him, rolled over me, calling to the wolf, making her hunger.

He sensed it. I don't know how, but he did.

"Look at me," he said softly.

His words were a command that whipped around me. When I didn't immediately obey, he chuckled softly and slid his finger under my bloody chin, lifting it up. The position had the muscles in my neck screaming and yet the pain was a distant thing, much like the alarm and fear and the desperation to be gone. I knew they were all there, but they just weren't touching me.

I wish the same could be said of Kingsley.

The heat and need in his eyes would have melted steel, and I have never claimed to be that strong. My body began trembling in response, my blood like quick fire through my veins.

His gaze blazed with power, and the energy of it ran over my skin, burning me, consuming me, in a way that went way beyond anything physical. And through it, a connection formed, a connection that wasn't telepathic, wasn't anything I recognized, but one I felt through every quivering inch of my body and soul. It was almost as if he were stroking me, teasing me, from the inside out, using that raw energy to strum the taut strings of my desire.

"You wish a completion?"

His free hand caressed my left hand, his fingers playing with mine. Something inside screamed a denial but it was still such a faint sound. I had no idea why his innocent action should cause such terror. Maybe it was just the fact that he was physically touching me.

"We can give it to you, you know," he continued. "Give you satisfaction of a kind you have never felt in your young life."

I didn't say anything. Couldn't say anything. My tongue seemed stuck to the roof of my mouth.

"Do you wish a taste, little one?"

My tongue unstuck itself, as if in preparation to say yes, and despite the fog, despite the distance, I bit down on it, hard. Acquiescence to this man—this dark god—was not a good thing. I had no idea why, and couldn't seem to battle the fog long enough to reach clearer thought processes. But I wasn't about to ignore it. Not when something more precious than life itself was at stake.

Kingsley laughed—a soft, seductive, and totally evil sound. His gaze moved from mine and he nodded briefly.

Jin's hand came down hard on my rear. I groaned, caught between desire and pain, wanting and not wanting.

Both men drew a deep breath, as if sucking in the taste of my pain and desire. Kingsley's fingers trembled against my wrist, evidence of a lust I could smell. Oddly enough, that lust still hadn't reached his cock. Maybe someone *was* listening to my prayers upstairs.

Jin hit me again, and again, until my muscles quivered, my flesh stung, and my traitorous body ached with a desire fiercer than anything I'd ever felt before.

I wanted. God, how I wanted.

Whatever they could give me. Whatever they would allow.

Sweat trickled down my forehead, tickling my cheeks before moving on to mingle with the blood still dripping from my chin. Some of that blood was now coming from my mouth, from my cut tongue. I was still biting it, still holding in the need to plead, to beg, for the ending my body so desperately required.

Just as I thought I could take no more, Kingsley nodded, and Jin thrust inside me. There was no gentleness about it, no smoothness in the way he withdrew and thrust, withdrew and thrust, but I couldn't have given a damn.

Besides, it wasn't Jin I felt, but Kingsley. He was all around me, all through me, filling me with his darkness, his desire. He touched me, caressed me, claimed me—not physically, but psychically, and in many ways, it was far more powerful than any mere touch. My body, my senses, responded eagerly, wantonly. Somewhere in the last few moments, I'd become his to do with what he wished, and there was absolutely nothing I could do about it.

Truth be told, I didn't *want* to do anything about it. I was lost in the moment, lost to the passion and intensity, drowning in it willingly. My heart pounded furiously, my body screamed for release, and every muscle, every fiber, felt so tightly strung that everything would surely break.

Then Kingsley took my left pinky finger into his mouth and began licking it, tasting it, and the sensation tipped me completely over the edge. I came, hard and fast and gloriously. In that precise moment, Kingsley's teeth pierced my flesh, biting deep and hard. Pain flowed through me, around me, only to smash against the raw energy that was Kingsley's presence in my mind and soul, mixing with it and becoming something so undeniably exquisite that I came a second time.

As I remembered how to breathe again, I became aware of Jin, still thrusting deep inside of me, his breaths short and sharp, speaking of a peak about to be reached. Became aware of Kingsley, still sucking at my finger.

There was an amazing lack of sensation coming from my littlest digit. Just a pounding, aching weirdness. And there was blood, lots of blood—so much so that even Kingsley's swirling, sucking tongue could not stop it from running down my hand and wrist.

And then I saw why.

My finger ended at the first knuckle.

Just like the women who'd ended up gutted on the floor of the warehouses.

That's what my clairvoyance had been trying to tell me. That's what it had seen, what it had feared.

I knew it now, when it was all too late.

I screamed. Internally, externally, I have no idea. I just screamed.

And then the darkness overtook me and I knew no more.

Chapter 12

Consciousness came back slowly, accompanied by a pounding headache that had spots dancing crazily before my closed eyelids and my stomach doing an accompanying jig. And I couldn't even begin to describe the pain radiating up from my left hand.

Better to ignore it. Pretend it wasn't there, even if the sheer force of it had sweat rolling down my forehead.

Or maybe *that* was the heat. It was hot here, wherever the hell "here" was. My skin burned, and it wasn't just the aches that caused it. The air was thick and humid, and filled with the rank scent of mustiness and old earth. Lingering underneath those two were the finer aromas of blood and death and sorrow and pain, some of them ancient, some of them fresh, all of them raw.

Which suggested that this place was not only

underground, but somewhere that had seen more than its fair share of death.

As had the table on which I lay. Misery and death seemed embedded in the stone itself, and the chill riding up from it ate into my spine and butt, making them ache. I resisted the temptation to shift position, and concentrated on what was going on in the room itself.

Somewhere to my left, fire crackled. I couldn't smell smoke, but there didn't seem to be even the faintest trickle of fresh air and it just didn't feel like a hearth-type fire complete with chimney. Given who had more than likely lit the flames, it was a fair bet to say it was probably magic in origin. I very much doubted Caelfind had been the only practitioner. Surely a dark god would know a bit about the dark arts of sorcery, as well.

Rising beyond the crackle of flame was the sound of chanting. I listened for several seconds, trying to understand the melodious words, but they didn't seem to be in any language I recognized. But the voice I knew—it belonged to Jin.

A tremor ran through my soul. I might not know where I was, but scent, sensation, and instinct were giving very strong indications of what this place was used for.

This was Quinn's gateway. The place where Kingsley did his sacrifices or feedings or whatever the hell they actually were. Why he transported the bodies to warehouses afterward, I have no idea. Maybe he simply didn't want the stink of rotting flesh hanging around his place of sacrifice.

I was tempted to open my eyes and look around further, but until I was sure Jin and I were alone in this place, I couldn't risk even the slightest twitch.

I drew in a breath—slowly but deeply—tasting the air, sorting through the thick scents of death and age and power, looking for the one that was Kingsley.

Nothing.

He wasn't here—a thought that was surely backed up by the fact I was relatively clearheaded. No longer was I the compliant, needy little bitch I'd been in the house, and my thoughts were free of the foggy distance that had made me so pliable earlier. Of course, there were now a thousand little miners working away on the inside of my skull and within my hand, but the pain—eye watering as it was—was a good one. Because I could think. I could feel. And after the events of the last few hours, that alone felt like heaven.

But the bitter, metallic taste in the back of my mouth very much suggested that my distant state had probably been artificially induced, that perhaps both the wine and water had been drugged. They had to have been—it was the only explanation for what had happened. What I'd allowed to happen.

And with my will suppressed, Kingsley had a relatively easy time of getting through some of my shields and making me do what he'd wanted me to do.

But only when he was close. My brief attack on Jin had proven that.

The one good thing about this whole situation was the fact he obviously hadn't gotten through *all* my shields. Otherwise, he would have known I wasn't any old sacrifice victim, but a werewolf and a guardian. And they surely would have taken far more precautions with me if they'd realized what they actually had.

Because I wasn't restrained in any way. I might be naked, but my arms were resting by my sides and my legs were stretched comfortably straight out. And while I mightn't have my shoes, I could still feel the two knives disguised as hair clips in my hair. I had weapons—good weapons—when I needed them.

My very first instinct was to get up and run while Jin's attention was caught elsewhere, but I quelled it quickly. Though I could smell only him in the room, I had no idea what else might be here as well. There might be nasty little—or not so little—beasties like the hellhound waiting in the shadows. And I seriously doubted I'd have the strength to battle *them* as well as Jin.

No, better to wait for the right situation. Like, sometime before they started gutting me.

I drew in another slow, deep breath, trying to sense something else about the room we were in. Nothing more than the aromas I'd already tasted touched the air. I'd have to risk opening my eyes.

I cracked one eyelid open. Warm light danced across the shadowed, earthy walls, highlighting the faint hieroglyphics etched into the rough-hewn walls. Some of the hieroglyphics were familiar, because they were the same as the ones on the back of the ring I'd found in the corner of the skinned thief's house. As to what the others were, I had no idea, yet just looking at them had an odd sense of dread rolling through me. I don't know why, but they left me feeling terribly alone and afraid.

The fear that had, up until now, taken a backseat to

pain and sensation came back with a rush, and again it was all I could do not to get up and run.

I blew out a soft breath, trying to stem panic, trying to keep my breathing slow and easy, and continued to carefully survey my surroundings.

If I was going to get out of here, I needed to know where all the players were, and what the entire situation was. I might suspect where I was and what my fate would be, but I needed to suss out the entire situation before I made any plans.

Which meant shifting a little to get a better view.

It was dangerous. I could see Jin standing in the shadows to the right of the flame, softly chanting, but I had no idea if there was something—or someone—waiting just beyond the range of my senses.

Still, the chance had to be taken.

Heart hammering, I carefully inched sideways—shifting, then waiting; shifting, then waiting—until I was lying at a slight angle across the stone. My stomach was a mess of knots by the time I finished, and my body flushed with the heat of fear, but my head was nearer to the edge of the giant table, and I had a far better view of a good half of the room.

Only it wasn't a room carved out underground, as I'd suspected, but a real cave. An old cave, one whose walls looked worn by the grime of time. From this angle, the hieroglyphics looked far younger than the walls, the symbols carved into the earth like open wounds, fresh and bleeding.

Another shiver ran through me, and I tore my gaze away. Jin was standing to my far left, dressed in a black robe that covered him from neck to feet. Interestingly, the dragon had very little body heat under infrared. It was dark and purplish, not even resembling the heat of a body on the verge of death. It was something totally different, something totally alien.

But then, I guess I was dealing with the ancient spirit of a dragon, not a human in any sense of the word beyond the borrowed body.

Behind him was a door. It was a heavy, modern metal thing, so at odds with the feel of this place. Yet for some reason, just seeing it made me feel better.

If there was a door, people could get here. People could still rescue me if by chance I couldn't actually rescue myself.

It gave hope, when part of me hadn't really wanted to hope until now.

Midway between me and that door was a small stand. A leather cloth covered the top, and on this rested a wickedly curved knife and a heavy silver chalice.

Both items smelled of death and age, though up until that moment, I would have sworn silver could never retain a smell.

My gaze went from the small table to Jin and back again.

That knife might be my one chance of freedom. *If* Maisie hadn't been lying when she'd said the best way to kill the dragons was to behead them.

I studied Jin again. His eyes were closed, his concentration on the chant I couldn't understand. If it was a spell of some kind, it didn't appear to be aimed at me. At least, not aimed at restraining me. It could well be doing something else, something that would affect me when I moved.

But the only way I was going to find out was to actually move.

I blew out a soft breath, then wrapped myself in shadows and slipped off the stone table. The chanting went on, a rhythmical sound that showed no awareness of change.

I stepped across the stones, the warmth of them caressing my skin, sending little tingles of itchy energy spiraling up my legs. I ignored it, wrapped my hand around the black hilt of the curved blade, raised it high, and ran at Jin with all the speed I could muster.

I was a dhampire. I had not only the speed of a vampire, but the strength of a werewolf *and* a vampire behind me. And no one, not even the spirit of a dragon, could counter them. Especially when taken unawares. Jin looked up at the last possible moment, his words stuttering to a halt and his eyes widening just a fraction before the knife sliced through flesh, muscle, and bone, severing his neck swiftly and cleanly. That almost comical look of surprise froze on his face as his head rolled from his neck and dropped to the floor. A second later, his body followed, crumpling in an untidy heap, blood spurting from the stump of his neck and pooling around his head. Almost like a dark halo.

Wispy tendrils began to rise from his body. I raised the knife and quickly retreated to the circle of stones. I had no idea if a dragon's soul could actually attack, or whether the silver blade or the circle of stones would protect me, but it sure as hell felt safer than standing next to a rising soul that belonged to the master of pain.

The tendrils swirled, pulling together, finding shape, finding form. Becoming that of a serpent without wings.

The serpent hissed, the sound echoing around the chamber and making me wince.

But it didn't attack, merely pulled apart once again and drifted away.

Going back to the hell where it had come from, hopefully.

It seemed Maisie hadn't lied to me, after all.

I looked beyond him, through the doorway. The next room seemed haunted by shadows. I couldn't see anyone, couldn't sense anyone. And yet . . . I had a feeling I was no longer alone.

A suspicion that was confirmed when one of those shadows moved.

For a moment, my heart leapt, and joy flooded through me. Rhoan. It had to be Rhoan, even if I couldn't feel his presence. He would have sensed I was in trouble, and come hell or high water, he would come for me.

Then the fresh air moving in from the other room hit me, accompanied by the noxious scent of unwashed flesh.

I almost laughed at the irony of it.

It wasn't Rhoan.

It was Gautier.

How totally, absolutely, fuckingly appropriate.

For a moment, the mad instinct to run, to rush past him and just get out, hit, and I took several steps forward before I forced myself to stop.

Truth was, I had no idea what waited beyond that door and Gautier. It could be the other dragon. It could be the dark god himself. Three against one just wasn't good odds in any way, shape, or form.

Besides, I might very well land myself in a room that offered absolutely no fighting—and more important, no running—space. If I had to fight Gautier, then this larger chamber was the place to do it in.

I glanced down at the stones surrounding the table. Unfortunately, now that Jin's chanting had stopped, there was no feeling of power coming from them. No purplish light coming from the writings on the wall.

Fate, it seemed, had no intention of helping me out any more than she already had. Not that I was surprised. Fate and I had never been chummy.

"What are you doing here, Gautier?"

He didn't answer immediately, instead squatting down next to Jin's body and dipping a finger into the thick pool of blood. He raised it to his mouth and sucked on it lightly. His eyes were filled with a madness and fury that was Gautier and something more. Something alien and deadly.

"A dragon's blood tastes like human blood, in case you were wondering."

"I wasn't, but thanks for the update, stinko."

He smiled and rose. From behind his back he produced a knife—longer and brighter than the one I was holding. "It'll be interesting to see whether your blood is as sweet as other wolves', or if it holds the sharpness of your tongue."

My knuckles went white with the force of my grip on the curved knife. "Tell me one thing before we do this, Gautier."

"Grant a dying wish? It is not usually in my nature to do so, but seeing we've had such a sweet and caring relationship over the years, go ahead and ask."

"How did you get into Dunleavy's town house uninvited?"

"Ah." His smile mocked as he ran his finger up the edge of his blade, drawing blood and not seeming to care. "I am the creation of a lab, a vampire endowed with the powers of other races. Because of it, I have never had the threshold restriction of a vampire."

Meaning he could walk through *any* doorway uninvited? That sure went a long way to explaining how he'd become our greatest guardian. That and the fact he was a psycho who loved to kill.

But at least it explained how he'd left that note in the apartment Jack had sent us to, to keep us safe when Gautier had first fled the Directorate's leash. A chill ran through me. He could have gotten us anytime he pleased, anywhere he'd pleased. Even in the places we'd felt the safest.

"If you are the death head of the dragon, how did you retain your soul when the others did not? And why didn't you tell your dark master that I was a guardian?"

He stepped past Jin's body. Just one step, but it was enough to have my heart just about leaping through my chest. "That's three questions."

"In the scheme of things, it's not going to kill you to answer a couple more questions."

"In the scheme of things, you will die slowly, in agony, with the full knowledge that the help that waits just beyond these doors will never ever find you or this place. And you will die with the knowing that I will kill all that you hold dear, and then I will kill as I want. Because no one will be able to stop me. I am death, and you are *mine*."

"You know, this death spirit you're sharing bodyspace with has made you a lot more eloquent, but he sure as hell talks as much shit as you do."

His gaze narrowed, just a fraction, but the sensation of danger swirled around me and the hairs along the back of my neck stood on end. It had never been a sane idea to annoy Gautier, but how much stupider was it now that he shared space with the spirit of death? Still, if I was going to die, then I sure as hell was going to die spitting in his eye and throwing barbs all the way.

"We will enjoy killing you."

"But are we going to answer the questions?"

He smiled again, and it was the smile I knew. All oily confidence and belief in self.

"The others were human and easily swept away. I am, as I've already said, a lab-born vampire. It is not so easy to get rid of me."

Didn't we know *that*. "And not telling Kingsley who I was?"

"He has other victims upstairs. He will not take mine. And in this place there is no cavalry to save you. It's just you and me."

I stared at him for a moment, then took a deep breath, gathering courage, and stepped over the stones, moving into the center of the circular cavern. It was bigger than I'd originally thought, filled with shifting shadows that wouldn't do either of us any good.

I rolled my shoulders, trying to ease the ache, then shifted my feet, letting the grit and dirt dig into my heels and enhance my grip. Once I was ready—or as ready as I was ever going to get—I lifted my free hand and gave him a quick "come on" sign. "Let's do it, stinko."

He laughed, and it was the most joyous sound I'd

ever heard escape his thin lips. In one smooth movement, he sheathed the knife behind his back, then he came at me, a blur of energy and heat and sheer bloody murder.

There was little I could do but try to survive. I weaved and dodged and blocked, using every skill pounded into my body over the last few months, every instinct, every ounce of speed. He was fast, super fast, with instincts and fighting skills honed far sharper than mine ever would be. But I was fighting for my life, and that gave me a huge advantage in the survival stakes. Enough to survive, anyway.

We moved, weaved, dodged around the room. Dirt clouded the heavy air, making it thicker, harder to breathe. Or maybe that was simply fear, weighing heavier and heavier on my flesh. Our dance was a vicious one, done in silence, except for the occasional smack of flesh against flesh or the heavy thump of a step against dusty ground. Blow after blow got through my defenses and rained upon my body, cutting and bruising but not breaking. Not yet. And every time he hit me, every time his teeth or nails scraped me, I kept the pain inside. If he wanted it, he was going to have to work a darn sight harder for it.

It was a frightening thought that he probably could. And would.

Still, after long minutes of heavy fighting, I was still upright, and still relatively unhurt. But God, I was thankful when he paused. As much as the wolf within begged to attack, to slash and bite and generally tear chunks off his stinking form, common sense held sway. I couldn't keep such intensity up. I might have the strength of a wolf and a vampire within me, but Gautier was a *whole* lot more now—who knew what strengths the dragon gave him? I had to pace myself, had to play this his way, until I got the chance to play it mine.

He breathed deep. Rapture flared in the depths of his flat eyes. "Ah, the sweet taste of your fear, Riley. So much more exquisite than blood."

I backed away a little farther, and swiped at the sweat running down my forehead with a bloody arm. Confidence fairly oozed from his pores, and, really, who could blame him? I stunk of sweat, effort, and blood, as well as the aforementioned fear, and there was no point in denying any of it.

"Enjoy it while you can, psycho, because it'll be the last time that you do."

He reached back behind him and drew the knife free once again. In the flickering torchlight, the silver blade seemed to glow with an odd red-gold luminescence. As if it were already coated with my blood.

I shivered and ignored the blade, watching his hands instead. With normal psychos you watched their eyes for their moves, but Gautier was far too devious to give the game away so easily. If he was going to throw that blade, I'd get the warning in the brief flick of his fingers.

He didn't throw it.

Just laughed. The sound rolled across the silence, sawing at my nerves.

I flexed my fingers and waited.

He smiled and casually swung the blade back and forth, back and forth.

When he finally came at me, it was so fast I barely had time to blink. I spun and lashed out with one bare foot. My heel skimmed his stomach, forcing him backward.

His free hand chopped down, his blow barely avoiding my shin; then he was following the impetus of the movement, spinning and kicking and slashing in one smooth motion. My knife went flying from suddenly nerveless fingers. His knife whistled mere inches from my nose, and probably would have sliced open my face if I hadn't bolted backward.

That angered me, for some reason. Beating me to a pulp I could handle, but cutting my face just went beyond the bounds of decency. I might not have a whole lot of prettiness to be worried about, but I was attached to what I had.

Gautier's fingers flexed, just the once, around the blade's shaft, then he blurred. His steps were featherlight on the dusty ground, little more than whispers of air. I wished I could say the same about his scent. It was thick with the reek of death, so vile that it snatched my breath and made it even harder to concentrate.

I tracked him with infrared, waiting until he closed in, then dropped and spun, lashing out with one foot, trying to bring him down. He avoided the kick easily, then his fist was arcing toward me. I dodged, felt the breeze of it scrape past my cheek, and dove forward, tackling him at knee height and bringing him down. We both hit the ground with a grunt and rolled in a mess of arms and legs and slashing teeth. I called to my alternate shape, felt her roil through my body eagerly, and slashed at his stomach with my teeth. Blood and flesh filled my mouth, a foulness worse than even his scent. Bile rose, and I hawked, spitting out his taste as I scrambled away. Silver glittered through the air. I dodged, lunged in a second time, tearing at the hand, the fingers, that held the blade.

He cursed, then his free fist was in my side, burrowing deep. Something snapped within, and everything went red as the force of the blow battered me away from him. I tumbled over and over in the dirt, changing shape along the way, until I hit the far wall in human form and with spine-jarring force.

But there was no time to lie there. No time to get my breath. The air was screaming with the scent and force of Gautier's follow-up leap. If he pinned me, that would be the end of it. I knew *that* from the one and only fight we'd had before now.

I rolled away and slashed sideways with my heel. The blow connected low, smashing into his leg just below his knee. Flesh and bone gave way under the power of it, and I swear I heard a crack. He grunted, fury flashing across his dead features, then he spun and grabbed my leg even as I tried to scramble away. A gasp escaped my lips and he chuckled.

I twisted, lunging up, fingers like daggers as I went for his eyes. He reared back, and I changed the blow, chopping down on a pressure point instead, trying to break his grip on my leg.

He swore, and swung, throwing me across the room a second time. I hit the wall with a smack that knocked the air from my lungs and left me gasping. Or maybe it wasn't the blow. Maybe there wasn't any air to begin with, because my lungs burned and I couldn't seem to breathe, no matter how much I gasped.

And he was coming at me again.

Somehow, I got up. Somehow, I forced myself to move. I felt rather than saw the sweep of the blade, and threw myself out of the way. Felt the silver point slash my calves as it whooshed past, leaving a trail burning fire in my flesh.

I rolled to my feet, scrambled around the table, putting its bulk between us. There I stood, watching him as I gasped for breath, my body shaking, aching, and bloody. It didn't matter. I was still standing, still fighting. The great Gautier hadn't beaten me yet, and he fucking well wouldn't. No matter what he did. No matter how bad it got.

He came at me again, and this time the knife was a deadly silver blur, leaving me with little option other than to back away. I didn't expect him to lunge forward, and the move took me by surprise. I jumped backward, but my foot caught against something solid—Jin's body, I realized with despair—and suddenly I was falling, sprawling, across the floor. Right next to the curved sacrifice blade—which was at Gautier's feet.

He laughed, a sound of pleasure and victory combined, and raised the knife, the bloody blade glittering as the torchlight caressed it.

I had one hope left and I tried it.

"Rhoan," I gasped, looking past Gautier. "Blow the bastard's brains out."

Against all the odds, against all reason, Gautier turned. I grabbed the curved knife, bucked upright, and swept the bright blade from left to right, removing Gautier's head from his shoulders.

I saw incredulity bloom in his eyes before his body crumpled and his head rolled away into the shadows. Which was good, because I didn't want to look at his ugly mug any more than I had to.

I dropped to my knees beside his body and took a

deep, sobbing breath. Rhoan had once told me that old tricks would never save my life. How wrong he'd been.

I'd won the battle I never thought I could win. I'd beaten the great Gautier, and had done it with a trick as old as time itself.

And yet, the danger wasn't over for me. Two dragon heads might now be dead, but there was one left, as well as the dark lord. I had to get out of here, while the going was good.

But it seemed that fate had helped me as much as she intended to. Because as I stumbled to my feet, John Kingsley walked back into the room.

His gaze swept from the altar to the bodies of the two men and then to me. If he was at all annoyed at the death of his dragons, it didn't show. He appeared amused, if anything. Though I guess a dark god could probably bring back the souls of his dragons easily enough.

"It seems Gautier was right. I did underestimate your strength."

I clenched my fist around the ceremonial knife. "People tend to do that."

His gaze slid down to the knife I held so firmly, and a smile teased the corners of his thin lips. "So who, precisely, are you?"

"So Gautier really *didn't* tell you?"

"Gautier was distressingly closemouthed when it came to details about you. A point he paid the ultimate price for."

"I'm a guardian," I said. "And I'm here to stop you."

He laughed, and it was a sound so warm and enticing, fear skidded down my spine.

I thought I was free of the dark god's influence.

I was very, very wrong.

Kingsley raised his hands and began to chant. His rich voice seemed to evoke a power from the hieroglyphics on the wall, because they began to glow with a muted purple light. Energy swirled around us, pungent and acidic, caressing my skin with a warmth that felt like water, and yet stung sharply as salt in a cut.

My skin began to tingle, my toes and fingers jump. As I breathed the suddenly thick, aromatic air, the aches and pains rolling through my body began to ease, until it was all but a muted ache.

I remembered the smile his other victims had died with. Remembered the feeling they'd died wanting the death and agony Kingsley had given them.

Realized that this power, whatever it was, was the reason. It didn't only ease the pain, but eased will, as well. I couldn't afford anything to affect clear thought—not if I wanted to stay alive.

I raised the ceremonial blade. Under the odd, purplish fire coming from the hieroglyphics, the blade gleamed with a deep red glow. As if it had a life and blood of its own.

"Stop whatever you're doing, Kingsley, or I'll chop something vital off." Because I couldn't kill him, not without pinning his soul to his body first.

And that would take the concealed silver knives that were miraculously still in my hair. But using them would mean getting closer, and that was something I just didn't want to do.

He smiled. Power swirled around me, through me, tugging at my resolve, dampening my will.

"You will drop the knife, young Riley."

I gripped it harder. The power became thicker, richer, stirring my senses, pulling at desire. I was a wolf and lust was part of my nature, but the desire he was promising was not the sweetness of orgasm but rather death.

Sweat trickled down my spine. "Kingsley, this place is surrounded by the Directorate. If they're not already busting into your lair, they soon will be. Give up, while you can."

"They will never find this place. We are deep underground, and protected by magic. Fighting me is useless, little one."

And the magic swirled, becoming a crescendo from which there was no escape. I wanted to fight it, I desperately wanted to, but it was as if someone had pulled the plug on the sink that was my courage and determination. It all just floated away, and that odd detachment came back full force.

I couldn't beat him. Not alone.

"Come here," he said.

My feet moved me across the room. I fought every step and it didn't matter a damn. Kingsley smiled, and touched a hand to my cheek. His fingers were cool and clammy, reminding me of dead flesh, and the part of me that was still free wanted to scream in horror.

"Look at me," he said softly.

His words were a command that whipped around me, and there was nothing I could do but obey. This close to him, his will was extremely strong, flaying my flesh with power and heat and desire. Despite everything, my body began to respond, my blood flicking like fire through my veins once again.

His gaze was ablaze with hunger and power, but what he hungered for this time was not sex, not emotion, but something far more powerful.

Death.

"Do you wish a completion?"

It was the same question he'd asked in the room with the stocks. Then, as now, I held my tongue, biting down hard on the need to answer.

If I did, it would be the end for me.

"I can give it to you, you know," he continued. "Give you satisfaction of a kind you have never felt."

I didn't say anything. Couldn't say anything. My tongue seemed stuck to the roof of my mouth.

"Do you wish a taste, little one?"

The power swirled, brighter and harder, until my whole body thrummed with it and the need to give in was a wave that was gathering pace toward an eager shore.

And then one of the shadows moved in the other room and awareness shot through me. I was no longer alone in this fight and the thought had energy surging, bolstering floundering will and determination.

"What I want," I said, my words little more than a pant of air, "is for you to fucking die, as horribly as all those women died."

And in one smooth movement, I grabbed the knives from my hair, flicked off the protective covers with my thumbs, and plunged them deep into Kingsley's chest.

Fury filled his eyes, and the power in the air became a weapon that hit with the force of a hammer, throwing me hard across the room. I hit the wall with a grunt, smashing the back of my head as I slid down to the floor.

My vision wavered. Stars danced and shadows moved as Kingsley strode toward me. Blood and steam were dribbling from the wounds but he didn't really appear to notice.

I scrambled away on all fours, but he grabbed my foot and yanked me to a halt.

"For that, you will pay with pain before I kill you."

"Bastard," I panted, kicking out with my free foot. "Let me go."

"Or you'll what? Kill me? Heard that threat once before, little one, and it is as ineffective as these little knives sticking in my flesh."

I didn't say anything. Didn't have time. Because at that moment, a sound rang out.

Not just a sound, but a gunshot.

The bullet shot Kingsley's fucking brains through the side of his head and splattered them across the wall.

I didn't even have the energy to cheer.

As Kingsley's body slumped to the ground, Rhoan stepped fully into the room.

"Why will you bad guys never listen?" he said, talking to Kingsley as if he were still capable of hearing and thought. And I guess if the silver-threaded knife had done its job and trapped his spirit inside his lifeless body, then he *was* still capable of understanding. He just couldn't reply. "I keep warning and warning, and nobody seems willing to listen. One of these days someone is going to wake up to the fact that I'm serious when I say never to attack my sister without looking over your shoulder for me."

I dragged myself into a sitting position and leaned wearily against the wall. "Maybe you should send out a pamphlet to bad guys' headquarters. It could be the only way to make sure they know."

"Now, that sounds like a plan." He hefted the weapon onto his shoulder, and gave me a grin. "And thanks for saving the good bit for me."

I laughed. At the irony in his words. In sheer, bloody relief at still being alive.

Laughed until the tears started flowing and the pain hit full force.

Laughed until I knew no more.

Chapter 13

Rhoan plopped down on the roadside curb beside me and offered me one of the two coffee cups he held. "It's only regular."

"I couldn't give a damn." I wrapped my hands around the cup, letting the hot liquid chase the chill from them. "How's the cleanup going?"

He shrugged. "Same as usual. How's your hand?"

I glanced down. My little finger stuck out at an angle, all swollen and angry looking. Shifting shape had stemmed the bleeding, but it would never, ever replace what was taken. I'd have a permanent, stumpy reminder of my time with a dark god.

"It's sore."

"Jack wants you to be checked out in a hospital."

"Jack's already been told what he can do with that

suggestion." I glanced at him. "So he's sent you to try and con me?"

Rhoan sipped at his coffee, then nodded. "He thought it worth the try."

"Hospitals suck."

"That they do."

"And they stink."

"Yes, they do."

"And I *will* heal without going there."

"Eventually."

I grinned. "*Not* pressuring me won't work either, you know."

"I can but try." His gaze met mine, gray depths filled with so much concern my determination wavered. "You lost a lot of blood, sis."

I grimaced. "Nothing a good steak won't fix."

"Not according to Quinn, and he *is* the expert in all matters blood related."

I took a sip of coffee as my gaze found its way to the house across the road. According to Rhoan, Quinn had arrived in the downstairs chamber about five seconds after I'd fainted. He'd ordered my brother to carry me out and had slammed the metal door shut behind him.

Finally finishing what his family had failed to finish so long ago.

I understood his actions, understood his need to complete what had been left undone for so long, and yet, at the same time, part of me was angered by it.

If he'd cared for me as much as he said, shouldn't his first instincts have been to take care of me himself? Take me upstairs, look after me? To hold me, kiss me, reassure me that the dark one was trapped, that he could never escape, that nothing of him lingered within me? The chamber and the dark god weren't going anywhere, after all. The silver knives had done their job, and his spirit was trapped, as Quinn's sister had been trapped.

But no. It was always business before pleasure with Quinn. Always mind before emotion.

I sighed and rubbed my good hand across my eyes. What was the good of dwelling on it? Quinn wasn't going to change, any more than I could. And I was never going to find what I wanted with him. Because what I wanted was my soul mate, and kids, and a quiet life.

Some of that dream might have disintegrated, but not all of it. And I had every intention of hanging on to the little that *did* remain as fiercely as I could.

There was still hope for me. And right now, I had a wolf ready and willing to explore those options with me.

He deserved a chance.

We deserved a chance.

I took another sip of coffee. "Is Kingsley going to be mummified and sealed away like Caelfind?"

Rhoan nodded. "Deep in the vaults of the Directorate. Quinn will magically seal the coffins and vault doors. They won't ever get free."

"Good." I looked beyond him, studying the sky. The softest of pinks was beginning to infuse the night, heralding the start of yet another day.

"A new day, a new start," I said softly, then met his gaze again. For no good reason, tears formed. "I wish I could begin again."

He put down his coffee, wrapped an arm around my shoulder, and drew me close. For several minutes, he didn't say anything, just held me against his chest and hugged me tightly. My rock, my island. The one bit of sanity left in the insanity that my life had become.

"There's nothing done that can't be undone," he said eventually, his breath stirring the hairs across the top of my head. "Nothing so wrong in your life that can't be changed."

I snorted softly against his chest. "There're lots of things that can't be changed and we both know it."

"But it isn't lots of things causing you grief. Only one." His hand slid down my arm, rubbing gently. "I think what you need is a break. A nice long holiday to regain strength will do you wonders, I think."

I half laughed, half sniffed, as I pulled away from his grip. "Has Kellen been in your ear?"

He smiled. "No. You're the one that mentioned he wanted to take you away on a holiday. Why not extend it? Why not explore the depth of your relationship with him? You've got nothing to lose, and everything to gain."

"I don't think Jack—"

He held up a hand, forestalling my argument. "Jack's agreed to give you time off."

"*What?*" I stared at him blankly. "How did *that* miracle occur?"

Rhoan smiled. "It's wonderful what the threat of losing his best two guardians can do. You have six weeks."

"Six *weeks?*"

"Yes. Use the time wisely, young pup."

I smacked his arm. "I'll use it to harass and annoy you if you're not careful."

"Which is what you normally do, and the aim of this time off is new directions."

New directions. A new start and the time to explore

dreams. Just the possibility had a smile breaking out. Six weeks of doing nothing except what *I* wanted to do. Six weeks of exploring new horizons, new places, new people.

Six weeks of finding out if Kellen and I really could be soul mates.

Excitement bubbled through me. I wanted that. Wanted it badly.

But new beginnings also meant endings, and there was one thing I needed to do before any fresh start could truly begin.

Quinn chose that moment to come out of the house. His gaze swept the darkness and came to rest on mine. Even from this distance, I could feel the turmoil in him.

It pretty much matched the turmoil within me.

I held out the coffee cup to Rhoan. "Hold this for me. I won't be long."

He didn't say anything, just accepted the cup. I rose and walked toward Quinn. The soft breeze swirled around us, tugging at his dark hair, catching his scent and spinning it around me. Heat prickled across my skin, and my hormones did their usual giddy dance.

I couldn't ever imagine not wanting him. But I was not the sum of my hormones, and I was tired of our game. I needed this new start Rhoan had offered, I truly did.

We stopped in the middle of the street. His gaze met mine, his eyes obsidian stone and expression shuttered. The emotions I'd sensed earlier were gone, carefully concealed behind the wall of his deliberate non-expression.

It only served to reinforce the rightness of my decision.

"It ends here, tonight."

"It'll never end between us, and you know it."

"What I know," I said softly, "is that you've used me, and continued to use me, these last ten months. You swear to care, and yet I am never first in your thoughts, never the one you rush to when things go wrong. Your own aims and needs are always first and foremost. You proved this by using the link we'd formed to leash and control the very desires that make me what I am."

"What did you miss out on?" he said, a touch of anger in his voice. "A few nights with strangers? Big deal."

I stared at him, unable to believe he couldn't see the wrongness in what he'd done. "What you did is really no different from what Talon, Misha, or even Starr have all done to me. You tried to force me down a path that was not my choosing. Dammit, you hated it when it was done to you, Quinn. You stripped your so-called fiancée of her identity and her life in retaliation. And yet here you are, using a psychic connection rather than a drug to force me down a path of your desiring."

He didn't say anything. Hard to refute something that was nothing more than the truth, I suppose—though I am surprised he didn't try. He usually did.

"Jack's given me six weeks off work," I continued. "And I want double that to sort out my life. During that time, I don't want any contact from you. I don't want to see you, I don't want to hear from you, I don't want you in my thoughts or in my dreams. I want a total and absolute break."

"For only three months?" His voice was still flat, and yet I had an odd feeling he was controlling himself very tightly.

Which was half the damn problem.

How could I trust what I never, ever saw?

How could I trust emotions he kept telling me about but never really showed in action or deed?

"After three months, I'll see where my head is at. There's no guarantee whatsoever that I'll ever be with you again, Quinn."

He didn't say anything for several heartbeats, just stared at me, his obsidian eyes darker than the night and a hell of a lot more dangerous.

Then he grabbed my arms and crushed me against him, his mouth finding mine almost savagely. I could have fought. I really could have. But I didn't want to. If this was a good-bye, then I sure as hell intended to enjoy it.

And if it wasn't? I'd enjoy it anyway, and smack him later.

Because this kiss was like nothing I'd ever felt before. It was a wild, erotic, and very unapologetic affirmation of what he wanted. What he felt. He might never, ever have said the words or hinted at emotions, but it was there, right there now, in his kiss, in the press of his body, in the thick, desperate heat that swirled around us.

But it was too little too late. I needed time. I needed to think. I broke off our kiss, pulled out of his grasp.

"No," I said, holding out a hand and backing away from him. "Enough. You owe me time, Quinn. If nothing else, you owe me that."

"Don't ask for things you don't really want," he said, voice little more than a harsh rasp. "Because you might just get them."

With that, he wrapped the shadows around his body,

spun around, and walked away. I let out a slow, shuddery breath.

"Well, that went a whole lot better than *I* expected," Rhoan said from across the road.

I laughed softly and spun around.

And suddenly, gloriously, felt *free*.

"How about we go to the pub and I buy you a steak and a beer?" I shoved my hands into the pockets of my borrowed coat and offered him my arm.

He handed me my coffee, then hooked his arm through mine and began walking down the street. "And after?"

"I call Kellen and start making plans."

"Good."

It *was* good.

Because, for the first time in ages, I was actually looking forward to the future. *My* future.

And that, after everything that had happened over the last ten months, was an excellent place to be.

Smart, sexy, and suspenseful, the Riley Jenson novels
are rapidly gaining fans worldwide.

Turn the page for an exclusive preview of the next
thrilling instalment:

Embraced by Darkness

by

Keri Arthur

Available from

Piatkus

EMBRACED BY DARKNESS

Chapter 1

The only trouble with getting away from it all was actually getting away from it all.

Six weeks of lazing around on secluded and luxurious Monitor Island, with nothing to do except eat, drink, and lust after the occasional hot-bod sounded like heaven itself. And it was.

For the first three weeks.

But now, with the fifth week done and dusted, the wolf within was beginning to hunger for the company of my own kind. Werewolves are not, by nature, solitary souls, and we tend to live in packs just as much as our animal counterparts.

My pack might now only consist of my twin brother Rhoan, his lover Liander, and my lover Kellen, but I was missing them all something fierce.

Especially Kellen. He'd been here for the first three

weeks, and the result had been a deepening and strengthening of our somewhat fragile relationship. Even so, I hadn't really expected to miss him *this* much. Not after only a couple of months of being together—and especially considering we'd probably spent more time apart than together in those months. Of course, I knew now that a lot of that separation was due to Quinn, the enigmatic vampire who swore his feelings for me ran deep—even as he used me to achieve his aims of killing the people who had destroyed his lifelong friend and creator. Even now, despite the feelings I had for Kellen, part of me still hungered to be with Quinn. Would probably *always* hunger to be with him.

Because there was a connection with Quinn that I'd never found with any other man. Not even Kellen.

But Quinn was out of my life for the moment—maybe even permanently—and I couldn't really regret that. I'd never condoned force in *any* relationship, and that's basically what Quinn had done when he'd used his vampire wiles to curb my very nature. His methods might have been psychic rather than physical, but in the end, it was the same thing. *Anything* that forced someone down a path they would not otherwise have taken was abuse, no matter how prettily the situation was wrapped.

What I needed to do was forget him. Just get on with my life, and stop remembering he was ever a part of it. Even if the very thought made my soul ache and my heart weep.

But the last two weeks alone had basically left me with nothing to do at night except think about the people in my life and the events of the last ten months or so. And all *that* was supposedly what I was here to forget.

I rubbed a hand across tired eyes, then leaned my

forearms on the balustrade of the small patio lining the front of my pretty little villa unit.

The breeze coming off the sea was cool, teasing my short hair and sending goose bumps flitting across my bare flesh. I briefly thought about going inside to grab a shirt, but in the end, I couldn't be bothered moving.

I let my gaze roam across the waves, watching the foam hiss across the white sand. It was a peaceful sound, as peaceful as the night itself, which made me wonder what the hell had woken me in the first place.

Certainly there was no noise coming from any of the other half-dozen villas that lined this section of half-moon beach. Not even the newlyweds were stirring, and they'd been at it nonstop since their arrival five days ago.

And I thought *werewolves* had stamina.

I smiled and plucked a leaf from the nearby eucalyptus branch that was draped over the railing, then flicked the leaf skyward from the stem, watching it twirl all the way to the ground.

What I wanted was to go home. To get on with my life and my job. But I had just under a week of my vacation to go, and while I might be going slowly insane with boredom, I just couldn't pack up and leave. Rhoan and Liander had given me this holiday as a gift to help me rest and recuperate after a particularly shitty year, and I couldn't—wouldn't—hurt their feelings by returning before my time was up.

"Riley." My name whispered across the gentle wind, a demand rather than a mere attempt to get my attention.

I straightened quickly, my gaze searching the moonlit night for some sign of the caller; some hint of where the voice had come from.

A difficult task when it seemed to come from everywhere and yet nowhere.

"Riley."

Again the voice rode the night, stronger than before and male in its resonance.

It wasn't a voice that belonged to any of the men who inhabited the other villas in this small cove. Nor did it belong to any of the staff members who looked after the villas or who worked in the main resort complex one beach over.

But there were three other accommodation areas scattered across the island, and I hadn't really had much to do with the guests or employees there. Even if it *had* been one of those people, why would they know my name? And why would they be calling me in the dead of the night?

It was odd, and the mere thought that something odd might be going on had the thrum of excitement racing through my veins.

Which was a rather sad statement of just how bored I was. Or perhaps how addicted I'd become to the adrenaline rush of being a guardian. Hell, I'd give away the killing bit any day, but not the thrill of the chase. The hunt was all to a wolf, and no matter how long I might have denied it, I was a hunter every bit as much as my brother.

I studied the night for a moment longer. The gentle wind whispered through the trees, void of any voice but its own. I could sense nothing and no one near, and yet something *was*. The electric charge of awareness raced across my skin, making the small hairs on my arms stand on end.

I spun on my heel and walked back into my room. I

didn't mind walking around sans clothes, but most of the guests currently on the island were human, and humans tended to get a little antsy about the whole naked thing.

I pulled on a low-cut T-shirt and a baggy pair of shorts, then headed back out onto the patio.

"Riley, come."

The voice swirled around me, rich and arrogant. A man who used, and probably abused, power. And my wolf soul reacted to the sense of command in that voice. But not in the way I expected her to. Not fiercely, not with anger, but meekly. As if she wanted to do nothing more than tuck her tail between her legs and cower before the power behind the voice.

And there could be only one reason for that.

The voice belonged to a pack member. Not just any pack member, but the alpha. The wolf who ruled the pack as a whole.

Only the voice didn't belong to *my* alpha, the man who had ruled the pack for as long as anyone could remember. I would have recognized the voice of my own grandfather.

What the hell was going on?

Frowning, I walked down the steps, then strode through the trees and out onto the moonlit sand. The wind was sharper without the cover of the eucalyptus, and filled with the scent of the sea.

And nothing else. No musky male scent. No hint of wolf. Nothing to suggest there was another soul awake and aware out here on the beach.

A shiver ran down my spine. Maybe I was imagining it. Maybe this was nothing more than a dream, and any minute now I'd wake up and laugh at my own stupidity.

After all, our pack had threatened to kill us both if we

ever contacted—let alone went near—any pack members. And not even our mother had dared to contradict that particular order.

Not that I thought she'd even tried. Though I had no doubt she loved us, she'd always seemed as relieved as the rest of the pack to see the back of us.

"Riley, come."

Again the order ran across the night, stronger than before. I closed my eyes, concentrating on the sound, trying to define just where the voice was coming from.

After a moment, I turned around and padded up the beach. The beach villas gave way to thicker strands of eucalyptus and acacia trees, the strong scents of both filling the night and my nose.

It didn't matter. I wasn't relying on my olfactory senses to track this particular trail, but rather, my "other" senses. The senses that were new and somewhat unreliable.

The part of me that could see souls rise.

Of course, seeing—and hearing—the souls of dead people wasn't a gift I particularly wanted. Hell, I had enough trouble dealing with the *living* dead without having to worry about the spiritual side popping along anytime it pleased.

But as was often the case in my life of late, it seemed I had little choice in the matter. The experimental fertility drug I'd been forcibly given by an ex-mate had not only kick-started latent psychic skills, but had given them a little twist, just for the fun of it. Clairvoyance had been one of those latent skills—until recently, anyway. Seeing dead people walk through the shadows was the not-so-tempting twist.

Though, until tonight, they'd never actually contacted me long range. I'd only ever seen them close to their own bodies. Well, mostly, I thought, shivering as I remembered the lingering, insubstantial wisps in Starr's bloody arena.

Not that I was entirely sure I was hearing the dead now, but it just seemed odd I couldn't see or smell anyone else near. My senses were wolf sharp—if someone had been close, I would have known.

I padded along the white sand until I reached the peninsula rocks. The wind here was sharper, the sea rougher, slapping across the smooth, round rocks and sending white foam flicking skyward. The tide was up, so I'd be getting wet if the voice wanted me to clamber around to the next beach.

I stopped and scanned the horizon. Awareness tingled across my skin, as sharp as needle stings. Whoever the voice belonged to, he was close.

"Riley, turn around."

For the first time, memories stirred. I'd known that voice in the past. I turned and studied the trees.

A man stood among them. Though at first glance he appeared solid, a more careful study revealed an almost gossamer look to his hands and feet. As if by the time he got to his extremities he didn't have the strength to maintain reality.

He was a tall man, rangy in build, with strong arms and blunt features. Not attractive, not ugly, but somewhere in between. But even if he'd been the ugliest spud on the planet, it wouldn't have mattered, because the sense of authority and power that shone from his green eyes and oozed from his tanned skin were all that would ever matter to any wolf.

And *this* wolf wanted to hunker down before it.

But I wasn't just wolf, and the other half of my soul bared its teeth and got ready for a fight. I locked my knees and skimmed my gaze up to his hair. Thick and red. Definitely red pack. Definitely *my* red pack. But who?

As I dropped my gaze to his, recognition stirred again. I knew those eyes, knew the cold superiority behind them. But I'd be damned if I could dredge up a name.

"Why are you calling me?"

Though the question was soft, my voice seemed to echo across the silent night. A tremor ran down my spine, and I wasn't sure whether it was due to the chill wind hitting my bare legs and arms or the sudden sense of trepidation creeping through my soul.

Amusement sparked briefly in the translucent green depths. "You do not remember me?"

"Should I have any reason to remember you?"

This time the amusement reached his thin lips. "I would think you'd remember the wolf who threw you off a mountainside."

Shock rolled through me. Oh my God . . .

Blake.

My grandfather's second in command, and the wolf who would have killed us if he could. The wolf who almost *had* when he'd thrown me off that cliff. Ostensibly to teach Rhoan a lesson about never backchatting the pack second.

Hate followed the shock, swirling through me thick and sharp. I clenched my fists and found myself fighting the sudden urge to run forward and punch the cold amusement from his thin lips. He wasn't real, he wasn't here, and I'd only look like a fool. So I simply said, voice low and venomous, "What right have *you* got to call *me*?"

"My right is pack given."

"The Jenson pack ceded its rights over me and Rhoan when they kicked us out."

"Pack rights are never surrendered, no matter what the situation or current politics. Once a pack member, always a pack member."

"*You* threatened to kill us if you ever saw us again."

"A statement that still stands."

"So why the *hell* are you contacting me? Fuck off and leave me alone. Trust me, I want as little to do with you as you do with me."

I turned on my heel and began to walk back down the beach, away from him. Part of me might have been curious as to why he was suddenly contacting me, but curiosity didn't have a hope against old anger and hurt. None of which I wanted to relive in *any* way.

"You will listen to what I have to say, Riley."

"Fuck off," I said without looking at him. Even as my wolf cowered deep within at my audacity.

"You *will* stop and listen, young wolf."

His voice was sharp and powerful, seeming to echo through the trees and ring in my ears. I stopped. I couldn't help it. My very DNA was patterned with the need to obey my alpha. It would take a great deal of will and strength to dare disobey, and right now, it seemed I had neither.

Even so, I didn't turn around. Didn't look at him. "Why the hell should I listen?"

"Because I demand it."

I snorted softly. "I was never one to listen to demands. You of all people should know that."

"So very true. And it *was* one of the reasons you and your brother were ostracized." Amusement laced his harsh tones. "Your grandfather feared you would challenge him."

Surprise rippled through me. I swung around. He was still in the trees, still in the shadows. Maybe the wind meant coming out onto the beach wasn't practical for a man who was little more than spirit. "Why would my grandfather fear that? Neither Rhoan nor I were ever allowed the illusion we were anything more than an inconvenience to our mother and the pack. And inconveniences don't rule." Especially if they were female. Or gay.

"You have a long pattern of doing the unexpected, Riley."

"Yeah, and I have the scars to prove the foolishness of that."

He grinned. It was a harsh, cruel thing to see. "You never did learn your place."

Oh, I learned it all right. I just didn't always cower down like I was supposed to. I thrust my hands on my hips and said impatiently, "As much as I just adore reliving old times with you, it's fucking cold out here. Tell me what you want or just piss off and leave me alone."

He studied me for a minute, green eyes abnormally bright in the darkness, his form waving slightly as the wind swirled through the trees.

"The pack needs your help."

"You want *my* help?" My sudden, unbelieving laugh was a cold and ugly sound. "That has to be the joke of the century, doesn't it?"

"There is nothing amusing about the situation, believe me."

"So why me? There have to be hundreds of other people you could ask."

Which *wasn't* an overstatement. The Jenson pack might be one of the smaller red packs, and it might be the poorer cousin when it came to wealth and land status, but Jenson pack members were to be found in all avenues of government and throughout much of the legal system. I had no doubt those pack members could muster up something—someone—far more influential than anything I could manage.

Amusement flared briefly in his eyes. "We have need of your guardian skills."

Again surprise rippled through me. "And how would you know I am a guardian? Why would you even bother keeping track of two outcast and useless pups?"

"We didn't. It came to my attention during investigations."

"Investigations into what?"

He shifted his weight and his form wavered, briefly becoming as insubstantial as a ghost. Which he wasn't, so how in the hell was he projecting himself?

"My granddaughter, Adrianne, disappeared a week ago."

He had a granddaughter? Good lord, that made me feel old. Though, in wolf terms, I was still very much a youngster. "Which of your sons was careless enough to lose a daughter?"

It was a cruel thing to say, but I just couldn't help it. Blake and his sons had been the banes of my existence while growing up—and the reason behind many of the scars Rhoan and I now had. Of course, if I'd just shut my mouth and bowed down like I was supposed to, things might have been different.

Though I very much doubt it.

His gaze narrowed to thin slits of dangerous green. "Adrianne is Patrin's oldest."

The image of a red wolf with black points came to mind, and my lip curled in response. Patrin was the youngest of Blake's get, and only a few years older than me. To say he delighted in following the family tradition of hassling the half-breeds would be the understatement of the century.

"How old is the daughter?"

"Nineteen."

Nineteen? Meaning he'd been fifteen when he'd sired his first? Randy bastard. But I bet Daddy had been *so* proud, especially given the pack's inherent fertility problems.

"If she's missing, contact the police. The Directorate doesn't do missing."

"You do if there appears to be a pattern in the disappearances. Three people have disappeared the same way as Adrianne, Riley."

I crossed my arms and tried to ignore the pulse of interest. I didn't want to get involved with Blake or our pack, because it could only ever end badly—for me, not for them.

"Then contact the Directorate. Give them the information. There's nothing I can do without the official go-ahead anyway."

Which was only a teeny-tiny lie. If I were so inclined, I could investigate just about anything. Guardians were the super-cops, the hunter-killers, of the nonhuman world, and we had free rein to investigate where we willed. Though, if I *did* investigate and *did* find something, I'd have to report it back to my boss. A full investigation could only go ahead with his official approval.

"All I'm asking you to do is an initial investigation. If you feel there's nothing the Directorate can do, then I'll try other sources."

He sounded altogether too reasonable all of a sudden, and my hackles rose. Blake and reason just didn't sit well with my memories of the man. "You were ordering me a few moments ago."

"Perhaps I'm seeing the error of my ways."

"And perhaps tomorrow they'll put a woman on Mars." I shifted from one foot to the other. I wasn't trusting this new and improved Blake to last more than a second, but it didn't hurt to play along anyway. "Why do you think her disappearance is a Directorate matter?"

"There's a pattern. For a start, they all stayed at Monitor Island for more than a week."

"And?"

"And they all disappeared within a week of returning. . . ."

KISSING SIN

From Melbourne's gleaming skyscrapers to its edgy night-clubs, Riley Jenson's world is fraught with danger and desire. A drop-dead-gorgeous werewolf – with a touch of vampire coursing through her veins – Riley works for an organisation created to police the supernatural races. But when she wakes up naked and bruised in a deserted alley, she knows only that she must run for her life.

Within moments, Riley collides with steely, seductive Kade, who is fighting a life-and-death battle of his own. With old lovers and enemies gathering around her, Riley knows she is being pursued by a new kind of criminal. Because in Riley's blood is a secret that could create the ultimate warrior – if only she can survive her own dangerous desires.

978-0-7499-3814-7